Levi wondered if Sarah realized how pretty she was with the new morning light streaming through the window bathing her face in golden light.

To his eyes, she grew more beautiful with each passing year. It was no wonder Daniel had fallen in love with her.

Levi dropped his gaze to his feet, afraid his thoughts would somehow show in his eyes. "Do you mind?"

"Do I mind what?" she asked at last with an odd inflection in her tone.

He waved his arm to indicate the shop. "That I made changes."

"*Nee*, it is your work space," she said quickly.

"*Goot.*"

"What needs doing in here today that Grace would normally do? I'm at your beck and call, so put me to work."

"I don't need anything." What he wanted was for her to go home. The workshop was his sanctuary. How could it be a place of peace with Sarah in it?

After thirty-five years as a nurse, **Patricia Davids** hung up her stethoscope to become a full-time writer. She enjoys spending her free time visiting her grandchildren, doing some long-overdue yard work and traveling to research her story locations. She resides in Wichita, Kansas. Patricia always enjoys hearing from her readers. You can visit her online at patriciadavids.com.

Dana R. Lynn grew up in Illinois. She met her husband at a wedding and told her parents she'd met the man she was going to marry. Nineteen months later, they were married. Today, they live in rural northwestern Pennsylvania with enough animals to start a petting zoo. In addition to writing, she works as a teacher for the deaf and hard of hearing and works in several ministries in her church.

USA TODAY Bestselling Author

PATRICIA DAVIDS

A Hope Springs Christmas

&

DANA R. LYNN

Amish Christmas Abduction

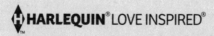

HARLEQUIN® LOVE INSPIRED®

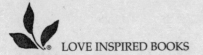

LOVE INSPIRED BOOKS

Recycling programs for this product may not exist in your area.

ISBN-13: 978-1-335-47017-1

A Hope Springs Christmas
and Amish Christmas Abduction

Copyright © 2019 by Harlequin Books S.A.

A Hope Springs Christmas
First published in 2012. This edition published in 2019.
Copyright © 2012 by Patricia MacDonald

Amish Christmas Abduction
First published in 2017. This edition published in 2019.
Copyright © 2017 by Dana Roae

www.Harlequin.com

Printed in U.S.A.

CONTENTS

A HOPE SPRINGS CHRISTMAS

Patricia Davids

This book is lovingly dedicated to my daughter Kathy and her husband, Tony. Thank you for your help and love. You both mean the world to me.

Let your light so shine before men, that they may see your good works, and glorify your Father which is in heaven.

—*Matthew* 5:16

Chapter One

"You can tell me the truth, dear. How are you really?"

Sarah Wyse dropped her gaze to the pile of mending in front of her on the scrubbed pine kitchen table without answering her aunt. How was she? Frightened.

"Tell me," her aunt persisted. Emma Lapp didn't believe in beating around the bush. She had a sharp eye and a gift for two things, matchmaking and uncovering gossip. How had she found out so quickly?

Sarah had expected to have a few days before having this conversation, but that wasn't to be. "I'm fine, *Aenti* Emma. Why do you ask?"

"You put on such a brave face, child. I know how hard the holiday season is for you. To lose your job on top of everything, my heart goes out to you. You must remember the Lord never gives us more than we can bear. Put your trust in Him."

"All is as God wills, even when we cannot comprehend His ways."

Christmas brought Sarah more painful memories than joy. Too many of her holidays had been marked by funerals. She dreaded the arrival of winter each year with its long, dark, lonely nights. It was her job that kept her sane. *Had* kept her sane.

What would she do now? What if the crippling depression she struggled to overcome got the upper hand?

"How will you manage?" Emma asked.

Sarah raised her chin and answered with a conviction she didn't feel. "As best I can. Would you like some tea?"

"That would be lovely."

Her aunt's sudden arrival was a blessing in disguise. Sarah had been sitting alone in her kitchen, wallowing in self-pity. It solved nothing. She needed to be busy.

She rose and crossed to the cupboard. Taking down a pair of white mugs, she carried them to the stove and filled them with hot water from the kettle steaming on the back of the cooktop.

"I know how you depend on the income from your job, Sarah, being a widow and all. Your *onkel* and I will help if you need it."

"Don't fret for me. It's only for a few months. Janet is moving her mother to Florida and wants to make sure she is settled before coming back. She plans to reopen Pins and Needles after Easter." Surely, she could hang on that long.

Emma cocked an eyebrow. "Will she be back? I heard she might stay."

A flash of panic hit Sarah, but she suppressed it. Janet would be back. Then things would return to normal.

"I'm sure she'll be back. Her business is successful. She enjoys the shop and loves the town. I have ample savings and the income from the rent of the buggy shop. I'll be fine."

Things would be tight, but Sarah would manage financially. Emotionally, that was another story.

Emma said, "Pins and Needles is successful because of the long hours you put into it. Anyway, you can depend on your family and the church to provide for you."

"I know." Being the object of sympathy and charity again was something Sarah preferred to avoid. She knew her attitude was prideful. Perhaps that was why God had set this challenge before her—to teach her humility.

Emma folded her arms over her ample chest. "You must find something to keep you busy."

"I was making a to-do list when you arrived." Sarah indicated a spiral notebook on the table.

"*Goot.* Have you thought of inviting your brother and his family for a visit? You haven't seen them in several years. The girls will be grown women before you know it."

After having been raised with only sisters, her brother, Vernon, had been blessed with two girls of his own and finally a boy. He and his wife were expecting another child in the spring. It would be good to see them. Having children in the house might help dispel the gloom that hung over her holidays.

"That's a fine idea. I'll write to Vernon first thing in the morning and invite them for a visit. There isn't much room here for the children to play. I hope they won't mind a stay in town." The family lived on a large dairy farm outside of Middlefield where the children had acres of woods and fields to roam.

Emma grinned. "You'll have to take Merle fishing if you want to keep that little boy happy. The last time we went to visit them, that was all he wanted to do and all he talked about. The girls entertain each other."

Sarah suffered a stab of grief. Her husband had liked to fish. It wasn't something she cared for. She should have tried harder to enjoy the things he liked, but how was she to know their time together would be so short?

Regrets were useless, but sometimes it seemed as if they were all she had.

She said, "I'll offer to take Merle on a fishing trip, weather permitting, if that will persuade his parents to come."

Emma chuckled. "He will nag them until they do."

Sarah placed a tea bag in each mug and carried them to the table along with the sugar bowl. As she sat down, a commotion in the street outside caught her attention.

A horse neighed loudly followed by raised voices. "I never want to see you again, Henry Zook! Do you hear me? Go ahead and marry Esta Barkman. See if I care. She—she can't even cook!"

A slamming door from the house beside Sarah's punctuated the end of the outburst.

"Goodness, was that Grace Beachy shouting in the street? Has she no *demut?*"

Oh, dear, her neighbor and friend Grace would soon find her quarrel public knowledge unless Sarah could stanch it. What on earth had Henry done to upset her so? Sarah cast a rueful smile at her aunt. "Grace has humility, *Aenti.* She is normally a quiet, reserved young woman."

"You couldn't tell it from her behavior just now. I understand the twins, Moses and Atlee, are the ones most often in trouble." Emma held her head cocked to hear any additional outbursts.

"They have been a trial to live beside," Sarah admitted as a frequent recipient of the teenage pair's numerous pranks.

The boys had turned seventeen in October. They were in their *rumspringa,* the "running around" years enjoyed by Amish youth from age sixteen up to their mid-twenties prior to taking the vows of the faith. Like many, the twins were making the most of their freedom, but they had always been on the wild side.

Sarah had grown up with an identical twin sister who rivaled the boys for getting into mischief. She missed her sister dearly. Bethany had left the faith to follow her English husband to the other side of the world. They died together in a car accident in New Zealand. In a way, Grace had become a substitute for Sarah's lost sister. She loved the girl.

Emma's eyes were alight with curiosity. "It sounded as if Grace is sorely put out with Henry. It would be a shame if the courtship ended this way. The bishop's son would be a fine match for the Beachy girl. I know Henry's mother is pleased as punch that her wayward son appears to be settling down."

If Grace married and left home, Sarah shuddered to think what the twins would be up to without her intervention. Levi, the eldest of the family, chose to ignore their less than perfect behaviors.

Emma couldn't resist the urge to learn more. "I want to see how Henry is handling this. I can't imagine he's happy to have his girlfriend shouting at him. His mother will want to hear of this."

Rising, she went to the kitchen window that overlooked the street and used her sleeve to rub an area free of frost. Winter had a firm grip on the town of Hope

Springs, Ohio, although it was only the first week of December. Peering through the frosty glass didn't give Emma a clear enough view so she moved to open the door.

Sarah quickly stepped between her aunt and the chilly night. Emma's nosy nature knew few bounds. "Leave the young people to sort out their own problems, *Aenti*."

Emma relented but she was clearly miffed at being denied more food for gossip. "How can I tell Esther Zook what happened if I can't see how her son is taking this rejection?"

"I'm sure if Henry Zook wants to discuss it with his mother, he'll find a way."

"She should know how his girlfriend is treating him."

Sarah pressed a hand to her chest and widened her eyes in disbelief. "You don't mean you'll mention this to the bishop's wife."

"I might, if the opportunity presents itself."

"You are a brave soul. I could never bring myself to tell Esther Zook that I heard her son was playing fast and loose with Grace *and* Esta Barkman."

Her aunt nibbled at the corner of her lip, then said, "It did sound that way, didn't it?"

"Grace is a sweet girl and would never raise her voice without serious provocation. I know Esther dotes on Henry and won't hear a bad word against him. I can only imagine how upset Esther would be with someone who spread word of his poor behavior. You know how much sway she holds over the bishop."

Her aunt's frown deepened. "I see your point. We don't actually know what happened, do we?"

"*Nee,* we don't. A lover's spate is all I heard. Not worth mentioning."

"You could be right."

"I know I am." Sarah waited until her aunt gave up trying to see over her and returned to the window. Sarah grinned as she started to close the door. Across the street, she caught sight of Levi Beachy standing motionless at the door to his shop. He'd obviously heard his sister's commotion, too.

His breath rose as white puffs in the cold night air. Their eyes met across the snow-covered street. Sarah couldn't see the color of them from this distance, but she knew they were as blue as a cloudless summer's day. They contrasted sharply with his dark hair and deeply tanned skin.

She rarely saw his eyes, for Levi kept them trained on his feet unless he was working. He was painfully shy, and she wished there was something she could do to help him overcome it. He had been a wonderful help to her when her husband was sick.

A quick frown formed on Levi's face before he turned away with a shake of his head.

"Great, now I'm the one who looks like the nosy neighbor," Sarah muttered. She sometimes had the feeling that Levi disapproved of her, although it wasn't anything she could put her finger on.

"What was that?" Emma asked.

Sarah pasted a smile on her face as she closed the door and returned to the kitchen table to resume her mending. "I saw Levi across the street. He's working late again."

"The poor fellow. He was saddled with raising his younger sister and those unruly brothers at much too early an age. He should have had the good sense to send them to his father's sister or even let his grandfather raise them. Reuben Beachy would have been glad to take care of the children."

Since Reuben was well past seventy, Sarah wasn't sure he would have been able to handle the twins any better than Levi did. "I'm sure Levi loves his family and wants to take care of them himself."

"I don't know how anyone could tell. The man hasn't spoken more than a dozen words to me in all his life. I think he is a bit simple."

Sarah leveled a hard gaze at her aunt. "Levi is shy, not simple."

Emma lifted the tea bag from her mug and added two spoonfuls of sugar. Stirring briskly, she said, *"Even a fool, when he holdeth his peace, is counted wise: and he that shutteth his lips is esteemed a man of understanding. Proverbs 17:28."*

Coming to her neighbor's defense, Sarah said, "Levi works very hard. He builds fine buggies, and he always pays the rent for the shop on time. He is a good man. I don't like to see him maligned."

"Gracious, child. I'm not maligning the man. I know several women who think he would make a good match, but I've had to tell them all that he is a waste of time. Levi Beachy will never find the courage to court a woman, much less propose. I've rarely met a fellow destined to remain an old boy, but Levi is one."

An old boy was the Amish term for a confirmed bachelor. Since only Amish men who married grew beards, a clean-shaven face marked a man as single no matter what his age. Like her, Levi was nearing thirty. She knew because they had attended school together until the eighth grade. She'd known Levi her entire life. He'd been the first boy to kiss her.

That long-forgotten memory brought a blush to her cheeks. Why had it surfaced after all these years? She bent over her mending.

"What about you, dear? It's been nearly five years since Jonas's passing. Are you ready to think about marriage again? I can't tell you the number of men who have asked me that question. One in particular." Emma eyed her intently.

Sarah should have known this wasn't the simple social visit her aunt claimed. She met her aunt's gaze as sadness welled up inside her. For once, she couldn't stop it. Tears stung her eyes. "No, *Aenti*. I've made my feelings on the subject clear. I won't marry again."

Sarah was laughing at him. She and her aunt were having a chuckle at the expense of his odd family. Levi knew it the way he knew the fire was hot—because he'd been burned by both.

It was wrong to dwell on the past, childish even, but the embarrassing incident came to mind when he least expected it. He'd long ago forgiven Sarah, but he hadn't been able to forget her part in his humiliation.

He had been fourteen at the time and the least athletic boy at school. His shyness made it easy for others to make fun of him, but Sarah had seemed kinder than his other classmates. She sat one row up and across the aisle from him.

How many hours had he spent dreaming about what it would be like to simply hold her hand? Too many.

Then one day, he found a note on his desk saying to meet her down by the creek after school if he wanted a kiss. He'd been ecstatic and frightened all at the same time. Of course he wanted to kiss her. What boy didn't? It took all the courage he could muster to make the short trek to the meeting spot.

She was waiting on the creek bank with her eyes closed just as the note said, but when he caught her by the shoulders and kissed her, she pushed him away. He never knew if it was by design or by accident that the fallen tree limb was right behind him. He tumbled backwards, tripped and landed in the water with a muddy splash.

On the other side of the creek, a dozen of his schoolmates began laughing and hooting, including Sarah's twin sister, Bethany. Mortified, Levi had trudged home in wet clothes and refused to go back to school. Working beside his father in his carpenter shop was the only thing that felt normal to Levi.

Less than a year later, both his parents were killed in a buggy accident. Levi was forced to sell his father's business. No one believed a fifteen-year-old boy could run it alone. Jonas Wyse bought the property and started a harness shop and buggy-making business in Hope Springs. He hired Levi, who desperately wanted to earn enough to support his sister and little brothers. The two men quickly became friends. Within five years, they had a thriving business going making fine buggies. They stopped repairing harnesses and focused on what they did best. It was a wonderful time in Levi's life.

Then Jonas decided to marry Sarah and everything changed.

Levi shook off his thoughts of the past. Sarah was his landlady and the widow of his only true friend. Levi was determined to treat her with the respect she deserved, but he sometimes wished he hadn't promised Jonas he would look after her when his friend was gone. That promise, made on Jonas's deathbed, was a binding one Levi could not break. Not if he planned to face Jonas in heaven one day.

Levi's gaze traveled to the colorful calendar on the shop wall. It was out of date by several years, but he'd never taken it down. His Amish religion didn't allow artwork or pictures to decorate walls, but a calendar had function and even one with a pretty picture was permitted. The one he never removed featured a panoramic view of the Rocky Mountains.

The dusty eight-by-ten photograph showed snow-capped mountains thrusting upward to reach a clear blue sky. Their flanks lay covered with thick forests of pine, aspen trees and spruce. It had long been Levi's dream to move to Colorado. Several of his cousins from the next village had moved to a new settlement out west and wrote in glowing terms of the beauty there. The idea of raising a family of his own in such a place was a dream he nurtured deep in his heart.

Colorado was his goal, but Sarah Wyse was the rope keeping him firmly tethered to Hope Springs.

He had loved Jonas Wyse like a brother. When his friend pleaded with him to watch over Sarah until she remarried, Levi had given his promise without hesitation. A year or so wasn't much to wait. The mountains weren't going anywhere.

It wasn't until Sara remained unmarried for two years that Levi began to doubt the wisdom of making his rash promise. Five years later he was still turning out buggies in Hope Springs and handing over rent money to help support her while his dreams of moving west gathered dust like the calendar on the wall.

He knew several good men who had tried to court Sarah, but she had turned each and every one of them aside. Levi had to admit none of them held a candle to his dear friend. But still, a woman Sarah's age should be married with children.

The thought of her with another man's babe in her arms brought an uncomfortable ache in his chest. He thrust aside thoughts of Sarah and replaced them with worry about his sister.

He hoped Grace was all right. He should go see, but he didn't know what to say to her. Women didn't think like men. Whatever he said would be sure to make her angry or make her cry. Perhaps it would be best to stay in the shop and wait until she called him for supper.

Half an hour later, he heard Sarah's aunt's buggy drive away. He went to the window and looked out. Sarah was alone again, as she was every night. She sat at her kitchen table working on some stitching. Why hadn't she remarried? What was she waiting for?

She was a devout Amish woman. She wasn't too old. She was certainly pretty enough. She kept a good house and worked hard. When the buggy shop needed repairs or upgrades he couldn't do himself, she was never stingy about hiring help or buying new equipment.

As he was looking out the window, he saw his sister approaching. He picked up a file to finish smoothing the edge of a metal step he was repairing.

Grace opened the door. "*Bruder,* your supper is ready."

"*Danki,* I'll be in shortly." He glanced up. His sister didn't leave. Instead, she walked along the workbench, looking over the parts he was assembling for a new buggy. She clearly had something on her mind. When she didn't speak, he asked, "Is everything okay?"

Her chin came up. "Why wouldn't it be?"

Because you were screaming at your boyfriend at the top of your lungs on a public street and giving our neighbors food for gossip. "Just wondering, that's all."

"Levi, can I ask you a question?"

He didn't like the sound of that. "Sure."

"Why haven't you married?"

That took him aback. "Me?"

"*Ja.* Why haven't you?"

Heat rushed to his face. He cleared his throat. "Reckon I haven't met the woman God has in mind for me."

"God wants each of us to find the person who makes us happy, doesn't He?" Grace fell silent.

Levi glanced up from his work to find her staring out the window at Sarah's house. Because her question so closely mirrored his thoughts about Sarah, he gathered his courage and asked, "Why do you think Sarah Wyse hasn't remarried?"

"Because she loved one man with her whole heart and her whole soul and she knows no one can replace him," Grace declared with a passion that astounded him.

She suddenly rushed toward the door. "I'll be back in a few minutes. Your supper is on the table."

"Where are you going?"

"I need to talk to Sarah about something."

When the door banged shut behind her, he sighed. It was just like his sister to leave him in the dark about what was going on. He hoped Sarah could help because the last thing he wanted was a home in turmoil, and unless Grace was happy, that was exactly what was going to happen.

* * *

After her aunt had gone, Sarah stared at the snow piled on the sill of her kitchen window. Dismal. There was no other word for it. Christmas would be here in less than a month, but there wasn't any joy in the knowledge. The Christmas seasons of the past had brought her only heartache and the long winter nights left her too much time to remember. At least this year her only loss was her job. So far.

She closed her eyes and folded her hands. "Please, Lord, keep everyone I love safe and well this year."

Second thoughts about inviting her brother for a visit crowded into her mind. He was all she had left of her immediate family. At times, it seemed that everyone she loved suffered and died before their time. What if something should befall Vernon or his wife or children while they were here? How would she forgive herself?

No, such thinking only showed her lack of faith. *It is not in my hands, but in Your hands, Lord.*

Still, she couldn't shake a feeling of foreboding.

She opened her eyes and propped her chin on her hand as she stared at the notebook page in front of her. The kerosene lamp overhead cast a warm glow on the mending pile and the sheet of paper where she had compiled a list of things to do.

Clean the house.

Mend everything torn or frayed.

Make two new kapps.

Stitch the border on my new quilt.

She had already finished the first item and was on to the second. They were all things she could do in a week or less and she had a lot more time on her hands than a mere week. Spring seemed a long way off. Inviting Vernon and his family was one way to help fill the days.

She added three more items to her list.

Don't be bored.

Don't be sad.

Don't go insane.

Six days a week for nearly five years she had gone in early to open the fabric store and closed up after seven in the evening. Without her job to keep her busy, what was she going to do? Work had been her salvation after her husband's passing.

Had it really been five years? Sometimes it seemed as if he'd only gone out of town and he would be back any minute. Of course, he wouldn't be.

She had tried to convince Janet to let her run the shop until spring, but Janet wouldn't hear of it. Instead, her boss said, "Enjoy the time off, Sarah. You work too hard. Have a carefree Christmas season for a change."

Janet didn't understand. Time off wouldn't make the holidays brighter. Six years ago Sarah and Jonas learned he had cancer only a week before Christmas. He battled the disease for months longer than the doctors thought he could. He died on Christmas Eve the following year. A month later, her sister ran away, leaving Sarah, her parents and her brother to grieve and worry. Their father died of pneumonia the following Thanksgiving. Her mother passed away barely a year later. Vernon said they died of a broken heart after Bethany left.

Bethany had been the light of the family. Her daring sense of humor and love of life were too big for Hope Springs and the simple life of the Amish. It had been two years ago at Christmas when Jonathan Dresher came to tell Sarah that Bethany was dead, too. Since that day, Sarah faced the Christmas season with intense dread, waiting and wondering what the next blow would be.

She sat up straight. She wasn't going to spend this winter cooped up in the house, staring at the walls and dreading Christmas. She had to find something to keep the bleak depression at bay. To her list, she quickly added *Find Another Job!* She circled it a half dozen times.

The sound of her front door opening made her look up. Like most Amish people, she never locked her doors. Knocking was an English habit the Amish ignored for they knew they were always welcome in another Amish home. A brief gust of winter wind came in with her visitor. Sarah's mood rose when she recognized her friend and neighbor, Grace Ann Beachy.

"Gut-n-owed," Sarah called out a cheerfully good evening in Pennsylvania Deitsch, sometimes called Pennsylvania Dutch, the German dialect spoken by the Amish.

"Sarah, I must speak to you."

Sarah was stunned to see tears in Grace's eyes. Fearing something serious had happened, Sarah shot to her feet. "Are you okay?"

"Nee, I'm not. I love him so much." Grace promptly buried her face in her hands and began sobbing.

Sarah gathered the weeping girl in her arms. Matters of the heart were often painful, but never more so than when it was first love. "There, there, child. It will be all right." Sarah led Grace to the living room and sat beside her on the sofa. The two women had been friends for years. They were as close as sisters.

Between sobs, Grace managed to recount her evening with Henry Zook from the time they left the singing party. The whole thing boiled down to the fact that Henry had grown tired of waiting for Grace to accept his offer of marriage. The conversation soon turned to a quarrel. Henry, in a fit of anger, said Esta Barkman had been making eyes at him all evening. Maybe she was ready to settle down and marry.

Sarah lifted her young neighbor's face and wiped the tears from her cheeks. "If you love him, why don't you accept him? Is there someone else?"

Grace rolled her eyes and threw up her hands. "There's Levi and the twins and the business. How can I leave my brothers? Levi can't manage the business alone. He can barely speak to people he knows. He's terrible at taking care of new customers. They'll go elsewhere with their business and where will that leave him? You depend on the income from the shop, too."

"Your brother could hire someone to replace you. I know Mary Shetler would welcome the chance to have a job in an Amish business."

"I'm not sure she would want to work with the twins, knowing what they did."

Grace was probably right about that. Mary Shetler had left the Amish and wound up living with an English fellow who turned out to be a scoundrel. Just fifteen and pregnant at the time, Mary had been terrified to learn her boyfriend planned to sell her baby. She had the child alone one night while he was gone. Planning to leave her boyfriend for good as soon as she was able, she hid her infant daughter in an Amish buggy along with a note promising that she would return for her.

The buggy belonged to Levi Beachy. The twins had taken it without permission and sneaked out to see a movie in another town. It wasn't until they were on their way home that they discovered the baby. Afraid their midnight romp would get them in trouble if they brought the infant home, they stopped at the nearest farmhouse and left the child on the doorstep in the middle of the night.

Fortunately, the home belonged to Ada Kauffman. Her daughter Miriam was a nurse. She and Sheriff Nick Bradley finally reunited mother and child but not before Mary suffered dreadfully believing her daughter Hannah was lost to her.

"All right, Mary was not a good suggestion, but I'm sure there are other young women who could work with Levi."

"Maybe, but what about the twins? They could burn the town down or who knows what if someone doesn't keep an eye on them. I know I haven't done a great job, but I'm better than Levi. When he's working, he could be standing in five feet of snow and not notice. I can't leave knowing no one will look after them."

"I'm sorry you feel trapped by your family, Grace. You know I would help if I could."

Grace grabbed her arm. "You can."

"How?"

"Help me find a wife for Levi."

Chapter Two

Sarah stared at Grace in stunned disbelief. "You must be joking. How could I find a wife for your brother? I'm no matchmaker."

"But you are," Grace insisted. "Didn't you convince your cousin Adrian Lapp to court Faith Martin?"

"Convince him? *Nee,* I did not. If I remember right, I cautioned Faith against losing her heart to Adrian because he was still grieving for his first wife." Sarah knew how it felt to mourn for a spouse.

"And that was exactly the push Faith needed to see beyond his gruff behavior. They married, and they are very happy together. Besides, you're the one who convinced me to give Henry a chance."

"I don't remember saying anything to you about going out with Henry."

"If you hadn't told me how your Jonas settled down from his wild ways after you were married, I never would have given Henry the time of day. But I did, and now I'm in love with him. I want to marry him. You have to help me. I will just die if he marries someone else."

Sarah leveled a stern look at her young neighbor. "That's a bit dramatic, Grace."

Drawing a deep breath, Grace nodded. "I'm sorry. I don't know what to do. I can't leave Levi and the boys, but I can't expect Henry to wait forever, either. I'm caught between a rock and a hard place with no way out."

"I hardly think finding a wife for your brother is the answer."

"It's the only one I can come up with. I'm afraid if I ask Henry to wait much longer he'll find someone else."

Sarah took pity on her young friend and tried to reassure her. "Henry Zook will not marry anyone else. I've seen the way he looks at you."

"I believe he loves me. He says he does, but he wants an answer."

"Henry is used to getting his own way. His mother has done her best to spoil him. He will be a good man, but right now he has the impatience of youth. What you and Henry need is a cooling-off time."

"What do you mean by that?"

The last thing Sarah wanted was to see her friend pushed into something she might regret. "You two have been seeing each other almost daily. I think both of you could use some time apart. Rushing into marriage can cause a lifetime of misery."

Grace shook her head. "Oh, Sarah. I don't know. What would Henry think?"

Sarah could see that Grace's dilemma was taking its toll on her friend. There were shadows beneath her eyes that didn't belong on a girl who was barely twenty. Her cheeks were pale and thinner, as if she'd lost weight.

There had to be some way to help her. Suddenly, an idea occurred to Sarah.

"He can't object if you tell him you're going to visit your grandmother in Pennsylvania. I know you've wanted to see her for ages. It will give Henry a chance to miss you while you're gone, and it will give you a chance to relax and think about what you want to do without worrying about Henry or about your brothers."

"But what if Henry doesn't miss me?"

"Wouldn't you rather know that before you are wed?" Sarah asked gently.

"*Grossmammi* has asked me to come for a visit many times. She's getting on in years. I would like to spend some time with her, but that means I would miss the quilting bee for Ina Stultz and the hoedown that's coming up."

"I'll take your place at Ina's quilting bee, and there will be other hoedowns. Of course, once you marry, that kind of fun is over." To marry, an Amish couple had to be baptized into the faith, which meant their running-around time was ended. Barn parties and such gatherings would give way to family visits and community events that bound together all members of their Amish faith.

"What about the business?" Grace asked.

"Levi will understand that you need some time to make up your mind about marrying. Besides, he's a grown man. He can manage without you for a few weeks. I can help if worse comes to worst. I used to work there every day."

"Oh, it'll come to worse very quickly. I don't doubt you could do all that I do, but what about your job?"

"The fabric shop is closing for a few months, so

I have some extra time on my hands." A lot of extra time, but was working beside Levi the way she wanted to spend it?

Grace's face lit up. She grabbed Sarah's hand. "You are so clever. You can work with Levi and find out what kind of wife would suit him all at the same time. I won't feel a bit bad about leaving him, knowing you're there."

Sarah held back a smile. If this is what it took to get Grace to leave town for a few weeks, Sarah would agree. "I hadn't thought of it that way, but you may be right. In spite of the fact that Levi was Jonas's friend and has been my neighbor for years, I don't really know him well."

Grace sat back with a satisfied smile. "I can tell you anything you want to know about him. Go ahead, ask me something."

"All right, what does Levi like to do for fun?"

A furrow appeared between Grace's eyebrows. "He doesn't really do anything for fun. He doesn't have a sense of humor, that's for sure. He works in the shop all day and sometimes late into the night."

"I know he is hard-working, but does he like to hunt or play checkers or other board games?"

"I don't think so. I mean, I've known him to go hunting in the fall when we need meat, but I don't think he enjoys it. The boys and I like board games, but Levi doesn't play with us."

What kind of wife would want a husband who didn't interact with his own family? Sarah said, "He used to go fishing with my husband. Does he still do that with his friends?"

"He goes fishing by himself sometimes. Levi doesn't

really have friends. Everyone says he makes right fine buggies, though."

Sarah knew that for a fact. She drove one he and Jonas had built together. It was solid and still rode well after eight years. However, Levi had to have other traits that would make him attractive to a potential wife. "What does your brother like to read?"

"He reads the Bible every night, and he reads *The Budget*."

The Budget was a weekly newspaper put out by the Amish for the Amish. Everyone read it. It was good to know he read the Bible. A devout man usually made an excellent husband. "Does he read other kinds of books?"

"Books? No, I don't think so." Grace shook her head.

Sarah never suspected Levi was such a dull fellow. What had her outgoing husband seen in him?

"You've been a big help, Grace. I'll look over my list of single friends and think on who might find him appealing." Right off hand, she couldn't think of anyone.

"Do you really believe I should leave town?"

"I do. It will do you, your grandmother and Henry a world of good. Trust me on this."

Grace nodded bravely. "I do trust you, Sarah. I'll do it."

Sarah grinned. "That's the spirit."

Grace jumped to her feet. "I must ask the Wilsons down the block if I can use their phone. I need to find out when the bus leaves and call my grandmother's English neighbors so they can tell her I'm coming."

"But it's getting late, child. You should go home and talk this over with your family."

"*Nee.* If I'm to do this it must be now." She leaned

down and pressed a kiss on Sarah's cheek. "You're the best friend ever, Sarah Wyse."

Without a backward glance, she rushed out as quickly as she had rushed in, slamming the door behind her.

"I'm not sure your brothers are going to feel the same," Sarah said to the empty room.

Levi tugged his suspenders up over his shoulders as he walked down the stairs from his bedroom on the second floor of the house. When he reached the kitchen, he paused. Instead of the usual aromas of toast, bacon and scrambled eggs, the forlorn faces of his twin brothers sitting at a bare table greeted him.

A suitcase sat beside the front door. His sister, Grace, entered the room, tying her best bonnet beneath her chin. "I left sliced ham in the refrigerator for sandwiches. You boys can heat some up in a skillet for breakfast if you'd like or make oatmeal. After today, you're on your own as far as getting something to eat. There is plenty of canned fruit and vegetables in the cellar along with canned meats. If you don't want to cook, the Shoofly Pie Café serves good food, and it's reasonable."

She picked up her suitcase and gave her younger brothers each a stern look. "I expect the house to still be standing when I return."

Levi found his tongue. "Grace, what are you doing?"

"I'm going to visit *Grossmammi* for a few weeks." She had a smile on her face, but it was forced.

He scowled at her. Grace was impulsive, but this was odd even for her. She hadn't said a word about visiting their relative. "Is Grandmother ill? Is that why you're going?"

"*Nee,* she's fine as far as I know."

"You can't take off at the drop of a hat like this."

Atlee spoke up, "That's what we told her."

"But she told us she was going and that's that," Moses added.

Grace's smile faded. "Please, Levi. Don't forbid me to go. I need you to understand that I have to get away for a while."

How could he understand when she hadn't told him anything? He opened his mouth but nothing came out. She took it as his consent and her smile returned. He never could deny her what she wanted. She and the twins had lost so much already.

She rushed to his side and pressed a kiss to his cheek. "Thank you, Levi. Sarah said you would understand. I've got to run or I'll miss my bus. This was a wonderful idea. I'm so glad she suggested it. I can't wait to see *Grossmammi* again."

Sarah suggested it? He should have known. "Grace, who will take care of our customers?" he asked as panic began to set in. He couldn't deal with people. Words froze in his mouth and he looked foolish.

"Sarah will help you. Be kind to her." Grace gave him a bright smile as she opened the door. A flurry of cold air swept in as she went out.

When Levi blinked he was still standing in his kitchen not really sure what had just happened. He looked at his brothers. They both shrugged.

Atlee said, "I'd like dippy eggs with my ham."

"I want mine scrambled." Moses folded his hands and waited.

Levi stared at the black stove with a sinking feeling in his gut. How on earth would they manage without Grace?

An hour later, Levi left the house and headed for his retreat, his workshop, where nothing smelled like burnt ham or charred eggs and he couldn't hear his brothers' complaints. He'd left after telling them to do the dishes.

A body would have thought I told them to take the moon down and polish it the way they gaped at me.

When he left, they were arguing over who should wash and who should dry. He didn't have time to referee because he was late, and he was never late opening his business.

He still didn't know why Grace had to leave town so suddenly. He hoped she hadn't gotten herself in trouble. That wasn't the kind of thing a man wanted to ask his sister. All Atlee and Moses knew was that after an argument with her boyfriend, Grace had decided to visit their grandmother for a few weeks. How many was a few? Three? Four? She didn't intend to stay away for a month, did she?

One thing Grace said stuck in Levi's mind. She'd said Sarah had suggested it. He suspected that Sarah Wyse was a whole lot better informed about his sister's abrupt departure than he was.

Two men in Amish clothing were standing in front of his store when he approached.

"Did you decide to sleep in today, Levi?" one man joked.

Levi tried to think of a snappy comeback, but nothing occurred to him. He kept his eyes down and wrestled with the key that refused to unlock the door.

"Reckon he wants to start keeping banker's hours," the second man said with a deep chuckle.

Levi hated it when people made fun of him. He searched his heart for forgiveness and offered it up to God, but he still felt small. He always felt small.

When the stubborn lock finally clicked open, he rushed inside. He hadn't had a chance to get the stove going and the building was ice-cold. The two men waited by the counter while he stoked the fire. When he had a flame going, they both stepped up to warm their hands.

Levi cleared his throat and asked, "How can I help you?"

The outside door opened, but Levi couldn't see who had come in. The men blocked his line of sight. He hoped it was the twins because he didn't like dealing with customers. Not that the twins would do better. They were likely to pull some prank and then disappear, leaving him to deal with the fallout.

The taller of the two men said, "We're wanting to order a pair of courting buggies for our oldest boys. They're good sons and they are willing to help pay some of the cost. Before we place any orders, what kind of deal can you give us for ordering two buggies together?"

Levi scowled. "A buggy costs what a buggy costs."

"That's not what Abe Yoder over in Sugarcreek told us. He's willing to take ten percent off for a double order."

Levi struggled to find the right thing to say. Grace always knew just what to say. Why did she have to take off and leave him to work alone? She knew how much he hated dealing with people.

Abe Yoder's offer was a good one, but Levi didn't want to send these men back to his competition. He couldn't cut ten percent off his price or he'd be making the buggies for free. He cleared his throat again and felt heat rising in his face. Why was it always this way? Other people didn't have trouble talking.

Behind the men, a woman's voice said, "If Abe Yoder says he can cut ten percent off he's overcharging to begin with."

The men turned around as Sarah Wyse approached the stove. She was looked straight at him. "Isn't that right, Levi?"

He nodded and followed her lead. *"Ja."*

She waited, as if expecting he would say more, but when he didn't she gave her attention to the men. "Come up to the counter, neighbors, and let us talk about what you think your sons will like and what they can live without. Once we have an idea of the amount of work that will be needed, we can give you a fair estimate. You'll find our prices are as good as Abe Yoder's and our quality is better."

Levi blew out a breath of relief. Everyone's attention was on her and not on him. Now he could think.

She stepped behind the counter and began opening drawers. "If I can just find our order forms."

"Top left." Levi supplied the direction she needed.

She opened the correct drawer and said, "Ah, here we are. Changes can be made later, but that may affect the price once we've started work. Do you know what color of upholstery they want on the seats? Do they want drum brakes? How about cup holders and storage boxes? I assume these will be open buggies as you said they are for courting."

She waited, pencil posed, with a friendly smile on her face that could charm anyone. Levi was grateful for her intervention until he remembered that she had sent Grace out of town in the first place.

Once again, Sarah seemed bent on making his life difficult.

Chapter Three

Sarah took down the information the men provided along with their addresses and promised them an estimate would arrive in the mail in a few days. They left, content with that.

When the door closed behind them, Sarah found herself alone. Levi was nowhere in sight. Silence surrounded her except for the occasional crackling and pop of the fire in the potbellied stove. She had time to look around. This cavernous building had been Jonas's favorite place.

There was nothing fancy about the shop. The bare rafters were visible overhead. Thick and sturdy, the wooden trusses were old and stained with age and smoke. A few missing shingles let in the light and a dusting of snow that had melted into small puddles here and there.

Buggy frames in all stages of completion were lined up along one side. Wagon wheels were everywhere, leaning against the walls and hanging from hooks. Some were new and some were waiting to be repaired. Wheel repair made up the bulk of their business. A good buggy wheel could last five years or more, but eventually they all needed to be fixed or replaced.

Down the center of the shop were two rows of various machines. Although their Amish religion forbade the use of electricity, in their church district it was possible to use propane-powered engines to operate machinery. While some of the equipment was new, much of it was older than the hills.

Sarah walked to the ancient metal bender and grasped the handle. The bender used heavy-duty iron gears and wheels to press bands of steel into symmetrical rings. The steel ring was then welded together to form the outside rim of a wagon wheel.

How many rims had she cranked out when she worked beside Jonas and Levi? Two hundred? Three hundred? She could still do it, but it would take a while to build up her muscles. Carrying bolts of fabric wasn't nearly as physical.

Turning around, she noticed the back of the shop held various pieces of wood waiting to be assembled into buggy tops and doors. In the far corner of the building, an area had been partitioned off and enclosed to make a room for cutting and sewing upholstery. The old sewing machine was operated with a foot pedal. She knew it well.

Although almost all the buggies they made were black, as required by their church, a person could order anything from red velvet to black leather for the buggy's interior and seats. Jonas's courting buggy had dark blue velvet upholstery. When he sold it two years after their wedding she cried like a baby.

She smiled at the memory, but she wasn't here to relive the past. She went looking for Levi. Would he

have something to say about her usurping his authority in dealing with customers? She found him working
on the undercarriage of a buggy at the very back of the
building. Or rather, she found his feet.

The sole of his left shoe was worn through. He had
used a piece of cardboard inside to keep his socks dry.
Did his socks have holes in them, too? She imagined
they did for the hems of his pant legs were worn and
frayed. Grace was wrong. Levi didn't need a wife. He
desperately needed a wife.

Someone with housewifely skills to mend and darn
for him and to make sure he was properly clothed.
Someone to insist he get new shoes for the winter instead of making do with cardboard insoles. She'd paid
no attention to the business books after Jonas died, pre-
ferring to leave all that in Levi's hands. Was the business doing poorly? Or was Levi frugal to the extreme?

Clearly, it was time she got her head back into the
business. "Levi, may I speak with you?"

A grunt was her answer. Was it a yes grunt or a no
grunt? Only his feet moved as he struggled with some
hidden problem. She decided to be optimistic. "I'd like
to take a look at the ledgers."

His feet stilled. "Why?"

She crouched down trying to see his face. "I realize
that I've left the running of the business to you alone
for far too long. We are partners in this, are we not?"

He wiggled backward out from under the carriage
and sat up to glare at her. "I don't cheat you."

She pressed a hand to her chest. "Goodness, I never
thought you did. I simply want to begin doing my share
again. Jonas and I used to do the books together. I know
what I'm looking at."

"Jonas is gone. I do the books now." He lay down and started to inch back under the buggy.

Sarah was sorely tempted to kick the sole of his miserable excuse for a shoe, but she didn't. More flies were caught with honey than with vinegar. "I don't mean to step on your toes, Levi, but I am the owner of this shop, and I have a right to see the books. I'm sure you understand my position."

"Help yourself," came his muffled reply.

"Fine." She left him to his work and headed for the small enclosed place that was used as an office. A wooden stool sat in front of a cluttered desk. Off to one side, a stack of ledgers and catalogs were piled together. She started by searching through them, but soon realized they weren't what she needed.

She went back to his feet. "Where are the current ledgers, Levi?"

"Ask Grace."

She blew out a huff of frustration. "I can't very well ask Grace. She's on her way to Pennsylvania."

He came out from under the frame and rose to his feet. "*Ja,* she is. I wonder why my sister chose to go running off during our busiest season with inventory to do and four carriages to finish. No, wait. I know why she left. You told her to go."

It was the longest speech he'd ever spoken to her. Sarah curbed her ire at his tone. "Grace didn't tell you why she went to visit her grandmother?"

"All she said was that it was your idea."

"Oh." No wonder he seemed upset. Where should she start?

He folded his arms and stared at his shoes. "Is Grace in…trouble?" he asked, his voice low and worried.

"Trouble? You mean… Oh! No, no, it's nothing like that. I hope she would confide in me if that were the case. No, she and Henry have gotten serious so quickly that I thought a short cooling-off time would give her a chance to decide if she really wanted to marry him or not."

"Marry? Grace?"

Levi looked astonished by the idea. It was almost comical. Sarah struggled to hold back a smile. "That's what young people do when they've been courting."

"She's too young to marry." He turned to his tool chest and grabbed a second wrench.

"She's the same age I was when Jonas and I married. I was twenty and he was twenty-seven."

"That was different." Levi didn't look at her.

"How?"

"It just was. Grace Ann is a child." He returned to his position under the buggy.

"*Nee,* Levi, your *shveshtah* is a grown woman. You must be prepared for her to marry and start a family of her own."

A second grunt was her reply.

If Levi hadn't considered where his sister's courtship was leading, then Sarah really had her work cut out for her. Not only did she need to find a woman who could put up with his stoic ways, she needed to help him see that Grace was an adult. This could certainly make the coming winter months more interesting.

Sarah stared at Levi's worn-out footwear. First things first, who did she know that might be ready for a husband?

Several women came to mind. There was the current schoolteacher, Leah Belier, a sweet-tempered woman in her late twenties. But having had the twins in school until two years ago, would she be willing to take them on a permanent basis? It would take a brave woman to do that.

It was too bad Susan Lapp had married Daniel Hershberger last month. While it was an excellent match for both of them, Susan would have been perfect for Levi. Big-boned and strong with a no-nonsense attitude, Susan was a woman who could keep Levi and the twins in line with one hand tied behind her back. Yes, it was too bad she was already taken.

There was Joann Yoder, but she was a year older than Levi. Sarah couldn't see them together. Joann was nearly as shy as he was.

Mary Beth Zook was also a possibility. Sarah wondered how the bishop and his wife would feel about two of their children marrying into the Beachy family. Perhaps Mary Beth wasn't the best choice, but Sarah didn't rule her out.

Another woman who came to mind was Fannie Nissley, the niece of David and Martha Nissley. She had come to Hope Springs to help the family when Martha had been injured by an overturned wagon a few years before. Martha was fully recovered, but Fannie stayed on because she liked the area.

Sarah guessed her age to be twenty-five or -six. As far as she knew, Fannie wasn't seeing anyone. This coming Sunday after the prayer service would be a good time to find out for sure. Aunt Emma would know if any of the single women in the area had already made a commitment.

Sarah suddenly thought of Sally Yoder. Sally currently worked for Elam Sutter in his basket-weaving business. Sally was only in her early twenties, but she might be ready to settle down. She had a good head on her shoulders and could help Levi manage the business.

Sarah looked around the building and remembered the many hours she and Jonas had spent poring over the company books and inventory, trying to stretch a nickel into a dollar to make ends meet. They hadn't seemed like good times back then, but now she cherished every moment she and her husband had spent working and struggling together.

God took him too soon.

Memories, both good and not so good, filled her mind. As she looked around, it was easy to see traces of Jonas everywhere. The chair where he sat as he ordered supplies was still waiting at the counter, as though he might return at any minute. Of course, Levi used it now.

The workbench Jonas made from scrap lumber had stood the test of time, but it had been shifted from its original position. So had the boxes of parts that once lined the wall above it. Now, they stood along the west wall, closer to where the bulk of the woodwork for the buggies took place. It was a better spot, and she could see why Levi had done it.

She said, "You have made many changes in here. I see you moved the workbench to beneath the south windows. Was that for better light?"

He didn't answer. Sarah crossed to the workbench Jonas had fashioned and laid her hand on the worn wood. She could almost feel him here beside her. Looking out the window, she realized that Levi had an unobstructed view of the narrow street outside and of her kitchen window across the way.

How many times had she sat at that table and cried,

worried and prayed since Jonas's passing. Had Levi seen it all?

She glanced toward the buggy frame. He was no longer underneath it. He stood, wrenches in each hand, watching her with a guarded expression on his face.

Levi wondered if she realized how pretty she was with the early morning sunshine streaming through the window, bathing her face in golden light. Her features were as delicate as the frost that etched the corners of the glass behind her.

Her white *kapp* glowed brightly, almost like a halo around her heart-shaped face. Her blond hair, carefully parted in the middle and all but hidden beneath her bonnet gave only a hint of the luxurious beauty her uncut tresses must hold. Only a husband and God should view a woman's crowing glory. For a second, Levi envied Jonas's right to behold Sarah's hair flowing over her shoulders and down her back.

The ribbons of her *kapp* were untied and drew Levi's attention to the curve of her jaw and the slenderness of her neck. To his eyes, she grew more beautiful with each passing year. It was no wonder Jonas had fallen in love with her.

Levi dropped his gaze to his feet, afraid what he was thinking would somehow show in his eyes. She was his best friend's wife. It was wrong of him to think of her as beautiful.

"Do you mind?" he asked.

When she didn't answer, he looked up. She glanced out the window and then at him.

"Do I mind what?" she asked with an odd inflection in her tone.

He waved his arm to indicate the shop. "The changes?"

"*Nee,* it is your workspace," she said quickly.

"*Goot.*" He returned his tools to the wooden tray and carried it to the workbench, sliding it into its place on the end of the counter where Jonas had kept it.

Levi hadn't been much younger than the twins were now when the local sheriff brought word that their parents were dead. They had both drowned when their buggy was overturned and swept away while they had been trying to cross a flooded roadway.

Jonas had come to the house and offered Levi a job when he was ready. Levi never forgot Jonas's kindness in treating him like an adult, like a man with responsibilities instead of like a boy who needed someone to look after him and his siblings.

As Jonas taught Levi the buggy-building trade, Levi had quickly realized Jonas would have been smarter to hire someone who already knew the business rather than an untried teenager.

When he mentioned his thoughts on the subject, Jonas had laid a hand on Levi's shoulder and said, "I want to work with someone I respect and enjoy being around. You and I are a good fit. Besides, if I teach you how to do a thing, I know it will be done right."

Levi never forgot that moment. He became determined to learn everything Jonas had to teach so that his respect was not misplaced. In that, Levi believed he had succeeded.

Sarah had followed Levi to the counter. She asked, "Do you mind my helping out until Grace returns?"

"Not much choice," he conceded gruffly.

"I'm sorry that my advice to Grace sent her racing off so quickly. I honestly thought she would talk it over with you and the two of you could decide when a good time for her visit would be. I didn't mean for this to happen."

"Grace can be impulsive." To his surprise, it wasn't all that difficult to talk to Sarah. His throat didn't close around the words and keep them prisoner as it usually did.

She laughed aloud at his comment. "That's an understatement."

Levi cringed and felt the heat rush to his face. Was she laughing at him or with him? Did it matter?

Sarah said, "I'm at your beck and call, so put me to work. What needs doing in here today that Grace would normally do?"

What he wanted was for her to go home. The workshop was his sanctuary. How could it be a place of peace with Sarah in it? She disrupted everything, including his thinking.

He said, "Nothing I can't handle." Now maybe she would leave.

"I can at least clean up." She turned around, grabbed a red rag from the box he kept them in and began straightening his workbench, moving his tools around and brushing at the bits of loose wood on the countertop.

He didn't like people touching his stuff. "Don't mess with my tools."

She paid him no mind. "I'm not messing with them, I'm cleaning off your workspace."

"Stop," he pleaded.

She held up a lone drill bit. "Where does this go?"

"Take it home with you," he snapped abruptly.

He shut his mouth in horror. He'd never spoken harshly to anyone.

Sarah stared at him for the longest moment and then chuckled with delight. "You are so amusing, Levi. And Grace told me you don't have a sense of humor. Take it home with me, how funny. I'll find where it goes. You get back to work and pretend I'm not even here."

Like that was possible. He turned away before he said something he would surely regret.

She kept dusting. "I'll have this cleaned up in no time. I remember how to do inventory, too. It won't be long before the end of the year. Might as well get a jump on it. I'll start on that when I'm done with this."

"No need." Inventory would take days. Days with Sarah underfoot wasn't something he wanted to endure. He needed to be able to concentrate. She didn't take the hint.

"I don't mind. I'd forgotten how much I enjoy being out here. Don't you love the smell of leather and wood? It's comforting knowing that each piece on the walls around me has a place and a function. I'm glad I told Grace I would help. This place could use some sprucing up, though."

Jonas had often said that Sarah had a one-track mind when she wanted to do something. Levi didn't know how true that statement was until three hours later when she was using a long-handled broom and an overturned bucket to reach cobwebs that had hung from the rafters longer than she had been alive.

Unless he took her by the arm, led her to the door and locked it behind her, he was going to be stuck with Sarah until Grace returned.

Please, Lord, let Grace's visit be a short one.

Levi drew a deep breath. It was almost lunchtime, and he hadn't gotten nearly enough done. His eyes were constantly drawn to where Sarah was working.

He had orders to fill and much to do in the coming weeks. When there was snow on the ground, many Amish families brought their farm wagons and buggies in to be repaired while they used their sleighs. With Christmas less than a month away, he was sure to get swamped with work soon.

Moving to the carriage body he was working on, he studied the list of accessories Grace had written out for him to add. The buggy was for Daniel Hershberger's new bride. The well-to-do businessman was sparing no expense for his wife's buggy. As Levi marked out the wood for the extra-sturdy seats to be added, Sarah began humming a hymn. After a few bars, she began singing softly. She had a lovely voice, soothing and sweet.

Levi gripped his handsaw and drew it back and forth across the board. The sound blocked Sarah's voice and he stopped.

She must have noticed because she asked, "Does my singing bother you?"

He looked toward her and found her watching him intently. "*Nee,* it's nice."

She gave him a sweet smile and went back to work, humming as she did so. Maybe having her around for a few weeks wouldn't be so bad after all.

The outside door opened and Henry Zook walked in. He nodded to Sarah and crossed the room to stand in front of Levi. "I must speak with Grace. Is she about?"

Levi could feel his throat growing tight. This was not

a conversation he wanted to have. He cast a speaking glance at Sarah. This was her doing. She would have to make it right.

Chapter Four

Sarah caught the look Levi darted at her. It was imploring, half-accusing. He clearly wanted her to take over the conversation with Henry. Instead, she retreated to his small office to give the men some privacy.

Yes, it was her fault that Grace had left town so quickly, but Levi needed his eyes opened to exactly how serious Henry was about Grace.

The office had four walls but no ceiling to separate it from the rest of the building. She had no trouble hearing their conversation.

"Please, Levi, I must to speak to Grace. It's important."

"You can't." Levi's reply was barely audible.

"What do you mean, I can't?"

"She's gone."

"Gone? Gone where?" Henry demanded.

"She took off with her handsome English boyfriend early this morning." A new voice entered the conversation.

"*Ja,* he was driving a fine red car."

Sarah was so startled to hear the voices of the twins

that she leaned around the doorway to see where they were. She hadn't heard them come in. How long had they been inside?

"Yup, bright red his car was," Atlee agreed with his brother. "Took off with the tires throwing gravel every which way. Grace didn't look none too sad to be leaving this place."

They both sat on the seat of a wagon waiting for repairs with identical smirks on their faces. They elbowed each other with mirth.

Poor Henry. He looked from Levi to the twins with growing disbelief. "Grace would not do such a thing."

The boys hooted with laughter. Moses said, "Proves you don't know our sister as well as you think."

Why didn't Levi say something? Sarah was ready to intervene when Levi spoke at last. "Enough!"

The twins fell silent, but didn't wipe the smiles off their faces. It was clear they didn't think much of their sister's suitor.

"Grace went to visit our grandmother." Levi walked away from Henry as if the conversation was over.

Henry wasn't about to leave without more of an explanation. He followed Levi into the office, forcing Sarah to back into the corner. "Grace never mentioned going out of town for a visit. Has your grandmother taken ill?"

"Nee," Levi replied and pulled open a drawer to search for something. Sarah found herself stuck in the small room with both men for there wasn't enough room to get past them. They both ignored her.

Henry raked a hand through his thick blond hair. "Then I don't understand. Why would she suddenly leave without letting me know? We had a disagreement, but I didn't think she was that upset."

Levi jerked a thumb in Sarah's direction. "Ask her."

Levi found the sheet of paper he was looking for and walked out of the office, leaving Sarah to face Henry alone. He waited for her to speak, confusion written across his face.

Sarah squared her shoulders and indicated the empty chair beside the desk. "Henry, sit down."

He took a seat. "When is Grace coming back?"

"I'm not sure when she'll be back."

"But she will be back, right?" His eyes pleaded for confirmation.

"Of course. She needs some time to think things over without feeling pressured."

He blew out a long breath. "I'm a *nah*. I shouldn't have pushed so hard."

Sarah smiled gently. "You are not a fool, Henry. You're in love. You are impatient to be with her as a husband. That is only natural. Grace has many concerns, but she says that she loves you. If she is the woman God has chosen for you she is worth waiting for."

"I could accept that if I knew how long she wants me to wait. She won't set a date."

He glanced over his shoulder and lowered his voice. "I know she is worried that her family can't manage without her. Can you convince her she has to start thinking about what is best for her?"

"That's exactly what she is doing. If you love her, you must trust her. I suggest you write her and tell her how you feel."

"I feel confused."

Sarah gave him a sympathetic smile. "Do not fret.

Things will work out. Now, go home and write Grace a long letter telling her how much you miss her, how sorry you are for your impatience and how you look forward to seeing her again."

"I'm not all that good with words, Frau Wyse."

"They are in your heart, Henry. Look for them there."

He nodded and rose to his feet. "*Danki.* I will do that."

When he left, she walked out into the area where Levi and the twins were putting the top on a buggy. When they had it set in place and bolted on, she said, "I have chicken stew simmering at my house. Levi, if you don't have other plans you are welcome to eat with me for I know Grace usually does all the cooking."

The twins rushed toward her. "We're starving," they said, together.

She held up a hand to stop them. "Psalm 101:7. *He that worketh deceit shall not dwell within my house: he that telleth lies shall not tarry in my sight.*"

The boys looked at each other. "What does that mean?" Moses asked.

Levi walked by with a small grin tugging at the corner of his mouth. "It means you're on your own for lunch. *Danki,* Sarah. I'll be happy to break bread in your home."

"But we were only teasing Henry," Atlee insisted.

"*Ja,* it was a joke," Moses added.

"It was cruel, and you took pleasure in his discomfort. But I forgive you, and I'm sure Henry will, too, when you ask him." She turned to follow Levi out the door.

"So we can eat with you?" Moses called after her.

Sarah paused at the door and looked back at their hopeful faces. She smiled at them. "No."

Their shocked expressions were priceless. She softly closed the door behind her.

Levi opened Sarah's front door and allowed her to go in ahead of him. The mouthwatering smell of stewing chicken and vegetables made his stomach grumble. His poor breakfast had been hours ago.

Sarah said, "You can wash up at the sink. It will only take a few minutes to get things ready. Are you upset that I refused to feed the twins?"

His family never asked him if their actions were upsetting. He wasn't sure what answer Sarah wanted to hear. He chose, hoping for the best. *"Nee."*

"I'm glad. I don't want you to think that I intended to discipline them without asking your permission. I simply wanted to make it clear to them that actions have consequences. They were intentionally unkind to Henry."

He turned on the water and picked up a bar of soap from the dish. As he washed his hands, the scent of lavender mingled with the delicious smell of the cooking meal. He held the bar close to his nose. It smelled like Sarah, clean, fresh, springlike.

He put the soap down and quickly rinsed his hands. He dried them on a soft white towel hanging from a rod on the end of the counter. It didn't feel right using her things.

When he turned around, Sarah was staring at him. She asked, "You do understand, don't you?"

He hadn't been listening. "What?"

"Why I told the twins they couldn't eat here."

"Sure."

She waited, as if she expected him to say something else. Nothing occurred to him. He slipped his hands in the front pockets of his pants. Could he feel more awkward? Not likely.

Nodding, she said, "*Goot.* Sit."

She indicated the chair at the head of the table. Jonas's place. Okay, that was going to feel more awkward.

Levi pulled his hands from his pockets and took a seat. Sarah moved around the kitchen, gathering plates and silverware. He rubbed his hands on the tops of his thighs. He was hungry, but he hadn't realized how intimate it would feel eating alone with Sarah. They weren't doing anything wrong. He knew that, but being this close to her set his nerve endings buzzing like angry bees.

Even sitting in this chair felt wrong. It was Jonas's chair. It didn't matter that Jonas was gone. It didn't seem right to take the place that was once his. Memories of their last hours together poured into Levi's mind.

He could hear Jonas's hoarse whisper as plainly as if they were back in the upstairs bedroom before his death.

"Watch over Sarah when I'm gone, Levi. Promise me you'll watch over her until she decides to remarry."

"You'll get better."

"Nee, my time is up, my friend. God calls me home. I want Sarah to find happiness with someone again, though I pray she doesn't remarry in haste. I know women who have and regretted their decision."

"Sarah was wise enough to choose you in the first place. She'll be fine."

"You know my Sarah well. I'd rest easier knowing she loved someone strong, from a good family, with a

fine farm or business. Promise me you'll watch over her until she meets him, Levi. Promise me this. It's all I ask of you."

Sarah set a glass of fresh milk on the table, jarring Levi's mind out of the past. He picked up the glass and took a long drink. Her gaze remained focused on his arm.

He stopped drinking. "What?"

"I can mend that rip in your sleeve right quick if you'll slip your shirt off."

He turned his arm trying to see what she was talking about and splashed milk out of his glass in the process. Embarrassed, he looked for something to clean it up with. She was quicker, placing a kitchen towel over the puddle and trying hard not to laugh. Why was he so clumsy when she was around?

"Sorry," he muttered.

"Don't worry about it. Accidents happen. Shall I fix your sleeve?"

He didn't care if his entire arm was hanging out of his clothes. He wasn't about to take his shirt off in front of her. He muttered, "Grace will fix it later."

"All right." Sarah then carried a steaming black kettle to the table and placed it in front of him. She returned a few seconds later with a plate of freshly sliced home-baked bread and a tub of butter, setting them within his reach. She took her seat and bowed her head.

Levi did the same and silently said the prayers he dutifully prayed before every meal. When he was finished, he looked up and waited. Sarah kept her eyes closed, her hands clasped. He cleared his throat. She took it as the sign the prayer was finished. Looking up, she smiled at him and began ladling steaming pieces of chicken and vegetables into his bowl.

She was so pretty when she smiled. It did funny things to his insides.

She said, "I hope you like this. It was one of Jonas's favorites. The recipe belonged to his mother."

Levi suddenly found his appetite had fled. He laid his spoon down

Sarah's eyes filled with concern. "Is something wrong?"

"This is Jonas's place, his chair. I shouldn't be here."

"Levi," Sarah said gently, "I miss him, too, but his place is with God in heaven. You are free to sit in any chair in this home. You were Jonas's friend, and I hope you are my friend, too. He would welcome your company as I do. I know you were very fond of him."

He had been more than fond of Jonas. He had loved Jonas like a brother. When Jonas gave him a job, Levi had no idea what a great friend and mentor Jonas would become. All these things ran through his mind, but he had no idea how to tell Sarah what Jonas meant to him.

She patted his arm. "It's okay. He was fond of you, too. He would like it that you have come to eat at his table. He would be upset that I haven't invited you sooner. Now eat, or your food will get cold."

Levi nodded. He was here for a meal and nothing more. He wasn't here to try and replace Jonas. He could never fill those shoes.

After eating in silence for a few minutes, he said, "You should give Grace this recipe. It's a whole lot better than her chicken stew."

Sarah laughed. Levi felt his face grow red. Had he said something stupid? Once again she touched his arm. It was as if touching came easily to her. It wasn't that way with him. He felt the warmth of her hand even through the sleeve of his shirt. It spread to the center of his chest and pooled there.

She chuckled and said, "I have given this recipe to Grace. She has assured me that everyone in the family enjoyed it. Maybe what she needs is a few cooking lessons."

She wasn't laughing at him. Levi was able to smile, too. "She needs more than a few. Her biscuits are as heavy as stones."

He fell silent again.

Sarah said, "I hope you've saved room for some peach pie. I made it last night."

"Peach is my favorite."

"Mine, too." She smiled warmly at him.

They finished the rest of the meal in companionable silence. When he was done, Sarah rose and began gathering up the dishes. "I'll bring the rest of the stew to your house this evening. I'm sure the twins will be even hungrier by supper time."

He pushed back the chair and stood. "The meal was *ser goot*, but I must get back to work."

"I will be over as soon as I finish these dishes. Is there anything special you need me to do?"

He shook his head, but then changed his mind. "If customers come in, I would appreciate your help finding out what they want so I don't have to stop work each time." "I can do that. I'll keep watch out the window while I finish up here. If I see anyone I'll come right over."

Levi nodded his thanks and walked out the door.

Sarah watched him go with a strange sense of loss. There hadn't been a man at the head of her table since

Jonas's passing. While it felt odd, it also seemed right that Jonas's best friend should have been the one sitting in his place. He'd been like a little brother to her husband. Levi grieved for Jonas as strongly as she did.

Since Jonas's passing, she often felt that Levi was avoiding her. Maybe it wasn't because he disapproved of her. Maybe it was simply that she reminded him too much of his loss.

Sarah shook off the sadness that threatened to bring tears to her eyes and instead concentrated on a plan to see which one of her single friends might be right for Levi, and most important, how to get them together.

It wasn't like Levi was going to attend the singings or gathering that were held on Saturday and Sunday evenings so the young people of the community could mingle and met potential mates. He was past that age and so were the women she had in mind for him.

Levi rarely left his work place, so if Levi wouldn't come out, she needed to find a way to get the women to come in.

The meal today gave her an idea. She would invite her friends, one at a time of course, to join her for a meal when Levi was present. She would have to include the twins and Grace, too, when she returned, but that couldn't be helped. It would look odd if she only asked Levi to come to dinner. People would say that she was running after him herself. That wouldn't do.

Perhaps having him and his family over to eat wasn't such a good idea. Who knew how many times she'd have to invite them before he found someone he liked? The twins could put away a lot of food.

Maybe she could ask her friends to help with inventory. That would be logical excuse to have them spend the day where Levi was working. She might even convince some of them to come in and look over the used buggies that Levi had for sale or buy a new one. If she remembered right, Leah Belier's buggy was old and worn. Sarah could drop a few hints about a good price and then leave Levi to show the teacher what was available. That might work.

Satisfied that she had a few plausible reasons to get Levi to spend time with some eligible women, Sarah closed the door and began to clean up the kitchen. While she might be new at matchmaking, she had been around her aunt Emma enough to know how it was done. If all went well, Levi would find a woman to take care of him and Grace would be free to marry.

Sarah placed the glass Levi had used in the soapy water. His shirtsleeves were threadbare, and his shoes had holes in them. He did need someone to look after him.

So why did the idea of Levi getting married suddenly cause an ache in her heart?

The twins were seated inside Levi's office when he returned to the shop. "Was it a fine meal?" Moses asked.

"Fine enough."

"Better than our church spread sandwiches, I reckon," Atlee grumped.

Levi loved the peanut butter and marshmallow crème spread served for Sunday lunches after the prayer service. "About that good, I guess. Did you finish the wheel we're fixing for Gideon Troyer?"

"Not yet, but we got the fire going good outside," Atlee said in a rush.

"And we finished the upholstery on the front seat for

the Hershberger buggy," Moses added. The boys exchanged a lively glance. It was rare that they did work Levi hadn't asked them to do. Perhaps Sarah's scolding had paid off.

"*Danki.* We'd best finish the wheel, though. Gideon will be by to pick it up this afternoon."

"I don't get him." Atlee shook his head.

"Me neither," Moses added.

Levi looked at his little brothers. "What do you mean?"

Atlee said, "He traded in flying airplanes to go back to driving a horse and buggy. Why?"

Levi understood their confusion. Very few of the young men who left the Amish came back and were content to do so after being out in the English world for as long as Gideon had.

From the doorway, a man said, "The outside world held many things that drew me away, but I discovered God's will for me was to return to my Amish roots."

Levi turned to see Gideon walking toward him. He liked the man that had married their cousin Rebecca and not only because he'd helped her regain her sight after years of blindness. He was a likeable fellow in his own right.

Atlee said, "You came back because of a woman."

Gideon gave a sharp bark of laughter. "God's ways are wondrous to behold, as I'm sure you will discover when you are older. Your cousin Rebecca's love was the prize I won for following God's will rather than my own."

Levi looked down at his feet. "Your wheel's not done."

"Mind if I hang around while you finish it?"

"*Nee*. It won't take long." Levi moved toward the side of the building where he assembled the finished wheels. The steel rim Gideon was waiting on had been welded together but it needed to be placed around the wooden rim.

Levi carried the steel ring along with a pair of tongs and a large mallet outside where the twins had build a fire in the pit they used for heating the metal. The flames had died down to a bed of coals that glowed bright red. Levi could barely stand the heat on his face as he laid the steel circle on it. Stepping back, he waited for the fire to do its work and expand the metal.

Moses carried the wooden wheel out and laid it on a scarred slab of wood near the pit. He looked at Gideon. "Tell us what it was like to fly in a plane. Were you scared to be so high?"

Gideon cocked his head to the side as he regarded the boy. "Why would I be scared?"

"Because you might fall out of the sky," Atlee answered.

Gideon grinned. "Falling out of the sky doesn't hurt you."

"It doesn't?" Atlee and Moses looked at each other in disbelief.

"No. Not a bit. It's that sudden stop when you hit the ground that hurts." Gideon winked at Levi as the twins groaned at his joke.

Levi chuckled. "That's a *goot* one."

As the boy begged Gideon for stories about flying, Levi concentrated on watching the fire. He knew the rim was ready when it began to glow red. He motioned to Atlee. He and the boy thrust the tongs into the hot coals from opposite sides and together they lifted the rim from the fire. They carried it to the waiting wheel. Because the heat had expanded the metal, Levi and Atlee were able to slip it over the wooden rim. Levi laid his tongs aside and hammered the steel into place.

Quickly, as the wheel started to catch fire, Moses came with several buckets of water and began dousing it. The hot metal hissed. Steam rose up in a thick fog. After a few minutes, Levi lifted the wheel by the rungs and set it in a water trough. He turned the wheel rapidly to make sure it cooled evenly.

A friend of the twins called to them from the street and they both ran out to talk to him, leaving Levi to finish the work alone. Again.

After a few minutes, he pulled the wheel out of the water and checked the fit over the wooden fellows. It looked good. No gaps, his weld was solid. He was pleased with it. It would last many years. He rolled the wheel to Gideon who inspected it carefully, as well. Levi looked up to see Sarah had come out of the shop.

Gideon spied her at the same moment. "Sarah, how nice to see you."

She gave him a warm smile. Too warm, Levi thought as a frown formed on his face.

"Gideon, you're just happy to see me somewhere besides the shop where your wife spends all your hard-earned cash on fabric for her quilts."

"You have that right. What are you doing here?"

"Helping Levi for a few weeks while Grace is out of town. The fabric shop is closed for the winter, if you didn't know." She moved to stand close beside Levi. He caught a whiff of her lavender soap and drew in a deep breath of it. His heart began racing.

Gideon said, "We heard about the closing. Rebecca

was bemoaning the fact that she will have to go all the way to Sugarcreek for her quilt backing. I reckon she'll wear out a couple more buggy wheels this winter traveling over there. Because, according to her, a woman can never have too much fabric."

"I'm sure my boss would agree with her."

Looking at Levi, Gideon said, "You're a lucky man to have such a pretty helper, for even a few weeks. How much do I owe you?"

Levi said, "Sarah will write up your ticket."

Sarah blushed. Rising on tiptoe, she leaned close and whispered in his ear. "I don't know how much to charge him."

Her warm breath caressed the side of Levi's neck and sent every nerve ending in his body into high alert. He hugged his mallet to his chest and struggled to find his voice. "On the counter."

She leaned closer. "On the counter, what?"

"Paper…with prices."

"*Danki.* I'll go find it, and I'll fix that shirt later." She gave him a bright smile and hurried toward the shop's back door.

He closed his eyes; thankful and sorry all at the same time that she was gone. He reached for his tongs.

Gideon grabbed his wrist. Levi looked at him in surprise and then glanced down at his hand. Comprehension dawned. Levi had been about to grab the end that was still smoking hot. Gideon had saved him from a nasty burn.

He nodded his thanks. *"Danki."*

Gideon glanced from Levi's face to Sarah's retreating form. He chuckled and let go of Levi's wrist. "It's like that, is it?"

Levi frowned. "What do you mean?"

"I was the same way when I realized I was falling for Rebecca. I fell, literally, at her feet on an icy street. Love makes it hard for a man to concentrate."

"Me? Falling for Sarah? *Nee,* it is not so." Levi shook his head violently.

Gideon laughed. "Whatever you say, my friend. Many men with two good eyes are blind to the desires of their hearts."

Chapter Five

As Gideon walked away, Levi sought to dismiss the man's disturbing words. Gideon had seen something that didn't exist. Levi refused to think about his feelings for Sarah because he didn't have any past his responsibility to her. Her behavior that day at the creek, not to mention her marriage to his best friend, had put an end to his infatuation.

No, Gideon was wrong. Levi was not in love with Sarah, and she clearly was not love with him. Only a fool would think she would consider Levi Beachy as a replacement for Jonas Wyse, the finest man Levi had ever met.

He carried his tools inside to put them away, determined to think no more about it. The problem he was determined to ignore was seated at the counter with her chin propped on her hands. She smiled sweetly at him, and his foolish heart skipped a beat.

She said, "I found the price list. I don't know why I never noticed it before."

He swallowed hard and nodded, not sure he trusted his voice to answer her.

Sitting up straighter, she said, "Of course, I haven't been in here in the last few years, so perhaps it is understandable. I'll try to learn where everything is so that I don't have to interrupt you with a lot of questions."

"I don't mind." Levi couldn't believe those words actually escaped his lips. He didn't want her questions. He certainly didn't want her to whisper them in his ear.

The memory of her closeness, the way he could smell her freshness, the sensation of her warm breath against his skin was enough to send heat rushing through his body once more. "I must to get to work."

"I understand. I'll stop talking. You can pretend I'm not even here."

He'd already learned that wasn't possible. He would forbid his sister to leave in the future.

"When Grace decides to marry, you'll have to hire a replacement for her. Someone with a sunny disposition would be nice. Can you think of anyone who might interest you? As a replacement for Grace, I mean."

"Nee." He didn't want to think about Grace marrying, either. Turning around, he walked to the back corner of the building and started his lathe. The noise of the grinder would cover any more comments by Sarah. He began to work with vigor, building new wheel hubs as fast as he could shape the blocks of wood.

Sarah heaved a sigh of exasperation as Levi busied himself as far away from her as possible. Trying to figure out what kind of wife would suit him would be next to impossible if he wouldn't say more than a dozen words to her.

He hadn't been exactly talkative during their meal, but perhaps in his own home he would open. He and the boys would appreciate her cooking while Grace was gone, she was certain of that.

She could seek information about Levi's likes and dislikes from the twins, but involving them came with its own set of drawbacks. They were bright and inquisitive. They might put two and two together and foil her plans by telling Levi what she was up to. Would he mind?

She didn't know, and she hoped she never had to find out.

She finished the day by getting things ready to do the inventory the following week. Only two customers came in and their requests were easy to handle. Levi managed to stay out of her way completely. No matter where she went, he was just leaving the area with long determined strides. Who would believe they couldn't exchange as much as a sentence when they were both inside the same building all afternoon? It was almost like he was *trying* to avoid her. Was he still angry about her advice to Grace?

Rather than become discouraged, Sarah grew more determined. She would discover the real Levi Beachy if it took her all winter.

Admitting only a temporary setback, she stopped trying to corner the man and settled herself with paperwork in the office. As she went through the previous year's records, she was pleased to see Levi was an excellent bookkeeper. While Grace might take care of the public part of the business, Levi clearly managed the rest with a deft hand. It was something a prospective wife would be impressed with.

When five o'clock rolled around, Sarah went home and gathered what she would need to feed the Beachy family supper. Along with the leftover stew, she packed a loaf of bread and two jars of vegetables she had canned from her own garden. She added a second loaf of bread when she remembered the appetite her brother had during his teenage years.

She carried the makings of the meal to the house next door with a simmering sense of excitement. No wonder her aunt Emma enjoyed matchmaking. Sarah had no idea how exciting it was. Her somber mood and worry about the season had taken a backseat to her enjoyment of the challenge she faced.

Levi had seen her coming. He held open the door. She squeezed past him, brushing against his side in the process. "*Danki,* Levi."

His face flushed deep red. "I—I forgot something."

He rushed out the door, leaving her staring after him. Really? Could he not sit still even in his own home? Miffed that he had once again escaped her, she turned back to see his brothers sitting at the kitchen table, looking at her with wide, hopeful eyes. They resembled a pair of starving kittens in front of an empty milk saucer.

"*Gut-n-owed,* Sarah," they said together.

"Good evening," she replied.

Atlee said, "We're right sorry we upset you with our teasing Henry Zook today."

She inclined her head slightly. "It's forgiven and forgotten. As long as it doesn't happen again."

Moses said, "It won't. When you pull a good joke on a fellow, it's only funny the first time. He might be expecting it a second time."

She leveled a stern gaze at him. "If you have no remorse, I can take supper home with me."

Stifling a grin at their frightened expressions, Sarah

glanced at the large box in her arms and the basket hanging on her elbow. "Your supper will appear much faster if I could get a little help."

They were up like a shot and took her burdens from her. They set everything on the counter and stood aside. Sarah began unloading her goods. To her surprise, the countertop was grimy. The stove was, too. She ran a finger along the back edge of the counter.

This much cooking grease hadn't accumulated in a single day. Grace clearly didn't devote much effort to housework. Poor Henry. He would be in for a shock after the wedding if Grace didn't improve. His mother's home was always as neat as a pin.

Sarah tried to remember the last time she'd been in the Beachy home. It had been years. Grace was forever dropping by to visit at the fabric shop or coming to Sarah's house. After Jonas's death, Sarah had curtailed her visits to friends and neighbors. It became too hard to pretend she was doing better when she wasn't.

She added one more item to her mental to-do list for the winter. Help Grace get her house in order.

The twins had been smart enough to make sure there was a fire going in the stove. Sarah put on the apron she'd brought with her and got to work. It wasn't long before the smell of steaming beets, buttered carrots and chicken stew filled the small kitchen. Glancing over her shoulder, she noticed the boys were hovering near the table but they hadn't taken a seat.

She lifted the lid on the stew and stirred the contents. "It's almost ready. Will you set the table?"

An alarming amount of clatter followed her request. When she turned around, plates, cups and flatware had been haphazardly set for three places.

"You don't want me to eat with you?" she asked sweetly.

The twins looked at each other. Atlee said, "I reckon that will be okay."

"If Levi says it is," Moses added.

She arched an eyebrow. "Perhaps one of you should go ask him."

Moses elbowed Atlee. "You go."

Atlee rubbed his side. "Why me?"

Folding her arms, Sarah asked, "Does Levi object to company?"

Atlee started toward the door. "I don't know. We never have any."

How had this family become so isolated in the midst of a generous and caring community? "Surely, your grandfather and your cousins come to visit on Sundays and at the holidays."

Atlee shook his head. "We normally go to their homes. It's more fun and the food is better. Grace isn't a great cook."

Sarah said, "It's nice to know that Levi enjoys visiting his family."

At the door, Atlee said, "Levi never goes if he can help it. He don't like it when people make fun of him."

"Why on earth would your family make fun of Levi?"

Moses grimaced. "Grace said he used to stutter when he was little. Our cousins and other kids made fun of him back then."

Sarah vaguely recalled Levi's affliction. Was that why he never spoke much? "He doesn't stutter now."

"Now, he doesn't say much of anything. Our uncle calls him Levi Lockjaw," Atlee said and went outside.

Sarah turned back to the stove and resolved to treat Levi with more kindness in the future. She hadn't realized how much of a loner he'd become after Jonas's death. Then again, how could she? She had been wrapped up in her own grief and worries, unable to focus on anything but her work.

The outside door opened a few minutes later. Atlee returned without Levi. "Brother says you may eat here, Sarah. We're to go ahead. He said he'll fix something for himself later."

"He's not coming in?" she asked in amazement.

Atlee shook his head and took a seat at the table.

Sarah pondered the turn of events as she dished up the meal. Did Levi have that much work to do, or was he simply avoiding her?

The twins fell upon the food like starving dogs. Sarah barely touched hers. Was her company so distasteful that Levi would rather spend the evening in a cold building instead of at his own table if she were there?

If that were the case, she would leave. She stood and carried her plate to the sink.

"Where are you going?" Atlee asked.

"Home. I'll see you both tomorrow at church." She gathered her belongings, grabbed her coat from the hook beside the door and went out.

Instead of going home, she entered the shop by the back door. Only one overhead lamp had been lit. It cast a soft glow where Levi sat on a stool at his workbench. He had a new hub wheel in a vise and was chiseling out the slots for the spokes. He hadn't heard her come in so she had a chance to study him as he concentrated on his work.

What she noticed first about him was his hands. He had sturdy hands, scarred by years of work at his craft, yet he wasn't clumsy. His movements were sure and deft. His body was relaxed, not tense the way he had carried himself all day.

She decided not to interrupt him. Before she could slip back out the door, he suddenly stiffened. She realized he'd caught her reflection in the window glass.

Gathering her courage, she came forward with her icy fingers gripping each other. "I wanted to let you know I was leaving so that you could come in and eat your supper before it grows cold or the twins devour it."

"Danki." He didn't turn around but kept his back to her.

She couldn't leave like this. She didn't want him angry with her. "I'm sorry, Levi."

"For what?"

She waved her hands in a helpless gesture. "Everything. I'm sorry Grace took off and left you in a lurch, but mostly I'm sorry that you're angry with me."

"I'm not angry with you," he said quietly.

"You're not?" She took a step closer. When he didn't say anything else, she moved to stand at the counter beside him. She gestured toward the hub he held. "You do good work."

"I'm not angry," he said again.

"It feels like you are. You won't look at me. You wouldn't come in to supper. Something is wrong. Is it because I can't do the work as well as Grace?"

"Nee."

She held her frustration in check. "Talk to me, Levi. I don't know what to change if you don't tell me. Do

I have to get a blackboard so you can leave me messages?" she teased, trying to get him to smile.

"It's a joke to you, isn't it?" he asked stiffly.

Her teasing had backfired. "Of course not."

"Grace, the twins, me, we're all a joke to you."

"Levi Beachy, what a mean thing to say. Grace is my dear friend. The twins frequently make me cringe or smile, but I don't see them as a joke. I see them as outgoing, boisterous boys."

"I saw you and your aunt laughing at Grace and Henry's argument. I reckon everyone will be talking about my sister's poor behavior tomorrow."

She sighed. So that was it. "Levi, I was grinning at my own cleverness because I had convinced my aunt not to mention the incident."

He cast a sidelong glance of disbelief at her. "You did?"

"Grace is my friend, Levi, just as Jonas was your friend. I had hoped that you and I could be friends, too."

He was silent for so long that she realized she had her answer. For reasons she didn't understand, Levi wouldn't accept her friendship. The knowledge hurt.

"I'll write to Grace and ask her to return as soon as possible. I'm sorry for the trouble I've caused." She turned to leave.

"Sarah, wait."

She stopped and looked back. His bright blue eyes were gazing intently at her. A strange quiver centered itself in her chest, causing a catch in her breath.

He said, "I am now, and have always been, your friend."

The catch moved to her throat. "I'm sorry I didn't recognize that. Thank you, Levi."

"It's what Jonas wanted."

He was right. Jonas would have wanted them to be friends. Why didn't that cheer her? Perhaps because she wanted Levi to like her for herself and not because of her husband.

Early the next morning, Sarah decided to walk to the church service instead of driving her buggy. The preaching was being held at the home of David Nissley and his wife, Martha. Their farm was little more than a quarter of a mile beyond the Hope Springs town limits.

A warm southern wind was melting the snow, making the sunshine feel even brighter. Rivulets of water flowed in the ditches, adding occasional gurgling to the symphony of morning sounds that surrounded her. Numerous Amish families, some on foot, most in buggies and wagons, were all headed in the same direction. Cheerful greetings and pleasant exchanges filled the crisp air. Everyone was glad to see a break in the weather.

Sarah declined numerous offers of a ride, content to stretch her legs on such a fine morning. The icy grip of winter would return all too soon.

She turned in at the farm lane where dozens of buggies were lined up on the hillside just south of the barn. The horses, most still wearing their harnesses, were tied up along the fence, content to munch on the hay spread in front of them or simply doze in the sunshine until they were needed to carry their owners home.

The bulk of the activity was focused around the barn. Men were busy unloading backless seats from the large, gray, boxlike bench wagon that was used to transport the benches from home to home for the services held every other Sunday. Bishop Zook was supervising the unloading. When the wagon was empty, he spoke with his two ministers, and they approached the house.

Sarah entered the farmhouse ahead of them. Inside, it was a beehive of activity as the women and young girls arranged food on counters and tables. Most of the small children were being watched over by their elder sisters or cousins. The young boys were outside playing a game of tag.

Catching sight of her aunt Emma visiting with her daughter-in-law Faith, Ada Kaufman and Mary Shetler, Sarah crossed the room toward them and handed over her basket of food. *"Guder mariye."*

"Good morning, Sarah," her aunt replied. "Isn't the weather wonderful?"

"It is." Turning to Mary, Sarah grinned at the child she held, "Goodness, how this little girl is growing. May I hold her?"

"Of course." Mary handed the baby over with a timid smile.

Sarah took Hannah, enjoying the feel of a baby in her arms. Mary's life had not been easy, but did she know how blessed she truly was?

Ada said, "She should be growing. She eats like a little piglet." There was nothing but love in her aged eyes as she gazed at her adopted granddaughter. Ada had opened her home and her heart to the once wayward Amish girl and her baby.

Emma said, "I see the bishop and ministers coming. We'd best hurry and join the others in the barn."

As she spoke, Bishop Zook and the ministers entered the house and went upstairs where they would discuss the preaching that was to be done that morning. The three-hour-long service would be preached from memory alone. No one was permitted the use of notes. Each man had to speak as God moved him.

Sarah handed the baby back to Mary. The women quickly finished their tasks and left the house.

The barn was already filled with people sitting quietly on rows of backless wooden benches with the women on one side of the aisle and men on the other side. Tarps had been hung over ropes stretched between upright timbers to cordon off an area for the service. Behind them, the sounds of cattle and horses could be heard. The south-facing doors were open to catch what warmth the sunshine could provide.

Sarah took her place among the married women. Beside her, Katie Sutter sat with her three small children, the youngest, Roy, born four months ago. Rachel, the oldest, only four years old, slipped off the bench and crossed the aisle to sit on her father's lap. The remaining child, little Ira began to pout and fuss at his sister's desertion.

Katie slipped a string of beads and buttons from her pocket. She handed them to her little one. He was then content and played quietly with his toy.

From the men's side of the aisle, the song leader announced the hymn. There was a wave of rustling and activity as people open their thick black songbooks. The *Ausbund* contained the words of all the hymns but no musical scores. The songs were sung from memory and had been passed down through countless generations. They were sung slowly and in unison by people opening their hearts and minds to receive God's presence without the distraction of musical instruments.

The slow cadence allowed everyone to focus on the meaning of the words.

At the end of the first hymn, Sarah took a moment to glance toward the men's side. She spotted Levi sitting just behind the married men. His brothers sat near the back. The twins were chewing gum and looking bored. Sarah considered asking Katie if she had any additional toys. In truth, the twins were not the only teenagers looking restless. Levi, on the other hand, held his songbook with a look of intense devotion on his face.

He glanced in her direction, and she smiled at him. He immediately looked away and she felt the pinch of his rejection. Why was it that he turned her every overture aside?

The song leader announced the second hymn. *O Gott Vater, wir Loben Dich* (Oh God the Father, we praise You). It was always the second hymn of an Amish service. Sarah forgot about Levi and his brothers as she joined the entire congregation in singing God's praise, asking that He allow the ministers to speak His teachings, and praying that the people present would receive His words and take them into their hearts.

At the end of the second hymn, the ministers and Bishop Zook came in and hung their hats on pegs set in the wall. That was the signal that the preaching would now begin. Sarah tried to listen closely to what was being said, but she found her mind wandering to the subject of Levi and who might make him a good wife.

Covertly, she studied the single women in the congregation. She quickly ruled many out as being too old or too young to suit him. It would be wonderful if Mary were older, for Levi would make her a strong and steady husband, but she was only sixteen. One by one, Sarah weighed the pros and cons of the remaining women. She ended up with the same women she had considered the day before. Sally, Leah and Fannie.

Confident that one of them would be right for Levi, she focused her attention on the sermon once again.

Levi sat up straight and unobtrusively stretched his back. He was stiff after sitting for nearly three hours. The wooden benches were not made for comfort. At least he hadn't fallen asleep the way Elam Sutter was doing. After Elam's daughter had moved back to her mother's side, the basket maker started nodding in front of Levi. When Elam began to tip sideways, Levi reached up and caught his arm before he tumbled off his seat.

Elam jerked awake. *"Danki,"* he whispered as he gave Levi a sheepish grin.

Levi ventured a guess. "Working late?"

Elam shook his head. "Teething baby."

He leaned forward to look toward the women. Following his gaze, Levi saw Elam's wife sitting across the aisle. Katie Sutter was sitting up straight with her baby sleeping sweetly in her arms. Her face lit with an expression of pure happiness when she caught her husband's glance. Sarah sat beside her.

What Levi wouldn't give to see Sarah look at him with such light in her eyes.

He quickly focused on his hymnal. Such daydreaming was foolishness.

Elam sat back and rubbed his face. He whispered to Levi, "I'm a sorry husband if I can't stay awake to thank God for all the wondrous gifts He has given me."

"I reckon God understands. Our Lord must have been a teething babe at one time, don't you think?"

Elam grinned and nodded. The minister who wasn't preaching at the moment cast a disapproving glare in their direction. They both fell silent. Twenty minutes later, the bishop stopped speaking, and the song leader called out the number of the final hymn. Levi ventured a look in Sarah's direction. She held her songbook open for Elam's daughter Rachel seated beside her. She pointed out the words as she sang them.

Sarah should have children of her own. She would make a good mother. He couldn't imagine why God had chosen not to bless her and Jonas with a baby. It didn't seem right.

The song drew to a close at last. The twins were up and out the doors the second it ended. Teenage boys were expected to sit at the back. Levi always thought that was so their late arrivals and quick getaways didn't disrupt others. He followed more slowly. His eyes were drawn to Sarah as she walked toward the farmhouse with the other women.

How much of his life had been spent watching her from afar, wishing for something that could never happen? Years.

Once she wed Jonas, Levi realized he would have to leave Hope Springs or grow bitter watching Jonas enjoy the happiness denied him. His dream of going to Colorado provided Levi with a goal. He embraced the idea. Only, he had waited too long.

What if Sarah never remarried? How much more of his life was he prepared to give up because of his promise to a dead man?

Sarah joined the women in the kitchen as they prepared the noonday meal while the men rearranged the wooden benches and stacked them to create tables. The majority of the congregation would eat out in the barn, but the bishop and many of the elders would be served inside the house where it was warmer.

Sarah positioned herself beside her aunt, slicing loaves of homemade bread into thick slices. "*Aenti* Emma, I have need of your assistance."

"Anything, child. What can I do for you?"

"I need some help with matchmaking."

Emma looked up with a wide grin. "Has some fine man finally caught your eye?"

"*Nee,* it is not a match for myself. I have a friend who needs a wife. How do I go about getting him to spend time with a possible mate?"

Emma scrutinized Sarah's face. "Is this someone I know?"

"I would rather not say."

"Now I'm intrigued," Emma said, reaching for a second loaf to begin slicing.

"I don't want either party to feel they are being pressured into a relationship."

"In that case, you must find something they have in common or give them each a task that requires the help of the other person."

Sarah looked over and saw Fannie Nissley enter the room. "Aunt, do you know if Fannie is seeing someone?"

Emma looked around to see who might be listening and then leaned closer. "She and Elijah Miller have been keeping company all summer. I expect her father will make an announcement soon."

Sarah crossed Fannie off her list. Just then, Sally Yoder approached the table and put down a box.

Sally said, "I've made a dozen peach pies. Here is the first half if you'd like to slice them. I'll bring in the rest."

Peach pie was Levi's favorite. It was like a sign from the Almighty. Sarah laid her knife aside and said quickly, "Sally, let me give you a hand."

Chapter Six

Levi stood near a group of men all about his own age. The majority of them wore beards indicating their married status. The recently harsh weather and the price of hay and grain dominated the conversation. Levi didn't farm, and the price of feed meant little other than it would cost more to keep his horses over the winter.

Like many of the Amish who no longer lived on the farm, he kept two buggy horses in a small stable behind his house. Soon, the twins would start asking for courting buggies and high-stepping trotters. He wouldn't begrudge them the cost even though the money would come out of his bank account. Money he'd worked hard to save so that he might one day buy his own shop in far away Colorado.

He had always assumed his family members would be content to move with him, but now he wasn't so sure. Was Grace really ready to marry? If the boys started courting, would they want to leave Hope Springs?

He was surprised out of his musings when Sarah spoke beside him. "Levi, will you help us carry in some of the food?"

Sally Yoder stood slightly behind Sarah. He didn't mind leaving the men, for he was rarely more than an onlooker in the group. He nodded and followed them toward the buggies lined up along the lane.

At the fourth one, Sally stopped and opened the back door. He accepted a large cardboard box from her. She picked up a smaller one.

"Be careful with that, Levi," Sarah cautioned. "It's full of peach pies that Sally baked herself. Peach is Levi's favorite kind of pie. Did you know that, Sally?"

"I didn't." Sally gave her a puzzled glance.

Sarah smiled. "You two go back to the house. I'll be along in a moment."

When they were out of earshot, Sally said, "I could've managed on my own, Levi. I don't know why Sarah thought I needed help."

"I don't mind," he mumbled.

"Danki." She blushed as she glanced at him.

She was a pretty girl with bright red hair, fair skin and a dusting of freckles across her nose. She was about the same age as Grace, but he didn't know her well. He couldn't think of anything to say. He was glad to be doing something useful, but the box wasn't heavy. Sally was right. She could've carried it easily.

He glanced over his shoulder. Sarah was still standing by the buggy with a satisfied grin on her face. When she saw him looking, her grin vanished. She immediately started walking toward the barn. He couldn't shake the feeling that she was up to something, but he had no idea what.

At the house, he handed over his box of goodies and started back toward the group of men. He caught sight of the twins sitting on the corral fence, talking to a group of boys about their own age. Not far away stood a group of girls casting coy looks in the direction of the boys.

His brothers would spend most of the day visiting with their friends. After the noon meal, games of volleyball, horseshoes or other diversions would get underway since the weather was nice. Tonight, there would be a singing, a get-together for the teenagers and unmarried young adults. Levi was happy to consider himself past the age of joining such pursuits. He hadn't enjoyed them even when he was younger. He never felt as if he fit in.

He rejoined the men and listened to the conversation with half an ear. His thoughts kept turning back to Sarah. It wasn't long before she approached him again.

"Levi, would you do me a favor? Leah Belier thinks there is something wrong with her buggy. Would you mind taking a look at it for her?"

He gave Sarah a funny look. This was definitely odd. She seemed determined to see that he stayed busy. "Can't she bring it by the shop tomorrow?"

"No, silly, she has to teach school, and it's too far for her to walk in this weather."

Since the day was bright and sunny he raised an eyebrow. Sarah clasped her hands together and smiled at him. He decided to let her comment slide. "All right. I'll take a look."

"*Goot.* Wait here, and I'll get Leah."

She entered the house and came out a few moments later with Leah in tow. She smiled at the schoolteacher as she said, "Levi would like to take a look at your buggy."

"My buggy? Why?" Leah stared at him in surprise.

"Because you told me it didn't feel right when you were driving it."

"I said it doesn't drive like it did when it was new."

Sarah beamed at her. "Well, Levi's the perfect person to examine it. You don't want to break down on the road, do you?"

"Of course not."

Sarah stopped beside Levi so Leah stopped, too. Sarah took a step back and shooed her along with her hands. "Go on. Levi will check out your carriage and then we can have lunch together when it's our turn to eat."

Levi and Leah exchanged puzzled glances. Levi started walking toward the buggies lined up on the hillside, and Leah fell into step beside him. She said, "Thank you for doing this."

"Sure."

She glanced over her shoulder. "Is it just me, or is Sarah acting a bit strange today?"

"It's not just you."

"I heard that the fabric shop is closed for the winter. Maybe she's feeling lost without her job. I know I would."

"But you must give it up someday."

"Only if I marry. I don't expect that will happen anytime soon."

"Why do you say that?" He studied her intently, wondering why she, like Sarah, seemed to have no interest in marriage.

She blushed and said, "There are many younger and prettier girls in Hope Springs for the men to choose from. I have accepted the fact that I won't have children of my own, so I will continue to teach and love each of my students. I didn't see Grace this morning. I hope she isn't ill?"

"She's gone to visit our grandmother in Pennsylvania."

"Oh, how nice."

Nice for Grace, not for him.

Leah said, "I would love to travel. I've always had a desire to go out West and see the Rocky Mountains."

He looked at her in surprise. "So have I."

"Really?" Her smile brightened.

"I have second cousins who live near Mont Vista, Colorado."

"I've read about the Amish settlements out there. I think it must be wonderful and yet frightening to move so far away. I might like to visit, but I'm not sure I would like to stay. What about you?"

"I plan to move there one day."

"Do you? I'm sure many people in Hope Springs will be sorry to see you go."

Not that many, he thought. Not as long as there was a carriage maker and wheelwright to take his place.

By this time they had reached her buggy. He checked it over carefully. Leah stood with her arms crossed beneath the black shawl she wore over her dark blue dress. She finally broke the growing silence. "Is there anything seriously wrong with it?"

"Your back axle is bent."

"Will it be expensive to replace? Can you straighten it?" she asked.

"It would be better to replace it. I can't tell what it needs until I spend some time under there. Bring it by the shop this week."

"*Danki,* Levi. Is it safe to drive until school lets out Friday afternoon? That way I can leave it overnight."

"Can't say for sure. Have someone follow you home today."

"I will, but I must get to school on Monday and someone can't follow me all week."

She'd done so much for the community over the years. Here was his chance to do something in return. "I'll come by and give you a ride to school and look at your buggy while you're teaching. If it isn't safe, I'll leave one of my used buggies for you to drive until I can fix it."

"That would be much appreciated. I'm glad Sarah thought of this because I wouldn't have had it looked at until it broke down."

"Even a well-built carriage needs maintenance."

"I expect that's true. How are the twins? There was never a dull day when they were my students. I haven't had to check my lunchbox for frogs in two years."

"I'm sorry they were such trouble."

Her eyes narrowed. "I've always wanted to know how they got that skunk into the coatroom without getting sprayed themselves. The school smelled for weeks."

Levi ducked his head. He'd had plenty of notes from Leah about his brothers' behavior over the years. His talks with them hadn't improved their actions. He often wondered how his parents would have handled the boys. He was a sorry replacement for their father.

Leah said, "I'm sure the boys will straighten out."

"Do you think so?"

"It may take a few years. Most rowdy boys get their come-uppance when they become fathers and are blessed with children just like themselves."

"Those boys as parents? God help us all."

Leah smiled. "It is a prayer I utter often. Thank you for checking my buggy."

He said, "I'll see you tomorrow."

She left and returned to the house.

Levi rejoined the group of men beside the barn. When it was his turn to eat, he entered the house and filled his plate. Sarah was at the serving table. With a bright smile, she dished him a large slice of the peach pie.

"Sally Yoder made this one. It's absolutely delicious. She is one woman who knows her way around the kitchen."

Levi accepted Sarah's offering and moved away. He spared one backward glance. She was watching him intently. Something was definitely not right. He didn't have long to think about it because Bishop Zook sought him out.

The bishop said, "I didn't see Grace this morning. I hope she's okay."

"She has gone to visit a relative in Pennsylvania."

Bishop Zook chuckled. "That explains why my son has been moping around the house these past few days."

Levi had no idea what to say so he kept silent.

"I think it will be a good match, don't you?" The bishop looked at him hopefully.

"Haven't given it much thought. Grace is mighty young."

"Ah, but she is old enough to know her own mind. I just wanted you to know that I approve of my son's choice." The bishop winked and walked away.

Levi's appetite deserted him. Was he the only one who hadn't seen how serious Henry and Grace were becoming? He wasn't prepared for his sister to marry and leave home. He wasn't sure he could manage without her.

"Is something the matter, Levi?" Sarah asked.

He hadn't been aware of her approach. "*Nee,* why do you ask?"

"I saw you talking with Bishop Zook. Was it about Grace?"

"*Ja.* He said he approved of the match."

"That is good to know."

"She's too young."

"There are younger wives and mothers here. Why don't you join me for lunch?"

He normally ate with his family, but since the twins were nowhere in sight, he nodded his acceptance.

"Wonderful. Sally and Leah have saved us a place outside."

His spirits dropped a notch. He should've known she didn't want to eat with him alone. That might have started baseless gossip about them.

Leah and Sally were sitting on the open tailgate of a farm wagon. They scooted over to make room for Sarah. Levi held her plate until she got settled. Instead of making them crowd together, he chose to stand beside the wagon.

Leah said, "I was just telling Sally about your plans, Levi."

"What plans?" Sarah glanced between Levi and the schoolteacher.

"Levi is planning to move to Colorado. I think it sounds like a wonderful adventure."

For an instant, Levi was sorry he'd mentioned his desire to Leah, but he reconsidered that thought as he studied Sarah's face. She would have to find out some day. What did she think of the idea?

Sarah managed to swallow the fried chicken she was chewing without choking. She stared at Levi in disbelief. "I didn't know you planned to leave Hope Springs."

"It's nothing definite, but I'll do it one day. Don't worry. You'll be able to rent the business to someone else. Perhaps for more money."

Leah began chatting about the Colorado settlement and its proximity to a wildlife refuge where whooping cranes gathered on their annual migration. Sally was full of questions about the place. Leah tried to include Levi, but to Sarah's chagrin, he kept his focus on his plate.

Sarah gave up trying to listen. She had no idea Levi planned to move away. He was as much a part of her life as the house she lived in and the business Jonas had built.

Levi had always been there. She need only mention to Grace that she was low on firewood and the next morning Levi was stacking a cord of wood along the side of her house. If her horse began limping, Levi showed up to check the animal's shoes and feet for problems. If the business needed upgrades, he came to her with a list of what was needed, how much it would cost and where she could buy what they needed. She had taken his presence for granted. It was hard to imagine life without Levi next door.

"What do you think of the idea, Sarah?" Leah asked.

Sarah realized everyone was looking at her. "I'm sure it doesn't make any difference to Levi what I think."

Leah frowned. "I was asking what you think about having a winter picnic out at my place?"

Sarah felt a blush heat her cheeks. "Sorry, I guess I wasn't listening."

Sally said, "We can have a bonfire and roast hot dogs and marshmallows. We would have to make sure there is plenty of hot chocolate to keep everyone warm."

"I think it sounds like a wonderful idea," Sarah agreed.

"When will it take place? Can we make it a Christmas party on the fifteenth?" Sally asked.

Leah shook her head. "I'll be busy with the school Christmas program until the nineteenth. Let's make it Saturday the twenty-second. I'll need help getting things ready the day before. Levi, would you be able to help me set up some straw bales for seats and boards for tables?"

"I reckon I could."

"Wonderful." Leah beamed at him.

Sarah sat back with a self-satisfied smile. She couldn't have planned that better if it had been her own idea. She took a bite of the mashed potatoes on her plate. If Levi took a wife, he might be much more reluctant to move away.

Sally asked, "Sarah, are you coming to the quilting bee for Ina Stultz? It will be at our home."

"*Ja,* I told Grace I would come in her place."

"We should have a good turn out. Her *mamm* has so much to do with two weddings this year that I offered to host the bee."

"That was very kind of you, Sally. Wasn't it, Levi?" Sarah glanced from Sally to Levi. This was his chance to say something flattering to the girl about her thoughtfulness. He nodded and kept eating. Sarah rolled her eyes.

For the rest of the meal, Sarah studied Levi's reaction to her two friends. His polite response to their questions was usually a monosyllable reply, but neither of the women let that stop them from including him in the conversation. Sarah couldn't detect any interest on Levi's part for either woman. He finished his plate and made his escape, much to Sarah's dismay.

Sally said, "He doesn't say much, does he?"

"He's the strong, silent type," Leah answered.

Sarah quickly added, "He's a hard worker, he's a kind neighbor and a nice-looking man. A woman could do much worse for a husband."

Leah grinned. "Sarah, I didn't know you were on the look out for a *mann*. Levi would be a fine choice for you."

"For me?" Sarah squeaked. She shook her head violently. "I'm not looking for a husband. I was talking about some other woman."

"Sure." Sally winked at Leah.

Sarah saw her plans blowing up in her face. If these women thought she had her eye on Levi, they wouldn't go out with him.

She lowered her gaze and spoke with quiet sincerity. "Levi is a fine man and would make a wonderful husband, but I'm not planning to marry again. No one could replace Jonas. I was simply making conversation."

Sally laid a hand on her arm. "We're sorry to tease you."

Sarah smiled. "I forgive you, but I must ask a favor in return."

"Ask away," Sally replied.

"I need help. I'm taking Grace's place at the carriage shop while she is gone. I'm supposed to do the inventory this week. I simply can't do it alone. Levi and the twins are much too busy to help me. Could you spare a day or two to give me a hand?"

Sally grinned. "Absolutely. We aren't that busy at Elam's shop now that the tourist season is over. I'm sure he can spare me for a few days."

"I would be more grateful than you know." Sarah took a bite of the peach pie on her plate, satisfied that things were back on the right track. Sally really did make a good pie. Surely, Levi had noticed that.

Levi stayed at the Nissley farm until late afternoon. He enjoyed watching Atlee and Moses play several games of volleyball. Unlike their older brother, the twins were outgoing and well-liked by their peers. They never had trouble fitting in.

When it grew late, Levi helped Eli Imhoff and a few others load the seats back inside the bench wagon. When he finished, he went looking for his brothers. He found the twins waiting for him by the front porch. He said, "It's time to go."

"We were thinking of staying for the singing. We'll walk home later," Atlee said.

Both boys had their eyes focused on a group of young people gathered at the side of the barn. Levi noticed the pretty Miller sisters glancing frequently in his brothers' direction. The girls were twins and the same age as his brothers. Levi accepted that he was on his own for the short drive home.

He fetched his horse from among the few still remaining and backed Homer between the shafts of his buggy. When he finished harnessing the gelding, he turned to get in and found Sarah once again at his side.

"I hate to be a bother, Levi, but is there any way you can give me a lift home? I walked this morning, but it feels like I have a blister forming on my heel. I really would appreciate a ride."

Sarah had never gone out of her way to spend time with him. What was going on? "*Ja*, I can give you a lift."

She got in without waiting for him. He climbed in after her. The inside of his vehicle had never felt so small. Their knees were almost touching.

He swallowed hard and slapped the reins to get the horse moving. As they rolled down the lane, he wondered what he should say.

Sarah had no difficulty talking. "It was a very nice sermon today. Bishop Zook has a way with words that makes you feel that God is speaking through him."

"I reckon He is."

"You're right. Did you enjoy Sally Yoder's peach pie?"

"*Ja.*"

"I knew you would. Peach is your favorite, isn't it?"

"*Ja.*"

"I remember that because it's my favorite as well. Sally is a very nice girl, isn't she? Not a girl really, she's a young woman. Certainly old enough to be courting."

"Nice enough, I reckon."

"Leah Belier is another nice woman. Did you enjoy your conversation with her?"

He slanted a glance at Sarah. "She wanted to know how the twins got the skunk into the coatroom at the school without getting sprayed themselves."

Sarah laughed out loud. It was a delightful sound and made him smile, too. She said, "It was a mean trick, but it was pretty funny. I doubt anyone will be able to top that anytime soon."

"For Leah's sake, I hope not."

"I have to wonder if she isn't ready to give up teaching and get married. She would certainly make a good wife. We all know she has a way with children. Don't you think she would make someone a fine wife?"

"I reckon."

After a long moment, she asked, "Have you thought about it?"

"Thought about what?"

"Honestly, Levi, what have we been talking about?"

"Peach pies and skunks?"

"You are being deliberately obtuse."

"You've been talking about Sally and Leah."

"And if Leah might be ready to wed. Have you thought about marriage?"

He didn't care for the topic. "Have you?" he countered.

She grew somber. "No."

"Why not?"

She stared at her hands. "Because I'll never find someone as special as my Jonas."

It wasn't what he hoped she would say, but one thing Levi knew for certain. He wasn't anyone special.

Chapter Seven

Sarah counted the number of lynchpins in the wooden box and added the total to the sheet of paper on the clipboard beside her. Inventory was tedious work whether she did it at the fabric store or here. It was part and parcel of a business. It had to be done.

It was her second day of working with Levi since riding home with him after the preaching. She could count on one hand the number of words he'd spoken to her since that evening.

"If he gets past ten words, I can make a tally sheet for him and keep it on my clipboard," she muttered to herself.

The twins were outside working on the church district's bench wagon. Eli Imhoff had brought it in that morning. The rear axle had cracked and needed to be replaced. Fortunately, Levi had an axle that would work and gave the project to the twins to finish before the day was done.

The wagon would be needed to carry the benches to Samuel Stultz's farm for a wedding service the day after tomorrow. The first of his five daughters was getting married. A second daughter, Ina, would be wed in three weeks' time. Sarah had promised Grace she would attend the quilting bee for her early next week. Weddings were wonderful events, but they were also sad reminders of what God had taken away from her.

Through the closed window, Sarah could hear the sounds of the twins' heated debate as they disagreed over the best way to undertake the bench wagon repair. It reminded her so much of the conversations she'd had with her sister when they had been teenagers. Her mother used to say they fought like cats and dogs. Sarah knew that wasn't entirely true. She had loved her sister unconditionally, even if she didn't always approve of Bethany's actions or her choices. She had loved Bethany and God had taken her, too.

If she never loved anyone else, she would never have to suffer such loss again. It was the main reason she wouldn't consider marrying again.

Suddenly, Sarah caught the mention of Leah Belier and she listened more closely.

"He did not," Moses said

"He did," Atlee insisted.

"Levi took Leah Belier, the teacher, riding in his buggy?"

"I saw them together yesterday with my own eyes. What do you think it means?"

"Nothing. It doesn't mean nothing."

Atlee said, "It doesn't mean anything. Have you forgotten all your English classes with Leah?"

"I try to. Give me a hand with this wheel or get lost."

The boys continued to quarrel, but they had given Sarah something to think about. So Levi had taken Leah for a ride. That was promising.

Letting her mind wander for a minute, Sarah shifted her gaze from the twins to where Levi was affixing a new tongue to a farm wagon. In spite of the cool temperature in the building, he had his sleeves rolled up. His light blue shirt was darkened with sweat between his shoulder blades. He was hatless, and she could see the beads of perspiration clinging to the hair at his temples.

He lifted the heavy wooden bar with an ease that surprised her. When he finally had it seated to his satisfaction, he stood back, dusted his hands together and propped them at his hips.

Why hadn't she noticed before what a fine figure of a man he was? While he wasn't a brawny fellow like her husband had been, his slender frame was well muscled. All in all, Levi was an attractive man. She hoped the women she had in mind for him would notice.

Sarah tipped her head slightly as she studied him. She already knew his crystal-clear blue eyes were his best features. His forehead was broad, and his chin jutted out slightly, giving him a look of determination. His nose was a little big for his face, but not overly so. She smiled. He could have been blessed with his grandfather Reuben's nose. Fortunately, he hadn't been.

He didn't smile often, but she knew there was a dimple in his right cheek. It made him look less severe, less aloof. He didn't smile enough.

Sarah was ashamed to realize how much she had ignored Jonas's friend over the past few years. Now that Grace had brought Levi's needs to her attention, Sarah was determined to find him a wife. Her aunt Emma might think he was destined to be an old boy, but Sarah didn't believe it.

She had a plan to change that, and she'd already set

it in motion. Levi deserved someone who cared about him, who could work beside him and bear his children to carry on his business.

She stopped when she realized how much that sounded like the hopes she once held dear. It wasn't to be for her.

She shook off the sad thought. Because that dream wasn't what God had planned for her didn't mean it couldn't come true for Levi and his wife.

A buggy pulled up outside. Glancing out the window, Sarah grinned. Part two of her plan was about to get underway. Sally Yoder stepped down from her carriage.

Sarah hurried to hold open the door for her. "*Guder mariye,* Sally. I'm so glad you could come."

"Good morning, Sarah. I hope I'm not late."

"Not at all."

"Isn't this the strangest weather we're having? Cold and snow one week, sunny and warm the next."

"I'll take sunny and warm any day."

Sally shook her head. "I like snow during the holiday season. Not a lot, just enough to make everything look sparkling and new."

Sarah kept her opinion of snow to herself. She glanced in Levi's direction and found he was watching them. Taking Sally by the elbow, Sarah led her toward him.

"Levi, I forgot to mention that I asked Sally Yoder to give me a hand with the inventory. You don't mind if she helps, do you?"

"I reckon not."

Sarah thrust her clipboard into his hands. "Wonderful. If you have a few minutes, can you show her what needs to be done? I would appreciate it. I've got something on the stove I have to check on. I'll be right back."

She hurried out the front door leaving the two of them together.

Levi had never considered Sarah a flighty woman until she had started working with him. He vowed to be less critical of Grace when she returned. Sally stood waiting for his instructions.

He handed her the clipboard without meeting her gaze. "This is a list of things to be counted. The shelves and bins are labeled. Write down the number of items you find in each one."

Sally glanced at the clipboard. "That's it?"

"That's it." He nodded and returned to work on the farm wagon.

"Levi, what is an axle nut?" Sally asked as she stood looking at the eight-foot-tall wooden cabinet filled with drawers that covered the west wall.

He put aside the hardware meant to hold the tongue to the front axle and crossed the room to show her the correct drawer. Pulling it open, he said, "It's used to hold the wheel on the axle."

"I thought as much." She counted the ones in the drawer and pushed it closed.

"Anything else?" he asked.

"No, I've got this." She opened a second drawer and began counting.

Levi returned to wrestling with the wagon waiting to be finished.

"Why do you have left and right axle nuts?"

He exhaled in frustration. "Because the nut on the

axle had to be threaded to turn right on one side and left on the other side."

"Why?"

"To prevent the nut from being spun off when the wheel is going in the same direction. If that happens, the wheel falls off." He lay down to tighten the bolts under the tongue.

"I see. What is a clip bar used for?"

He finished tightening the bolts, wiped the sweat from his face and rose to walk past to her. "Moses will be in to help you. I have work to do outside."

He rolled down his sleeves, donned his jacket and escaped out the door. How many questions could one woman ask? Outside, he found young Ben Lapp unloading a wheel from his wagon. Ben was a few years older than the twins. He rolled the wheel toward Levi. "I've got a broken fellow on this one. Any chance I can get it replaced today?"

Behind Ben's wagon, Daniel Hershberger was helping his new wife out of their buggy. He had a second horse tied on behind.

Atlee and Moses came hurrying up. Moses took the wheel from Ben. "We can't get to it today. It will be tomorrow afternoon at the earliest."

Ben nodded. "That will work. I also need a new left axle nut."

Levi pointed over his shoulder. "Sally Yoder can find you one."

Ben's eyes brightened. He looked with interest toward the building. "I didn't know Sally was working here." He headed inside without another word.

Dan Hershberger, with his bride, Susan, at his side,

approached Levi. They made an imposing pair for both were tall with ample figures and stern expressions. Dan said, "I understand my wife's new carriage is done."

Levi nodded. Atlee said, "I'll hitch your horse for you. The two of you can take it for a ride around the block to make sure it's to your satisfaction."

Susan folded her arms and gave Levi a stern glare, ignoring the twins completely. "I would prefer that my husband harness the horse."

She wisely didn't trust his brothers. Neither of the boys looked disappointed, so perhaps they didn't have a prank in mind. Levi said, "It's this way."

Levi walked toward the back lot. Dan followed, leading his spare horse. It was a high-stepping and spirited coal-black mare. Glancing over his shoulder, Levi saw Susan waiting near their buggy. She was keeping a close eye on the twins.

The open carriage was sitting in the center of the back lot. Dan's stern face broke into a wide grin when he saw it. "This is exactly what I had in mind. Susan will love it. I hope she will love it, for a happy wife makes a happy life."

The two men hitched up the horse and led her to the front of the building. Susan walked around the buggy, tested the doors, and ran her hand over the leather upholstery. Turning to her husband, she finally smiled. "It is wonderful, *danki, mie* husband."

"It is my joy to see you happy." He opened the carriage door and assisted her to climb in.

Levi happened to catch a glimpse of Atlee's gleeful face from the corner of his eye. A cold feeling settled in his bones. What had they done?

* * *

Sarah finished her cup of coffee and took the blue enameled pot off the stove. She hadn't lied. She did have something on the stove—her coffee pot. Glancing at the clock, she wondered if twenty minutes was enough time to leave Sally and Levi alone. Hopefully, he had spoken more than a handful of words to her.

Sarah was anxious to see how the couple was getting along. She rinsed her cup and set it to dry on the side of the sink. When she opened the front door, she saw Dan and Susan Hershberger sitting in their new carriage. Levi was with them and not with Sally. Sarah scowled. She hadn't taken into account that they might have customers.

As Sarah descended her steps, Dan tipped his hat in her direction. Susan lifted her hand to wave as Dan slapped the reins against the rump of his horse. The mare surged forward. Sarah heard a sharp crack. Dan and Susan both fell backward as their seat gave way. The mare trotted smartly down the street with her passengers' legs sticking in the air.

Horrified, Sarah dashed out her front gate. Levi was already in hot pursuit of the couple. Moses and Atlee were clinging to each other as they laughed hysterically. Sarah stopped in front of them. "Oh, how could you?"

"They are such a pompous pair," Atlee managed to say when he caught his breath.

"Ah, Levi's got their horse already," Moses said with a pout.

Sarah looked down the street and pressed her hand to her heart in relief. "Thank heavens. What if the horse had run into traffic or upset the buggy?"

Moses shrugged. "Nothing bad happened. I was hoping they'd go clear through town that way."

Sarah wanted to box his ears. "We're lucky they didn't. Dan Hershberger could buy and sell this business ten times over. He is an influential man. If he decides to make trouble for us, we could lose most of our business."

Atlee said, "He won't make trouble for you, Sarah. You're a widow. The church elders would never stand for that. Here they come. We better get out of here."

The boys took off, leaving Sarah and Levi to face their irate customers alone.

It was an ugly scene. It took the better part of half an hour to soothe Dan and his wife's ruffled feathers. Sarah ended up letting them have their carriage at cost. Levi promised to deliver it to their home tomorrow after thoroughly inspecting it. When they finally left, Levi and Sarah turned to face each other.

"Where did they go?" he asked in a tired voice.

She knew he was talking about his brothers. "They took off running toward the center of town. God only knows where they are by now."

"I can't believe they pulled this off. I knew they were up to something, but if I can't trust them to work for me, what will I do with them?"

"Send them to work for someone else," Sarah suggested.

He thrust his hands in his pockets and stared at his feet. "Who would have them?"

"Your grandfather perhaps?"

"Maybe. I will speak to him."

The silence stretched between them. Sarah glanced

at Levi just as he looked at her. She couldn't hold back a grin. "It was kind of funny."

Levi's hangdog expression changed to a reluctant smile that tugged at the corner of his mouth. "*Ja,* it was. Susan Hershberger wears pink bloomers."

"She does?" Sarah choked on a chuckle. Their eyes met. The ridiculousness of the prank hit them at the same time. They both started laughing.

"Snap, wee!" Sarah threw her hands in the air. Levi laughed harder. Sarah pressed her hands to her face as tears blurred her vision.

"Stop," Levi begged her, holding his sides.

"Snap, wee! Pink I see!" Unable to stand because she was laughing so hard, she fell against Levi and grasped his arm. His hands came up to steady her. She looked at his smiling face and her mirth slowly died away.

Their eyes met. Sarah realized that she was practically in his arms. She took a quick step back. His hands dropped to his sides.

She said, "It was funny, but it could've been so much worse."

Levi nodded. His gaze once more dropped to his feet. "Reckon I should get back to work."

"As should I. I have left Sally alone for too long."

"I forgot. Ben Lapp needed a part. Sally must be having trouble finding it for him."

"I'll take care of it." She took another step back but discovered she was reluctant to leave him. The frown had returned to his face. She knew he was once again thinking about his brothers.

"Levi, would you like me to ask Bishop Zook to have a talk with the boys?"

"Do you think it would help?"

"It can't hurt."

"I will speak to him about them. They are my responsibility."

"And none of mine. I understand." She gave a half-hearted, embarrassed smile and hurried toward the carriage shop front door. She heard him call her name. She stopped and glanced back.

He said, "I'm grateful for your counsel."

Her heart grew light again. "I only want to help."

She pulled open the door and went inside. She found Ben Lapp leaning against the counter. Sally stood on the other side, smiling at him as she said, "The right hub nut is threaded to the right and the left hub nut is threaded to the left so they won't spin off the wheel while it's turning."

"For only working here one day you sure seem to know a lot about the equipment."

Sally blushed a becoming shade of pink. "I try to pay attention. Some people think I ask a lot of questions, but it's only because I want to learn new things."

Sarah walked behind the counter with Sally. "And I'm sure that Levi was happy to answer all your questions."

"Actually, he didn't seem happy to answer any of them. Ben helped me finish the inventory of the tall cabinets. He's been wonderfully patient with me." She smiled sweetly at him.

He shrugged off her compliment. "It was no trouble. What are you doing for Christmas, Sally?"

"*Mamm* is cooking a big dinner for the family on Thursday. We have cousins coming from Kilbuck to visit for the long weekend. What about you?"

"That's funny because my folks and I are traveling

to my uncle Wayne's place. My grandparents live with his family. His farm is down near Kilbuck. My family goes there and your family comes here."

The young pair were so focused on each other that Sarah began to feel invisible. "Ben, Levi said you needed a part. What can I get for you?"

Sally answered her. "He needed a left hub nut. I found it for him, but I didn't know how much to charge. We've just been waiting for you or Levi to come back."

Sarah rang up the amount on the cash register. "I'm sorry to have kept you waiting, Ben. There was a problem with the Hershbergers' buggy."

"I didn't mind." He hadn't taken his eyes off of Sally.

"Are you staying in Kilbuck long?" she asked.

"Just until Friday evening."

"That means you'll be back in time for the barn party on Saturday." Sally spoke with a nonchalance that was a dead giveaway his answer was important.

"I'll be back in plenty of time. Who's having a hoedown?"

"There's going to be one at Ezra Bowman's farm. Maybe you could come by for a while."

Sarah looked at Sally in surprise. "I thought that was the night of Leah Belier's winter picnic?"

Sally shrugged. "It is. I didn't hear about the hoedown until last night. It should be loads more fun than an old picnic. Leah will understand if I don't come."

A troubled look crossed Ben's face. "Ezra Bowman belongs to the Sparkler gang, doesn't he? Do you run with that crowd? I hear they're a pretty wild bunch."

Sally raised one eyebrow. "We're not goody-goodies, but you shouldn't judge us without getting to know us. Some of them are kind of wild, but most them are like me. Ordinary Amish kids just looking to enjoy their *rumspringa*."

Ben pulled out his wallet and handed Sarah the money he owed. "I'll think about it. It could be fun."

"It will be."

His smile returned. "Okay. I'll see you there and maybe I'll see you tomorrow when I come back for my wheel."

"I'll be here," she said brightly.

When he left, Sally turned and grasped Sarah's arm, bubbling over with excitement. "I can't believe Ben Lapp actually spent the better part of an hour talking to me. He's so fine."

Sarah saw her hopes for a match between Sally and Levi going out the window. She wasn't one to give up easily. "Levi is a fine-looking fellow, too. He's hard-working and much more mature than a boy like Ben."

Sally rolled her eyes. "I know he appeals to someone older—like you—but not to someone like me. We should get back to work or we're never going to get finished here."

Sarah picked up the clipboard. Her first serious attempt at matchmaking was a failure, but Sally was right. They still had a lot of work to get done. "We can move to the upholstery room. That has the second largest number of small items."

Sally followed along behind Sarah. "Why is the upholstery room enclosed? None of the other rooms have ceilings over them."

"To keep the dust out of the cloth in there."

"How much cloth do you keep?"

"It depends on how many orders we have. Often, we

have to special-order fabrics, but if we find a good deal on something our customers like, we'll order in bulk."

As they counted needles, threads and bobbins, Sally continued to pelt Sarah with questions. Before long, she realized that working with Sally was more tiring than working alone. Her patience began to wear thin. After another twenty minutes and as many questions, she said, "I can finish up in here. You've been a big help. Why don't you go ahead and go home?"

"It's barely noon. I'm not going to leave you to do this by yourself. I said I could work for two days and two full days is what you will get. Why are the threads arranged according to size and not according to color?"

"Because they are."

Sarah heard the large double doors at the side of the building open. She stepped out of the workroom and saw Levi pulling the Hershberger carriage in. He was struggling with the heavy vehicle and could barely move it. She put down her clipboard and rushed to help him. Together, they were able to pull it inside.

"Danki," he said and blew out a long breath.

"You should have called me to help. It's too heavy for you to manage alone."

"Don't scold. I thought I could do it." He raised his fist to his mouth and coughed sharply.

Concern sharpened her tone. "You deserve a good scold. If you don't take care of yourself, who will?"

"Grace is normally here to help, but someone told her to take a vacation. Oh, wait, that was you."

"You're not going to start harping on that again, are you? What's done is done."

"Gee, you two sound like an old married couple," Sally said from the upholstery room doorway.

Levi scowled. "I reckon a wife would not talk to me like I was a child."

"Sometimes you act like a child," Sarah said quickly.

"As do you," he snapped back.

Sarah's mouth dropped open. She shut it and marched back into the workroom without another word. Sally moved out of her way. "Sorry."

"That's quite all right. Where were we?"

"Nylon thread, size eight."

Sarah opened the bin. "Four spools."

Consulting the clipboard, Sally said, "Cotton thread, size eight."

"Six spools."

"Are you sure you aren't upset with me?"

Sarah closed her eyes. "I'm not upset with you."

She wasn't upset with Sally. She was upset with herself for promising Grace she would try and find a wife for Levi. She had no business being a matchmaker. She didn't know the first thing about helping people fall in love.

Sally said, "I've learned so much today. Plus, I had the chance to make an impression on Ben Lapp. I've been hoping for a chance to do that for ages, and he'll be back tomorrow."

Her comment gave Sarah pause. Maybe she'd been going about this the wrong way. It might not be about who she thought Levi would like. It could be she needed to find out who liked Levi.

"Sally, earlier you said Levi was attractive to someone who was…older. Were you thinking of someone specific?"

"I shouldn't have said you were older. You're not old."

"Never mind that. Were you thinking of someone else?"

"You have to promise you won't tell her I said anything."

"I promise. Who is it?"

"My cousin Joann."

Joann Yoder? The one woman Sarah had crossed off her list as being too shy. On second thought, the spinster might be the perfect woman after all. She wasn't likely to speak to Levi like he was a child even when he acted like one.

How could she get them together?

"I don't know your cousin very well. What is she like?"

"Quiet, shy, but she has a heart of gold."

That sounded familiar. "What kind of things does she enjoy doing?"

"Joann? She likes to garden and she loves quilting. She's coming to Ina Stultz's quilting bee. You're coming, right?"

"I am." Sarah couldn't envision a way to get Levi involved in quilting.

"*Goot.* Joann likes to cook. She likes to visit. Oh, and she really likes to fish. Yuck. I hate handling worms, but she doesn't mind. She goes with my brothers when they have time."

"She likes fishing? That's very interesting." Sarah smiled. Levi used to go fishing with Jonas. Could he be persuaded to toss a line in with Joann? How?

Sally's eyebrows shot up. "Do you like fishing?"

"It can be…rewarding. I love the taste of fresh trout." As long as she didn't have to clean it before she cooked it.

She would have to get up a fishing trip of her own. If all went well, using Levi Beachy as bait might just land him the perfect mate.

Chapter Eight

"I know that silly thing is in here somewhere." A crash followed Sarah's muffled words.

Levi, splitting kindling in her backyard, stopped swinging his ax and glanced toward her back porch. It was late in the day and they had finished at the shop an hour ago. The sound of something heavy hitting the floor made him put his tool down. "Sarah, are you okay?"

"I would be if I could just find that rod. Do you know where it is?"

Puzzled, he walked toward the building. He stepped inside and saw Sarah down on her hands and knees pulling out baskets and boxes from beneath a wooden storage bench. "What kind of rod are you talking about?"

"Jonas's fishing rod. I know I still have it. It has to be here somewhere."

"Why are you looking for his rod?"

"Because I'm going fishing."

It was the last thing he expected her to say. "You hate fishing."

She glared up at him. She had a smudge on one cheek

and a look of steely determination in her eyes. "I don't hate fishing. I simply didn't like it as much as Jonas did. Which was why I was always glad he went with you. Why can't I find his rod?"

Levi arched one eyebrow. "I distinctly remember hearing you tell him you wouldn't go fishing until God started making fish that weren't slimy and didn't stink."

She turned back to searching under bench. "I must have been having a bad day."

Levi stepped past her and lifted a four-foot-long black tube off a nail on the back wall. He handed it to her. "Is this what you're looking for?"

She glanced at it and shook her head. "No. I'm looking for a red fiberglass rod with a silver reel thing on it."

He opened the end of the tube and pulled out two rods. One was a dark blue fly fishing rod and the other one was a red spin-casting rod. They had been taken apart to let them fit inside. "I bought Jonas this case after one of my brothers stepped on his favorite rod and broke it."

She rose to her feet looking sheepish and adorable. *"Danki."*

"Du bischt wilkumm." He handed them to her.

She took them from him and looked them over. "The pieces just fit together, right? Where are the hooks?"

"In the tackle box you threw aside."

"Oh." She looked at the mess on the floor.

"Are you really going fishing?"

"I can see it may be a more complex undertaking that I first imagined, but I do intend to go. I have to."

"Why?"

"To be out in the fresh air. To enjoy the glories that

are the world God has given us. To be at one with nature."

"I ask again, why are you going fishing?"

She closed the lid of the bench and sat down. "I invited my brother and his family to come for Christmas. Apparently, his son loves to fish. I offered to take my nephew fishing if the weather was nice enough while they were here. It was snowing when I wrote the letter. How was I to know it was going to warm up? I received an answer this morning. They are coming for a visit, and Merle is very excited that he is going fishing with his aunt. Can you give me a few pointers so I don't look like a complete fool?"

"Like how to tell a tackle box from a picnic basket?"

"You enjoy poking fun at me, don't you?"

He folded his arms over his chest and stroked his chin with one hand. "I've never gotten to do it before. *Ja,* it's kind of fun."

"Levi, will you take me fishing or not?"

How could he deny her anything? "All right."

"When?" she demanded eagerly.

"Tomorrow?"

"It can't be tomorrow. I'm going to a quilting bee."

"That's just as well. I need to deliver Susan Hershberger's repaired buggy. How about the day after tomorrow?" He had plenty of work to do, but the prospect of spending an afternoon alone at the lake with Sarah was too tempting to pass up.

"I think the day after tomorrow will be fine, but I'll have to let you know tomorrow for sure. What time would we leave?"

"I'll pick you up at one o'clock."

"Where will we go?"

"Down to the old stone quarry. I think the bass fishing will be good there."

Sarah grinned. "It sounds like a wonderful time."

She looked so excited and happy that his heart gave a funny little skip. He never imagined she would be thrilled to spend time in his company.

She went inside the house and he returned to the woodpile. Picking up his ax, he began whistling as he worked.

Over a dozen buggies and two-wheeled carts lined the lane leading up to Sally Yoder's home. Sally herself greeted Sarah at the front door. "Come in and welcome. Nearly everyone is here except the bride and her family."

"She'll be here." Sarah remembered how excited and nervous she had been at her own quilting frolic, for she knew she and her new husband would spend many nights together beneath the quilt she had designed and pieced together. She had chosen the Birds in the Air pattern in shades of blue, soft creams and bright greens. That quilt was packed away now, for she couldn't bear to sleep beneath it alone.

Inside Sally's home, twelve women were already seated around the large kitchen table. The air was filled with lively chatter. The mouthwatering smells of fresh coffee, warm donuts and freshly made cinnamon rolls added to the party atmosphere.

Sally's father and three of her brothers were setting out straight-backed and folding chairs around the edges of a large quilting frame in the front room. The furniture in the room had all been pushed against the walls to make room. Sunlight streamed in through the south-facing windows. The quilt top was a beautiful Sunshine and Shadows pattern with blocks in shades of blue, green, magenta, pink and violet alternating with rows of black. She wondered what had made Ina choose this particular pattern and fabrics.

Sarah scanned the faces of the women who ranged in age from seventeen to seventy. They were all women she knew well. Nettie Imhoff and her daughter-in-law Katie Sutter were talking to Karen, Nettie's stepdaughter, who had recently wed Jonathan Dresher. Faith Lapp and Rebecca Troyer sat beside Naomi Wadler. Esther Zook, the bishop's wife, was locked in deep conversation with Susan Hershberger. They darted compassionate glances in Sarah's direction.

No doubt, the bishop's wife was getting an earful about the Beachy brothers. Poor Grace would have her work cut out winning over Henry's mother when she came home.

Looking for Joann Yoder, Sarah spied her standing alone near the back door and staring with longing out the window. She was dressed in a drab gray dress with a black apron. Her hair was mousy brown beneath her black *kapp*. Her shoes were coated with drying mud.

After accepting a cup of coffee, Sarah moved to stand near her. "I almost wish it were rainy and dreary out today."

Joann looked at her in surprise. "Why?"

"It's such a beautiful day, cool but not chilly, with plenty of sunshine to tempt a person away from the chores inside. After all, how many more nice days can we expect this late in December?"

"Not many, but a quilting bee is not really a chore."

Joann lowered her gaze again, as if she was afraid she'd said too much.

She reminded Sarah so much of Levi that she wanted to give the woman a hug. Not that Sarah was tempted to hug Levi. That wouldn't be proper. Okay, she did feel the urge to hug him sometimes, but only because he worked too hard and his family didn't appreciate all he did.

Sarah said, "You're right, a quilting frolic is much more than stitching. We'll hear familiar tales from the grandmothers, and catch up on their grandchildren's antics. Perhaps we'll even hear some of the latest gossip. We'll sing and laugh together. Later, there would be oodles of food. I can smell the ham cooking already, can't you? The only thing better than this would be a day spent fishing."

For you and Levi, not for me.

Joann looked up with interest. "You enjoy fishing?"

Sarah couldn't outright lie to her. She decided to sidestep that comment. This was for Levi. She forced a smile and said brightly, "*Enjoy* is hardly the word I would use. My husband took me when we were first married. I never seemed to have time after I started working at the fabric store."

"I know what you mean. I don't get to go as often as I would like, either."

This was her opening. Sarah tried not to sound too eager. "Levi Beachy is taking me over to the old quarry tomorrow. Would you like to join us?"

A look of delight filled Joann's eyes, but it quickly died away. "I'm sure the two of you would rather go alone."

"Not at all. You would be doing me a great favor by

joining us. Levi is a much better fisherman than I am. I know he'd enjoy the company of someone who isn't a novice."

"Do you really think so?" The fearful hope in her words fueled Sarah's determination. Here was a woman who didn't need to be convinced of Levi's good traits. She just needed a way for him to notice her.

Sarah laid a hand on Joann's arm. "He'll be thrilled. Please say you can come."

"Well, if you're sure it's okay."

"Perfect. We're meeting at my house at one o'clock. Levi said the bass fishing should be good over at the old quarry."

"After this nice warm-up, I reckon it will be. I hooked into a big one there a month ago, but it broke my line. I'm ready to try and land him again."

Sarah felt a sudden pang of envy. Joann and Levi might find they had many things in common besides fishing. That was the reason Sarah had suggested the outing. So why did the look of anticipation on Joann's face leave her feeling jealous?

Sarah faced the true cause of her discontent. She wanted to feel that rush of attraction again. She wanted her heart to skip a beat when the name of a certain someone was mentioned.

Such thoughts were pure foolishness. God had given her the best possible husband, but for some reason, she didn't deserve to know years of happiness with him. The fault lay in her, not in her husband, she was sure of that. Joann and Levi deserved a chance at the happiness that eluded her.

Joann asked, "What's the matter? You look so sad."

Sarah managed a smile as she shook her head. "It's nothing."

The front door opened and Ina Stultz came in with her mother and both her grandmothers. Sarah went to say hello, glad for something else to think about.

Now that the bride-to-be had arrived, Sally's mother invited everyone to find a place at the quilting frame. With so many eager hands, Sarah knew the project would be finished by day's end. She followed the others into the front room and took a seat beside Joann.

Out came the inch-and-a-half-long quilting needles, called "sharps" or "betweens" and spools of thread. For a few minutes, the chatter died away as the women got down to work threading their needles and studying the areas to be outlined. The quiet didn't last long.

"Do you remember when I used to make a play fort under your quilting frame?" Ina asked her mother.

"I do. It wasn't until you were ten that you decided to watch me quilt while you stood beside me instead of playing at my feet."

"Does this quilt have a story?" Rebecca asked, running her hand over the colorful pattern.

Ina smiled. "My mother and her mother both used the Sunlight and Shadow pattern for their wedding quilts."

"To remind us that our lives will be filled with both gladness and sorrow, but that the comfort of the Lord will always be over us," her grandmother explained.

There were murmurs of agreement from around the room.

"From the time I first started setting stitches I wanted to become as good as my grandmother." Ina smiled at her family.

Sarah nodded. Hand-quilting was a journey of personal accomplishment for each Amish girl. Like Ina, Sarah had spent years striving for consistent lengths, working to make straighter lines and improve her stitch count.

For Sarah, her personal best became ten stitches per inch. A goal few quilters could reach. But then, most Amish girls married and began raising families—work that took them away from their craft until their children were grown and they had more time again. Without a husband or children to care for, Sarah had been free to devote her evenings to quilting. She often made two a year. Naomi Wadler sold them for her to the tourists who stayed at the Wadler Inn.

Sarah chose a starting place on Ina's quilt and began to rock her needle through the three layers of fabric stretched on the frame, the solid backing, the batting in the middle to make the quilt fluffy and warm and the top sheet, which bore the pattern. By rocking the needle back and forth, she was able to load as many stitches as possible before drawing the thread through the layers.

Looking up from her work, she saw smiles on the happy faces around her. These women had come together to do something for one of their own. It was a wonderful feeling to join them, young and old alike, as they worked on a craft they all loved.

The skill levels were diverse in such a large group. It was one reason that quilts done at a bee were kept by the families and not offered for sale. Having been employed by an Englishwoman and having met many of the English tourists who came to the store, Sarah knew they prized uniformity in the stitching of the quilts they came to purchase. Such quilts were usually done by one woman.

Joann leaned close. "Watch, Sally will start a contest soon to see who can make the shortest stitches."

Sarah looked over the women. "Anyone who can beat Rebecca Troyer will deserve a prize. You may be a contender. You have a very neat hand at this."

"*Danki,* but my skills are nothing compared to Rebecca's," Joann said.

Rebecca was a renowned quilter in the community. She once suffered from a disease that gradually robbed her of her sight. She had supported herself and her aged aunt by making quilts to sell. With the help of many, and Gideon Troyer in particular, the community had raised enough money for Rebecca to undergo surgery to restore her sight.

By the grace of God, she could now see as well as anyone, but she still kept her eyes closed when she was quilting. She said the sight of so many colors and shapes distracted her from the feel of her needle.

The afternoon passed quickly and Sarah enjoyed the company of her friends. It was getting late when Naomi Wadler spoke up. "Sarah, lead us in a song. Your voice is so sweet."

"Sing 'In the Sweet By and By,'" Ina said quickly.

Closing her eyes, Sarah began, *"There's a land that is fairer than day, And by faith we can see it afar; For the Father waits over the way, To prepare us a dwelling place there."*

Everyone joined in the hymn's refrain. *"In the sweet by and by, We shall meet on that beautiful shore; In the sweet by and by, We shall meet on that beautiful shore."*

When the song was finished, Ina said, "Choose another one, Sarah. What is your favorite?"

* * *

Levi trudged along the highway with his horse walking behind him. He was on his way back to Hope Springs after delivering the repaired carriage to Daniel Hershberger's farm. Having driven it over with his own mare, Levi now led his docile Dotty along the edge of the roadway. A few cars zipped past, but the mare kept her head down and walked quietly beside him. The steady *clip-clop* of her hooves on the blacktop provided a soothing sound to their walk.

He'd made one other stop before dropping off the buggy. He had stopped at Bishop Zook's farm. He'd had a long talk with the bishop. He felt his brothers would benefit from the minister's wisdom.

It was late in the afternoon now and the air was growing chilly. The newspaper that morning said to expect two more days of sunshine before the cold weather returned. It looked as if the weather would stay fine for their fishing trip, if Sarah decided she could join him.

Throughout the day, he'd had a hard time keeping his mind on his work. Thoughts of spending a quiet afternoon alone with Sarah kept intruding. He was eager for this day to end and for tomorrow to arrive.

As he crested a hill, he noticed a line of buggies in the lane of the house off to right. He recognized Sarah's gray gelding hitched to the white rail fence.

Dotty lifted her head and whinnied a greeting. Several of the buggy horses replied in kind including Sarah's gray.

He patted Dotty's neck. "Must be the quilting bee Sarah spoke about."

He hoped she was having a good time with the other women. She didn't get out much except to go to work and church and occasionally visit her family. Since Jonas's death, the joy had gone out of her eyes. Levi knew several widows who had remarried and found happiness again. Why hadn't Sarah? Was her grief so deep?

As he passed by the lane, he heard the sounds of singing coming from inside the house. Someone must have opened a window. It was an old hymn, one he particularly liked called, "Savior Like a Shepherd Lead Us."

He stopped to listen. Dotty dropped her head and snatched a bite of grass growing along the roadside. Levi recognized Sarah's pure, clear voice leading the song. He stayed where he was, listening to the words that stirred his soul and embodied his faith until the last note died away.

Sarah had beauty inside and out. What would it be like to have such a woman as a wife? He couldn't imagine the joy that must have been Jonas's.

Levi settled his hat firmly on his head and started walking again. More and more, he found he couldn't stop thinking about Sarah, about her smile and her laugh, about the way she scolded his brothers and put the shop to rights. Tomorrow, he prayed he would see her smile and maybe even laugh, not at him, but with him.

The urge to sing overtook him but he settled for quietly whistling the hymn Sarah had been singing. Tomorrow couldn't come soon enough.

Chapter Nine

Levi left the shop at noon and went home to eat a hasty lunch. Sarah had stopped by the previous evening to say she could go fishing with him. He didn't want to keep her waiting, but there was one thing he had to do first.

The twins came in to eat a short time later. They had been making wheel spokes and were covered with wood shavings from the lathe. They'd been a quiet pair following the incident with Daniel's buggy. It wouldn't last. He knew they'd be up to something else before long.

He said, "I'm going fishing today. You will stay and run the shop while I'm gone."

The boys looked at each other. Moses said, "We'd like to go fishing, too."

"I would have liked to be paid for the work I put into Daniel Hershberger's carriage. Thanks to you, I labored for nothing."

Scowling, Moses said, "You shouldn't have agreed to give it to him at cost. It's not like he can't afford it."

"Sarah made the offer, and I had to agree to it. She is the owner of the shop we work in. I think you forget that sometimes. The place is not ours to do with as we will."

"How can we forget it? The sign says Wyse Buggy Shop in big letters." Moses had a mulish expression on his face that troubled Levi.

He said, "I like a good joke as well as the next fellow, but you two crossed the line this time. Someone could have been hurt."

"No one was," Atlee countered, looking chastised.

"No one was—this time. It pains me to say this, but I'm giving you both two weeks' notice. You will have to find jobs elsewhere."

"What?" They gaped at him in disbelief.

"If I cannot trust you to keep the safety of our customers foremost in your minds, you can't work for me. You are free to seek employment elsewhere."

Atlee said, "You can't run the place by yourself."

"I will hire a man I can trust. Perhaps working for someone other than your brother will teach you to value the work you do."

"You mean you're going to stop paying us? How will we get our spending money?"

"That is no longer my problem."

Moses said, "It's not that easy to find a job. Who will hire us both?"

Levi didn't want to punish his brothers, but he had ignored his responsibilities toward them for far too long. He wasn't their father, but he was an adult who knew right from wrong. It was past time they learned a hard lesson.

He gathered his pole and tackle box from the corner of the room. "Daniel Hershberger is hiring at his furniture factory. I heard he pays good wages."

"Ha, ha," Moses said dryly.

Atlee shoved his hands in his pockets and stared at

the floor. "We weren't thinking about needing a job from him. We planned to work with you."

Levi looked from one to the other. "You might want to consider something other than what's funny when you plan your next prank. There are some openings at the coal mine. They will bus Amish workers in. You could try there. One other thing, Bishop Zook will be by to speak to you both later today. Be here when he arrives. If I hear otherwise, you will be looking for a place to sleep as well as work."

With the uncomfortable confrontation behind him, Levi left the house and walked next door. Sarah stood waiting on the front steps of her house. She wasn't alone. Joann Yoder stood with her, pole and tackle box in hand.

Sarah came toward him with a wide smile. "Levi, look who has agreed to join us."

He nodded in Joann's direction. She blushed a fiery shade of red and stared at her feet. His happy anticipation dropped like a stone in a well. He wasn't going to be alone with Sarah.

"Shall we go?" Sarah asked, looking between the two. He nodded again.

"I'm ready," Joann mumbled.

"We are going to have such a nice time. Levi, I can't thank you enough for taking me. Isn't he kind to take time out of his busy day for us?" Sarah started toward his wagon waiting by the street.

He'd chosen to take it instead of his buggy because they would be going off the road and through a farm field to his favorite fishing spot, an old stone quarry now filled with deep clear water from a natural spring.

Besides his fishing gear, he'd put in a pair of folding chairs and two quilts in case the day turned chilly.

Sarah scrambled up onto the wagon seat without waiting for his help and scooted across the seat leaving Joann to sit in the middle. Joann smiled shyly and handed him her pole. She held a large bucket in her other hand.

He put her pole in the back of the wagon and said, "I only have two chairs. I'll get another one."

"Don't bother. I just turn my bucket upside down and sit on it until it's time to take the fish home."

Sarah said, "Isn't she clever, Levi? I never would have thought of that."

He took the bucket from Joann and put it in back. She climbed up onto the seat and he took his place beside her.

As they rolled out of town, he glanced over at Sarah. Joann had her pressed against the far side of the seat. He feared she would be knocked off if they hit a bump. He asked, "You okay?"

Sarah grimaced. "I'm a little crowded. Joann, can you scoot closer to Levi? He doesn't bite."

Joann giggled and slid over.

"A little more, please," Sarah said.

Joann moved closer until her hip was touching his. Did Sarah really need that much room? Their destination began to feel a long ways away.

He said, "Elam Sutter has a nice pond. It's closer than the quarry lake if you'd rather go there?"

Sarah quickly dismissed his suggestion, "The quarry sounds much better, doesn't it, Joann? I've never been there and I'm dying to see it. You've been there before, haven't you Joann?"

Joann nodded but didn't say anything.

After a few minutes of silence, Sarah said, "Joann was telling me that she hooked into a really big bass last month. Tell Levi about it, Joann."

"It broke my line."

"What weight were you using?"

"Five pound test."

"Six would have been better."

"That's what I have on now."

"Should be good enough." He couldn't think of anything else to say so he fell silent.

Sarah had no such problem. She continued to pelt them with questions about fishing and their best catches, what kind of lures they used and what type of fishing they liked best. He began to wonder if she had taken a job writing for a fishing journal. It wasn't until they reached the turn-off for the quarry that she finally seemed to run out of questions.

The ride across the field was rough, but it was less than a mile to the edge of the quarry. Levi chose a spot with a sloping shoreline exposed to the sun and drew the horse to a halt.

Sarah hopped down. "What a lovely lake. I think I'll explore a little before I start fishing."

She took off at a quick pace along the edge of the water. He got down and raised his arms to help Joann. She blushed scarlet, but allowed him to lift her down. He quickly stepped back.

Brushing at the front of her coat, she glanced up at him and said, "I hope you don't mind my coming along."

"*Nee,* it is fine." She wasn't to blame. He should

have known Sarah wasn't interested in spending time alone with him.

Joann scowled. "I didn't realize Sarah was such a chatterbox."

He looked over her head to where Sarah was walking at the water's edge. "She doesn't usually talk your ear off."

Joann cast a worried look in Sarah's direction. "If she keeps it up, she'll scare the fish away."

"Let me get our poles." If he couldn't spend the afternoon alone with Sarah, he might as well try fishing.

Sarah remained some distance from the wagon and covertly watched Levi and Joann. It looked briefly as if they were having a conversation, but they soon parted ways and actually began casting their lines in while standing fifty feet apart. This wasn't going as she had hoped. Now what?

She wandered father away and found a place on a flat rock between a pair of cedar trees. Leaning forward, she propped her elbows on her knees and settled her chin on her hands. Matchmaking was turning out to be much harder than she thought.

She was almost hoarse after carrying a conversation alone for five miles. Between Levi's stilted replies and Joann's brief comments, Sarah had been tempted to knock their heads together.

Reaching down, she picked up a rock and tossed it in the lake. She was about ready to give up. She had been foolish to think matching Levi up with her friends would be a way to avoid the winter depression that normally gripped her. Grace would simply have to find the courage to leave home without a wife for Levi to replace her.

Standing, Sarah picked up a flat rock and tried to skip it across the still surface of the lake. It sank two feet in front of her. She couldn't even skip a stone right, how could she manage someone else's love life?

"Point number one. If you throw rocks at the fish, they won't bite."

Startled, Sarah spun around to see Levi standing behind her.

He held out her casting rod. "You asked for some pointers, remember? Point number two. It helps to actually put your hook in the water."

"Right." She took the rod from him. She thought she remembered how to cast, but when she tried, her lure plunked into the water barely four feet from shore. Was she doomed to be a failure at everything?

Levi stepped closer. "Reel it back in. Let me show you how it's done."

He stood close behind her and wrapped his hand over hers. "Move your arm back like this, and then go forward. Keep your eyes focused on where you want your line to go."

As he moved her arm back and forth, mimicking the motion she needed, Sarah completely lost interest in fishing.

The firmness and warmth of Levi's hand over hers made her breath catch in her chest. He stood only a fraction of an inch behind her. If she leaned back just a little she could rest against him. She closed her eyes.

The urge to lay her head back and melt into his embrace was overpowering. She had been alone too long. She didn't want to be alone anymore.

He stopped moving her arm. She was afraid to open her eyes and look at him. What would she see written on his face? Indifference? Friendship? Or something more?

"I've got one!" Joann shouted. "Hurry, bring the net."

Levi stepped away from Sarah. The breath rushed back into her lungs. She trembled, but managed to say, "I've got this. Go help Joann."

As he strode away, Sarah called herself every kind of fool. She wasn't a potential wife for him. Even if she wanted to marry again, which she didn't, he hadn't shown the least bit of interest in her *that* way. He was a friend. She had no business thinking of him in any other light.

For Sarah, the afternoon passed slowly, although Joann and Levi both landed fish. An hour later, Levi landed a huge one. The sight of his excited happy face only made Sarah more aware of how attractive he was.

Joann looked as excited as he was. "It's a beauty, Levi! I think it's the very one that got away from me last month. What kind of jig are you using?"

"This is a black *Jig and Pig*."

"I'm going to have to get me a few."

"I've got several. Try one of mine."

Joann grinned. Her shyness had evaporated. "That's nice of you, Levi. I believe I will."

Sarah glanced between the two of them. Who would have thought something called a *Jig and Pig* could spark such interest between two people? The more relaxed they became with each other, the worse Sarah felt. Her plan was working, so why wasn't she happy?

Within an hour, they had a stringer loaded with eight fat bass. Sarah had a bite or two, but they got away. Her heart wasn't in the adventure. She wanted to go home and bury herself under the covers until her common sense returned.

She made the long ride home in silence. Joann, on the other hand, spoke with growing confidence. Levi gave his usual short replies, but occasionally expanded them to a full sentence or two. Sarah often felt his gaze on her, but she studiously avoided looking in his direction.

When they arrived back at her home, Levi took the fish to clean them. Joann followed Sarah into the house.

Once they were in the kitchen, Joann grabbed Sarah in a quick, strong hug. Just as quickly, she released Sarah and took a step back. She clasped her hands together. "Sarah, I had such a wonderful time. You can't even know."

"I'm glad." She was. One of them should be happy.

"Levi is such a fine fellow. I've never enjoyed a day fishing more than I enjoyed this one."

"I hope you get to enjoy other days together."

"That would be nice, but I'm not holding my breath."

"Why do you say that? You're good company, you enjoy many of the things Levi enjoys, I don't see why he wouldn't ask you out again."

Joann looked at her sadly. "Sarah, Levi isn't interested in me. It was exciting to imagine he might be for a while, but I know the signs. I've seen the way my brothers and cousins look at the women they want to court. Levi doesn't look at me that way. He looks at you that way."

Sarah's mouth dropped open. For the most part, Levi ignored her unless the business needed something. She'd lived beside him for years. "You are mistaken. Levi and I are friends, but nothing more."

Joann gave her a quick puzzled look and then stared at her feet. "I'm sorry I said anything. Forgive me."

"There's nothing to forgive."

"I must get home. Thank you again for inviting me." She hurried out the door.

Sarah moved to the window and watched her walk away. Joann was mistaken. Levi didn't harbor the kind of feelings that she suggested. Sarah would have known if that were the case. She would have seen it in his beautiful blue eyes.

She glanced toward his house and saw him standing in the yard. He wasn't watching Joann's retreating figure. His gaze was on Sarah's window, but he was too far away for her to read his expression.

Levi didn't know what he had done wrong, but Sarah wasn't speaking to him.

All day long on Friday, whenever he went in search of her, she was heading away from him. If he went to the upholstery room, she made some excuse about needing another type of thread and took off for her house. She handled the customers easily. She smiled and laughed with them, but when she was alone with him, she suddenly thought of things she needed to do elsewhere.

Twice, he cornered her in the small office, but each time she simply said, "Excuse me," and slipped past him. Short of grabbing her and demanding to know what was wrong, he had no idea what to do.

Not only had Sarah turned cold, so had the weather. A gusty north wind rattled the shutters of the building and low gray clouds blotted out the sky. The nice weather had come to an abrupt end as winter returned.

The weather forecast was calling for snow by the end of the week.

At four-thirty, Leah Belier drove up and came inside. Since he hadn't a clue where Sarah had gone, he was forced to leave the new carriage he was finishing and speak to Leah. At least she was easy to talk to. "Good afternoon. Are you ready to leave your buggy with me?"

She smiled. "I am. I have one of my students bringing in the used buggy you loaned me. I see you are building a new one."

"*Ja,* it is almost done."

"Who is it for?"

"This one is for someone who needs one right away."

"Like a family who has lost theirs in an accident?"

"Something like that. It's plain inside, but I can change a few things if someone wants to fancy it up. It's a good all-round buggy for a small family. I try to keep one or two finished samples on hand. This will make number three."

"Can I see it?"

"Sure." He led the way.

"Where is Sarah, today?" Leah asked.

"Around." He wasn't about to try and explain something he didn't understand.

Leah opened the carriage door and looked it. "The upholstery is lovely in this shade of gray. I would only change a few small things."

"Such as?"

"I'd need a bigger storage box added to the back and a cup holder up front. I like to sip my diet soda on the way to school in the mornings. It's my one vice."

"Diet soda isn't much of vice. Mine is fresh orange juice."

She laughed. "Levi, that isn't a vice. Orange juice is good for you. Didn't you learn anything in school?"

"Not enough, I reckon. I didn't have you for a teacher."

"Seriously, would you sell me this buggy? How much is it?"

He named a price and waited, expecting her to decline.

Instead, she said, "I'm tempted. Mine is almost fifteen years old and needs work. If I have to put out the money, I may as well get something I like. But not for as much as you're asking." She named a slightly lower price.

It was a fair offer. He didn't want to turn down a sale, but he wanted to make sure she wasn't doing this on an impulse. "You'd best think it over."

"I have been thinking about it ever since you told me what was wrong with mine. I'm ready to do this." She broke into a wide grin.

Could she really afford new on her teacher's salary? He said, "Why don't you take a look at some of the used carriages I have out back? They won't be as expensive."

"Honestly, Levi, you act like my money is no good."

"I want you to be happy with what you buy from me."

"I'm sure I will be. You haven't forgotten about helping me set up for my winter picnic have you?"

"I haven't. When should I come out?"

"There won't be a lot to do. If you come the evening before, that will be fine."

"It's the weekend before Christmas, is that right? I'll be there."

"Wonderful. I will look at your used buggies, but

I'm afraid only a new one will do now that I've made up my mind."

He led the way to the back door and held it open for her. The twins were outside cleaning the ashes from the fire pit. They both had folded kerchiefs covering their noses and mouths. As Atlee hefted a shovelful of ash into a wheelbarrow, a gust of wind sent a cloud of it swirling toward the shop door.

With a muffled cry, Leah covered her face with her hands and turned into Levi's arms.

Startled, he held still. "What's wrong?"

"There's something in my eye. Oh, it hurts. I think a cinder flew in it."

"Let me see. Hold still." He cupped her chin and turned her face up to his.

Sarah opened the front door of the workshop and looked around for Levi. She wouldn't be able to keep running away from him forever, but she wasn't ready to face him. Not if what Joann suggested was true. It couldn't be.

Yes, their friendship had grown in the past days, but it was only friendship. She wouldn't allow anything else.

It wasn't in her to love a man the way Levi deserved to be loved. To love a man as deeply as she had loved Jonas would mean facing the possibility of loss and grief again.

She couldn't live through another loss. It would be better never to love someone again.

She heard the sound of soft voices and rounded the counter to see if he was working in the back of the building. If he was, she could slip into the office and finish the day in there.

When she spotted Levi near the back door, she couldn't believe her eyes.

He and Leah were locked in an embrace not twenty feet from her. Levi tenderly cupped Leah's face and bent toward her. Was he going to kiss her?

Shock shook Sarah to her core. She quickly turned away.

Levi wasn't in love with her. He was in love with Leah. Why hadn't she seen it?

Instead of the elation that should have filled her at knowing her plan had worked, all she felt was disappointment. With astonishing clarity, she could imagine herself in Levi's arms, lifting her face to receive his kiss.

She quickly left the building. Outside, she leaned against the door and pressed a hand to her stinging eyes, surprised to find tears on her face.

Sarah squeezed her eyes closed but she couldn't shut out the sight of Leah in Levi's arms. She couldn't ignore the ache growing in her heart. He cared for someone else.

Leah was a lovely woman and a good match for Levi. Perhaps she was a bit too conservative for him, but none of that mattered if Leah truly cared for him. Did she? Or was she a desperate old maid leading him on so she wouldn't have to spend the rest of her life alone?

Sarah shook her head to clear her thinking. Such unChristian thoughts didn't become her. She'd started her matchmaking project to keep her depression at bay and to help Grace, but now she realized what she really wanted was for Levi to be happy.

To love and be loved in return was one of the most beautiful gifts God could bestow on a man and a woman.

Tears came to her eyes again. Grace and Henry would be happy. Levi and Leah would be happy. Everyone would be happy except her. Why had God chosen this life for her?

No, that was wrong. She mustn't question God's plan for her. Her life was blessed with her remaining family and good friends. She had her health and a church community that would rally around when she needed it.

She would grow old alone. So what? Many women did. If she wasn't content, that was something she would pray to overcome. Pressing the heels of her hands to her eyes, she stemmed the flow of tears. It was better for her to live alone than to suffer the constant fear of losing someone dear.

Wasn't it?

It was the belief she's clung to for years, the reason she refused to consider remarrying. So why did she question that decision now? Because in one moment of weakness she thought she wanted to be kissed? Such foolishness would pass.

She would do her best to be glad for Levi and Leah and pray that they would have many happy years together.

Chapter Ten

"Good morning, Levi. Isn't it a lovely Monday morning?"

Levi still didn't know what he had done to upset Sarah last week, but it seemed that she had forgiven him. He looked out the window. "It is pouring rain."

"Rain is nice sometimes. I can't believe Christmas will be here in two weeks. This year has flown by. Are you doing anything special for the holidays?"

At least she wasn't avoiding him anymore. He said, "The boys and I have been invited to Gideon and Rebecca's place for dinner next Sunday. I plan to have a quiet Christmas at home. When will your brother and his family arrive?"

"Next Monday evening. They intend to stay here for a few days and then go to visit Emma and her family."

"You should invite them to Leah's winter picnic."

Sarah's smile vanished for just an instant. When it reappeared, it was brighter than before. "That is a wonderful idea, but I'm not sure they will stay the whole week. Were you able to fix Leah's axle?"

"She has decided to buy a new buggy instead."

"Really, I had no idea you were such a good salesman."

Something in her tone made him look at her closely. "Sarah, are you okay?"

"Of course. Why do you ask?"

"No reason, I guess."

"You should get to work. I have plenty to do. I made chicken salad sandwiches for lunch and put them in your refrigerator. Where are the boys?"

"Out looking for new jobs."

"What?" She stared at him in astonishment.

"I had a talk with Bishop Zook. He made some suggestions and I took them. I fired Atlee and Moses. After their stunt with Daniel and Susan's buggy, I can't trust them to work here."

"Wow."

"I'm sorry if you disapprove."

"I'm not saying you're wrong. I'm just surprised."

"Hundreds of people ride in the buggies we make and repair. Many more than that depend on the wheels I've sold them. I take the safety of our people seriously. A faulty wheel, a carelessly tightened bolt could kill or maim. I will hire someone new to help me. Ben Lapp is a good boy. I will see if his father can spare him from the farm this winter."

Her eyes filled with sympathy. "It must have been hard for you to tell the twins they couldn't work with you. They're your family."

"The boys were only two when our parents died. Grace was only six. She became the little mother, but I never became the father. I didn't believe I had the right to take my father's place. They lacked discipline because of that. I pray I have not learned my lesson too late for them to become good and wise men."

She stepped close and laid a hand on his arm. Gazing into his eyes, she said softly, "I am pleased with you, Levi Beachy. If they become good, wise men, it is because they have a good and wise brother."

He covered her hand with his. "*Danki,* Sarah. You have made me see the error of my ways with them. They will have you to thank, as well."

She snatched her hand away and stepped toward the counter, avoiding his gaze. "I can't believe how quickly this place gets dirty. I must get to work and so must you. I have bread baking in my oven. I'll be back in a little while if that's okay with you."

"Of course."

She quickly went out the door.

Did his touch repulse her? Her rejection stung, but he called himself a fool for expecting otherwise. At least she wasn't laughing at him anymore. Her sympathy for his family dilemma was real.

After replacing the axle on Leah's old buggy, Levi worked at fixing up the inside, tightening the door hinges and adding a new shine to the old leather interior with saddle soap and elbow grease. When he finished, he surveyed his work. He now had a nice used buggy to resell. Maybe to a young couple just starting out who couldn't afford a new one yet or as a runabout for a grandmother to use. He glanced outside. The rain had stopped.

He went to the front of the shop and found Sarah cleaning. Didn't she realize she was never going to get this old building spic-and-span? He didn't like to see her working so hard at something impossible.

He wanted what Jonas had wanted for her. He wanted to see her happy, with her children around her and a man who loved her at her side. Then and only then, Levi could follow his dream.

His eyes were drawn to his calendar. Instead of the mountains he loved to look upon, a picture of a collie dog with puppies stared back at him.

He rounded on Sarah. "Where's my calendar?"

She stopped cleaning. "I tossed it on the rubbish heap. It was years out of date. I got you a new one."

"If I wanted a new one, I would've gotten it myself." He charged past her and out the back door and stopped in disbelief. Not only had she thrown it on the rubbish heap, but she had set the trash on fire. His calendar was charred beyond recognition.

"I'm sorry," she said from behind him. "I didn't think it was important."

It was only a picture. It held no value to anyone except him. The anger drained out of his body. "I wish you had asked, that's all."

It wasn't his dream going up in smoke. It was only a photograph.

"I'm sorry," she said again. "Why was it so special to you?"

"It was just a pretty place. I liked looking at it."

"That was where you hoped to live one day, wasn't it? Oh, Levi, I am sorry."

"I don't imagine I'll ever leave here. It was a pipe dream, nothing more."

He turned away from the fire. His promise was keeping him here. She was keeping him here. How much longer could he stay? Perhaps it was true that he was never meant to leave. The rain began falling again.

He said, "You should go inside before you catch your death." Without looking back, he crossed the lot to his house and went inside. The twins sat at the kitchen table with sandwiches piled on their plates.

He opened the refrigerator. There wasn't any left for him.

He took out the milk carton and poured himself a glass. Moses said, "We haven't had much luck today."

"Neither have I," Levi mumbled and took a seat at the table with them. He downed the milk and wiped his lips. Atlee pushed half a sandwich toward him.

He nodded his thanks and finished it in two bites.

Moses pulled an envelope from his pocket. "The mail came. You have a letter from Grandmother."

Atlee said, "I hope she's sending Grace home."

Levi did, too. He tore open the letter and began to read his grandmother's spidery handwriting.

"What does she say?" Atlee leaned closer.

"She is thrilled to have Grace with her. Looks like Grace intends to stay until the week after Christmas."

"That's not too long." Atlee didn't look thrilled with the news.

Moses rolled his eyes. "I thought she'd hot-foot it back here to be with Henry."

Levi read the next sentence and stopped. "This can't be right."

"What?" Moses and Atlee asked together.

"I'm to be thankful Grace's friend has agreed to be a matchmaker for me." Levi couldn't believe what he was reading. Grace's friend? Was she referring to Sarah?

Moses took a bite of his sandwich. "Grandmother must be getting senile."

"Reckon so," Levi said, but he kept reading.

Give somber consideration to each woman that is presented to you. A pretty face does not a good wife make. A woman who is devout, who loves God and keeps His commandments, that is a woman who has a beautiful soul. Love grows from respect and shared experiences. Be kind and receive kindness in return. Love and receive love in return.

Suddenly, all that had been happening since Grace left began to make sense to Levi. Sarah inviting Sally to work with them. Sarah convincing him Leah wanted him to look over her buggy. Sarah inviting Joann to join their fishing trip.

Sarah *was* matchmaking. Trotting him out like a prized horse for consideration.

As if he couldn't find a wife by himself if he wanted one! He hadn't looked seriously because a wife might not want to move to Colorado if she had family in Ohio.

It had been his father's dream long before it became Levi's. His mother had kept his father from going. She had refused to move one step farther west from her family in Pennsylvania. Levi remembered his father's caution on the subject of choosing the right spouse all too well.

Had Grace suggested this matchmaking scheme? Why? Oh, how Sarah must have laughed. The wretched woman, how could she? Were all her friends in on the joke?

He had waited patiently for Sarah to marry for five long years, and now she was wife-shopping for him?

Well, two could play at matchmaking. If he was fair game, so was she. There were any number of men who would be happy to hear that the pretty widow Sarah Wyse was finally on the lookout for a husband.

She hadn't asked him if he wanted to meet potential wives. He saw no reason to ask her if she wanted to meet potential husbands. When the shoe was on the other foot, she wouldn't be laughing then.

What he needed was a strategy. He couldn't think with his brothers staring at him. "I'm going out."

"But it's raining," Atlee pointed out.

"I've got a hat. A little water won't hurt me."

Sarah couldn't put her finger on what it was, but when Levi came back from lunch, something was different about him. He had a hard look in his eyes when he stared at her. His coat was soaked and his hat was dripping all over her freshly cleaned floor.

He said, "I'm going over to the café. The boys didn't leave me but two bites of a sandwich."

"I can make you some scrambled eggs or a grilled cheese sandwich if you don't want to go that far."

"No, I like the food at the Shoofly Pie Café. I won't be long."

"All right. Have a nice lunch."

He smiled, but it didn't reach his eyes. "It's going to be a fine one. I can feel it in my bones."

She puzzled over his comment, but didn't know what to make of it. He was back a little over an hour later. When he took his coat off, she saw his shirt was damp and he had a smear of what looked like blueberries across the front of it. She said, "It looks like the pie was good, how was the rest of your meal?"

He patted his stomach. "The meal and the company were fine. You have no idea how many men eat lunch at the café."

"Mostly the single ones, I reckon. Those who don't have a wife to cook for them at home."

He grinned and pointed a finger at her. "You are correct."

"You're soaking wet. You should go change."

"I'm a grown man. I'll change my clothes when I'm ready and not before. I'll change my life when I'm ready and not before."

"Levi, you're acting very strange."

"Am I? What could have brought that on?"

"Are you feeling well?"

His grin faded. "*Nee,* I'm not."

"Is there anything I can do?"

"You've done enough, Sarah Wyse. You've done more than enough." He left her and went into the office, closing the door behind him. She was left to puzzle over his behavior for the rest of the afternoon.

The sun came out shortly after one o'clock. When the twins came in, Sarah left them in charge at the counter and took the opportunity to go home and get her wash done. If the rain held off, her clothes would be dry by the time she left work.

She was back at the shop an hour later. The twins were where she had left them. They hadn't done much work at all. When four o'clock rolled around, she tapped on the office door.

"What is it?" Levi asked from inside.

"I'm going home now."

"Fine." He sneezed loudly.

Sarah frowned at the door. Was he upset with her? She hadn't done anything to anger him. Perhaps he and Leah had a quarrel after…after she saw them in each other's arms.

Whatever was wrong, it wouldn't be solved by lurking outside Levi's office. She had plenty of work waiting at home. She had oodles of baking to get done before her family arrived.

As she crossed the street, she noticed rain clouds rolling in again from the north. She rushed inside the house and grabbed a laundry basket, intent on getting her clothes in before the rain undid all the sun's work. She had just started taking down her sheets when the first sprinkles splattered against her *kapp* and face.

From behind her, she heard a man's voice. "Let me give you a hand with these, Sarah."

Startled, she turned to see Jacob Gingerich pulling clothespins from her pillowcases. "*Danki,* Jacob. What are you doing here?"

"I was passing by and decided to stop in for a visit. How are you?"

She bundled the last of her clothing into a basket and lifted it. "I'm fine. Won't you come inside for some *kaffi?*"

His grin widened. He took the basket from her. "I was hoping you would say that."

His joy seemed out of proportion to her simple offer of coffee. Sarah led the way inside the house.

Jacob Gingerich worked in Daniel Hershberger's lumber mill. He was fairly new to the Hope Springs area, having come from Indiana to find work. He wasn't married, and she knew him only from having seen him at the church services. She could think of no reason for him to be passing by her house because Daniel's mill and the farm where Jacob lived were on the other side of town.

She said, "Just set the basket on the floor and have

a seat at the table. It will only take me a few minutes to get some coffee going."

He set the basket down, then hung his coat and his hat on one of the pegs by her front door.

She moved to the sink to fill the coffee pot with fresh water. Looking out, she noticed Andy Bowman getting out of his buggy at her front gate. He had a large paper sack in his hand with the Shoofly Pie Café logo on the front. She looked at Jacob. "Are you expecting Andy Bowman?"

He frowned. "*Nee,* I'm not. Why do you ask?"

"Because he's coming up my front walk." She moved to open the door for him. "Good afternoon, Sarah Wyse," Andy said in a booming voice.

"Hello, Andy. What brings you here?"

He thrust the paper bag toward her. "I thought you might enjoy a supper that you didn't have to cook. I had Naomi Wadler pack up some of her fried chicken, potato salad and shoofly pie."

One male visitor was unusual. Two single men showing up at her door unannounced smacked of her aunt Emma's matchmaking meddling.

Sarah opened the door wide. "Come in, Andy. Jacob Gingerich and I were about to have some coffee."

She stepped aside. Andy hung up his coat and hat beside Jacob's. The men scowled at each other briefly, but were cordial to one another.

As it turned out, it was a good thing that Andy had brought food. By suppertime, there were four sets of coats and hats lined up beside her front door. Sarah had no idea what her aunt could have said to bring so many bachelors and widowers to her door, but she planned to give her aunt a stern talking to the next time they met.

Once the sparse meal was done and the second pot of coffee had been finished, her guests still made no move to leave. It seemed that none of them wanted to be the first man out the door. They stayed until Sarah finally had to ask them to leave.

As he left, each man promised to return at a more opportune time when they could be alone. When the last one was out the door, Sarah stood on the porch and watch them disperse. She glanced toward the carriage shop and saw Levi leaning against the open door jamb. He gave her a jaunty wave.

Sarah stepped back inside the house and closed her door with a bang. She considered nailing it shut but decided moving away might be a better option. She should have known her aunt wouldn't wait forever before deciding Sarah had been single long enough.

Levi suffered a twinge of conscience the following morning when Sarah came to work looking as if she hadn't slept well. Her eyes were puffy and she kept yawning into her hand. He hadn't slept that well, either. Today his throat was raw. He had a burning pain deep in his chest.

He said, "There isn't much work today. Why don't you go home? I'm sure you have a lot to do before your family arrives."

"I have a lot of baking to do, that's for sure. I had hoped to get started last evening, but that didn't happen."

"I noticed your party. I felt a little left out, not being invited and all."

"I didn't issue the invitations, but I'm surprised you

didn't get one. When I see my aunt Emma, she is going to get an earful."

So she didn't suspect him. That was good, but he didn't like the idea that she was blaming someone else. Still, like the twins, she had to learn that not everyone could be manipulated for her benefit. He pulled a chair up beside her. "Why are you angry with your aunt?"

"Emma Lapp loves the idea of being a matchmaker. I've told her for years that I'm not ready to marry again. I reckon she decided to take matters into her own hands. Hence, half the single Amish men over twenty-five were grouped around my table last night. No doubt the rest of them will show up tonight."

He stared at his hands. "What makes you so sure your aunt is behind it?"

"I can't imagine who else it would be."

"I sympathize with you, Sarah. I've been feeling like I've been put on display myself, lately."

She frowned. "You have?"

"It's not a comfortable feeling, as I'm sure you noticed."

Her frown turned to a look of speculation. "Levi, do you know something about the line of men in my kitchen last night?"

He folded his arms over his chest. "About as much as you know about fishing lines."

She had the decency to blush. "I did promise my nephew I would take him. Thanks to your help, I'm sure I won't embarrass myself."

"Thanks to Joann you mean. And our special thanks must also go to Sally for all her help with the inventory. Is it done?"

Sarah's voice grew smaller. "Almost."

"What sweet young thing can I expect to help you finish?"

"I'll be able to manage alone," she mumbled, her eyes downcast.

He hid a smile behind the hand he used to rub his chin. "That is *goot*."

He heard a horse stop outside. He glanced out the window. "Ah, I see you have another visitor at your house. I believe that is Amos Fisher. He's a long way past twenty-five, but he runs a nice hog farm. He told me yesterday that he has two hundred sows now."

Her eyes snapped to his, shooting daggers of loathing. "I think you are a sneaky, mean man, Levi Beachy."

He grinned. "I'm learning from the best."

Chapter Eleven

When Sarah entered the carriage shop the following morning she had every intention of giving Levi a piece of her mind. Three more suitors had darkened her door the previous evening.

She found Levi huddled in front of the stove with his arms wrapped around his body. When he looked up, his face was pale as a sheet. There were dark circles under his eyes. He shivered so violently that he nearly fell from the small stool he was perched on. The man looked sick to death. He coughed and the deep rattle in his chest frightened her.

"Levi Beachy, I never once considered you to be a fool until this moment." She advanced toward him.

"Go away," he muttered in a pitifully hoarse voice.

"You are the one who is going. You're going straight to bed. You look miserable."

"I'm fine. I just need a minute to get warm." He leaned closer to the fire.

Shaking her head, Sarah marched to the door and flipped the Open sign to Closed. Outside, Elam Sutter was just getting out of his buggy. At least she knew he hadn't come to court her. He was happily married to her friend Katie.

She opened the door and called out to him, "I'm sorry Elam, but the shop is closed today. Levi is sick."

"I've stopped by to pick up a part he ordered for me. I had a note in the mail that it had come in."

"All right, I'll find it for you, but you should stay outside. I don't want you taking sickness home to Katie and the *kinder*."

"*Danki,* Sarah. I'll wait right here."

Closing the door, she quickly checked the counter area but didn't find anything with Elam's name on it. She crossed the room and crouched beside Levi. He was looking worse by the minute. She touched his shoulder gently. "Levi, where is the part that came in for Eli Sutter?"

He opened bloodshot eyes. "On my desk in the back."

"I'll get it, and then you are going back to the house."

"I don't want to go to the house."

"You sound like a pouting child. You're going back to the house if I have to drag you by your suspenders. And don't think for a minute that I can't do it."

A ragged cough followed by a weak nod was her answer. She pulled off her coat and tucked it around his shoulders. He nestled into the warmth with a grateful sigh. Leaving him sitting by the fire, Sarah quickly found the part and carried it out to Elam.

He took it from her and asked, "Is there anything I can do for you or Levi?"

"*Nee.* Rest is what he needs now."

"My mother said a nasty flu bug has been making the rounds over in Sugarcreek. Looks like it's come to pay Hope Springs a visit."

"Levi got soaked yesterday and wouldn't go home to change. I hope it's the flu and not pneumonia. He's too sick to work, but he won't go to bed, either. Sometime men are more trouble than they are worth."

Elam chuckled. "My wife would agree with you."

"Good day, Elam. Give Katie and the children my love."

He promised to do so and drove away. Sarah hurried back inside just as Levi was struggling to his feet. He teetered and would have fallen if she hadn't rushed to hold him up. Staggering under his weight, she managed to keep both of them upright.

"I'm sorry," he mumbled against her *kapp*.

She had both arms around his waist. "Never mind. Let's get you to the house. What on earth possessed you to try and work today?"

"I thought I'd feel better in the shop."

"Why would you think that?"

"I always feel better here. Besides, I have work that must be done."

Sarah lifted Levi's arm and placed it around her shoulder. "The work will still be here tomorrow."

"If I don't get it done today, there will be twice as much work tomorrow."

"Let the twins do some of it."

"They're sick. I told them to stay in bed." So it was an illness that was going around and not because Levi had had a soaking. Still, it certainly hadn't done him any good.

"You told the twins to stay in bed, but you couldn't take your own advice."

A vicious cough stole his breath and left him wheezing and unsteady. She knew if he lost his balance she wouldn't be able to hold him up. Why had she sent Elam Sutter away? He wouldn't have had any trouble carrying Levi.

"Come. It's only a few steps to the house. We can get there together."

Thankfully, they were able to manage the short trek, although several times she wondered if they would make it. They were both sweating and out of breath by the time they reached his front door.

"Danki, mie goot Sarah," he said as he sank in a heap on the couch.

Why did she wish she were his good Sarah? It wasn't part of her makeup to be a loving wife. Hadn't that been made painfully clear to her?

She unlaced Levi's boots and pulled them off. As she had once suspected, both his socks had holes in them. She would have to have a stern talk with Grace when the girl came home. The art of good housekeeping wasn't reserved solely for a woman's husband.

Sarah pulled a folded quilt from the back of a rocker and spread it across Levi. She coaxed him to give up her coat and then tucked the quilt around his shoulders. She pressed her palm to his forehead. He was burning up.

"If I make you some hot tea will you be able to keep it down?" she asked.

"I think so."

"When was the last time you had something to eat?"

"I'm not hungry. I just want to sleep."

"Not until I get some fluids in you. I'm going to check on the twins."

When Levi didn't respond, Sarah took it as his consent. She quickly put the kettle on and made her way up the narrow stairs to the upper story of the house.

The first room she looked into belonged to Grace. It was painted a lovely shade of lavender with a large throw rug on the floor and a beautiful lavender-and-white quilt on the bed.

The next door she opened was to Levi's room. It was tidy and clean. The walls were a pale gray. His bed had a simple dark blue blanket as a spread. He was a tidy man.

The last room she looked in was not neat at all. There were clothes strewn on the floor, shoes had been tossed aside and lay where they'd fallen and numerous books and magazines lay helter-skelter around the room. From a set of twin beds, one bleary-eyed and one bright-eyed boy looked at her in astonishment. She marched to the bed closest to the door and laid her hand on Atlee's brow.

He was hot, but his fever wasn't as high as Levi's.

Moses drew his covers up to his chin when she came toward him. "What are you doing in here?"

"I'm seeing who is sick and how sick they are." She clapped a hand on his forehead. He was cool to the touch. His eyes were bright, his lips weren't cracked.

She fisted her hands on her hips and glared at him. "You aren't sick."

"I am. I ache all over. My stomach is churning. I feel terrible," he insisted.

"You'll feel better when you're done helping me."

"Helping you do what?"

"Levi is downstairs and he is very sick. I don't think I can get him up to his room by myself. You have five minutes to get dressed, and then I'm coming up here with a pail of cold water. If you're in this bed when I get back, you'll get a bath."

"You wouldn't?"

"Trust me, I would."

She turned to leave. Stopping by Atlee, she straightened his covers and said, "I'll bring you some hot tea with honey in a few minutes. Do you think you can eat something?"

"Maybe some toast if you don't mind making it." He coughed harshly.

"I don't mind a bit. Try and get some rest."

"Yes, ma'am." He closed his red-rimmed eyes with a sigh.

Downstairs, she found the kettle starting to whistle. She took it off the heat and filled two big mugs with the steaming liquid. She added tea bags and honey, and then set two slices of bread in the oven.

She checked on Levi. He was curled up on the sofa with the quilt pulled tight around his neck.

The poor man, he looked miserable, but there wasn't much she could do for him. "Levi, can you drink some of this?"

He shook his head and burrowed deeper under the quilt. Giving up, she carried the mug back in the kitchen.

Sarah glanced at the clock. When the five minutes was up, she found a saucepan and filled it with cool water. She flipped a towel over her shoulder and set the pan, the tea-filled mug and a plate with the toast on a tray. She carried it all up the stairs. As she suspected, Moses was still in bed, trying to look as if he belonged there.

Setting the tray down on Atlee's nightstand, she helped him sit up in bed by arranging his pillows at his back and gave him the mug of tea. He wrapped his hands around it and took a sip. "*Ach,* that's *wunderbaar,* Sarah. *Danki.*"

"You're welcome." Taking the pan, she walked around his bed and threw the water on Moses.

He came out of the covers yowling like a scalded cat. He stood in his pajamas, glaring at her while water dripped from his hair. She took the towel from her shoulder and held it out. "I couldn't find a pail. You're lucky all I found was a small sauce pan."

He snatched the towel from her. "I'll catch my death for sure now."

"I doubt I'll be so lucky. Get dried off, get changed, strip your bed and clean up this mess. All of this mess." She indicated the rest of the room.

Without waiting for him to reply, she turned toward the door. Atlee sat in his bed with a stunned expression of disbelief on his face. She said gently, "Finish your tea, dear. It will help bring the fever down."

He nodded. She smiled and walked out the door.

Twenty minutes later, Moses came into the kitchen. He was dressed in his work clothes. He held a bundle of sheets in his arms.

She took them from him. "I've made some scrambled eggs and hash browns. When you're finished with breakfast, you can help me get your brother up to his room. I may need to send you for the doctor later, so stay nearby."

He frowned and glanced in the living room. "Is he really that sick?"

"I'm afraid he may be." Her own father had died of pneumonia. His illness had started out the same way as Levi's. She always thought her father's stubborn refusal to see a doctor had contributed to his untimely death.

She wouldn't think about another death at Christmas. God would not do that to her. Besides, she didn't love Levi. There was no reason he might die.

She said, "I don't know if Levi took care of the horses this morning or not. Would you please check and take care of them if he didn't?"

"Will you pour more water on my head if I say no?"

She sighed heavily. "*Nee,* but I will be sorely disappointed for I have always thought you had the makings of a good man in you. I know Levi believes you do, and I trust his judgment."

Moses cast her a sheepish glance and then stared at his boots. "I'll take care of it. Keep my eggs warm, will you?"

"Of course."

He pulled on a coat and settled his hat on his head. When he glanced back at her, she realized how much he looked like Levi. Maybe he would grow into a good man after all. She prayed it would be so.

She spent the next half hour coaxing Levi into taking the cough medicine she found in the bathroom cabinet along with a couple of aspirin and sips of warm sweet tea. She could tell it was an effort for him just to raise his head, but he managed to swallow a full cup of the liquid. She left his side feeling better about his condition. Moses came in as she put the kettle back on.

"The stock is taken care of. I've stoked the fire in the shop. I can finish most of the work that Levi had planned for today. How is he?"

"He took some tea. Do you think we can get him upstairs?"

"It would be easier to bring one of the cots down here and move him onto that."

"That's a good idea, Moses. I'll let you do that while I get the laundry started. I need to get your sheets out on the line so you have someplace dry to sleep tonight."

"I can always sleep in Grace's or Levi's room."

"Won't Atlee feel better knowing you're close by?"

"I reckon you are right about that. I'll go get the cot."

Between the two of them, they got Levi moved to a more comfortable bed close to the fire. It didn't make him happy. He fretted for the next hour, more concerned about Sarah than about his own comfort.

"You must go home, Sarah. I don't want you to become ill because of me."

She tucked his quilt more tightly around him. "I'm a grown woman. I'll go home when I want to and not before."

"I wondered how soon that remark would come back to haunt me."

"Rest and don't worry about me. I feel fine. It is up to God if I catch your flu. Now hush. I will hear no more about leaving. Atlee is sick, too. Who will take care of him with Moses in the shop all day?"

Levi said, "I will see to the boy's needs."

Sarah was tired of arguing with him. She stepped back and raised her hands. "Okay, I was about to take some soup up to him, but you can do it."

"Finally, the woman is minding me. Praise the Lord." He pushed his covers aside and sat up.

When he didn't go any farther, Sarah said, "The soup is in the kitchen."

He teetered on the side of the cot. Closing his eyes, he lay back with a moan. "I can't do it."

"I told you so."

"You're laughing at me. You're always laughing at me," he muttered wearily.

"*Nee,* I have never laughed at you, Levi."

He opened his bloodshot eyes and stared at her. "Yes, you have."

"When?"

He started coughing again. She brought him a drink of water. He took a sip and lay back with his eyes closed.

She should let him sleep, but his comment bothered her. "When did I laugh at you, Levi? If you thought I was, it wasn't on purpose and I'm sorry."

"It was on purpose. You wanted me to kiss you… and then you pushed me in the creek. Everyone saw. Everyone laughed."

She recalled the day vividly. She was saddened to realize he thought she had acted deliberately. She reached down and brushed a lock of hair from his forehead. He needed a haircut. She was pleased to note his skin felt cooler.

"You startled me, Levi. That's why I pushed you away. I didn't mean for you to fall in the water. I'm sorry the others laughed, but I wasn't laughing."

He rolled on his side away from her. "I want to sleep now."

"All right. I'll be here if you need me." He didn't answer.

She left him alone and took a bowl of soup up to Atlee. She was pleased when he managed to eat most of it. She hoped Levi would be able to take some later.

With Moses working in the carriage shop, Sarah got busy on something she had been dying to do for days—putting Levi's house to rights.

She re-washed all the dishes in the cupboards. As

she suspected, some of them had had only a cursory cleaning. After that, she scrubbed down the kitchen walls and counters. She was getting ready to mop the floor when she heard the door open. Expecting Moses, she was surprised to see Nettie Imhoff and her aunt Emma coming in.

She rushed to stop them from entering. "There is sickness in the house, ladies. It would be best to visit another time."

Nettie set a large basket on the kitchen table. "My son Elam told me as much. Knowing that Levi is a bachelor, I came to see if I could be of use. I stopped by Emma's place and asked her to join me."

"Men are no good at taking care of themselves or anyone else when they're sick," Emma declared.

"You look like you could use a stout cup of coffee. I can do that much." Nettie untied her bonnet, hung it along with her coat on the peg by the door and smoothed her apron.

"That sounds lovely." Sarah kept her voice low so she wouldn't disturb Levi.

Nettie glanced at the cot in the other room. "How is he?"

"A little better, I think. I was very worried this morning. Atlee is sick, too, but his fever isn't nearly as high as Levi's."

Nettie said, "My friends in Sugarcreek wrote that this flu has been harsh, but it only lasts a few days. Levi and his brother will be better in no time."

Sarah felt the unexpected sting of tears in her eyes. "I'm silly to fret, but with Christmas coming I can't help but worry that something bad will happen again.

Jonas, my parents, Bethany, they were all taken from me at Christmastime."

Emma drew her into a comforting hug. "God has given you far too much grief for one so young, but do not doubt His mercy."

Sarah sniffed and wiped her eyes. "You're right. I must lean on His strength."

"What can we do to help?" Nettie asked.

"Until Levi or Atlee need something, I'm trying to put this house in order."

Emma frowned at the grimy floor. "The house is missing the mistress."

"I can't give Grace high marks in housekeeping. Levi seems to be the only one in the family who likes an orderly existence. The twins are slobs."

The older women chuckled and Sarah smiled. It was good to have them here. She hadn't realized how scared she had been. Having Levi laid up brought back so many bad memories of her husband's illness and death.

"A strong cup of *kaffi* first, then we clean," Emma declared. She glanced toward the living room and lowered her voice. "While the men are stuck in bed and can't mess it up before we're finished."

With the three of them working, they were able to scrub the kitchen floor, strip and air the beds, wash a half dozen loads of laundry and clean the bathroom, all before two-o'clock in the afternoon.

Sarah blew out a weary breath as she hung the last sheet on the line. She glanced down the rows of bed linens, shirts, pants and socks flapping in the breeze. Thankfully, the day was sunny. She'd be able to gather them in a few hours and begin the process of ironing, mending and putting them away. She'd forgotten how much work it was to do laundry for more than one person. She was tired, but in a good way.

At least her string of suitors wouldn't come looking for her over here.

Her aunt and Nettie left after exacting a promise that Sarah would send for them if she became ill or the Beachy brothers didn't recover as expected.

Levi refused any supper, but since he was keeping liquids down, Sarah left it at that. Atlee was feeling better while Moses came in looking worn to the bone. Sarah laid a hand on his forehead. "Are you feeling ill now?"

He shook his head. "It was a busy day, that's all."

"Levi will be pleased when he learns how you stepped in to take his place. I've left some soup on the stove and there is fried chicken staying warm in the oven. Just put the leftovers in the refrigerator."

He sniffed the air. "What's that funny smell?"

Sarah tried not to laugh. "Pine cleaner."

"Oh."

"Moses, I'm sorry about tossing water on you this morning."

He grinned. "I reckon Atlee and me played enough jokes on you that I had a little payback coming. Just remember what I said about pranks."

"It's only funny the first time?"

"Ja."

"I'll see you first thing in the morning. Don't be afraid to come get me if either of them get worse." She glanced once more toward Levi's bed. He would be fine. She had to have faith. So why didn't she?

* * *

Levi wasn't sure if he was still among the living, but he decided he must be when he rolled over and every muscle in his body protested.

Daylight streamed in through the window on the east side of the house. What time was it? How long had he been asleep?

He sat up in bed and discovered he could do it without getting dizzy. He was definitely on the mend. Maybe it had been Sarah's tea.

He realized he was thirsty. Rising, he made it as far as the kitchen. There was a pitcher of orange juice and several glasses on the table. He sat down and poured himself a drink. It tasted wonderful.

"You need a haircut." Sarah was standing behind his chair. He should have known she was in the house. When was the last time one of the twins made fresh-squeezed orange juice? Before he could form an answer, she was running her fingers through his hair.

His ability to speak vanished altogether. He stopped breathing. It was the first time a woman who wasn't his sister or his mother had touched him like this.

"I never realized you have such nice curls." She tugged gently, testing the length and thickness of the hair he battled into smooth submission with a brush each morning. His scalp prickled, and gooseflesh rose on his arms. A shiver raced through his body.

She stopped. "Are you cold?"

He wasn't, but he lied. "A little."

"Do you want to move closer to the stove?"

"Nee." He could already feel the heat building in his body. Did she realize how her touch affected him? He hoped not. He prayed not.

She said, "How foolish of me. A haircut can wait until you're feeling better."

Even if he had been at death's door it wouldn't have mattered. All he wanted was for her to keep her fingers in his hair. He managed to say, "I reckon a haircut is past due. Might as well get it over with. If you don't mind the chore."

"I don't mind at all. Let me get a towel." She seemed delighted with his capitulation. She left the room humming and returned a few moments later with a large white towel under her arm, scissors and a comb in her other hand.

Setting her tools aside, she shook out the towel and put it around his neck, fastening it behind him with a safety pin. Taking up the comb, she studied him for a moment. He glanced at her from beneath his lashes.

Her blue-green eyes narrowed as she assessed his head. She tilted her face first one way and then another. She ran the comb through his hair. It caught on a tangle and he winced.

"I'm sorry."

"It's all right." He prepared to withstand a few more pulls for his hair was matted from his fever.

She started combing again, more gently. "Levi, can I ask you something?"

"Ja."

"Yesterday, you said… Oh, never mind."

"I accused you of laughing at me. I know you weren't. You were only trying to help."

"That's true, but you said when we were in school that I…that I asked you to kiss me. Why did you say that?"

"It was a long time ago. Can we just skip it?"

"I want to know what I did that gave you that impression."

"Impression? You wrote me a note. It said to meet you by the creek if I wanted to kiss you. What other impression was I going to get?"

She stopped combing his hair. "I did not."

Anger rose in him. "Now you're saying I'm a liar?"

Taking a seat beside him, she faced him without flinching. "I don't know a more honest man than you, Levi Beachy. You must believe me when I say I did not write you such a note."

"If you didn't, why were you waiting under the willow tree?"

Her eyes widened, and she sat back with a stunned expression on her face. "She wouldn't have."

"Who?"

Her eyes narrowed. "Did the note say exactly where I would be?"

His anger drained away. He was tired, and he wanted to lie down again. He didn't want to rehash the most embarrassing event of his youth. "Does it matter?"

"I guess not, but I think I know what happened. My sister was a prankster equal to or better than your brothers. When school let out that day she said she had a surprise for me. I was to wait by the willow tree and keep my eyes closed. Then you came, and I forgot all about her surprise."

Sarah rose to her feet and resumed combing his hair. "I'm sorry she made you a pawn in her game, Levi. Bethany never thought how her actions would affect others."

All this time he had blamed Sarah, and she hadn't had anything to do with his humiliation. What a fool he had been. What a fool he still was. "I'm sorry I fell into her trap so easily."

"We were kids. It happened. It wasn't a bad kiss, you know."

Embarrassment made him want to sink through the floor. Why did she have to admit that now?

She stopped combing and bit the corner of her lower lip. "I need better light."

He started to rise, but she laid a hand on his shoulder. "Just scoot your chair a little closer to the window."

The legs of the chair grated on the wooden floor as he shifted closer to the light. She pressed her hand to his chest to stop his forward movement. "That's fine."

When his poor heart started beating again, Levi realized with a jolt what Gideon had recognized weeks ago.

Levi cared about Sarah. Not just as his responsibility, not because she had been Jonas's wife, but because she was a warm and vibrant woman. As much as he wanted to deny it, his heart would no longer be silent.

He was falling foolishly and hopelessly in love with Sarah, and she treated him like a brother.

She stepped behind him and carefully pulled the comb through his hair again. The rasp of the teeth over his scalp, the tugs when she encountered tangles, none of those small discomforts mattered, because each time she smoothed them away with her other hand. She started humming again.

No matter how he felt, he knew she would never return his feelings. She had loved her husband. Levi was a poor substitute for a man such as Jonas. It was pure foolishness to think anything else.

He would never embarrass her with unwanted displays of affection. He was good at keeping his feelings hidden. He would remain her friend as he had promised Jonas he would.

She ran her fingers through his hair again. "I haven't done this in a while. I hope I remember how. Are you sure you're not too tired to do this?"

If he said yes, she would stop. He should send her away. He opened his mouth to do so, but couldn't speak the words. Instead, he said, "I'm fine."

She said, "Here goes." He heard the snip of the scissors.

Levi closed his eyes and gave himself up to the forbidden luxury of her touch.

Chapter Twelve

She was making a terrible mistake.

Sarah knew it even before she began cutting locks of Levi's hair. Her barbering skills were adequate to the task, but what about her self-control?

Her desire to do this small, wifely task had seemed so innocent when it first occurred to her. Now, with her fingers entwined in Levi's curls, she admitted her motives were far from innocent. She wanted more than to run her fingers through his hair. She wanted to know what it would be like to be held in his arms, to be kissed by him.

How had this happened?

In the space of a few weeks she had come to see Levi as much more than the neighbor and friend that he had been for five years. Her plan to uncover the man behind his shy exterior was meant to help her find the right kind of woman for him. The real Levi was a man with a quiet soul, a big heart and a wonderful sense of humor…someone who thrilled her with the simple touch of his hand.

And he was courting her friend, Leah.

That was exactly what she had hoped would happen. Only now, she wanted to undo what she had done. She wanted to keep the man she had uncovered to herself.

How selfish she was. This wasn't about what she wanted anymore. Levi had become more important to her than she ever expected. She cared deeply about him.

She drew the comb through Levi's hair, measuring with her fingers and cutting away the excess. What would he do if she told him how she felt? Probably fall out of his chair. In five years he hadn't given the least hint that he saw her as anything more than his dear friend's widow.

Should she ask him about Leah? It wasn't any of her business.

What if he married Leah and they began happily raising their children next door to her? Could she watch from her kitchen window and not be jealous of their happiness? She wasn't sure.

Would it be better if he moved away? Or would not seeing him be worse? Would he finally follow his dream of living where he could see the Rockies from his front porch each morning? She was torn between praying for his happiness and praying for her own.

She drew his hair upward, snipping the long ends and letting them drop to the towel around his shoulders. She worked slowly, but she was finished all too soon. She plucked one perfectly formed crescent from the towel and slipped it into her pocket. She would keep it as a memento of today.

When he was gone or married, she would be able to remember the texture of his hair beneath her hands and how she longed to press a kiss to his brow.

She stood behind him with her hands resting on his

strong shoulders, relishing the feel of his strength beneath her palms.

After a few moments, he asked, "Are you finished?"

His voice was rough and raspy. She chided herself for keeping him sitting here while she indulged in a sad fantasy. "I'm finished. I didn't give you many bald spots."

"Lucky for me, I get to wear a hat."

She started to turn away, but he captured her hand and held it tight. The air around them became charged with electricity. She stopped breathing, waiting for him to speak.

She heard footsteps on the stairs before he could say anything. One of the boys was coming down. Levi released her hand, and she moved quickly to fetch the broom leaning in the corner of the kitchen.

"Guder mariye." Atlee entered the kitchen wearing a threadbare blue robe over his pajamas. His hair was disheveled and he looked tired, but his eyes were bright and his color was better.

"Good morning, Atlee. How are you feeling?" Sarah unpinned the towel from Levi's neck and began sweeping up the loose hair on the floor. She was careful not to meet his gaze. Her stolen time with him was over. She had to come back to the real world.

Atlee sat beside Levi at the table. "I'm a little better. Brother, how are you?"

"I think I'll live."

Sarah cringed at his jest. Life was short and precious and could be snatched away in an instant. *Please, Lord, grant him long full years here on earth before You call him home.*

"Where is Moses?" Levi looked toward the stairs.

Atlee yawned and propped his elbows on the

table. "He went out to take care of the stock about an hour ago. I reckon he's working in the shop. Delbert Weaver brought in his buggy late yesterday. His door was snapped clean off when a pickup sideswiped him. Moses is going to put a new one on this morning. Delbert said his son was hurt pretty bad. He might loose his arm."

"Which son?" Sarah asked. They had gone to school with several of Delbert's children.

"Roman. They took him to a hospital in Cleveland."

"How awful." Roman was only a few years younger than Sarah.

Levi shook his head sadly. "He was the star of our school's baseball team and a fine fellow. We must pray for his healing."

It would be a sad Christmas season for someone other than herself. She needed to put her own fears and worries aside and stop being selfish in her grief. "I must see if we can organize a quilt sale to help pay his hospital expenses. I have two quilts I can donate."

Levi smiled at her warmly. "I can't sew, but I can donate a set of wheels."

Atlee said, "We could hold an auction here after Christmas."

Sarah nodded. "What better way to celebrate the great gift God bestowed on mankind than to help someone in need?"

Levi met her gaze. His eyes were filled with an emotion she couldn't read.

Atlee sat up straight. "What's for breakfast, Sarah? My bellybutton and my backbone are getting to be best friends."

Levi dropped his gaze. What would he have said if they had been alone?

"I'll have oatmeal and bacon in a few minutes. Levi, what would you like? Toast? Poached eggs?"

"I reckon I'd like to lay down in my own bed for a bit. Thank you, Sarah, for everything." He smiled at her, but it was a smile tinged with sadness.

When he had gone upstairs, Atlee brushed a loose piece of hair from the tabletop. He had an odd expression on his face. He glanced at her several times, but couldn't seem to find a way to speak his piece.

"Is something on your mind, Atlee?"

"We had a letter from our *grossmammi* the other day."

"Is she enjoying Grace's visit?"

"I reckon. Grace is staying until the week after Christmas. Sarah, you haven't really been matchmaking for Levi, have you?"

Embarrassment flooded her face with heat. "What gave you that idea?"

"Grandma wrote that one of Grace's friends was matchmaking for him. Moses and me thought it might be you."

So that was how Levi found out. She sighed deeply. "I admit I was trying to help, but Levi has no need of a matchmaker."

"Course not. He's not the marrying kind."

"You may be mistaken about that."

"What do you mean? Is Levi is seeing someone?"

"I shouldn't say. When he is ready to wed, he will tell you."

"*Nee.* Who would marry my brother?"

"A very blessed woman, if you ask me."

Sarah suddenly glared at Atlee and shook a finger at him. "You must not play tricks or jokes on them, Atlee. Hearts are not playthings."

He held his hands in the air. "All right. We won't, but it would help if we knew who she was."

"I will not say, but if you open your eyes, you can put two and two together. You know who your sister has been seeing, don't you?"

"That wimp, Henry Zook."

"He is not a wimp. He is your sister's choice. She may wed him one day. You must respect that."

"Okay, but the only woman Levi has been around much is you. Is he courting you?"

An intense sense of loss settled in her chest. "*Nee,* he is not. I believe he has been seeing another."

"Wait, do you mean Leah Belier? The teacher?" His voice shot up an octave.

Perhaps now the boys would realize Levi's life no long revolved around them. "It is for Levi to say, not me. How do you want your oatmeal?"

"Oatmeal is oatmeal." His dejected tone made her smile.

"Not when you add brown sugar and cinnamon or raisins. Would you like to try it?"

"Levi can't be serious about the teacher. That would be awful. If she came to live with us it would be worse that being in school again. She has eyes in the back of her head. She'd make us toe the line day and night."

"Someone should."

He stayed silent, but he wore a belligerent expression that gave her pause.

"I'm sorry I said anything, Atlee. Levi may not be

serious about anyone. But if such a thing does happen, you must be happy for him no matter who his choice is."

Sarah noticed a lock of hair against the table leg that had escaped her broom. Leaning down, she plucked it from the floor and added it to the one in her pocket. Tonight, she would press them between sheets of tissue paper and place them in her Bible. Then she would pray for Levi's happiness and not for her own.

Levi made a rapid recovery. Sarah didn't come to his home again after she cut his hair. He would not soon forget those moments together, the feel of her hands, the whisper of her breath, the scent of her body so close to his. It had taken all the willpower he possessed not to take her in his arms and declare his love.

Would she have been repulsed by his actions, or would she have accepted his advances?

He wasn't half the man Jonas had been, but maybe Sarah could love him just a little. She didn't have to love him the way she had loved her husband. He could accept that. He would spend a lifetime trying to make her happy and keep her safe.

He didn't know what answer she might have given him. He lacked the courage to act.

He saw her only briefly the following day when she stopped in at the shop to tell him she wouldn't be able to work until after Christmas.

He understood, but he missed her and found himself spending most of the day looking out the window toward her house. At least two more men dropped by to visit her. Levi's punishment for his little joke was having to watch and wonder what was going on inside her home until each man left. Just because he lacked the courage to declare his feelings didn't mean another man would have such trouble. He prayed for courage and the chance to learn how she felt about him.

On Sunday evening, Levi joined his family at the home of his cousin Rebecca and her husband, Gideon. His grandfather Reuben and Reuben's wife were there, as well. Levi's grandmother died before he was born. Lydia was his grandfather's third wife. She had a sour disposition, but she was a mighty good cook.

The day was cold with occasional snowflakes drifting down from gray skies. The weather suited Levi's mood.

The company was good, as was the plentiful food. His grandfather's stories of holidays past had everyone chuckling. When the meal was over, Reuben stepped outside to smoke his pipe. Levi joined him. Few Amish smoked, but the occasional use of a pipe by an elder was permitted.

His grandfather's snow-white hair held a permanent crimp around his head from the hat he normally wore. His beard, as white as his hair, reached the center of the dark gray vest he had buttoned over his white shirt. His sharp eyes looked Levi up and down. "You are better?"

"I am."

"*Gotte es goot.* I heard those rascally brothers of yours played a pretty good prank on Daniel Hershberger and his new wife."

"I knew the story would get around quick. The twins rigged the seat to tip over backwards when the carriage started moving."

"So it is true? Daniel and Susan went rolling down the street with their feet in the air?"

Levi suppressed a grin. "Kicking like a pair of mad babies."

Reuben pulled his pipe from between his teeth and laughed out loud. "I wish I might have seen it."

"It was right funny, but what they did was no laughing matter. Had Daniel's horse run out into traffic, someone could have gotten hurt, or worse."

"True enough. What have you done about it?"

"I told the boys they had to find work elsewhere,"

"Did you?" Reuben looked surprised. He took a drag on his pipe and blew a ring of smoke in the air.

"Was I wrong?"

"That's not for me to say, Levi. You've dedicated your life to raising those boys. Many admire you for it, some call you foolish. A man rarely has the luxury of knowing if his decision was right or wrong in this life. How did they take it?"

"Better than I hoped."

"Have you thought about separating them?"

"What do you mean?"

"I'm thinking it might be good for them to get along without each other for a time. Your cousin Mark from over in Berlin could put one of the boys to work on his dairy farm. Leah Belier told Lydia her cousin was looking for help in his construction business in Sugarcreek. He and his family are staying with her until tomorrow if you want to talk to him about it."

"The twins have never been away from each other."

"Unless they plan to remain old boys all their lives, that will have to change eventually."

"I will think on it." He would ask Sarah for her opinion. She had a knack for handling the boys.

A shriek came from inside the house. They hurried

in to find Lydia beating the floor with a broom. The twins were doubled over with laughter.

Atlee said, "It's just a plastic spider."

"The look on your face was priceless." Moses caught sight of Levi's stern face and smothered his grin.

"Oh, you evil boys. I hate spiders, and you know it." Lydia left the room with a huff.

"You're lucky my wife didn't take that broom to your backsides." Reuben sent a speaking glance at Levi.

He knew what his grandfather meant. It was time the boys learned to go their separate ways. He would speak to his cousin Mark and to Leah's cousin.

He nodded. "I reckon you are right. It's time we should be leaving. Gideon and Rebecca, it was a mighty good meal. Merry Christmas to you all. Grandfather, please tell Lydia I'm sorry for her fright. The boys will be over this week to cut and stack a cord of wood for her."

The expressions on the boys' faces changed from amusement to outrage. Levi fixed his gaze on them and added sternly, "And they will be happy to do it."

Reuben grinned and patted the boys on their shoulders. "You will find many changes in store for you in the next few weeks. If I were you boys, I'd be on my best behavior."

Moses glanced from his grandfather to Levi. "What is that supposed to mean?"

Levi said, "We'll talk about it after supper tonight. It's time to go."

To his surprise, the twins didn't pester him for an explanation on the way home. When they arrived at the house, he waited until the boys got out, then he said,

"I've got to see someone. I'll be home in a couple of hours."

"Where are you going?" Atlee asked.

"To Leah Belier's place."

The twins exchanged hard glances with each other. Levi snapped the lines against his horse's rump and drove away. It was four miles to Leah's home. He would have plenty of time to wonder if he was doing the right thing before he reached her house. He half hoped her cousin would be gone by the time he arrived.

Sarah had been waiting for Levi to come home. When she saw them pull up, she hurried to put on her coat, gathered her gift and headed out the front door. But by the time she reached her front gate, Levi was turning the corner at the end of the street. The twins were standing in their front yard watching him leave.

Disappointed, she decided her gift might as well be given to the twins. She walked toward them with a large package wrapped in white butcher's paper in her arms and said, "Good evening to you both. I have a little something I thought you might like."

Atlee looked at her brightly. "What is it?"

"It's a smoked ham. I thought you might enjoy it for supper or keep it for Christmas dinner."

Amos Fisher had stopped by with it earlier. She didn't think he would mind if the Beachy family enjoyed some of his generosity. It would take her ages to finish so much meat.

"Where is Levi going?" She hadn't intended to show such interest, but she couldn't help herself.

"He's going to see his girlfriend," Moses grumbled.

"We don't know that Leah is his girlfriend," Atlee said, quickly.

Moses rolled his eyes. "I'm pretty sure he's not taking reading and writing lessons. Thanks for the ham, Sarah."

"Du bischt wilkumm," she replied, handing it to him.

They were welcome to the ham even though she had hoped to make Levi smile when she told him where it came from. Amos Fisher had only one hundred and ninety-nine sows left now. Tonight, Levi wouldn't be smiling at her joke. He'd be smiling at something Leah said or making her laugh.

Sarah sighed and looked at Moses. "Are you going to the winter picnic at Leah's place on Saturday?"

"Are you?" Atlee asked.

"I'm not sure. My brother and his family are coming to visit. It depends on when they leave. What about you?"

Moses scowled. "That's a party for old folks. We don't want the gang thinking we're part of the goody-goody crowd. We're going to the hoedown at Ezra Bowman's farm."

"I heard Sally Yoder mention it. Ben Lapp seemed to think it might be a wild party."

"That's the best kind," Atlee said with a grin.

"You boys will be careful, won't you? I've heard that some of the kids in that gang drink and do drugs."

"We'll be careful. We don't need to drink to have a good time," Moses assured her with a twinkle in his eyes.

"That's very sensible."

"We don't need to, but it helps!" Atlee yelled.

The boys dashed up the steps and into the house before she could say anything else.

She curbed her need to scold them and held tight to the knowledge that most Amish boys gave up their wild teenage ways and became good husbands and fathers. She would pray that Levi's brothers soon discovered worldly pleasures weren't as satisfying as leading a quiet, plain life with their loved ones and friends close at hand. It would break Levi's heart if they strayed from the Amish way of life and were lost to the wickedness of the world.

Sarah looked up to heaven. "Lord, what those boys need is a sign from You to make them see the error of their ways."

When she thought of all Levi had done for them and how little they seemed to care, she frowned. "I dearly wish I could see You deliver it."

Chapter Thirteen

Levi got his wish. Leah's cousin had already gone by the time he reached her home. She gave Levi her brother's address in Sugarcreek and encouraged him to write and ask about a position for one of the boys. Like Levi's grandfather, she thought spending some time apart would be good for them.

Over the next several days, Levi saw little of Sarah. Her family had arrived and she was kept busy with her houseful. On the Monday before Christmas, he had a chance to become reacquainted with her brother when he came by the shop.

Vernon was several years older than Levi, but he remembered him from school. "You're the boy my sister shoved in the creek, aren't you? I heard about that from the girls."

The reminder wasn't as painful as it once had been. "I reckon I deserved it."

"It was Bethany's doing. She thought it was a pretty good joke, but I don't think she ever told Sarah. Poor Sarah, she felt so bad. She always thought she was the reason you left school before graduation."

"My dad needed me in the shop."

"I thought that must be it. That last year of school was a waste for me. I wanted to be out and working. I thought I'd be working in the mill alongside my father. Instead, I married a woman with a dairy farm. Luckily, we have her nephews who help us or we wouldn't be able to come for this visit. Cows never take a day off."

Levi smiled at the boy hanging on Vernon's leg. "What's your name?"

"Merle."

"Nice to meet you. How old are you, Merle?"

"Five. I'm gonna go to school next year." He was dressed exactly like his father, with dark pants, a dark coat and a wide-brimmed black hat.

"Are you enjoying your visit with your aunt Sarah?" Levi asked.

"She's gonna take me fishing today," the tyke announced proudly.

Leaning down, Levi propped his hands on his knees and said, "I'd stand clear when she tries to cast if I were you. She's not very good at it."

"I heard that," Sarah said from the doorway.

He saw her approaching with a woman he assumed was her sister-in-law and two little girls.

Vernon introduced his wife, Alma, and his daughters Rosanna and Phoebe. Rosanna, who looked to be about eleven or twelve, stood quietly by her mother's side. She reminded him of Sarah at that age. Phoebe was a few years younger. She hung back behind her mother's skirts and clutched a blank-faced doll.

Alma said, "I can't wait to do some of my Christmas shopping. What a treat it is to stay in town. Vernon, are you sure you'll be okay with the *kinder* while I'm gone?"

"Don't worry about us. Come, children, let us hitch up your aunt Sarah's buggy for Mother so she doesn't have to walk the streets with her arms full of packages." He herded the kids out the door.

Alma said, "Sarah, I forgot my shawl in the house. I'll be right back."

Levi found himself alone with Sarah. The ease with which he'd once spoken to her deserted him. He wanted nothing more than to take her in his arms and hold her close. He needed to know how she felt about him. He needed to know if there was any hope for him. Could she love him even a little?

The questions he wanted to ask stuck in his throat. Fear made him keep silent.

When her family left the shop, Sarah crossed her arms and smiled after them. "I can't believe how much those children have grown since I last saw them. Rosanna has put off her *eahmal shatzli*."

The *eahmal shatzli* or "long apron" was the traditional dress of young Amish girls. When a girl was allowed to "put it off" and wear the short apron and cape like her mother, it was a sign that she was moving into womanhood.

Levi said, "She looks like you did at her age."

"She's much prettier than I was and so bright. She reminds me of Bethany."

"Sarah, I need to speak to you," he blurted out in a rush.

From outside, Alma called, "Sarah, I'm ready."

The door opened and young Walter Knepp came

in. The teenager looked around and asked, "Where are the twins?"

Sarah took a step closer to Levi. "You look so serious, Levi. What's the matter?"

He couldn't do it. Not with people watching and waiting on them. He needed to find a time when they wouldn't be interrupted.

"Never mind. It can wait. Enjoy your shopping trip. Walter, the twins are at the harness shop chopping wood for their grandfather."

Walter left but Sarah remained. "Are you sure it can wait?"

He nodded. "I'm sure."

"Okay."

She started to leave but paused at the door. "We're going to eat at the café tomorrow evening. Would you like to join us? The twins are welcome, as well."

He felt as if a weight had fallen off his back. "I'd like that."

Her eyes sparkled with delight. "Wonderful."

Sarah had been right about one thing. Having children in the house kept her from dwelling on the sadness of holidays past.

Rosanna was a quiet child, but Merle never walked if he could run and he ran as often as possible. Her fishing trip with him to Elam Sutter's pond was half a success. She had a nice visit with Katie Sutter, and Merle caught four fish but none that were big enough to keep, much to his disappointment.

The following evening, Levi was waiting beside her gate when they came outside. Sarah looked around. "Where are the twins?"

"I decided not to risk spoiling your brother's visit by subjecting his family to them."

"So you didn't invite them?"

"Nope. I decided not to spoil my evening by subjecting myself to them."

"They aren't that bad, Levi."

"That's what you think."

As her family piled in her buggy, Sarah found herself wedged between Levi and the children in the backseat while her brother drove through the quiet streets of town. Along the way, they enjoyed the Christmas lights and display in the English homes and businesses.

"Oh, how beautiful," Rosanna said when they passed the stately pine in the center of the town square. It was covered with multicolored lights and bore a shining silver star on the highest branch.

Phoebe turned to her father. "Why can't we have a tree like that at our home? We have big pines."

Vernon shared a knowing glance with his wife and then said, "Sarah, do you remember asking Father that question? Why don't you tell Phoebe what her grandfather had to say about the subject?"

Sarah smiled softly at the warm childhood memory. "We were traveling to visit Aunt Emma, and we passed by this very tree. It was smaller then and so was I. I said, 'Papa, why can't we have pretty trees like the *Englisch?*'"

"What did he say?" Merle asked.

"He said that when our Lord and Savior was born, no one decorated a tree for him. No one put fancy lights on the roof of the lowly stable. Jesus came to us quietly, in a plain and simple way. We have no need of glowing lights to remind us of His coming, for His light is bright and strong in each of our hearts. And when Jesus looks down from heaven to see how we are celebrating his birth, He looks for the simple light that shines from inside us, where it counts. All those of us who keep His light in our hearts make a more beautiful display to His eyes than any English tree."

Vernon looked at his daughter. "So, Rosanna. Do you want God to see lights in our pine trees or do you want him to see the light in your heart."

"I want Him to see the light in my heart," Rosanna answered quietly.

"Me, too," Phoebe said.

"Me, three," Merle chimed in.

"Me, four," Sarah added. Levi took her hand and gave it a squeeze. She had let the light of God's love grow dim in her heart. The sorrows of the past could not be forgotten, but they could be endured.

Sarah couldn't remember when she'd had a more enjoyable evening. The food was excellent and made better by the fact that she didn't have to cook or clean up afterwards. She had pork roast so tender it fell apart when she put her fork in it. The green beans were steamed to perfection and the sweet potato fries were delicious. She didn't have room for dessert when she finished her meal. Levi had no trouble putting away a slice of peach pie topped with vanilla ice cream.

As they were getting ready to leave, Elam and Katie Sutter came in with their family. Seeing Levi, Elam stopped by the table with his infant son in his arms. The chubby baby sported a pearly white bottom tooth when he grinned at Merle and Phoebe's baby talk.

Levi looked to Elam. "Are you getting more sleep these days?"

"Finally."

The men grinned at each other and Elam left to join his wife and children in a booth at the back of the room.

Sarah's heart warmed as she imagined Levi with a child of his own. He'd learned some hard lessons raising his brothers and sister. Sarah suspected he would do things differently with his own son or daughter, for the better.

Vernon covered his mouth and coughed deeply, then he grimaced and rubbed his chest.

Alma looked at him with concern. "Are you sick?"

"I've got a scratchy throat, that's all."

Levi said, "Take care of yourself. There's a nasty flu bug making the rounds. I had it myself, and it wasn't fun."

He glanced at Sarah, but she couldn't tell what he was thinking. She looked away, afraid he would see how much that time alone with him had meant to her.

On the way back to the house, Sarah wished she lived miles from the inn instead of a dozen blocks. If she did, she'd be able to sit snuggled beside Levi for hours. As it was, they reached their destination all too quickly. Watching him walk home, she began to miss him before he was even out of sight.

Whenever Levi was near, she only wanted to keep him near. When he was away from her, all she wanted to do was to see him again.

The intensity of her feelings frightened her. How long could she keep them hidden if he loved another? How could she keep them from growing stronger?

Later, when she was ready for bed, Sarah knelt beside her mattress and prayed. She prayed that her feeling wouldn't grow into love.

She slept poorly, but it was the only rest she would get for many hours. Before dawn, there was a knock on Sarah's door and her sister-in-law came in.

Sarah sat up in bed. "What's wrong?"

"It's Vernon. He's very ill. Can you come help me?"

"It sure seems quiet over at Sarah's place. Has her family gone home?" Atlee stood at the workbench looking out the window.

Levi stopped working. "Their buggy was still parked beside Sarah's barn when I fed our horses this morning."

Atlee said, "Merle is normally up and about this time of the day. Usually, he's running back and forth along the fence hitting the pickets with a stick. It beats me why he gets such a thrill out of it."

Levi rose from his stool at the counter and moved to the window. Movement at Sarah's kitchen window caught his eye. It looked as if Sarah's sister-in-law was crying and Sarah was comforting her. He said, "I think I'll go over and see if everything is all right."

He left the shop and hurried across the street. Sarah's front gate squeaked when he opened it. He would have to tell Atlee or Moses to oil it. Sarah opened the door before he reached it. Merle stood at her side.

"Is everything all right?" Levi asked.

"Papa is sick and we have to be quiet," Merle told him solemnly.

Sarah said, "I think it's the same flu that you had. So far, none of the rest of us are sick. What did you need?"

"Nothing. Atlee noticed Merle wasn't out banging on the picket fence. I wondered if everything was okay."

"Mamm says I can't make noise so *Daed* can sleep." Merle looked sorely disappointed.

"What can I do to help?" Levi asked.

She smiled, but she couldn't hide the fear in her eyes. "I am low on some medicines. Could you go to the drugstore for me?"

"Of course." He came inside while Sarah wrote up a list of things she needed. He wanted to hold her close and offer his comfort, but he didn't dare. He didn't know if she would welcome his attention. If only he had spoken before. As soon as he was granted another chance, he would accept it gladly. He couldn't bear not knowing how she felt.

After fetching her supplies, he returned as quickly as he could. He handed them over. "Would you like me to sit with Vernon for a while? You look tired."

"I didn't sleep well. I'm not worried about me. I'm worried about Alma. She's four months' pregnant, and it hasn't been an easy pregnancy for her. This stress isn't good for her or the babe. If we can't get Vernon's fever down in a few hours, I will send for the doctor."

"I'll be close by if you need me."

Her grim expression lightened. "I never doubted it for a minute. Can I ask you one more favor?"

"Anything."

"Can you take Merle with you for a few hours? He's restless."

"Sure. Atlee and Moses can take him to the park. I imagine he'd like the slide and the swings. They can take the girls, too. It's a cold day, but if they dressed warm, they should be okay."

"That's a great idea. I'll make sure it's okay with Alma, and I'll send them over when they're ready. Thanks for stopping by, Levi. You're a good friend."

He reached out and grasped her hand. "We're more than friends, Sarah. I hope you know that."

Panic flashed in her eyes, but she quickly subdued it. "Best friends," she said and withdrew her hand.

He had to leave it at that.

An hour later, Phoebe and Merle arrived at the shop. Levi looked out the door. "Where is Rosanna?"

Phoebe said, "She wanted to stay home even though *Mamm* says she can't be in Papa's room because she might get sick, too."

Atlee and Moses came forward when Levi beckoned to them. Moses said, "I can't believe we have to babysit. What if somebody from the gang sees us?"

Levi frowned at him. "You'll live. Do not forget all Sarah has done for us. This is the least we can do to ease her burdens."

Although the twins grumbled about being stuck with a pair of babies, they left the shop with the children happily tagging along behind them.

Levi waited, but Sarah didn't come get him that morning. He figured Vernon must be better. Sarah wouldn't hesitate to involve the doctor.

The twins returned with two tired children just before noon. When questioned, Levi discovered his brothers actually enjoyed spending time with the little ones. Merle was so taken with Moses that he asked if Moses would take him to the park again tomorrow.

Moses ruffled the boy's hair. "Sure, kid. Why not?"

Late Friday morning, Levi stopped in to check on Sarah again. She looked worn to the bone and more worried than ever. She offered him a seat at the kitchen table and a cup of coffee.

He asked, "Is Vernon worse?"

"No, but Alma has made herself sick with worry and work. I went to the Wilsons' down the street and used their phone to call the doctor. He's with Alma now."

"Is it the babe?"

Sarah nodded. "I can't bear to think of her losing her baby. Why can't we have one Christmas with something joyous to remember?"

The sound of the doctor's footsteps coming down the stairs had Sarah out of her seat. Her hands were clenched tightly together.

Dr. White came in the kitchen. A tall, dignified man with silver hair, the elderly physician was well past eighty, but still practiced in the community that he loved with the help of a partner. "I won't beat around the bush. She needs rest. She needs to stay in bed for a week at least. I'm going to send my granddaughter-in-law, Amber, over to give you a break, Sarah."

"*Danki,* Dr. White."

"Don't mention it. Alma is worried about her other children. Is there someone in the family who can keep them for a while? I think it would ease her mind and help her rest."

"I'm sure my Aunt Emma will be happy to take the children for a few days."

"Good. Call me if anything changes, Sarah."

Levi walked him outside. The doctor asked, "How are you? No lingering ill effects from your bout with this mean virus?"

"I feel fine."

"That's great. I hear there is a winter picnic out at Leah Belier's home tomorrow. I remember what fun they could be."

"You're welcome to come."

"No, these bones are too old to sit on hay bales around a bonfire. You young people go and enjoy yourselves while you can. See if you can get Sarah to go. She needs a break. She doesn't say anything, but I can tell she's under a lot of strain. It can't be easy having her only remaining sibling ill and lying in the same room where her husband died. For some reason, she thinks she is to blame because she invited them."

"I thought Vernon was getting better."

"Oh, he is, but I'm not sure Sarah can see that past the painful association she has with past events. It isn't rational, but for her it is a very real fear."

Levi shook his head. "I doubt she'll go to a picnic. I plan to stay home, as well. Someone should be close by if she needs help."

"You're probably right. I'll stop in at the Wadler Inn and ask Naomi Wadler to put the word out that Sarah could use an extra pair of hands."

The doctor settled his gray fedora on his head and glanced at the gray overcast sky. "My old bones think it's going to snow. They're usually right." He nodded to Levi and walked briskly up the street toward his clinic.

Levi was preoccupied with thoughts of Sarah as he entered the shop. The twins were working on a banged-up courting buggy that had ended up in a ditch when the driver should have been paying attention to the road and not the girl beside him.

Levi looked at the clock. It was getting late.

He spoke to the boys. "I've got to get going. Leah Belier is expecting me. If Sarah needs anything, I know she can count on you until I return."

Moses tipped his head to the side. "You've been seeing a lot of Leah lately. Is there something you want to tell us?"

"Not right now. Maybe later." He didn't want to say anything until he heard back from Leah's cousin about a job for only one of them in Sugarcreek.

"What does that mean?" Atlee asked.

"It means I may have news to tell you later but I don't have anything to say about it now."

Moses tipped his head toward the door. "Come on, Atlee, let's get the buggy ready for Levi while he gets cleaned up, or he'll be late for his date."

"And she may not wait." Atlee chuckled at his rhyme, but Levi just shook his head.

Moses said, "Leah hates it when people are late."

When Levi came out of the house a half hour later, his horse and buggy were waiting outside the front door. The twins were nowhere in sight. He caught sight of Sarah back by her barn slipping a headstall on her gray. Where was she headed?

He walked toward her. As much as he wanted to take her in his arms, he knew his timing couldn't have been worse. She had too much on her plate at the moment. She didn't need to hear his lovesick utterings. If only he could manage some time alone with her, then he might find the courage to tell her how he felt.

"Sarah, can I give you a lift somewhere? My horse is ready to go."

She turned around with a grateful sigh. "I need to take the children out to my Aunt Emma's farm. Naomi Wadler and Amber are sitting with Alma and Vernon so I thought I would go now and be back before dark."

Her aunt's farm wasn't exactly on the way to Leah's

place, but he didn't mind the detour. Not if it meant spending time with Sarah. "I'll drive you out."

"Really? But where were you going?"

"To help Leah set up for the winter picnic. I honestly don't mind going a little out of my way."

"That's hardly a little out of your way." She bit her lip.

"Okay, I don't mind going a lot out of my way. I'll drop you off and pick you up in a few hours. You can fill Emma in on what's been happening and not have to rush off." Would she accept? It might give him the opportunity he'd been hoping for. Time alone with her.

"All right. I'm so tired, I was worried I'd fall asleep and who knows where old Gray would take us. I'll go get the children."

Levi could barely contain his excitement. Without the children in the buggy, he and Sarah would be alone on the ride home. He'd have a chance to tell her how his love for her had grown and discover if she could return those feelings.

His hands were ice-cold when they finally got underway. He wanted to blame it on the rapidly deteriorating weather, but the truth was he was as nervous as a man could be. Merle was excited about the trip. Rosanna put up a weak protest. She didn't want to leave her mother. Phoebe was quiet and held tightly to her doll. Sarah kept up a running conversation in an effort to reassure the children.

He put his horse into a fast trot. The sooner he delivered Sarah and the children to her aunt, the sooner he could finish his work at Leah's and be back in this same buggy for a leisurely ride home with Sarah at his side.

The snow quickly changed over to sleet, and then

back to snow as they traveled. The road became slippery, even for his surefooted mare. A half hour later, they were rounding a curve on a steep hillside when Levi felt something shift in the buggy beneath him.

The horse felt it, too, and cocked her head to the side. Her move carried the vehicle to the shoulder of the road. Sarah grasped his arm just as the buggy lurched sharply.

In horrifying slow motion, the buggy tipped over and tumbled down the ravine. He heard Sarah scream his name and then everything went black.

Chapter Fourteen

Levi pressed a hand to his aching head. He winced when he felt the lump above his right eye. The sound of whimpering slowly registered in his foggy brain. He tried to sit up, but someone lay sprawled across his chest. Forcing his eyes to focus, he realized it was Rosanna.

He moved her gently to the side. "Rosanna, are you hurt?"

"Yes."

"Where, honey?"

"My face hurts."

He sat up and looked. She had a knot forming on her cheekbone that would turn into a bad bruise and a nasty gash on her chin. The good news was that it had stopped bleeding. He searched for the other children. Where were they? Where was Sarah?

The buggy lay smashed against a tree at the bottom of a steep hillside. Snow was quickly covering the splintered wood. A large black shape moved off to one side. He realized it was his mare. She was on her knees and struggling in the tangled harness.

"Sarah!" he shouted into the night.

"Levi?" came a weak reply. It was Merle.

Levi crawled toward the sound. He found the boy sitting on what once had been a door. "Merle, are you okay?"

"I'm scared."

"I'm scared, too. Where is Phoebe? Where is Sarah?"

"I don't know. What's wrong with your horse?"

"I'll see to her in a minute. I have to find the others. Sarah!" he shouted as loud as he could.

"She's with me." The voice belonged to Phoebe and it came from up the hillside.

Levi took the boy in his arms and carried him back to Rosanna. "Stay here."

He quickly worked his way up the steep slope where he found Phoebe sitting beside Sarah who lay sprawled sideways across the hill.

To his relief, she was breathing.

Thank You, dear Lord, for sparing her.

He looked at Phoebe. "Are you injured, child?"

"My hand hurts real bad."

"Let me see." She held it out. She had two dislocated fingers. His stomach took a wild flop, but he knew what he had to do. He searched around and found her doll nearby.

"Phoebe, I want you to bite down on your dolly's legs as hard as you can. Will you do that for me?"

"I don't want to bite her."

"This is important. She's going to help make your hand better, but you have to close your eyes and bite hard. She won't mind. She wants to help."

"Do as he says, Phoebe." Rosanna called from below.

Phoebe bit down on her doll and he quickly jerked her fingers back into place. She screamed and then fell back.

Rosanna struggled up the hill toward her.

Levi said, "She's okay. She just fainted."

He turned his attention to Sarah and lifted her gently in his lap. "Sarah, speak to me," he begged.

Her *kapp* was missing, and there was blood covering the side of her face. After a moment, her eyes fluttered open. Relief made him giddy.

Thank You, God. I will never again miss the chance to tell this woman how much I love her.

Sarah gazed up at him. Slowly, she raised her hand and touched his face. "You're alive."

"We all are."

"The children?" She tried to sit up, but he wasn't willing to let her go.

He glanced over his shoulder. Phoebe was sitting, supported between Merle and Rosanna. "They're banged up, but nothing too bad as far as I can see. What about you? Tell me where it hurts."

"I'm not sure." She touched her head and winced. Squinting, she moved her hand in front of her face and stared at her fingers. "Is that blood?"

Pellets of sleet mixed in with the snow stung Levi's face. He needed to get her and the children to shelter. "Do you think you can stand? We need to get out of this weather."

"I'll try."

He lifted her to her feet but she crumpled against him with a cry of pain. "My knee. It won't hold me."

He lowered her to the ground. "Which one?"

"The right one. This is all my fault. I shouldn't have

invited them to visit. I knew something bad would happen."

"Sarah, you didn't cause this."

"You don't understand. Everyone I love is in danger."

She must have hit her head harder than he thought. She wasn't making sense. He sought to soothe her. "Don't fret. The children are going to be fine."

With gentle fingers, he examined her leg. Her knee was already swelling. "I can't tell if it is sprained or worse."

She looked at her nieces and nephew huddled together. "If you can help me to the buggy, Levi, I'll wait here while you take the *kinder* to safety."

"I'm not leaving you."

"I'll be fine. Just take care of the children. Please, Levi."

"This is going to hurt." He slipped his arm beneath her knees and lifted her. She clutched his shoulders and bit her lip but didn't cry out. He carried her to the wreckage of the buggy. It was useless as a shelter. He lowered her to the snow-covered ground. There was no way he was going to leave her here alone. He looked at the children. They would all have to go together.

Leaving them briefly, he moved to his horse. She had stopped struggling and lay quietly on the ground. "Easy, my girl. I'll get you loose." He managed to unbuckle and lift the harness from her. She surged to her feet, but limped heavily as she managed a few steps. She wouldn't be able to carry Sarah or the children.

He searched for a suitable place to leave her and found it beneath a leaning cedar. Leading her slowly, he tied her under the makeshift canopy knowing she would be safe until he could return for her.

Moving back to Sarah and the children, he surveyed what they had and what they would need. The first thing was to get up the hill to the roadway and hope they could flag down a passing vehicle. It was unlikely this time of day and in this weather. Barring that, they would simply have to walk to the home of Sarah's aunt.

He said, "Rosanna, I need you to unbuckle one of the long lines from my horse's bridle."

To his relief, she quickly did as he asked. When she came back with the leather strap he said, "Now, I want you to make three loops for handholds about three feet apart."

"Like this?" she asked as she tied the first one.

"Ja."

"I'm cold," Phoebe whined.

Merle said, "I want Mama."

Sarah said, gently, "Darling, Levi is going to take you to *Aenti* Emma's. I want you to do as he tells you."

Rosanna held up the rein with three loops in it. "Is this right?"

He took it from her. "Couldn't have done better myself."

He tied one end around his waist, and then squatted so he was eye level with the children. "I want each one of you to put your hand through a loop. Rosanna, I want you on the end so that the little ones are between us. If everyone holds on, no one can get lost. Okay?"

The children nodded. He looked at Phoebe. "I need your apron to make a bandage for your sore hand. Is that okay?" She nodded. He fashioned a makeshift sling and some padding for her arm. It was the best he could do.

Rosanna quickly fastened the loops around her sister's good hand and then placed one over Merle's.

Levi moved to pick up Sarah. She tried to push him away. "You can't carry me all the way to my uncle's farm. I will only slow you down."

"Sarah, the longer you keep talking, the longer these children have to stand here in the cold." He scooped her up in his arms and ignored her hiss of pain. It couldn't be helped.

He stared up the hillside. It would be a steep climb at the best of times. At night, in the snow, with Sarah in his arms, it was going to be a nightmare.

He looked at the children lined up behind him. "Ready?"

They all nodded. Levi began making his way up the slope with careful steps. The wet snow made the climbing treacherous. It wasn't any easier for the children behind him. Each time one of them slipped and fell, he felt the jerk on the line at his waist. He struggled to keep his feet.

His arms ached with the strain, but he didn't stop. By the time they reached the top and the roadway, everyone was out of breath and panting. Merle began crying.

"The hard part is over, dearest," Sarah said with her face buried in Levi's neck. Her voice had grown weaker.

The steep part was over. Levi wasn't sure they were past the hard part. "This way," he said, and started walking.

They had only gone a little ways when Rosanna called out, "Can we rest now?"

"Sure." Levi dropped to one knee, allowing Sarah's weight to rest on his leg and give his aching arms a much-needed break. She still had her face buried against his neck. If the children weren't present, he would have kissed her and professed his love again and again.

That would have to wait until they were all safe, but the sun would not set tomorrow before he found a way to be alone with Sarah and make his feelings known. Did she care for him at all? He prayed that she could find it in her heart to love him a little.

He struggled to his feet. "Time to go."

Merle refused to get up. "I can't go on. I'm tired. I want my *daed* to come get me."

"Great," Levi muttered as he sank to his knee again. He couldn't carry Sarah and drag the children, too.

"They are scared, Levi. Talk to them. Take their minds off what they have to do." Sarah's voice was weaker. He worried about the blow to her head. How serious was it?

He said, "Merle, I heard you're quite a fisherman. Is that true?"

"Ja," came the small reply.

Levi rose to his feet and hefted Sarah to a more comfortable position. "What's the biggest fish you've caught?"

"I caught a four-pound bass at our pond." Merle's voice grew stronger. "It was a whopper."

Levi cocked his head to the side and said in mock disbelief, "Four pounds? *Nee, not* a little fella like you."

Merle rose to his feet. "I'm stronger than I look."

Levi hid a grin. "I believe you. Girls, what about you?" He started walking. The children moved close to his side.

Rosanna said, "I caught a six-pound blue cat down at the river."

"Are you sure it was a blue catfish and not a channel cat? Merle, did you see it?"

"It was a blue cat all right."

"Some channel cats can look blue." Levi kept a slow pace, even though his mind screamed at him to hurry for Sarah's sake.

Merle said, "Channel cats have spots on their sides."

Levi asked, "Did it have spots, Rosanna?"

"Not a one."

Phoebe said, "I caught a pumpkin seed."

"You did?" Levi pretended to be impressed.

Merle looked up at Levi. "It wasn't very big."

"But it was real pretty," Phoebe insisted.

Levi said, "I reckon it was. I think pumpkin seeds are about the prettiest fish around. What about you, Rosanna?"

"I saw a goldfish in a store once. It was beautiful. It had a long tail that looked like a ribbon."

"You don't say?"

"I saw it, too." Merle jumped in to support her claim.

Phoebe said, "I'm cold. Can we stop now?"

"Not yet, Phoebe. We still have a little ways to go."

"How far?" she demanded.

"Look up ahead. I see a light in the window. Do you see it?"

Phoebe said, "I don't see anything."

"I do," Levi insisted. It was an exaggeration on his part. He couldn't see more than twenty yards through the snow, but he knew a light was shining in the darkness, waiting to guide them to safety.

"Is it a Christmas candle?" Rosanna asked.

He smiled down at her. "That's right. It's a Christmas candle in your aunt's window. It's meant to remind all of us that Christ is the light of the world."

Merle said, "Christmas is God's birthday."

"It's His son's birthday. We did a play about the birth of Jesus for our school program," Rosanna told them.

Levi's aching arms couldn't hold Sarah any longer. He said, "Let's rest a moment."

He dropped to one knee again. *Please, Lord, give me the strength I need.*

"I'm so sorry this happened. I can stay here while you go on." Sarah's voice was weak, her words slurred together.

He redoubled his resolve and struggled to his feet. "I was just giving the kids a break. Rosanna, tell us about your play while we walk."

Phoebe said, "I was one of the angels."

Sarah's arm slipped from around his neck. "Stay with me, Sarah. Did you hear? Phoebe was an angel in her school play."

"I know." Relief flooded him at the sound of Sarah's voice.

"Who did you play, Rosanna?" she asked.

"I played the innkeeper's wife."

Merle said, "I'd be Joseph if I was old enough to go to school."

"You will be old enough one day, Merle." Levi squinted to see ahead of them. Was it his imagination? No, there was a light.

"Are we there yet?" Phoebe asked.

"We are. This is the lane and up ahead is your Aunt Emma's house. Can you see it?"

"I see it." Rosanna's voice brimmed with relief.

"Me, too." Merle dropped his loop and ran ahead.

When Levi and the girls arrived, Emma and her husband were at the door. Emma quickly stripped the wet coats from the children and wrapped them in quilts while her husband helped Levi carry Sarah to the sofa.

When she was safely surround by her family, Levi said, "She needs a doctor. She hit her head pretty hard. May I use your buggy?"

Abe patted Levi's shoulder. "You get out of that wet coat and warm up, son. I'll fetch the doctor."

Levi gave his coat to Emma and sank into Abe's chair.

"Levi?" Sarah called his name and raised her hand. He was on his knees beside her in an instant.

He took her cold hand in his. "What, Sarah?"

"I've never heard you talk so much in all the years I've known you. You were wonderful. You saved us all."

"Rest, Sarah. I'll be right here if you need me."

"I never doubted it for a moment." She closed her eyes and drifted off to sleep. Levi closed his eyes, too, and gave thanks to God for sparing the life of the woman he loved.

Sunlight was streaming through the window when Sarah opened her eyes. The room in which she lay was vaguely familiar. A sharp headache pounded behind her eyes. Slowly, the events of the previous night came back to her and she realized she was in her aunt's home.

She tried to sit up but the effort was too much. It made her knee hurt insanely. She grimaced and lay back. Memories of their horrid mishap flashed through her mind. Levi and the children had come so close to death. Once again, the ones she loved had been made to suffer. She folded her hands and bowed her head.

Thank You, Lord, for sparing Levi and the children. Please, God, I won't love him if only you'll keep him safe. I'll be happy for him and Leah, I promise. Have pity on me. Don't make me endure another loss.

"Are you awake, child?" her aunt asked from the door.

Sarah opened her eyes. "I am. How are the children?"

"Their cuts and scrapes have all been tended. They are fine, but Merle seems to be particularly upset. He says he won't go back inside a buggy."

"The poor child. And Levi? He was so sick only a week ago." Only bad things had happened to him since her feelings for him had begun to change. She couldn't cause him more pain. She wouldn't.

"Levi seems fine for a man who didn't get a wink of sleep for worrying about you. He did put away a good breakfast this morning. That's always a sign a man is feeling well. He wants to see you when you're awake. Shall I send him in now?"

Could she face him without revealing her love? Somehow, she had to. "I will see him."

Her aunt went out. The door opened again and Levi peeked in. "How are you?"

"Oh, look at your poor face. You have a black eye." It was all her fault. If he had gone straight to Leah's home, none of this would have happened. Why did everyone she love end up getting hurt?

"I've had worse than this." He dismissed her concern.

He might pretend it didn't bother him, but Sarah knew better. It must hurt as much as her knee. How had he found the strength to carry her so far?

Don't think about how much you want to be held in his arms again.

She stared at the quilt pattern on the bed. "What happened last night?"

"We lost a wheel and tipped over in the worst possible spot. But we are all alive to tell the tale. God was merciful."

God had shown mercy last night, but what about next time? She couldn't bear the thought of losing Levi. It would be painful to see him happy with Leah, but she could live with that if he was safe.

He moved closer and pulled a chair to the side of her bed. Her heart started beating like crazy.

He took her hand and gazed into her eyes. "I'm so thankful you are safe, Sarah. Last night, when I came to in the buggy and couldn't find you, I thought I would never have the chance to tell you this. I love you, Sarah."

Her eyes flew open wide. "No, you don't."

"I know my own heart. I do love you. What I don't know is how you feel."

Terrified. Wonderful. Sad. If only I could love you in return, but I don't dare. My heart is breaking, but you can never know that.

She looked out the window. "You're simply feeling guilty about the accident. You don't love me. You are in love with Leah."

"Leah? Why would you think that?"

She looked at him and saw astonishment written on his face. "I saw you kiss her."

He shook his head. "I don't know who you saw kissing Leah, but it surely wasn't me."

Had she been mistaken? No, she had seen Leah in his arms. "The day you sold her a new buggy, I saw you holding her in the shop. She was in your arms. You were about to kiss her. And that's fine. She is a wonderful woman."

"She had a cinder in her eye. I was trying to get

it out. I wasn't going to kiss her. The thought never crossed my mind. It is you I wish to kiss, Sarah Wyse. If you can love me even half as much as you loved Jonas, I will spend my life trying to make you happy. Say that you will marry me."

Sarah froze. She couldn't draw a breath. Here was what she had longed for and what she feared. For a few wonderful seconds she thought that happiness could be hers again, but she forced that dream out of her heart. He'd almost been killed last night. As much as she wanted to return his love, she knew what she had to do.

She closed her eyes. She couldn't love him. If she did, he might be the next to die. Dying herself would be easier than losing him.

Please, Lord. Don't do this to me. Levi needs a woman who will love him without doubt and without fear. I'm not brave enough.

She turned her face away. "I don't love you, Levi."

The moment the words left her lips she knew they were a lie. She did love him. With all her heart.

Silence hung thick in the air. He let go of her hand. She heard his chair scrape back. What had she done?

At the sound of the door opening, she looked to him. "Levi?"

He paused without looking back.

"We can still be friends, can't we? Like it was before?" Oh, how she needed to have him near. It wasn't enough, but it was something.

He left the room without answering. When he closed the door, she burst into tears.

She was still sobbing when her aunt came in a short time later. Murmuring, "There, there." Emma gathered her close and held her until her tears finally ran dry.

Emma put a hand under Sarah's chin and lifted her face. "You refused him?"

Sarah sniffed. "How did you know? Did he say something?"

"Nothing needed to be said. I could tell from the way the light died in his eyes that you sent him away. I thought… I hoped that you had found love again, Sarah. I'm rarely mistaken about these things. Do you love him?"

She couldn't utter the lie a second time. "Yes."

"Then why send Levi away?"

"God has shown me His plan for me. He took Jonas from me. He took my sister and my parents. I must live alone. It is His will."

"Nonsense!" Her aunt scowled at her.

"What if I accepted Levi and he died, too? You don't understand." Sarah was too tired to explain herself.

Emma said, "I understand fear. I understand regret. I understand that it is hard to trust that God knows best. Yes, you have suffered great losses, Sarah. No one can deny that, but to think God wants you to spend your life without love is to say that He doesn't love you. Surely you believe in God's love."

"Of course I do."

"He loves you beyond all understanding."

"I know that."

"So you say, but do you truly believe it?"

Did she? Or did she doubt God's love? Was that why it was so hard to trust that He would bring love back into her life?

She shook her head. "I'm tired, *Aenti*. I'd like to try and sleep now."

She wanted to close her eyes and let the darkness swallow her. She didn't want to think, didn't want to feel.

"Very well." Emma rose from the side of the bed.

At the door, she turned back to Sarah. "If you don't believe God wishes you to be happy, why has Levi stayed beside you all these years? Think about that. Don't let fear rule your heart and ruin your life. Give it to God."

After her aunt was gone, Sarah turned gingerly to her side. Outside the window, the snow was still falling. She hated the snow.

Why had Levi stayed? Was that part of God's plan for them? If only she could believe it.

Chapter Fifteen

Levi stepped down from Adrian Lapp's buggy. "Thanks for the lift."

"Not a problem. I'm happy to help. *Mamm* said they would bring the children back later this afternoon. Dr. White wants Sarah to rest her leg another day before trying to come home. He won't have any trouble keeping her and Alma in bed. There will be a half dozen women here to help take care of them by tomorrow night."

"That's good." The mere mention of Sarah's name sent a stab of pain though Levi's chest so sharp that he wanted to look and see if he was bleeding. She didn't love him. Not even a little.

He walked into his house and stopped in surprise. Grace stood at the kitchen sink peeling potatoes. She turned to smile at him and shrieked, "Levi! What happened to you?"

He heard his brothers pounding down the stairs. Moses said, "It must have been a hot date. You were gone all…night." He stopped dead in his tracks and his voice trailed away at the sight of Levi's face. Atlee bumped into him from behind.

Grace sped into action. "Sit down, Levi. Let me get some ice for you. Do you need to see a doctor?"

Could Dr. White reach inside him and put his shattered heart back together? If so, he'd go for treatment in a minute. "It's only a black eye, Grace. I didn't think you'd be home for another week."

"I learned what I needed to know so I came home. What happened to you?" she asked again as she gathered ice cubes from the freezer. The twins had come to stand on either side of him but they were surprisingly quiet.

"The left front wheel of the buggy came off when I was going around the hill out on Paint Road. The buggy swerved off the road, flipped over and rolled down the hill. I got off lucky. Sarah and the kids were banged up pretty good."

"Sarah and the kids were with you? Why? What were you doing on Paint Road?" Atlee demanded. His face had turned ashen.

Levi sat down and accepted the towel full of ice that Grace handed him. "I was going to drop them off at Emma Lapp's place so the children could stay there until their parents were well. The buggy is a complete loss."

Atlee went to look out the window. "What about Dotty? Where is she?"

"Jonathan Dresher came and got her with his horse ambulance. He's going to try to save her, but her front left leg is messed up pretty good. She'll never pull a buggy again."

"No!" Atlee grasped his hair with both hands.

Moses hadn't said a word. He sat down beside Levi. "How bad were the children hurt?"

"Rosanna's pretty face will have a jagged scar across her chin. She was badly bruised. Phoebe has bruises galore and two dislocated fingers on her hand." He shuddered when he thought about his crude fix for her.

"What about Merle?" Moses asked quietly.

Levi shook his head. "A few bumps and bruises on the outside, but he started screaming bloody murder when we tried to put him inside a closed buggy. Finally, we gave up. Ben Lapp is bringing him home in his courting buggy. Merle won't get into anything else."

Moses folded his arms on the table and laid his head on them. "We did it. We rigged the wheel to come off."

Levi placed a hand on his brother's head. "I know. This morning, I went back for our horse. I found the axel nut on the roadway where the wheel dropped off. I saw at once it was the one for the wrong wheel."

Moses looked up with tears in his eyes. "I'm so sorry, Levi. I didn't mean to hurt anyone."

"Why did you do it?"

Atlee said, "We didn't want you to court Leah Belier. We thought if you stood her up for a date she might get mad and not go out with you anymore. The road to her place is long and flat. We thought the wheel would just drop off and you'd have to walk home."

An amazed bark of laughter broke from Levi. He shook his head. "That was a really stupid reason made all the more idiotic by the fact that I'm not courting Leah Belier."

"But you've been taking her for rides in your buggy. You've never taken a woman riding before."

"I was helping a friend. I'm not sure either of you would understand that."

He looked at Grace. "You are free to marry the man of your choice. Choose wisely, little sister."

He glanced at his brothers. "You boys have a decision to make. I'm moving to Colorado. I'll be leaving the day after Christmas."

"You don't mean that." Grace stared at him in shock.

"What about us?" the twins demanded.

Levi sighed. "You may come with me, or you may stay here. If you stay here and run the repair shop, you will have to negotiate a new contract with Sarah. She is well within her rights to refuse you."

"Was Sarah hurt?" Grace asked

"She injured her knee and can't walk. She also has a concussion." He rose to his feet.

Grace grabbed his hand. "I'm so thankful you were not badly injured for I dearly love you, brother. Please, don't leave Hope Springs."

He *was* badly injured, but not all wounds were as visible as his black eye. "My mind is made up. Atlee and Moses, I forgive you for the harm you have done me. I must go and pack. I don't need any help. I'd like to be alone for a while."

He walked up the stairs, leaving stunned silence behind him.

Sarah used the crutches the doctor had given her to make her way into her house. Her aunt and uncle had taken the children home the day before. Inside, Vernon was pacing the floor. The moment he saw her, he rushed to her, took her by the shoulders and kissed both her cheeks. "Praise God for His mercy."

"How is Alma?"

"She was a wreck, but once the children arrived, she went straight back to bed as the doctor had ordered. She is reading them a story now."

The front door opened and Grace Beachy walked in. Her eyes were puffy from crying. She threw her arms around Sarah. "I'm so sorry for the pain my family caused you."

"It's all right. I'm glad you are back." She was happy to see her friend. It meant she wouldn't have to work in the shop with Levi any more. Things could get back to normal.

Levi would soon realize he didn't love her. They could be friends again. Tears stung her eyes at the thought.

"Sarah, Levi is leaving Hope Springs. He's moving away," Grace said between sniffles.

Sarah's heart dropped to her feet. "What?"

"He told us he is leaving town for good. His bus leaves at four o'clock the day after Christmas. We've tried to talk him out of it, but he won't be swayed. What are we going to do without him?"

"Where is he? I can't let him do this."

"He's in the shop."

Her brother said, "Shouldn't you be lying down? The doctor said to rest that knee."

"I will. After I've spoken with Levi."

He couldn't leave. How would she repair the damage she had done to their friendship if he moved away? He had to stay. She couldn't bear it if he left.

She hobbled across the street on her crutches, pulled open the door and went in. He was standing in front of the workbench sorting his tools. He didn't glance up. "What do you want, Sarah?"

He must have seen her crossing the street.

"Grace tells me you're leaving." She still couldn't believe it.

"I am." He didn't look at her.

Why wouldn't he look at her?

Tears gathered in her eyes, but she blinked them back. "Are you really going to Colorado?"

He carefully wrapped his tools in a length of canvas. *"Ja."*

She didn't want him to go. She needed him. Her life would go back to being empty with nothing but work to fill the lonely hours if he were gone.

You mean so much to me, Levi. Please turn around and look at me.

He didn't. Suddenly, the truth sank in. She had lost him. Her fear had robbed them both of a chance at happiness. A tear slipped down her cheek. "I hope you'll be happy there."

He threw down his tools and raised his face to heaven. There was such sorrow in his expression. "How can I be happy if I'm not near you?"

"Then why are you leaving?"

He turned to face her. The pain in his eyes cut her like a knife. "Not so very long ago, I told myself that I could be content if you loved me just a fraction of the way you loved Jonas. But I was fooling myself, Sarah. I'm a selfish man. If you cannot love me every bit as much or more than you loved Jonas, then I must go. I can't be satisfied watching you through the window anymore. I love you, but if you don't love me, leaving is all that is left."

"I care for you, Levi. You know that."

"But do you love me?"

How could she make him understand? "I want to."

He closed his eyes and turn away. She couldn't let him go. "I want to love you, but I'm afraid, Levi."

He turned back to her. "What is it you fear? Surely you know I would never hurt you."

"I'm afraid you'll die," she whispered the words, as if saying them aloud would give them power. She covered her face with her hands.

"What do you mean?"

"Everyone I love dies. You and the children were almost killed because of me." She tried to leave but stumbled on her crutches. He caught her and held her in his arms.

"Oh, Sarah." His voice softened. "The wreck wasn't your fault. My brothers rigged the wheel to come off."

She tried to turn her face away from him. "How it happened doesn't matter."

"You're right. I'm going to die. We are all going to die, Sarah. Not loving someone won't prevent that."

"It's all I can do. You have to be safe."

"You can't keep me safe any more than you can take the moon out of the sky. All you can do is make living bearable for me. Sarah, one day of knowing your love would make my entire life worthwhile, no matter how short or how long."

"Don't say that."

"Don't speak the truth? How can you ask me to lie? I love you, Sarah. How many times must I say it? God planted this love in my heart. He allowed it to grow into something strong and enduring. It will not die even after

I'm laid in my grave. I will love you through eternity, as God is my witness, I will."

She broke down and sobbed.

Levi couldn't bear the sight of her tears any longer. He gathered her into his arms and held her tight. Her hands grasped his coat as if she were afraid to let go.

"Don't cry, *liebschen*. Please, don't cry so."

She pressed her face into his neck and he cupped the back of her head to keep her close.

"Did you know that Jonas made me promise to watch over you until you remarried?"

She shook her head, but didn't speak.

"He did. Two days before he died, he made me promise to see you happily wed before I left town. He knew I wanted to go west. You know what else I think he knew? I think he knew that I was in love with you years before I knew it myself."

"Really?" She drew back to look up at him.

"I believe that."

"He was always thinking of others. I loved that about him."

"I love him, too, you know."

"Maybe he hoped I would eventually see the fine man hidden behind the shy boy who could barely speak to me."

Levi shook his head. "We are a sad pair, you and I. I was afraid to speak for fear of looking the fool. You're afraid to love because it may bring you more loss. Neither one of us trusted God enough to lay our fears at His feet and ask what He wished of us. I found my voice because of you, Sarah."

"You found it because you wanted to help the children. You're right about one thing. I need to give over my burden and trust in His mercy. I'm just not sure I can."

"Yes, you can. Close your eyes and feel His love. I feel it and it gives me comfort."

"Levi, when did you know you loved me?"

He sighed. "I knew it the day you gave me a haircut. You could have plucked out my hairs one by one and I would have endured it without a peep. I've never wanted anything as much as I wanted your touch."

"But what if in a few months or a few years you discover Leah or Sally is the woman God wants for you?"

"You're right. I should test my feelings." He smiled at her and then lowered his face and kissed her.

Swept away in the glorious sensation of his lips on her, of his body pressed against hers, Sarah gave herself over to delight. She never wanted it to end. She wanted Levi to hold her forever and she wasn't afraid. This was so right. Her doubts slipped away as she gave her fear over to God.

Levi drew back a few seconds later. Her mind was still spinning. "Shall we test this some more?" he asked.

She nodded and lifted her face to his. The second kiss was every bit as wonderful as the first. More wonderful, because she knew what was coming.

When he drew away again, he was as breathless as she was. "Tell me now that you don't love me."

He kissed her again before she could answer. When he drew away, she raised her arms to pull his head down to her and buried her fingers in his curls. Her crutches fell away, but she didn't need them. Levi was holding her up.

He placed a kiss on her forehead. "Say it, Sarah."

He placed another kiss on her eye. "Say it."

He nuzzled her cheek with his mouth a fraction of an inch from her wanting lips. "Say it, Sarah. I need to hear it."

"I love you, Levi Beachy."

"I knew you did."

A great weight lifted from her heart and she knew this was part of God's plan for her life. She smiled at Levi. He bent toward her and she raised her face for his kiss.

A long time later, she sighed and snuggled against him. He asked, "Are you cold?"

"Not a bit. I could stay here for hours."

"Your family will be missing you soon."

"I know, but can't we stay a little longer?" She never wanted this closeness to end. How blessed she was to have this second chance to love and be loved.

He looked over his shoulder. "I'm afraid we're about to be interrupted. My brothers are coming this way."

She took a step back and gave a small cry of pain.

He grasped her to keep her from falling and held her close. "Is it your knee?"

She nodded. "I reckon I've been up on it too long."

He wrapped his arm around her waist. "Lean on me. I will help you back to your house, unless I need to carry you."

She kept her face pressed against his shoulder. Breathlessly, she said, "I think you had better carry me."

He swung her up into his arms. "This is getting to be a habit."

She nuzzled his neck. "It's a habit I quite enjoy."

Levi stared into her eyes so full of love for him. "Tomorrow is Christmas Eve."

Sadness filled her eyes briefly, but it faded as she looked up at him. "I know."

"You haven't asked me what sort of gift I might like."

"Let me guess, a new rod and reel?"

"Not even close. All I want is your answer to a very important question, but I want it today, before Christmas. Will you marry me, Sarah Wyse?"

She bit her lip, then nodded. "I will."

He swung her around as joy pushed aside the last doubt from his heart. When she shrieked, he stopped and kissed her again. "Thank you. That is truly the best Christmas gift I have ever received."

"How soon are we moving to Colorado?" she asked with a grin.

He looked at her in surprise. "Just like that you're willing to go to Colorado? To leave all your friends and family? It might be years before we can come back for a visit."

"I know it will not be an easy thing, but I want you to follow your dream. You follow it. I will follow you."

"The decision is that simple for you?"

"I reckon it's as simple as can be. I want you to rise each morning and see God's glory in the mountains from our front porch."

He no longer needed to run away from the woman he couldn't have. "I've changed my mind about that."

"Really? Why?"

"Because God, in His goodness, has delivered to me something more beautiful than the highest mountains. I won't even have to walk out on my porch to see it. My beautiful wife, my best Christmas gift, will be lying beside me in our bed each morning when I open my eyes. Wherever you are, Sarah Wyse, there is my heart, my dreams, my very life."

He bent and kissed her once more.

Epilogue

When Sarah woke the morning of her wedding, she was tired but happy. Rushing to her window, she saw the sky outside was overcast with low gray clouds. The threat of snow hung in the air.

She crossed the room and opened her cedar chest. She took out the blue dress she had made with loving care years before. Her wedding dress. It would be the dress she would be buried in. She chose to wear it again for one simple reason. For Jonas.

He was the reason that she and Levi had fallen in love. If he hadn't asked Levi to stay and watch over her, Levi would have gone to Colorado and she might never have grown to love him. By wearing her first wedding dress, she was acknowledging her first husband's love and caring.

Her sprained knee had healed well enough in the two weeks since the accident that she could stand for small amounts of time and walk short distances. She was determined to stand unaided at her own wedding.

When she finally stepped down from her buggy at her aunt's house, she couldn't believe how nervous she was. Faith and Grace accompanied her. Sarah clenched her hands together and drew a deep breath.

"What's the matter?" Grace asked.

"My hands are like ice. I have butterflies the size of geese flopping around in my stomach."

Grace shook her head. "I can't believe you're nervous. You've done this before."

Faith gave her a hug. "I understand exactly how you feel."

Sarah knew that was true. Faith was also a widow who had found a new love in their small community.

"I think I'm more nervous than when I married Jonas. I don't know why I'm scared. I want nothing more than to spend the rest of my life with Levi."

Faith gave her a tiny push toward the front of her aunt's house. "That will not happen if you stand out here all day."

Sarah said, "Wait. It's starting to snow."

Grace looked up. "It is."

Flakes as large as duck down began floating to earth. They clung to Sarah's coat and settled around her feet. More and more followed until the air was thick with them.

Faith said, "We should go in. Everyone is waiting."

Sarah held out her hand and smiled at the white flakes sticking to her mittens. She looked out over the farm. The tall pine trees were catching the powdery fluff in their needles. She smiled at Grace. "Hear how quiet it has become? Isn't it beautiful?"

"Yes, it is," Faith agreed.

Jonas had loved the way snow turned the world into something clean and bright. Perhaps he had arranged this for her, a new start to her new life.

She said, "I used to hate the snow. There was snow on the ground when Jonas died, but from this day on, snowflakes will always remind me of my wedding day. I'm ready now."

Inside her aunt's home, the walls had been pushed back to open up the downstairs rooms. Benches were arranged in two rows, men on one side and women on the other just as they were for regular preaching services.

Levi, looking remarkably handsome in his new black suit, white shirt and black bow tie, waited beside his brothers at the front of the room. The look in his eyes said everything she wanted to hear. Her nerves quieted and she walked toward her place at the front of the house beside Levi.

Sarah reached for Levi's hand. He gave her fingers a quick squeeze. Soon they would be joined as husband and wife.

As Sarah stood before Bishop Zook with Levi at her side, she knew the questions that would be asked of her.

Looking at them both, the bishop said, "Do you confess and believe God has ordained marriage to be a union between one man and one woman? And do you believe that you are approaching this marriage in accordance with His wishes and in the way you have been taught?"

She and Levi said, "Yes," in loud, clear voices.

Turning to Levi, the bishop asked, "Do you believe, brother, that God has provided this woman as a marriage partner for you?"

"Yes." Levi smiled at her and her heart beat faster.

The bishop then turned to her. "Do you believe, sister, that God has provided this man as a marriage partner for you?"

"Yes, I do."

"Levi, do you also promise Sarah that you will care for her in sickness or bodily weakness as befits a Christian husband and do you promise you will love, forgive and be patient with her until God separates you by death?"

"I do so promise," Levi answered solemnly.

"Sarah, do you promise the same, to care for Levi in bodily weakness or sickness, as befits a Christian wife? Do you promise to love, forgive and be patient with him until God separates you by death?"

The question gave her pause. She knew it was coming, but she was still unprepared for the shaft of fear that hit her.

Would she someday be called upon to watch Levi die? Could she go through that agony again?

"Sarah?" the bishop prompted gently. He was waiting for her answer. The sympathy in his eyes said he understood her hesitation.

She focused on Levi. He was waiting, too.

Taking a deep breath, she nodded. She would be blessed to care for this man no matter how many or how few days were given to them. She raised her chin and said, "I promise."

The bishop smiled and nodded. He took her hand, placed it in Levi's hand and covered their fingers with his own. "The God of Abraham, of Isaac, and of Jacob be with you. May He bestow His blessings richly upon you through Jesus Christ, Amen."

She smiled brightly at Levi as he squeezed her hand. That was it. They were man and wife.

When the ceremony ended, the festivities began. Levi had but a moment to realize he was the luckiest man alive before he was quickly led away by his groomsmen. Looking over his shoulder, he saw Sarah being shepherded away by his sister and Faith Lapp.

The women of the congregation moved to the kitchen and started getting ready to serve dinner. The men arranged tables in a U-shape around the walls of the living room.

In the corner of the room facing the front door, the honored place, the *Eck,* meaning the corner table, was quickly set up for the wedding party.

When it was ready, Levi took his place with his groomsmen seated to his right. Sarah was ushered back in and took her seat at his left-hand side. It symbolized the place she would occupy in his buggy and in his life. Her cheeks were rosy red and her eyes sparkled with happiness. They clasped hands underneath the table. She was everything he could have asked for and more.

There would be a long day of celebration and feasting, but tonight would come, and she would be his alone.

Moses elbowed him in the side. "Put your tongue back in your head *bruder,* you look like a panting dog. Greet your guests."

Still unable to believe how blessed he was, Levi released Sarah's hand and began to speak to the people who filed past.

The single men were arranged along the table to his right and the single women were arranged along the tables to Sarah's left. Later, for the evening meal, the young, unmarried people would be paired up according to the bride and groom's choosing.

Levi leaned over. "You will have a chance to sharpen your matchmaking skills this evening."

"My skills are sharp enough. I found you a wife, didn't I?"

"*Ja,* and a right fine wife she is."

"I wonder who would do for Joann?"

"Look for a fellow with his own fly rod and a full tackle box."

Sarah rolled her eyes and shook her head. "Men are so limited in their thinking when it comes to matters of the heart."

"Are you saying I don't have matchmaking skills?"

"Let us see. Who do you want to pair with Amos Fisher?"

"Leah. I think she could make a silk purse out of a sow's ear."

"No. Leah needs someone quite special. I'll have to think on that one. Oh, I see Roman Weaver coming this way."

The pale young man stopped in front of them. He wore a sling. A thick cast covered his right arm. Sarah had heard he would never recover the full use of it. He said, "I wanted to thank you and your brothers for helping my family with my hospital bills."

"It was our pleasure, Roman," Sarah assured him.

"You would do the same for us," Levi added.

As Roman walked away, Sarah said, "I wonder if he and Joann know each other?"

"Ah, Sarah, one thing I know for sure. My life will never be boring with you by my side."

She smiled brightly and his heart turned over with happiness. "Say it again, my wife."

"Levi." She blushed and looked to see who might have noticed.

"Say it, Sarah, please."

She didn't even pretend to misunderstand. Leaning close, she whispered in his ear. "I love you, Levi Beachy, for now and for always."

It was exactly what his heart needed to hear.

* * * * *

AMISH CHRISTMAS ABDUCTION

Dana R. Lynn

Rachael, Bradley and Gregory.
There is not a day that I don't thank God for
the blessing of being your mom. Love you forever.

Brad…thanks for loving me and encouraging me
to live my dream. Love you!

Acknowledgments

To my family and friends, who supported me and
held me up in prayer…I appreciate you so much.
Thank you with all my heart.

To my editor, Elizabeth Mazer…thank you for
all your guidance. It's a joy to work with you.

To my agent, Tamela Hancock Murray…
thanks for believing in me. I am grateful
for all your efforts on my behalf.

To my Lord and Savior…thank You for
Your presence in my life. I am nothing without You.

Blessed are they that mourn:
for they shall be comforted.
—*Matthew* 5:4

Chapter One

"Didn't you see the sign? This is private property."

Irene Martello stepped back from the door, her raised hand falling to her side... The man who answered the door glared at her. It was the most vicious stare she'd ever encountered. Anger at being treated so rudely warred with apprehension. She was here alone...unprotected. Would this man turn violent?

"I'm sorry to bother you," she managed. "I was trying to find the Zilcher residence."

She shivered as he glowered, his heavy brows lowering over black eyes. It was difficult to see his mouth through the thick black beard, but she had the distinct impression he was scowling.

"You have the wrong house. They live there." He jerked his head sharply toward the house next door.

"Sorry..." She opened her mouth to apologize for any inconvenience, but stopped when there was a movement behind Black Beard. A young woman, somewhere in her late teens or early twenties, stood in an open doorway deeper inside the house. As the man whirled around and speared her with a glance, she fled back out of sight. Was that a child crying? Irene leaned forward instinctively, straining to hear. He returned that glare to Irene, and she straightened again. It was none of her business if he had children, she chastised herself. He narrowed his eyes at her, and she felt true fear at the way his eyes blazed at her.

Turning on her heel, she moved briskly back down the steps. Only the fact that the ground was covered with snow kept her from running as she hightailed it back to her SUV. After getting in, she started the engine with a shaking hand, then backed along the driveway and onto the dirt road. She drove past the mailboxes on the side of the road and realized that what she'd thought was a 1 had actually been a 7. A natural mistake to make.

In no time, she was in the driveway of the correct house. She fumbled around for her purse and laptop bag, completely aware that the man had moved outside and was watching her from his porch.

After pushing open the door of her SUV, Irene stepped from the vehicle, glad she'd opted for warmth rather than fashion as her heavy boots crunched the snow beneath them. Against her better judgment, she peeked at the man from house number seven. She instantly regretted it. His face had darkened even more. Turning quickly, her face heated as she felt his glare continuing to bore into her back. She took a deep breath, refusing to admit to herself how unsettling her encounter with the man had been.

Trying to appear calm, she pulled her belongings from the dark red SUV and shut the door with her hip. Slammed it, actually. Even though she refused to look, she was aware that he was still there. Now she was getting mad. Why was he watching her like that? What did he expect? That she'd drive back over to chat? Not likely.

Enough! She had a job to do. A job she loved, even though she'd only been working with the Early Intervention program for two months. Today she was meeting a new family. She shifted the red bag carrying both the laptop and her file of papers for the family to sign.

Determined, she made her way up the narrow walkway to the small house, careful to avoid looking at the man on the porch. It didn't help matters any that the family had requested a late meeting, due to the father's work schedule. It was already going on four o'clock. By the time the meeting ended, it would be almost five. LaMar Pond started getting dark around that time in December. At least it was Friday. After this appointment, she could pick up her own kids and enjoy a quiet evening at home.

Come on, Irene. One more home visit, then you're all done.

Once, only once, did she glance to the right. Her eyes switched targets as she became aware of movement from the side window. The same young woman she'd seen in the house was peering out of the blinds. She had the most hopeless face Irene had ever seen.

Something wasn't right.

The door in front of Irene opened. Taking her eyes off the creepy house, she forced herself to smile at the young couple waiting anxiously. For now, she needed to focus on work. But as soon as she was done with the meeting, she had every intention of calling her brother, Lieutenant Jace Tucker, and filling him in on the house and the woman. If her instincts were correct—and they usually were—that was a woman who needed help.

It might be nothing. But Irene knew she wouldn't rest easy until she had called. Maybe Jace wouldn't be able to do anything, but there was always the possibility that the police would keep a closer eye on the area.

Irene was very familiar with the police. Not only was her older brother a lieutenant, but she'd been married to a cop for six years, six wonderful years, before he'd been killed in the line of duty a little over three years ago.

The familiar ache in her chest when she thought of Tony was almost comforting.

Once inside the warm house, she was escorted into the dining room. She focused on the young family. The little boy she was there to evaluate was adorable, his little head bald except for a light fuzz. He was almost two years old, and had just been diagnosed with a vision impairment. Irene's job as the service coordinator was to decide if the child qualified for Early Intervention services. The meeting was merely a formality. Having a diagnosis almost always guaranteed that he would receive services.

In less than an hour, the meeting was completed and Irene was pushing her feet back into her winter boots.

"I will call you when I have the IFSP meeting scheduled," she told the mother, referring to the Individualized Family Service Plan meeting with the family and the therapists who would become part of the little boy's team.

After bidding the Zilchers goodbye, she pulled the door open and stepped outside. It had started to snow while she was inside. She tried to keep her focus on her car, but it was no use. The other house drew her gaze like a magnet.

The man was probably still home. There were three vehicles in the driveway—a truck, a Jeep and a small sedan. But no one was standing outside. The man must have gone inside.

Relief coursed through her. And quite a bit of embarrassment. Imagine getting so upset because someone was watching her! What a goose she was! It wasn't like he had threatened her or anything like that.

Getting to her car, she frowned. Her door wasn't locked. She must have been so rattled by that man that she'd forgotten to lock it. She shrugged. It wasn't out of the norm to leave doors unlocked in LaMar Pond, especially out on the back roads. She had friends who didn't even lock their house doors at night.

She quickly climbed into the car and shut the door, making sure to lock it the moment she was inside. After starting the car, she turned up the heat to help rid herself of some of the chill, not all of which was from the weather. Lifting her head, she froze.

There, in the Zilcher family's front room window, a large Christmas tree sparkled and shimmered. The tree hadn't been lit when she'd arrived or she would have noticed it, no matter how freaked-out she had been. It was probably on an automatic timer. It was beautiful, looking at it through the snow. She swallowed the lump in her throat. She wasn't looking forward to Christmas, just a few weeks away. It would be the third since Tony's death. Her boys would go through another holiday without their father. A father little Matthew hardly remembered. He'd only been two. Now he was five.

Seven-year-old AJ had more memories, but had forgotten so many details. It broke her heart.

A soft ping signaled an incoming text. Irene sighed. And this would be her mom, asking her to attend late-night services with her and the family on Christmas Eve. Just like Irene used to do every year before God abandoned her and her babies. She glanced at her phone. Oh, yeah. Just as she thought. She would hear about it later, but she was going to just ignore the text. For now.

A door slammed. Startled, her head jerked up in the direction of the sound. It had come from the man's house.

He was back, his eyes burning with anger. She could almost feel the menace emanating from him. Thankfully, he wasn't looking at her. He appeared to be searching for something, though, as his dark gaze swept over his yard.

Dropping her phone, Irene put her car into Reverse and started to back out of the driveway. Thankfully, there was no traffic on the road, so she could pull onto the street, away from the man, without waiting. But moments later, she heard a shout.

He was running her way!

Panicked now, she jerked the gearshift into Drive and peeled out. The vehicle fishtailed. Her grip tightened on the wheel. It straightened out and she continued, exhaling in relief.

Steering her SUV up the hill, she drove as fast as she dared before braking for the stop sign at the T on top of the hill. There was only one car coming. She edged her car forward, ready to turn right. She waited for the other driver to pass, drumming her fingers nervously on the steering wheel.

Come on. Come on.

Her back windshield shattered.

Irene screamed. What had just happened? A look in the rearview mirror confirmed her nightmare. The pickup truck she'd seen in the neighbor's drive was right on her bumper, and the man with the black beard was leaning out the window, some sort of rifle in his hand. She wasn't going to give him the chance to take a second shot. She shoved her foot down on the gas and whipped her car forward. She drove as fast as she could. She couldn't stop now to call the police. If she didn't concentrate on getting out of here, he'd get her for sure. But the moment she could pull over…

She heard a roar behind her. A glance in the mirror showed the pickup was coming up on her bumper. It was moving faster than she was, dangerously fast given the slick condition of the roads.

Now would be a good time to pray…if she still did that.

Since she didn't, she was on her own.

The truck slammed into the back of her SUV. She shrieked and pushed her foot down as hard as she dared on the gas pedal. She had never been so grateful for four-wheel drive. Pushing her foot down a little farther, the SUV lurched as it sped up. The truck stayed on her tail, then slammed into her again. Her SUV went into a full spin and slid off the road into a ditch. She was stuck.

Tears tracked down her cheeks. She was going to die! Her babies would be completely orphaned. Suddenly, her boycott on God no longer mattered. There was no one else who could help her.

Lord, help me. Please. Oh, please. Help.

* * *

Chief Paul Kennedy was driving back from a two-vehicle accident on the outskirts of LaMar Pond when the dispatcher announced shots fired near his location. A young woman had called 911, screaming that her neighbor was shooting at her son's service coordinator and had taken off in his truck after her.

Paul switched on his siren and pushed the hands-free button to answer the call. "Chief Kennedy here. I'm less than a mile away, heading that direction now. Send backup."

Disconnecting as soon as she confirmed, he said a prayer for the safety of all involved. It was never pleasant to handle road rage. Adding a gun and winter weather into the mix could prove to be a disaster in the making.

He came around the curve, his headlights cutting through the dark. The snowflakes caught in the beams made him think of a snow globe. Then they hit a sight that chilled his heart.

A red SUV was stranded in a ditch. He knew that SUV. It belonged to Irene Martello, his best friend's younger sister. The girl whose trust he'd shattered so many years ago. She was also the widow of one of his officers, shot down on his watch. Three good reasons he'd never, ever want to see her in danger of any kind. But it looked like that was exactly what was happening.

Directly behind her car, he could see a dark pickup truck had pulled off and parked on the side of the road. And not to help. The driver, a large man with a fierce scowl on his bearded face, had opened his door. He had started to step out of the vehicle, a rifle in his bare hands. This man meant to harm Irene.

The moment Paul appeared, though, he halted. The bright lights and the loud wail of the siren made the bearded man jerk back into his truck before speeding off in the opposite direction. Paul wanted to chase him, needed to stop the maniac. But he needed to check on Irene more. Quickly, he called in a description of the truck and the driver, and called for an ambulance.

Parking his cruiser on the side of the road, he kept his lights on to warn any oncoming traffic to slow down. Then he strode to the driver's-side door. She was watching him, her face bloodless. From fear, or was she in shock? Either way, he sent up a silent prayer of thanks at the sight of her alive and alert. He rapped on the window. It wasn't necessary. She was already rolling it down.

"Irene? Are you okay?"

"Paul!" She choked out his name. For the first time in years, her gaze wasn't cool when she met his eyes. Fear and gratitude took precedence over wounded pride. "I thought he was going to kill me!" Her voice wobbled slightly, but she wasn't crying. Anymore. The streaks left by earlier tears were evident.

He needed to calm her down, see if she was injured. "Easy, Irene. He's gone. Are you hurt anywhere? Anything broken?" He scanned her carefully.

She shook her head, then winced. His gaze narrowed in on her forehead. She wasn't bleeding. There was a dark shadow on her temple that concerned him. It could have been nothing, or a bruise forming. Hard to tell without proper lighting.

"Did you hit your head? It looks bruised. Any dizziness, or blurry vision?"

"I did bang it against the steering wheel when I went into the ditch. But I don't think I'm really hurt."

Hmm. He'd have her checked out when the ambulance arrived, just the same.

"What happened?" He kept his voice calm, even though he was feeling anything but.

"You know I started working at the Early Intervention program a couple of months ago?" He nodded. He remembered Jace saying something about that. "I was finishing a home visit. It was my last one of the day. When I first arrived, I accidentally went to the wrong house. That man answered the door and he was very angry to see me there. It was downright creepy. Then, when I was leaving his neighbors after my visit, he came out of the house and started looking around. Not at me, but like he was searching for something. I started driving and he started running after me. I didn't wait, just took off. Then next thing I knew, I was waiting at the stop sign, and he came up behind me and boom—" she slapped a hand on her steering wheel "—he'd shot out my back window and was coming after me. He rammed his truck into me, twice. The road was icy, and I lost control. I really think he would have killed me if you hadn't arrived. How did you know I was in danger?"

He had to draw in three deep breaths before he could speak around the red haze threatening to overcome him. His normally calm demeanor was failing him as he tried to keep from thinking of what would have happened if he had been farther away. *Thank You, Lord, for placing me here in time to help.* Paul was a firm believer that the Lord was in charge.

"The family you'd visited with called nine-one-one. They were able to give the operator the address of the neighbor who attacked you. I was on my way there when I came across your vehicle. I need to check in and make sure an officer is on the scene. Then we can go from there."

She nodded, relaxing briefly in her seat. Only for a moment, though. Her eyes widened slightly and she sat ramrod straight in her seat, grimacing. Maybe she was more bruised than she'd let on. "There was a woman inside the house when I arrived. Young, nineteen, maybe twenty or twenty-one. I don't know what was going on in there, but she looked scared, Paul. Really scared."

"I'll get it checked out, Irene. I promise." Paul moved to the front of the car and thumbed the radio on his shoulder to get an update. When he was told that several officers were en route to the scene, he gave the order that they inform him immediately of any findings. He took one step back toward Irene, then stopped. Jace's shift would be ending soon. He'd want to know what had happened. Paul was his chief, but he was also his best friend. Jace should hear about it from him. Before he could change his mind, he reached back, pulled his cell phone from his pocket and dialed the familiar number.

"'Lo, Chief."

Paul winced, even though he'd expected him to answer. He loved Jace like a brother, and this would not be an easy conversation. Jace was used to dealing with violence, but telling him that the shooting target had been his sister this time was not going to go over well.

"Lieutenant Tucker." Paul hesitated. He always tried to keep things professional when they were at the station. They weren't at the station, however, and this was an unusual situation.

"Jace…" He addressed the man as a friend. "She's okay, but the woman shot at was Irene."

Silence. Then Jace's deep voice exploded over the phone.

"What? What happened? You're positive she's okay? Where are you?"

Paul gave him his location. "He rear-ended her, and her car went into a ditch. Her forehead looks bruised, but she seems lucid and aware. I'm sure she's fine, but I have an ambulance coming, just to be safe."

"She's not going to want to ride in an ambulance."

Didn't he know that? If he knew Irene, her first priority would be to get back to her kids as quickly as possible. Plus, she had never liked hospitals.

"Did you get the guy?" Jace's voice was calmer now.

"No. He ran off when he heard my siren. And I wasn't about to leave Irene on the side of the road, especially not knowing if she was injured or not."

"Appreciate that."

Paul moved back to the side of the car.

A distant siren rent the air. The ambulance. Finally. It was starting to snow harder, which would make the roads more treacherous. Before this night was done, there would be more than one accident for the crew to work on. He would feel much better knowing that Irene was taken care of.

"The ambulance is here now," Paul said to Jace. "Why don't you call your mom and let her know what's going on so she doesn't worry."

"How bad does Irene look?"

Bad? Paul nearly smiled. Irene never looked bad. Even bruised and shaken, the red-haired woman was perfect. Of course, he couldn't say that, although he had a suspicion that Jace was on to him.

"She looks fine. Maybe a little shaken." Blue eyes glared up at him. "Make that mad, will you?"

An unexpected chuckle floated down the line. "She's glaring at you, isn't she?"

"Sure is. And I much prefer that."

A pause. "Yeah. Me, too."

An angry Irene was much easier to deal with than a shaken or frightened one. He got that.

"Put her on, will you?"

Paul handed the phone to Irene, then moved away again to give her some privacy. When the ambulance crew came over, she returned the phone to him.

Paul gave them room to do their job. And he did his—setting up flares to warn oncoming traffic to take precautions. By the time he returned to the car, Irene was done being checked out. The paramedics were recommending a trip to the hospital to get her head checked out. As expected, she was set against going.

"You should go to the hospital to get checked out." Paul bent over for a closer look at the bruise. She rolled her eyes, making him grin.

Irene sighed. "I need to get home to my kids."

"I had Jace tell your mom where you were. He will make sure that they're taken care of. Besides, your car will need to be towed. There's no way you can drive it with the back window blown out. Go to the hospital, and we will bring your car back when it's drivable. If all it needs is a new windshield, that should be tomorrow morning."

He received another glare for his trouble. Why did it have to be this hard? He kept hoping that she would forgive him. Then again, what would he do if she did? It wasn't like he would be any good for a fine woman like Irene. He had way too much baggage. Too many other responsibilities around his neck.

A sudden noise caught his attention.

Irene started to speak. He raised his hand. When she started to look huffy, he said, "Wait. Do you hear something?"

Irene tilted her head, her curls brushing against her cheek as she did. He averted his gaze and was momentarily distracted by the fact that her left hand was ringless. He was sure she had still been wearing her wedding band last time he saw her.

There it was again. A scratching noise. And now a faint mewling sound. Coming from inside her SUV. Paul moved closer and leaned in. Irene backed away from him. Whether that was because he was too close or because it was him, he didn't know. And now was not the time to ponder it. If something was in Irene's car with her, he needed to get to the bottom of it, fast.

"Irene, I need you to do exactly what I say." He kept his voice at a low murmur, the epitome of calm and casual, even though his heart was beating fast.

For once, the stubborn woman nodded without arguing. Guess she was still pretty freaked-out. And who wouldn't be?

"Go get in my cruiser. I need to see what's in your car, but I don't want you here when I do. I need to focus on this completely."

He didn't say, *And your presence is already too distracting to me.* Although he could have. He surely could have.

Paul made eye contact with her, making sure she understood how important this was. She moved towards his car, wobbling slightly on the uneven road. He held on to her elbow until she was steady, then let her go. He watched as the female paramedic led her safely to his cruiser. The paramedics wouldn't leave the site of an accident until the patient either joined them in the ambulance or signed a refusing-treatment form. So at least, she wouldn't be alone and unguarded.

The moment he felt she was reasonably safe, Paul shined his flashlight into the back of the car. Nothing was there that he could see. But then he heard the mewling again. This time it was louder.

Moving to the back, he grabbed his gun in one hand and the light in the other. Bracing himself for a fight or to duck, he flashed his light in the back window—and nearly dropped the light in his shock.

Curled up on the floor of Irene's SUV was a small child. A little girl, although he was unsure of her age. No more than two, he guessed. Judging by her dress and bonnet, she was Amish. She was shivering.

She was also covered in blood.

Chapter Two

Paul pushed his gun back into the holster and yelled for the paramedics.

"I have a child here! Possibly injured."

He opened the door, stepping back to let it swing upward. The dome light came on, causing the little girl's eyes to squeeze shut. She whimpered and curled into a tighter ball. The poor little thing was scared to death. Who did she belong to? And how on earth had she gotten into the back of the car?

"It's okay, little one," he crooned softly. "I'm going to help you. What's your name?"

No response. She didn't even look up.

Paul heard shuffling feet, and the male paramedic stepped up beside him, only his eyes showing the level of his concern. In a job working with those who were injured or dangerous, you learned quickly to remain calm at all costs. That was the only way you survived. Paul knew from experience that bad things could happen when you didn't. When you lost control, who knew what sort of damage would result? When the man started to climb into the back of the SUV, the child drew back in terror.

"Let me." Sydney, the female paramedic, moved forward and climbed in, making soothing noises. The girl still pulled back, but her distress seemed to lessen. When Sydney moved toward her, the girl whimpered but was calm enough for the woman to examine her.

He felt someone at his side and knew without turning that Irene was there. Of course. Why would she do what he asked and remain in the car? After all, he was only the chief of police. It wasn't like he had any authority. Not with her, at any rate. Even if she didn't like him, she knew him too well to be intimidated by his authority.

"She has Down syndrome."

"What?" He looked at the little girl again.

"You see her eyes, and her face—I'm a special-education teacher, remember?" Irene's voice was hushed, soothing. A mother's voice. "Oh, she's beautiful. And so scared. Paul, is that blood on her dress?"

Sydney beat him to it. "Yes, but I don't think it's hers. I can't seem to find any visible bleeding injuries on her. But she is dehydrated. When she opened her mouth, her tongue was white and seemed dry. Her eyes seem a little sunken, too. I wouldn't rule out abuse, either. She needs to go to the hospital."

"How is it we didn't hear her before?"

Paul wanted to know that, too.

Sydney tilted her head. "My guess? She was either momentarily stunned or the noise from everything else drowned out the sound."

Paul had another thought, one that chilled him. "Or she's been conditioned to make no noise." Irene and both paramedics looked at him, startled. Maybe even a little confused. But he could see the dawning horror as the meaning of his words sank in.

"You mean she might have been punished for making any noise."

He nodded. "Yeah, that makes the most sense to me. Sorry to say."

Sydney moved to pick up the child. The little girl backed away, eyes flaring wild. The male paramedic—Trey?—tried to reach in and get her. Immediately, she went into a frenzy, shrieking and biting.

"Oh, hey, don't do that!"

Irene moved forward. Paul reached out a hand to caution her to stay back, then felt his own jaw drop when the child launched herself out of the car and into Irene's arms. Her little arms wound up about the woman's neck and clung tight. Almost strangling Irene. Her grip looked painful, but Irene didn't flinch. She held the child securely in her arms, murmuring comforting sounds. The child settled down.

"I guess I'm going to the hospital, after all." She smiled at the girl. Her eyes were sad. Paul could almost see her thinking. Some mother somewhere was missing her baby. Suddenly, her gaze flashed back up to Paul's. "Oh, my! I was in my client's house for almost an hour and I forgot to lock my car. When I got in, I didn't even look back there. Paul, I think that this baby was from that house, the one where the man who was shooting at me lives. I remember thinking I heard a child cry out when I was there."

Paul shook his head. Not in disagreement, but in horror. "I wouldn't be surprised if this sweet little thing was kidnapped and he was shooting to stop you from getting away with her once he realized she was gone. But now I have to see how she got there."

He stepped back to allow them to move past him to the ambulance.

"I need to call this in, see if we have any reports of missing children from the Amish community."

"Would Rebecca know?"

Sergeant Miles Olsen had recently gotten engaged, and his future wife's family was Amish. Rebecca had left the Amish community years ago before she was baptized, allowing her to keep her ties with her family. She was also deaf, and sometimes communication with her family broke down. "I'm not sure. Somehow, I doubt it. And I also need to check with the officers at the scene."

Paul returned to his car and made a call to the station. As he'd expected, there were no reports of any young Amish children vanishing in the area. Considering the discomfort most Amish felt at the idea of involving the police in their community problems, he wasn't surprised.

His next call should have been to child services. He hesitated. If there was someone willing to shoot Irene to keep the identity and location of this child secret, he didn't feel comfortable letting her stay with a regular foster family, who wouldn't have the means to protect themselves and the other children in their care. No, for the moment, this was still police business.

And that brought another concern to the front of his mind. Irene would be in the hospital, but when she left, would that man still be after her? Things obviously weren't on the up-and-up, and she had gotten a very clear view of him. Not to mention his house and the vehicles. Would he come after her again?

And what about that sweet little girl? He called the station again. Remembering the girl's reaction to Trey and himself, he asked for Sergeant Zerosky, fondly known as Sergeant Zee. She picked up, and he sent her over to the hospital to keep watch. He knew she'd protect both Irene and the child.

He pushed the button on his radio again to speak with the officers on the scene.

"There wasn't much to find where the shooting happened. Some glass. Tire marks," Sergeant Gavin Jackson reported. "We're back at the house where the shooter lived. It's a mess. And Olsen found blood on the floor of the back bedroom. I can't tell how recent. It's dry. It's gonna take us a while longer to process this scene."

"Okay, this is a possible kidnapping, and maybe even a murder case. I have a child in custody, presumably kept in that house, who was then stashed away in a vehicle. She's on her way to the hospital right now. While you're processing the scene, keep your eyes peeled for anything that might help us to identify a small Amish girl. Oh, and Irene says she probably has Down syndrome."

"Irene? Jace's sister?"

"Yeah. She was visiting a nearby home. And the child was in her car when she came out—not that Irene noticed at the time, with that maniac chasing after her. We just found the kid about twenty minutes ago. Listen, someone will have to interview the neighbors, too. See what they know about the people at that house."

"Sure thing, boss. I'll keep ya posted."

Paul disconnected. He sat for a minute, musing about the sequences of events. He liked to be able to envision things in his head in order to understand how all the loose pieces fit together.

By the time the tow truck had arrived and pulled the SUV out of the ditch, Jace had appeared. He parked his cruiser behind Paul's, but kept his lights on. Jace stepped out of his vehicle, then sauntered over to meet Paul, looking like a man without a care in the world. Paul knew better. He could see the tense set of Jace's shoulders.

"Hey, Paul." Jace stopped beside him, his eyes grim as he watched his sister's SUV being towed away, a jagged hole where the back window should have been. "I'm going to go to the hospital to see my sister, then I will drive her back to my mom's house. She's got Reenie's kids."

Paul smiled. Only Jace could get away with calling Irene "Reenie."

"She's fine. She had been starting to refuse treatment—against my better judgment—when we made a little discovery."

Jace whistled after Paul had finished bringing him up-to-date. "Whoever said life in a small town was dull? And we have no idea where this child came from?"

"None. It's a mystery. I do want to head to the hospital to get a report on the child's condition." And on Irene's.

Paul drove back toward LaMar Pond. The struggle not to speed was causing his leg to ache with tension. The last thing he needed was to cause another accident on this snowy night, but he was so concerned about Irene that his nerves were taut.

She'd had more than her share of pain in her life. And she might not like it, but if she was in danger, then she'd just have to get used to having him around until she was safe again.

He wouldn't take no for an answer.

What kind of person could take another woman's baby? Irene's heart was shattered as she struggled to withhold the tears brought on by the child's fear and sorrow. It wasn't a hard jump to imagine a mother somewhere, suffering through a nightmare.

Irene held the little girl close as the doctor examined her. She knew the doctor was annoyed that she was getting in his way. She could hear it in his fussy voice and see it as he peered over the tops of his glasses at her. At them. But it made no difference. She had tried to set the child down. The doctors and nurses had tried to coax her away from Irene.

It was no use. The child fought and kicked out any time someone tried to take her from her chosen protector. Which was how it came to be that Irene was allowed to hold her while the doctor examined her. And it was she who had helped the child out of her blood-stained dress. The process was made difficult because the girl wouldn't completely release Irene. Eventually, it was managed. Irene was out of breath by that time.

"Well, the good news is that the child doesn't appear to be hurt. She needs some nutritious food, a bath and, I expect, rest."

Irene nodded. She had already surmised all that. "But the blood? Is any of it hers?"

Please say no.

"No."

She sagged slightly with relief, then caught herself and forced her tired back to straighten. She couldn't give in to the weariness that was dragging at her.

Someone knocked on the door. The child snuggled in closer. Irene leaned down and kissed the child's head, offering what comfort she could. The door opened and Paul peeked into the room. Some of the familiar annoyance surged up briefly. Then it faded, when she remembered how happy she'd been to see him earlier. There had been a time when she had dreamed of Paul noticing her, back when they were both teenagers. Then he *had* noticed her, and for a few short months, she'd been happier than she'd ever been. Until he'd broken her trust and wounded her young heart.

She'd been devastated.

She'd managed to get over that. Had told herself she was better off without him. He'd hung out with a rough crowd back then, she mused. Well, except for Jace. She'd been sure Paul would end up arrested or worse. Before that could happen, he'd moved away for a few years. She couldn't believe it when Jace said he'd become a cop.

Not that she'd cared. She had fallen in love, gotten married and started a family. And then he had come back and become Tony's boss. She had resented that, at first. After all, Tony had seniority. But Tony took it in stride, and, as time went on, Paul had proved to be a good boss. The reckless kid she'd known had learned to control his wild side and become dedicated to serving others. He'd also apparently developed a strong relationship with God.

She had held on to her doubt, waiting for him to disappoint her again.

But tonight, he had been a real gift. If he hadn't come around that corner when he had, she would be dead. And who knew what would have happened to the little girl?

"Hey," he said in a loud whisper. "Jace will be here in a minute. He's talking with your mom on the phone." He indicated the little girl with a nod. "How is she?"

"Well, she's not injured," the doctor replied. "Is someone from child services coming for her?"

Irene grimaced. She had known that would be the next question, and she didn't like it. Not that she had anything against child services. They did a job very few people had the stomach for. But she knew that her new friend was not going to go willingly.

"I have not called child services yet," Paul responded, his voice deep and sure.

What? Shocked, her gaze flew in his direction.

He met her eyes and shrugged. "As far as I'm concerned, this is still a police matter. Speaking of which, Doc, I will need her clothes with blood for DNA testing."

"I'll ask my nurse. Mary—"

All conversation stopped as the girl's head whipped around.

"Does she recognize the name, do you think?" Irene looked between the two men. They looked as surprised as she felt. "Maybe it's her name."

Leaning back so she could see the small face, Irene tested her theory. "Mary? Hi, Mary."

The smile she received was like a ray of sunshine. Mary giggled and hunched her shoulders. It may or may not have been affirmative, but it was better than calling her "the child."

"Okay, then. We will need to keep Mary with us for the time being."

At the name, Mary smiled at Paul. He blinked. An answering smile softened the edges of his mouth. When was the last time she had seen a tender smile on his face? Paul was always in total control of himself. Her heart fluttered as the memory of that same smile from her high school days floated up to the forefront of her mind.

Not going there. He had broken her trust and her faith before. She may have forgiven him, had even allowed his presence in her life and that of her children's due to his friendship with Jace and Tony, but no more. And even if she was willing to believe he could be relied on, if there was one thing she didn't need, it was an emotional entanglement with another cop.

"Where will she stay?"

Paul scratched the top of his head. She knew that mannerism. He was still trying to figure things out. To make all the pieces fit.

"I don't know." She smiled at the admission. She had known it. "I was thinking of having a protective detail with Sergeant Zee in charge. Thought Mary would be more at ease with a woman in charge."

Irene nodded, saddened. A protective detail made sense, but it was a shame that it was needed. This little girl should be with her mother. Hopefully, Mary would be reunited with her family soon.

Jace arrived. Without a word, he walked over and leaned in to kiss Irene's forehead, careful not to crush Mary, who had fallen asleep. Irene blinked at the sweet gesture. She understood. Years ago, their baby sister

Ellie had been killed. This night had reminded them all of their mortality.

The only good thing was that Mary slept through the transfer as Irene passed her off to the nurse who would finish cleaning up the child before turning her over to the police. Irene knew Sergeant Zee. The woman was competent and kind. She had also been a caretaker for her grandmother for a while. She would take good care of Mary.

If Mary let her.

Well, that wasn't Irene's problem. She tried to keep her mind from focusing on the little girl.

"Irene."

Oh, yeah. Paul.

She turned, lifting an eyebrow in question. In place of his normal unruffled demeanor, his brow was furrowed. He was a troubled man.

"I may need you to come in and look at the files to see if you recognize the man who attacked you if no one else can. I will check with his neighbors first. If we can't identify him, I will need to schedule an appointment with the forensic artist to come up with a good sketch we can pass around."

"Okay. I can stop by the station tomorrow, if you need me to."

Jace interrupted, "We won't be able to have anyone work with the artist until next week. You remember? Tara had surgery and won't be back until then."

Paul's mouth twisted. "I had forgotten. Well, if all works out, he'll be someone already in our database. Wouldn't that make life easier?"

Neither responded. Nor did he seem to expect a response.

"Come on, sis. I'll drive you home."

Irene started to head out with her brother. Then she stopped and turned to find Paul's deep brown eyes trained on her. His short dark hair was practically standing on end in places. He'd been running his hands through it. This had been a stressful evening for all of them.

"Paul? Thank you. I mean it. You saved my life tonight."

He nodded and flashed her a weary smile. "Anytime, Irene. I'm glad I was in the area."

Feeling they'd said everything that needed to be said, she left the room. She was so worn-out that she closed her eyes the moment she was seated in the passenger seat of Jace's cruiser.

All she wanted to do was go in and hug her boys. She needed to reassure herself that they were safe and happy. The image of little Mary with her bloodstained clothing was burned into her brain. She would remember that sight for the rest of her life.

At her mother's house, she marched quickly up the walk and in through the front door. Jace had obviously salted the sidewalk and steps, she was happy to note. Her mom met her in the kitchen. Irene endured her mother's scrutiny with as much patience as she could gather. Her mother needed the same reassurance she did.

"Mom, where are the boys?"

"They're watching a Christmas movie." Melanie Tucker, Jace's wife, moved into the kitchen, holding her year-old daughter, Ellie, in her arms.

Irene let the tension roll off her shoulders. She was

safe. They were safe. She stepped past her sister-in-law, running a finger down her niece's cheek.

In the living room, she heard the soft voices of her children. A sudden rush of tears caught her off guard. She struggled for control. They had almost lost her. If Paul Kennedy had been farther away, this night might have had a whole different ending. For the first time in a long time, she felt as if she was being watched over. She shrugged the feeling off.

And thought again of that little girl, left alone. What would become of her?

Then another thought struck. Would the man be able to find out who she was? He'd seen her at the neighbor's house. She had been carrying a bag with the Early Intervention logo on it.

Irene hugged her arms close to her. Would he come looking for her?

The day had started with so much hope. Now it was turning into a nightmare. As long as that man stayed at large, she didn't know how she would ever feel that she and her children were safe.

Chapter Three

"Chief, you need to come out here."

Paul shifted so his phone was wedged between his shoulder and his chin as he shrugged back into his coat. Sergeant Olsen's voice was slightly muffled, but he could still hear the words clearly. Jerking his shoulder to adjust the fit of the coat, he took the cell phone back in his hand and strode out the sliding doors and back into the cold, snowy night.

"I'm heading out now, Olsen. Just needed to wait for Sergeant Zee to get here." He felt a little guilty. She had no idea what was coming when Mary woke up. Maybe it would be fine and Mary would take to her the way she had to Irene. Maybe. But, somehow, he doubted it.

Thinking of Irene left a hollow feeling in his stomach. Was she safe? Jace would have called if something more had happened. But he couldn't get the image of the bearded man out of his mind. He didn't look like a man who would give up. One thing was sure—Paul wouldn't be able to focus as long as Irene was still in danger. He grabbed his phone and put in a call, directing that someone would drive past her house each hour. Being the chief of police definitely had its perks.

At the scene, he parked his cruiser in the driveway behind Olsen's vehicle. It was obvious that the driveway had not been plowed in the past few hours. He couldn't really tell if he was on the pavement or on the grass. Not that it mattered.

"Chief." Olsen trudged through the snow to meet him. "Jackson is with the neighbors right now. The people who called nine-one-one. I figured you might want to go over. And then there are some things in the house I want your opinion on."

Paul nodded. "Right. I'll head right over." He lifted his gaze to the house. It looked dark and ghoulish at night, very poorly lit. It had obviously not been kept up. Just what horrors did it hide inside? The sooner they finished processing this scene, the easier he would feel.

Sergeant Jackson was still talking to the family when Paul entered the room.

"Sir, this is Mr. and Mrs. Zilcher. They called in the shots when the man started shooting after Irene. I mean, Mrs. Martello."

Paul focused in on the stressed faces of the young couple. What a way to spend their evening.

"Folks, thanks for calling it in. Mrs. Martello is safe, no doubt because you were so brave." That was certainly true. He shuddered to think what would have happened if the couple hadn't notified the police. He wouldn't have known to head in this direction, and Irene…

He took in a deep breath, noticing that everyone was staring at him. Now was not the time to think of Irene. Pushing thoughts of the lovely widow out of his mind, he recommitted himself to getting to the bottom of the case. As soon as humanly possible. With lots of Divine help.

Lord, I place Irene, my officers, that child, and all involved in Your hands.

"Do you know the people who live in that house?"

Mrs. Zilcher bit her lip, then she ducked her head, as if ashamed. "I know it sounds bad, but we avoided them. They seemed, I don't know... Honey?"

She turned to her husband.

"The first time we saw them, the younger man—not the one who fired the shots—yelled at our older son for playing too near their property. Now, Joel is only six. He wasn't doing any harm, but that man scared him so much that ever since, we have just avoided them at all costs."

Paul nodded. It made sense. "And would I be correct to assume that your son never went near the house again?"

"Chief, this has always been a very safe area. But in the past two months since they arrived, I don't even let him go outside in the backyard alone. And it's fenced in."

Smart move.

"What about this afternoon? After the man pursued Mrs. Martello, did he come back?"

"No. But within half an hour, all of them took off." Mrs. Zilcher twisted her wedding ring. "I didn't see them come out, but I heard lots of loud revving, and then the truck and the car both left. I haven't seen them since."

The man who went after Irene must have warned them when he saw Paul's police car approaching.

Paul broke into their narrative. "Who is 'them'? Can you describe the people you saw there? Anything you can remember will help. Age, gender, descriptions… anything at all."

"Well, let's see," Mrs. Zilcher ticked them off on her fingers. "There was that young guy. Just an average-looking man. Maybe in his early twenties? Blondish hair, collar length. Average build. Really, no one you'd look twice at if you saw him on the street or at the store. Then the big guy who shot at Irene, our service coordinator. He was a handsome enough man. Well groomed. But he looked so fierce. Probably late thirties, early forties. Not overweight, but big. Definitely over six feet. The last guy I never got a real good look at." She turned to her husband.

He shook his head. "I didn't, either. He was usually pretty covered up. Hats, hooded sweatshirts, hunting coats. Got the impression that he tried to keep from being noticed. Only glimpsed him briefly when I did see him. And then I only really saw him from the back."

"Did you ever notice a young woman, maybe in her late teens or early twenties, at the house?"

Both of them shook their heads.

So how long had she been there? And was she one of them or another victim? Paul was starting to get a very ugly picture in his mind.

"What about any children?"

"Children?" Mrs. Zilcher blinked, startled. "No, I certainly never saw any children there."

Half an hour later, that picture was even darker.

Going through the abandoned house was not something that Paul was likely to forget. In the back bedroom, around where Irene would have seen the girl looking out the window, there was indeed dried blood on the floor. Recent blood. There was some on the wall, too. One spot looked like a handprint, tiny and low to the ground. Either from a very young person or someone who was very small. The team had already pulled fingerprints and would see if they could track down any matches. Hopefully, there would be something in their system that would connect to either Mary or the girl Irene had seen. Paul refused to think of what might have happened to her. She was gone, so there was a shot she was still alive, though his faith in finding her alive was fading. And it would continue to fade every hour that they couldn't find her.

His cell phone rang. It was Irene. His pulse spiked. Irene never called him.

"Irene? Are you okay? Is someone hurt?"

There was a moment of silence on the other end, then a breathy sound, almost a laugh but not quite. "Paul, I'm fine. You startled me. I'm not used to hearing you yell."

He *had* yelled, hadn't he? Stretching his neck to the side to relieve his sudden tension, he tried again, keeping his voice calm.

"Sorry. I didn't mean to yell. But you caught me at a tense moment."

"Oh. Is everything okay?" Her voice was reluctantly concerned.

"With me, everything's dandy. But this house, Irene, it's bad. Really bad." He shook his head, deciding not to say any more. She might have been married to a cop, but she still was a civilian. And he wanted to spare her from the rougher parts of his job. Not that she'd ever give him a chance to share anything more. He had more or less shattered any chance with her, now or in the future, when he'd abandoned her on that long-ago home-coming night. If only he could explain why…

He scoffed silently. That would make her even more resistant, knowing his secrets. No, his secret scars would have to remain that way.

"I just realized something, that's why I called. When I was thinking about the girl in the house, the one who was watching me? Well, I just realized that she looked like there was something around her neck. And now, thinking about it, I believe they were bonnet straps. I think she was Amish, too, just like Mary."

"What else was she wearing?"

"I couldn't tell. She was mostly out of view. I'm sorry. I'm probably not much help." Her voice was growing embarrassed.

"No, actually, you are. I have more information than I did before—that's always a good thing."

So now they needed to search for a missing child and a missing girl. They would start searching in the local Amish communities. If they didn't succeed there, then they would widen their search.

"Thanks, Irene. I mean it. Every detail helps."

"How's Mary doing?"

His heart softened. Irene, always thinking about the plight of others. She'd always been that way. "I left her with Sergeant Zee."

"Did she go quietly?"

"Yeah, but that was probably because she was asleep."

"Paul!"

He sighed, rolling his eyes. She couldn't see him, after all. "I will check on her first thing in the morning. Promise."

After disconnecting the call, he went to the room where Olsen was taking pictures.

"What did you want to see me about, Olsen?"

"Look at all this stuff, Chief. What do you make of it?"

There was a trunk full of children's clothes in various sizes and colors. All of them showed signs of wear. And there was a pair of Amish breeches on top. Beside the trunk, there was a bottle, still half-full, and a dirty sippy cup.

"Mary wasn't the only child these people have taken, is my guess. Maybe they still have one or two of them. What they were planning to do with them, I don't know. But we need to find them. Fast."

Before any more children were taken. Or worse.

Irene couldn't remember the last time she'd been so tired. Last night, she had tossed and turned. When she had finally fallen into a restless sleep, it was to be disturbed in her dreams by images of being chased at gunpoint. She finally gave up. It was only quarter after six, but she knew trying to fall back to sleep was hopeless. Throwing back the covers, she padded to the boys' bedroom and peeked in. Both were still sound asleep. She sighed, aching with tenderness at the sight of the peaceful children.

Since the peace wouldn't last, she might as well get ready for the day. She dressed in casual jeans and an emerald green turtleneck sweater. She lugged out her workbag, shaking off the memories.

Pulling out her laptop, she spent some time finishing an evaluation report. By the time it was completed, she could hear the boys arguing in the kitchen. They were up early. Normally, the thought of facing their fighting at seven o'clock on a Saturday morning would annoy her. The memory of the night before washed away any trace of aggravation. She was here, safe, with her kids. That was a lot to be grateful for.

She entered the kitchen, kissed her boys and ruffled their hair as she walked past. Their dog, Izzy, was peacefully snoozing under the table.

"Hi, Mommy!" Matthew peeked up at her with his ragged grin, his front teeth missing. "Can we have waffles for breakfast?"

That was Matthew. His stomach always came first.

"Waffles sound good to me. AJ?"

Her older son peered at her through his new glasses. My, he was looking so grown-up. When had her baby become such a big boy?

Tony would have loved this.

"Waffles are yummy. Can we set up the tree today?"

Ugh. The Christmas tree. One more thing she didn't want to face. But at least she could give her children the fun parts of Christmas.

She made them waffles, and then the boys helped her drag out the artificial tree and ornaments. She sat down in the center of the living room floor to sort the ornaments, AJ by her side. As she was unraveling the lights, Matthew stood at the window, his face intent. She frowned when she noted him standing on his tiptoes, straining to see something.

"Matthew, why are you staring out the window?"

"I'm watching the man, Mommy."

She set aside the strand of lights in her hands, unease dancing down her spine. It could be nothing, but she wasn't taking any chances.

"What man, darling?" *Calm. Stay calm. The last thing they need is for you to overreact.*

"That man across the street." Matthew hadn't turned around, still intent on the stranger.

"Matthew, come away from the window." How she was able to keep from raising her voice she'd never know.

Something in her tone must have said she meant business, though, because Matthew left his place and skittered down on the floor beside her, his small face pale. The freckles on his cheeks stood out.

"Mommy, I'm scared."

Her poor baby.

"It's okay, love, I'm going to call Chief Paul. He'll know what to do."

Crawling over to the end table, she grabbed her phone and dialed Paul's number with shaking fingers. It wasn't until the phone started ringing that she wondered why she'd instinctively called him and not Jace. Because Paul helped her last night? Of course that was why. She moved to the window and peered out, taking care to keep out of sight. There parked on the street across from her was a dark sedan. Was that the one that had been sitting at the bearded man's house?

"Hello."

Paul's deep drawl sent a shiver down her spine. She scolded herself. She didn't have time for that. Sure, he was strong and was well respected in LaMar Pond, but he was hiding something. She was certain. Only, right now, it didn't seem to matter.

"Paul," she whispered. "There's a man sitting in his car outside my house. He's watching us. And I can't be sure, but it may be one of the people from that house. The car looks familiar."

"Irene, are the boys with you?" His voice had lost all trace of the lazy, relaxed drawl. Its intensity communicated his concern over the phone.

"Yes, we are all here."

"Okay, this is what I want you to do. Make sure the doors are locked. And keep away from the windows. Whatever you do, do *not* answer the door unless it's me or Jace. I'm going to call him right now. He's closer to your house. I will be over as soon as I can."

Click.

She slid the phone back into her pocket and looked at the two frightened faces before her.

"Boys, let's go back to the kitchen."

"Aren't we setting up the tree?" AJ asked, disappointment on his face.

Matthew didn't argue. He was already halfway there.

"We'll make Christmas cookies first," Irene declared, coming up with an impromptu diversion. Both faces brightened.

Her phone rang again. Paul.

"Jace is on his way, too. Sit tight, Irene. We'll be there ASAP."

Her nerves were shot by the time Jace arrived. She saw his car pull around the corner from the kitchen window. Immediately, an engine revved. She heard tires squeal as a car raced in the opposite direction. The watcher had left. The cruiser's lights burst into a swirl of blue and red as Jace followed in pursuit.

Less than five minutes later, someone pounded on her front door. Yelping, she dropped the bowl of icing she'd just whipped together. The silver bowl bounced, flinging white icing on the cupboard doors and all over her blue jeans.

"Irene? It's me. Paul."

Paul. She placed a hand over her pounding heart and closed her eyes, fighting the urge to wilt against the countertops.

"Mommy, Chief Paul is here." AJ frowned as the chief called out again. "Should I let him in?"

"No! No, I will do it. You boys stay here and wipe up this mess. Please."

They looked less than thrilled, but both nodded. She had expected some protest. Especially from AJ. That neither boy offered even a token resistance told her that they had sensed the seriousness of the situation.

She moved to the door and opened it. She came face-to-face with Paul, his hand raised to knock again. Patent relief flashed across his face as he saw her. His gaze moved over her, checking for injury or signs of distress. She knew the moment he spotted the icing by the way his mouth curled up at the sides. Not exactly a grin, but she could tell he was amused.

Only for a moment, however. The smile vanished so fast she might have imagined it.

"Jace went after the guy," she informed him.

He nodded. "Yeah, he almost caught him, too. The guy got out and took off running across the interstate. Unfortunately, Jace didn't get a good look at him. The Zilchers are coming in to look through the data files. I think you should do that, too. Immediately, if not sooner. In the meantime, Jace is going to go over the car the guy abandoned. See what he can get from it."

There was no way she could refuse. If this was related to what had happened the day before, they had found out where she lived. The situation was as serious and urgent as it could get. "My kids..."

Paul laid a hand on her shoulder. She shivered. The warmth of his hand spread out. Not now. This was not a good idea. She moved back.

"Take them to your mom's house. Jace already called her."

She had no choice. Reluctantly, she agreed. The reluctance was partially because she didn't want to be separated from them right now. And, she admitted to herself, partly because she didn't like this awareness of Paul that seemed to be returning. The thought of spending more time alone with him was unsettling. She wasn't a high school girl anymore—what was wrong with her?

As she bundled them up for the trip to her mother's, she couldn't stop the dread quivering in her belly. She had to work hard to keep her apprehension from showing on her face. Kids were sensitive. They would pick up on her disquiet in a heartbeat.

But her mother's heart wouldn't let it go.

"Paul," she began as she made her way back to the living room with two boys wrapped up tight in their winter gear. She stopped. Paul was no longer alone. Jace and Miles were there, deep in conversation. The men stopped talking when she appeared.

Paul nodded at the other two men and approached Irene and the boys. "Hey, guys. How would you like a ride to your grandma's in a police car?" He grinned at the boys like he was suggesting an adventure, rather than moving to get them out of harm's way. "Sergeant Olsen was wanting to visit your gran. Think she'll have cookies he can swipe?"

AJ nodded, his face serious. "Yeah, Granny always has cookies. But he better ask first."

"And say please," Matthew added.

"I'm sure he will." Paul patted their heads affectionately.

His eyes, though, when he glanced back at Irene, were completely devoid of humor.

He's as worried as I am.

That scared her most of all.

Chapter Four

Two hours later, she sat back with a sigh, disappointed. No one in the mug shots looked familiar. But she really hadn't expected they would. Jace was more fortunate. Mrs. Zilcher had identified the owner of the car. Jace felt certain it was the same man who had escaped from him that morning. His runner was wanted for several assault charges. A man by the name of Niko Carter. Jace immediately put out the alert to apprehend the young man. Unfortunately, the car was clean of any evidence that could be connected to Mary or other missing children.

There was nothing left for her to do here.

"I guess I should get the boys and go back home," she said to no one in particular. "I don't have my car back yet. I'm going to need a ride."

Jace stood and stretched. "I can drive you. Just give me a few minutes."

Paul's voice stopped him. "It's okay, Jace. I want to talk with Irene about what we should do to keep her and the boys safe. I'll take her to your mom's. It would be more efficient."

Jace acquiesced, his lips twitching as he raised an eyebrow. Irene felt her skin warm as embarrassment—and something she wasn't quite ready to name—sizzled under her skin. As she walked out past Jace, she gave him her best narrow-eyed stare, daring him to tease. He shrugged, but continued to smile. Then he surprised her by standing and kissing her cheek. Jace might not have said it, but she knew he was concerned about her. After their sister Ellie had died, Jace had become over-protective of Irene. It had taken years for him to learn to let her have her space, but she knew it still ate at him to see her distressed or in any kind of danger. She reached out and squeezed his arm, silently telling him she understood.

Once she was seated beside him and they were on their way, Paul didn't waste any time bringing up his concerns.

"Irene." His deep voice settled between them.

She turned her head and raised an eyebrow.

"I talked with Zee while you were looking at the files. Mary's doing fine, although she's a little cranky."

"That's good to hear. Thank you for telling me."

He nodded, then continued. "I don't need to tell you that this is a potentially dangerous situation. I'm changing my orders. Instead of an hourly drive-by, I'm putting a detail on your house around the clock. Just until the danger passes."

She'd been expecting that, and as much as she treasured her independence, she accepted it gratefully. It wasn't only her life at stake here. Her boys were in danger, too.

"The department's going to be stretched tight between the detail on you and searching for Mary's family."

She nodded. Then a thought occurred to her. "What about my car?"

"I will check on the status when we arrive at your mother's house."

The boys were thrilled to see her arrive with Paul. They chattered happily about the time spent with their grandmother and the new puppies her neighbor's dog had just had that morning. Irene fended off subtle hints about getting a new puppy with ease born of practice. She could hear Paul talking to the mechanic about her car in the other room.

"Your vehicle's fixed," he announced as he entered the room. "The only problem was the windshield, and your insurance covered that. We'll drive by and pick it up on our way back to your house."

She smiled. It would be nice to have her car back. She thanked her mother, then gathered her boys and got them situated in the cruiser. Twenty minutes later, they had stopped to get her SUV, and were again on their way. It was comforting to look back in her review mirror and see Paul following her.

The closer they drove to her home, however, the more anxiety twisted in her gut. Would that man be watching the house again when they returned? Would she and her children be safe? She breathed a sigh of relief when she rounded the corner and no one was there. Still, she waited until Paul was parked behind her to get out of the car.

She scooted the kids inside as soon as Paul had checked the house and declared it was safe. When they looked like they wanted to complain, she reminded them that Izzy had probably been lonely and would need to be fed and walked. They hurried inside to see to the dog.

She nodded her thanks at Paul, then continued into the house. Paul pulled out his phone. She could hear his voice murmuring as she closed the door before moving into the kitchen.

Should she have stayed at her mother's house for a day or two? She pondered the idea for a brief moment before rejecting it. No. Her mom was a worrier. And she still had normal things to do. Like go to work. And the boys had to go to school. She'd have to consider her next step carefully.

She put a kettle on the stove. A cup of tea might help settle her nerves a bit. Paul walked into the room just as she began pouring hot water over the mixed-berry tea bag.

She indicated the tea with her free hand. "Want a cup? Or I can make some coffee."

A smile flickered briefly across his handsome face. "Nah. I'm good. Listen, we might have a slight problem."

She tensed. Apprehension skittered up her spine. What else could go wrong?

"I have a small gap in the morning where I will be without coverage for you. Jace and Miles are flying out tonight because they are witnesses in a trial this coming week. Sergeant Zee's looking after Mary. I have Thompson keeping an eye on her house. And the other officers have assignments they're working on. I'm the only one left, and I take my mother to church every week. She can't drive anymore. Her vision's too bad now."

Church. Did he expect her to go with him? She hadn't

gone inside a church since Tony had died unless it was for a wedding. Lifting her mug, she took a small sip, holding the hot liquid in her mouth to enjoy the subtle flavors.

Apparently, her ambivalence got through to him. Paul's expression was bland, but she could feel his withdrawal. "Of course, my mom will understand if I cancel one week. She can watch services on TV."

And now she felt mean.

"We'll go with you." What was she thinking? But it was too late to back down. "The boys and I will go with you and your mother to church."

Maybe, with all that was going on, maybe it was time she gave God another chance. Paul's expression lightened. It almost made up for the mass of nerves in her stomach. Almost.

Paul hung around until the first patrol showed up outside the house. She could see the officer inside the car. It was one of the older officers she'd known for years, and the sight of him was comforting.

The day passed smoothly, but by nighttime, her nerves were all jangled. The phone rang. She let out a shriek, startled by the noise.

Silly, she chastised herself.

"Hello?" she answered the phone.

Whoever it was hung up.

Wrong number. Or was it him? Had he called to see if she was home? Running to the living room, she stood beside the window and peered out. The current patrol was there. She could see the man inside the car moving around. She was safe.

An hour later, the phone rang again.

Again, the person on the other end of the line hung up.

Now she was freaked-out. Maybe she should run out and tell the cop. Tell him what? That someone had hung up on her? That was hardly a crime. And there was no way on earth she was walking outside and leaving her babies inside unprotected. They were in bed, but they would still be vulnerable.

No. She would wait.

After changing into sweats, she tried to sleep. She tossed and turned until, finally, she dropped off into a restless sleep.

Only to be awoken by the sound of the dog barking at five in the morning. Not just barking. But growling and lunging at the back door.

Irene jumped out of bed, her heart pounding. Running to the boys' room, she checked to make sure they were safe. Both were sound asleep.

Izzy continued to bark. Irene crept down the hall in time to see the dog lunge viciously at the back door, scratching the wood as she tried to get at whatever was threatening the family.

Izzy never did that. She had been too well trained.

That's when Irene knew. Something evil was out there. Or someone.

What was that noise? Paul had been feeling a bit sleepy after sitting in the dark for the past two hours, but now he was on full alert. There. He heard it again. From where he sat inside his cruiser in Irene's driveway, it sounded like it was coming from inside her house, though he couldn't tell from where.

Paul rolled down his window and listened.

Izzy was barking. And it wasn't a normal bark. It was the bark of a dog protecting her family. Adrenaline flooded his system. Irene and the boys might be in danger. He reached over and picked up the flashlight, shoving it in his pocket as he hopped out of his vehicle and ran up to her front door, mindful of the snow crunching beneath his feet. He would be of no use to her if he fell and injured himself on her driveway.

He pounded on her door.

She screamed from inside the house. His heart stopped at the sound.

"Irene!" He raised his hand to pound on the door a second time.

Footsteps, running toward him. Then the door was yanked open. He saw her white face for just a moment before she launched herself into his arms. Unprepared for the onslaught, he stumbled back two steps until he regained his balance. He hugged her and, at the same time, moved them both inside the house. Shutting the door, he gave her a squeeze, then released her. The dog was still growling at the back door.

"Are you and the boys all right?"

She opened her mouth, but only a broken sob emerged. All she could manage was a nod. That was fine. As long as she and the kids were unhurt. That was all that mattered.

"Mommy? Mommy!" AJ and Matthew hurtled into the room, tears on their cheeks. Nothing scared a child as much as knowing their parent was frightened. Irene visibly pulled her emotions under control.

Izzy was still barking at the back door, scratching frantically to get out.

"It's okay, boys. When Izzy started barking, Paul came to check on us. The noise of him knocking startled me, that's all." She bent and kissed the boys. They didn't look convinced, but allowed her to lead them back to their bedroom. Paul took advantage of her absence and checked the locks on the doors and the windows, nodding in satisfaction when all was secure. She returned to stand near him.

He absolutely should not be noticing the scent of her shampoo as she stood close. Moving to the door, he refocused on the job at hand. Irene pulled the dog back from the door.

"You stay here," Paul commanded, pulling the flashlight out of his pocket. He flipped it on, keeping the beam low. His service weapon was in his other hand. "Lock the door after me. Don't open it until I tell you to. No matter what."

The moment she nodded, he was out the door. He waited just a moment until he heard it latch and the dead bolt was slid back in place. Then he was off, searching for any sign of movement or disturbance. The snow was far too messed up by footprints from the Martello family and Izzy to really see if any new tracks were visible.

As he approached the backyard, he noticed that the barking inside the house had lessened. Then it stopped altogether. He sighed. Whoever or whatever had been there had likely taken off again. Who knows? Maybe it wasn't a person at all, but a black bear, instead. They sometimes woke up and left their dens, wandering around searching for more food. It wouldn't be the first time a confused bear had wandered so close to a home.

It was a possible explanation—but not a very likely one. He didn't buy it for a second. And a minute later, his gut was proved correct as he moved along the thick row of bushes that lined the perimeter of the property line. Near the north corner, he found a suspicious break in the shrubbery. A hole just large enough for some-one to slip through. Moving closer, he shined his light on the ground. There, showing up starkly on the white snow, were cut branches. No bear had done this. The branches were sawed cleanly off. Likely with a pair of heavy-duty shears. So whoever had done it had come prepared. Which meant that Irene was being watched by someone who knew there was a policeman parked out front and had taken steps to sneak in through the back. He used his radio to call in to the station. Ryan Parker and Gavin Jackson were on duty.

"Chief?"

Jackson. Concisely, Paul brought the officer up to speed on what he'd found.

"Okay. Parker and I will be out ASAP."

Paul hung up and looked again at the bush. Someone was very determined.

He shuddered. What would have happened if Irene hadn't had Izzy to warn him of the would-be intruder?

Stop. He couldn't let himself go there. Nor could he allow any of the emotional attachments he had for the family, or for Irene, to interfere with his focus. It was on him to keep Irene, AJ and Matthew safe. He would do everything in his power to protect them. Which meant putting the people out to get Irene behind bars.

If he could protect Irene and her family and get little Mary back to her family, he would be content.

He remembered the look on Irene's face when they'd found the little girl. It had been plain to see that her heart ached for the child's parents. Just thinking of Irene made him anxious to check on her again, make sure she was still all right.

"Irene?" Paul called, knocking. "Open up. It's me, Paul."

Subdued and worn-out, she let him in. It had only been a day and a half since this whole mess started, and yet it seemed to have aged her right before his eyes. How much could one person take?

Paul shut the door behind him, locked it, then faced her. His eyes narrowed as they took in her expression. Without a word, he reached out and enfolded her into his embrace. She let him. Which proved just how unsettled she was. After a minute, he felt her stiffen and pull back. Reluctantly, he let her go. Immediately, he missed her closeness and wanted to take her back into his arms, to smooth the strain off her pretty face. He resisted the impulse, knowing it wasn't the time. Nor did he have the right. Instead, he had to content himself with letting his eyes roam her face, just to assure himself that she was well.

"I'm okay. Really," she insisted as his right eyebrow nudged upward. "Just tired. And aggravated. Was it a bear?"

He wished he could tell her it had been.

Her shoulders drooped as he shook his head. "I don't think so. A hole has been cut in the hedges out yonder." He waved in the direction of the left corner of her lot. She and Tony had planted bushes all around the perimeter of the backyard. Thick bushes that would have been hard to fit through. "A hole big enough for a man to fit through. The branches were lying there, and they had clearly been cut with shears. Someone was here, but Izzy kept them at bay."

Tears welled up in her eyes. Oh, man. He hated to see her beautiful blue eyes filled with tears. It ripped his heart to pieces seeing her in pain. Irene rubbed the tears away, then knelt and gave the blond Labrador a hug. Izzy returned the favor in the form of doggy kiss with her wet tongue.

"Oh, yuck. Thanks, Izzy." Irene leaned her head back to consider Paul. "Don't take this the wrong way. I'm glad you showed up. But why are you here? Where is the officer on duty?"

He grinned.

"I *am* the officer on duty. We are short-staffed, re-member? I have two new hires that will be starting next week. Until then, we're making do. I have my shaving kit and a change of clothes for church in the car."

She grimaced.

He hesitated. "Or we could stay here if you'd feel safer keeping indoors?"

She vehemently shook her head. "No. I feel like I need to get out of here for a few hours. And it's church. What could happen there?"

Chapter Five

The church had changed since she'd last been inside it. Minor things. It had been painted, undergone some redecorating, and the social hall had been remodeled. It was easier to focus on these details than on what was happening around her.

Her emotions were a roller coaster. When Paul leaned over to grab the hymnal, she found herself inhaling deeper, enjoying the scent of his understated cologne. Realizing what she was doing, she jerked away from him. He gave her a quizzical look. She busied herself looking around, trying to ignore the heat rising up her neck and cheeks.

After the service, she found herself surrounded by people welcoming her back into the fold. Although there were those who just wanted to satisfy their curiosity or get some fodder for gossip, most of them were genuinely glad to see her back after so long. She didn't see Melanie and Jace. They had probably gone to an earlier service so he could attend church before he and Miles flew out.

When Paul made a general excuse that they should be on their way because his mother needed to get home, she agreed with alacrity. Disappointed to see her go, but unwilling to argue with the police chief, most of the crowd shuffled back into the aisle to make their way to the doors that led to the outside of the stone church building.

"Thanks for the rescue," Irene murmured as Paul put a warm hand on her elbow and motioned for her and the boys to walk ahead of him. "I never know what to say in situations like that."

"It's okay. I don't know what makes people do that."

Someone jostled her from behind. Irene startled and turned her head to see a strange young man. He gave her an apologetic smile.

It was a bit crowded. It must have just been an accident. She nodded and smiled back. She didn't recognize him, but then she hadn't been here for so long, there were bound to be new faces. She turned back to Paul. He had his phone out.

"In church?"

Okay, so now she sounded like her mother. She was way too young for that.

Paul grimaced, but slid his phone back into his pocket.

"Sorry, just checking on Sergeant Zee. Mary seems to be doing all right. Probably because Zee is a woman. And the red hair might have something to do with it." She hadn't considered it, but if Mary's mother had red hair, it might have been comforting for her—drawing her first to trust Irene, and then to trust Sergeant Zee.

"Any luck finding her family yet?"

"No. I will drive to Spartansburg soon. Take a look around. Want to come?"

Surprised that he would ask, she hesitated.

His face went blank. "You don't have to. I just thought that it would be easier if we could take Mary along, since the Amish community wouldn't be comfortable with us showing a picture of the child. And Zee has something else she needs to attend to."

Regret rose up. She hadn't meant to make him feel bad, but she sensed her hesitation had done just that. "Of course, I want to come. It can't be today, though. My neighbor across the street has her sister visiting today. I promised I would go over for a bit and show them how to set up Skype accounts. The sister is moving out of state."

Paul nodded, looking thoughtful. "What time?"

She shrugged, catching the end of her braid in one hand and twisting it.

"I don't know. Sometime after lunch. She'll text me."

He opened his mouth to say something, then shut it as they neared the pastor. They greeted the man, then scurried to catch up with Mrs. Kennedy and the boys, who were halfway across the parking lot.

Paul opened her door for her, and Irene started to slide into the back seat next to her sons. She looked up and stopped.

"Paul, do you know that young man?"

Paul looked over where she was pointing. The man who had bumped into her in church had been staring after them while talking on his phone. The intensity of his gaze made her shiver. He was now busy talking to some of the older women as they left. The women were laughing. So maybe they knew him. She felt like an idiot.

"I've never seen him before." Paul frowned. He discreetly held up his phone and took a picture of the man. "He could just be someone new to the area."

Irene ducked into the back seat with AJ and Matthew. Paul cast one last look at the man. Then he got in and yanked his seat belt in place.

"Y'all ready?"

They dropped off Mrs. Kennedy first. Irene had expected Paul to take her and the boys home first. Then she remembered. Understaffed. There was no one to keep an eye on them but him. Yeah, she had forgotten about that one. Sighing, Irene sank back against the seat, rubbing her hands against her thighs as she gazed out the window.

"Why don't you move up front?"

It would have been ridiculous to refuse. And she didn't mind sitting next to Paul. Frowning, she changed seats, not sure why she was suddenly feeling so low. She hated to think it was because Paul was spending time with her solely because it was his duty. Because that would mean that she wanted him to spend time with her by his own choice. And she didn't. Did she? She tried to convince herself she wasn't developing renewed feelings for the handsome man beside her.

"Looks like Nola's sister's arrived," she commented as Paul swung his car into her drive. A blue compact car was sitting in the driveway across the street.

"Have you ever met her sister?"

She opened her mouth to reply, but AJ exploded out of the car, Matthew hot on his tail. "Mommy! I'm hungry. Is Chief Paul eating lunch with us?"

Irene chuckled at her guys. They would give the Energizer Bunny a run for his money, that's for sure. "Okay, okay. I can only answer one question at a time.

Chief Paul is welcome to eat with us. As long as he doesn't mind cheeseburgers and French fries."

He grinned. "Yum. I will even help you make 'em."

She nodded, shooing the boys ahead of her. "You two change out of your church clothes, then you can have a few minutes of free time before lunch. But stay in the house." Her heart twinged at the way their shoulders drooped, but she needed to keep them safe. That had to be her priority.

"Aw, Mom!"

"Hey, Junior…don't sass your mama." Paul tussled AJ's hair, a crooked smile flashing across his face.

At the familiar pet name—the one her husband had used for AJ—Irene's stomach dropped. She realized she had been enjoying Paul's company and hadn't even thought of Tony until now.

Better get things back on track. "And no," she responded to Paul. He looked puzzled. "I have never met her sister. But she talks about her all the time."

The hungry group made their way inside. Soon, the aroma of sizzling meat and baking fries was pungent in the air. Paul set the table while Irene fixed the food. When it was ready, the children were called and they sat down to eat.

It felt like a normal family thing to do, Irene thought with a pang. And Paul was seated at the head of the table as if he belonged there. Tears stung her eyes. She blinked them away. Never had she been so grateful to hear her cell phone ping. *Great timing, Nola.*

"It's Nola. As soon as lunch is done, I'm going to go over."

Paul frowned. He didn't say anything, though, until

they were finished eating and the boys were cleaning up the dishes.

"I should go with you," he said in a low voice.

She snorted. Loudly. "Please. Paul, this is my neighbor. And these are plans we made before I was in danger. You can watch me cross the street. And I will text you before I start back. But I don't want to leave the kiddos alone, and they'd just be bored if they came with me."

She could see that he wanted to argue. She lifted her chin and crossed her arms, daring him. After all, she was an adult. And it was daylight. Not to mention the fact that there was a police car in front of her house. Anybody would have to be crazy to try to attack her with the chief of police just across the street.

She knew she'd won when he sighed.

"Fine. Do me a favor, though. Give me a thumbs-up when you get there to let me know everything's good."

Irene rolled her eyes. It sounded like something she would tell her boys when she dropped them off at a friend's house. Not like something you'd tell a woman who was almost thirty. Still it was sweet, in a way.

Grabbing her phone, she put on her coat and headed across the street.

Humming under her breath, she rang the doorbell. And waited. When no one answered, she shrugged and frowned. The doorbell must not be working. She knocked. Footsteps crossed the wooden floor just behind the door. Finally. She'd been starting to worry. The door opened.

"Hi—" The greeting that was ready on her lips died as she spotted the person standing behind sweet little Nola.

The young man Jace had identified in the police station. The one who had been watching her.

"You took long enough. Get in the house. Now."

The impulse to scream or throw some sort of fit was strong. Anything to let Paul know something was wrong, that she had walked into a trap. But she couldn't. Because he was holding a gun.

And it was pointed right at Nola.

Paul had watched from the doorway, growing increasingly uneasy the longer the door stayed unopened. The women were expecting Irene. What was the holdup, anyhow?

But finally the door opened, and Paul had seen the older woman standing in it. She looked frail from his position.

Why wasn't Irene going inside? She was a target out here.

And why wasn't she giving him a thumbs-up?

After an eternity, she began to move inside the house. He sighed in relief, glad she was getting out of the open. Her hand moved up behind her back to give him the requested thumbs-up.

Only she didn't.

She gave him a thumbs-down.

Then she was inside the house.

What? Something was terribly wrong. Paul grabbed his cell phone and called for backup. He started for the door, ready to dart across the road. Wait. The kids were in the house.

What could he do? He couldn't wait to go after Irene. She'd obviously walked into some kind of ambush.

"AJ! Matthew!" The boys came running. "Listen to me. This is very important. Are you listening?"

Both boys nodded, their young eyes flaring wide and anxious at the tone in his voice.

"Your mama needs my help. Now. I have to go across the street. I need you to stay in the house. Lock the doors. Keep Izzy with you and do not open the door unless it's me, your mama or one of the officers that you know. Don't even open to an officer you don't know. Clear?"

"Yes, sir," AJ said. Matthew nodded, his eyes fearful.

Man, he didn't want to scare the kids, but he had no choice. As soon as the door was locked behind him, he was off, running across the street to the house Irene had disappeared into five minutes earlier. He moved around the house, peering in windows. He couldn't risk barging in and maybe getting Irene killed.

The back door was open a smidgen.

He nudged it open a little farther. Weapon out and ready, he slid along the wall. Voices were coming from deeper in the house. An older woman's quavering voice. A man's angry growl. Irene's calming voice—the tone she used to restore peace when her kids were fighting.

A slap. A woman cried out. Irene. The sound of something hitting the floor. Hard.

That was it. Moving quickly, he came to the doorway and peered in. An elderly woman was on the couch, her arms tied behind her at an uncomfortable angle. A young man was standing in the middle of the room. But not just any young man. This particular man's photo was hanging up in the station and had been sent around to other stations in the area. He was standing over Irene, who was in a heap on the floor. And that man was pointing a gun at her, ready to shoot. Rage like Paul had never known surged through his veins. Instead of clouding his mind, though, he saw everything with startling clarity.

"Police! Drop your weapon!" Paul stepped into view, his service weapon held in front of him, trained on the would-be assassin.

With a roar, the man wheeled on Paul and whipped his own gun up. His intent was clear. He had his finger on the trigger. He shot. Paul dodged and the picture behind him shattered. With a yell, the man pivoted slightly and took aim a second time. This time at Irene.

Paul fired.

The man fell.

Paul knew immediately he was dead. Sorrow struck him. He hated taking a life. Any life. But he knew he'd had no choice. The man had been intent on killing Irene.

Paul replaced his weapon and hurried over to check on the two women. The older woman seemed unharmed though clearly frightened out of her mind. And who could blame her?

Irene was sporting a bloody lip from where she'd been struck. Otherwise, she seemed fine. He crouched down to her level. With a sob, she threw her arms around his neck, almost strangling him. He buried his face in her hair. He had nearly lost her. Five minutes later...

He couldn't bear to even think along those lines. A shudder ran through him.

"Chief!"

With one last deep breath to steady himself, Paul pulled away from Irene. Searching her drenched eyes, he was relieved to see she was calmer. He moved back more, and her arms fell from his neck. Immediately, he wanted to pull her close again.

Instead, he stood.

"In here, Parker!"

Sergeant Ryan Parker entered, his eyes widening as he took in the scene.

"My kids!" Irene bounded to her feet, her expression wild.

"Easy, Irene. They are okay. I had them lock themselves in with the dog. They know not to answer except to one of us."

"Can I go to them?" The words were meek, the expression was not.

He pitied the person who would dare to stand between Irene and her children. He certainly wouldn't. He had Parker escort her back across the street while he stayed to interview Nola. Halfway through the interview, her sister arrived. He had to wait through the new storm of tears. And then the paramedics arrived to check her out. There were no visible injuries, but since she had a known heart condition, they were taking no chances. He would have to visit her later to get the rest of her report.

"Sir, you might wanna see this."

"What do you have, Parker?" Paul slipped on latex gloves from the box Parker had brought with him.

Parker handed him a picture from the dead man's wallet. Paul had already recognized him as Niko Carter, the man who had been watching Irene's house the previous day. His collar-length blond hair made Paul fairly certain that this was one of the men the Zilchers had described. In the photo, Carter was standing next to another young man. Buzz cut. Belligerent stare. Black hoodie with the hood down. The third man from the house? Probably.

Paul called it in. "We know Carter's name and his record, but we're going to need to dig deeper. I want to know everything about him. Down to his shoe size and his favorite cereal. That includes everyone who's given him a job, partnered with him on a crime or shared a jail cell with him dating back to juvie. And I want to know it yesterday."

"Gotcha, Chief. We'll find everything we can."

"You do that, Parker. I am leaving the scene now to head over to Irene's. I want to interview her as soon as possible." *And I want to make sure she and the kids are okay.* He couldn't say that out loud, though. All he knew was that it took every bit of his considerable discipline to carry on as if this were a normal case, when his gut told him to go to her and stay there until the danger had passed. Not happening. Even if she was his best friend's sister, he still had a job to do.

Is that all she is to you?

He shoved the question from his mind. Whatever he had once felt for her was irrelevant. She was in trouble, and he was the chief of police. That was it. It had to be.

Jogging across the street to Irene's house, he kept his eyes roving the street for any signs of other possible dangers. There was no doubt now that she had become a target. The fact that one of the men after her was dead in no way mitigated the danger. There was still one, maybe even two men who were after her.

Some of the tension drained from him when he found Irene sitting with her boys on the couch. Although he could see the fear lurking in the blue depths of her eyes, she was doing a fair job of presenting a calm front to her sons. Still, the two kids were too smart not to have picked up on something. Instead of running around like usual, they were snuggled against each of her shoulders. He knew from talking with some of the officers who had kids that children seemed to have an instinct about what their parents were feeling. According to one of his lieutenants, Dan Willis, it was next to impossible to hide anything from his twin toddlers.

He had long ago accepted that he would remain single, but now, looking at those kids, his felt a pang in his gut at the knowledge of what he would never experience for himself.

Just then, Irene lifted her head. Her gaze latched on to his. The pit of his stomach dipped, like when he was riding a very steep roller coaster. It was not a feeling he enjoyed at the moment, so he ignored it. He needed to talk with her. Alone.

"Kids, go play in your room while I talk with Chief Paul."

Grumbling, the boys obeyed, their steps sluggish.

As soon as they were gone, Paul perched on the coffee table in front of Irene. He hated the weary look in her eyes. He needed to solve this case so she could relax.

"Irene, are you sure you're okay?"

She nodded. "Just spooked. I don't know how I'll ever step into that house again."

"Don't worry about that yet. Right now, I need to know what happened."

She took a deep breath. "I thought you were being paranoid when you insisted on the thumbs-up. Now I am really grateful." He nodded. So was he. "That guy, he planned to kill us both, so he didn't care what he told us. He said that the boss wanted me out of the way. I had interrupted a very important transaction. Mary had a family waiting for her. They've already paid money, so the kidnappers had to deliver her. I was a target because I had seen the leader's face up close."

Paul bit back the anger swirling in his gut. *Keep calm. Don't let yourself get off track.*

"He probably wouldn't have cared that you'd seen him until he realized you had Mary."

Irene sat up straight. One hand shot out and grabbed his arm. She held on so tight he could feel each individual finger digging in. He kept his face blank.

"Paul! He said they were going to get Mary back! His partner was the man from church—he heard us talking about her staying at Sergeant Zee's and texted the update to him and to their leader. It won't take them long to figure out who Zee is."

Paul pulled his cell phone out of his pocket and punched in Zee's number. "Come on, come on. Answer the phone."

Two rings. Three. When the phone rang four times and went to voice mail, Paul knew something was wrong. He barked out a message, warning her.

He only prayed they weren't too late.

Chapter Six

He needed to get to Zee's place, pronto. But he also knew that he needed to make sure Irene, AJ and Matthew were protected. There were two madmen still out to get her.

Shifting into command mode without thought, he started barking orders to Gavin Jackson the moment he came in the door. It wasn't Paul's normal style of command. He prided himself on his ability to keep his cool even when everyone else was losing it. It was a skill he had honed for years, after life had taught him some hard lessons. He had paid the price once for his lack of control. It had almost cost him his friendship with Jace. And it had cost him any chance he may have had with Irene.

Clenching his fists, he closed his eyes briefly, willing himself to control the anxiety spinning inside him. Then he murmured a quick prayer for guidance and strength. Right now, he desperately needed both.

Opening his eyes, he regarded Jackson, who had come to stand in front of him.

"Sir, a unit is on its way to Sergeant Zee's place. I also have an ambulance on standby."

"Very good, Jackson." He rolled his shoulders and took a deep breath. But then his pager suddenly started beeping. The dispatcher's voice came over the air, announcing an attempted break-in. The intruder was still on the premises. An officer was on the scene, requesting backup. There was a child present, although the dispatcher did not disclose the child's age or gender. She rattled off an address. Paul and Jackson looked at each other.

Dismay was dawning over Jackson's face. It was probably mirrored on his own. He made a decision.

"I'm going to head out that way, see if I can lend a hand. The other unit should beat me there, but I don't want to risk it."

"What's wrong?"

As one they turned. Irene was staring at them, concern furrowing her forehead.

Paul sighed and rubbed the back of his neck. There were so many things to factor in here.

"That call that just came through, that's Sergeant Zee's address," Paul replied. "There's a unit on the way, but I am going to head over there, too. We have no way of knowing how many intruders showed up to get Mary."

Irene lifted her coat from the back of the sofa and shrugged into it. "I'm going with you." Both men started to protest, but she cut them off. "Who else will be able to deal with Mary while you take care of the attackers?"

"We don't have time to argue." Paul faced Jackson. "Who's on duty here to protect Irene and the boys?"

"I guess that would be Parker."

Paul gave a single nod. Parker hadn't been with them that long, but he had already been tested and tried. Paul knew that he could handle watching over the kids. Just to be on the safe side, though...

He picked up his phone and dialed The second ring was interrupted as the call was answered.

"Parker." His voice was confident. Good. Paul needed someone who knew what they were about.

"Kennedy here. I need you to take the boys to their grandmother's house and stay with them there. Jackson will supply the details."

"Understood, Chief. Mrs. Russell just left in an ambulance with her sister, and the ME has removed the body. I'm coming over so Jackson can brief me."

He loved the way his officers worked together.

Paul strode at a brisk pace out to his car, aware of Irene following him. They passed Parker as he was on his way in. A tall man with short light brown hair and dark eyes, Parker looked like a laid-back young man with a carefree grin and a casual saunter. Until you saw him in duty mode. He wore his duty like some men wore aftershave. Effortlessly. Paul saw Irene dissect him with a glance, then smile. Parker had passed the mother exam.

Paul slid into his seat, shaking his head as Irene snapped her seat belt into place. It was, of course, completely insane to have her along on a police call. On the other hand, she had made a very valid point. Mary had been terrified of him previously. He hated to think it was due to abuse she had suffered, but knew it was the most likely scenario. It was essential that they protect the child, but if there was a situation brewing, Irene was the only one he knew of besides Zee who the little girl would allow nearby. If he could avoid traumatizing the child, he would. And that meant having Irene accompany him.

Sergeant Zerosky lived on the edge of town. While she didn't have neighbors as near as Irene did, there were other houses in the area. The ambulance had already arrived and had pulled into the driveway. Paul fervently prayed for the safety of Sergeant Zee and Mary. There wasn't room to park another vehicle in the narrow drive without blocking the ambulance. He edged his car snug against the curb, directly behind Thompson's cruiser, and put his hand on the door to open it. Before he pulled the handle, he glanced over at Irene. The whirling lights from Thompson's vehicle were splashing across her face.

"I need to know that you will listen to me immediately without asking questions once we're in there. It's the only way I will feel free to go in and do my duty." Irene had never been one to take orders well, but he knew she would do whatever she could to keep a child safe.

"I understand." Her voice was low, intense. He could already see it in her. She was determined to do what he said to protect Mary. Good. They were both on the same page.

Feeling like every second could mean life or death, Paul waited for Irene to exit the vehicle. When he realized that his fingers were tapping an impatient rhythm against his thigh, he forced himself to hold his hand still. As soon as Irene reached his side though, he grabbed hold of her hand and pulled her along toward the house.

He was slightly embarrassed when he reached the

house and realized that he was still holding her hand. And even more embarrassed when he realized how perfect her hand felt in his. But now was not the time to be noticing things like that. He had a child to save and an officer at risk.

When he reached the front door, he started to call out, then paused. Voices were coming from the deck at the back of the house. What were they doing outside?

Refusing to allow himself to hesitate, Paul continued at a brisk pace through the house to the sliding door in the rear that led onto the deck. He paused. He could clearly see Sergeant Zee, lying down on the deck but conscious, although she seemed a little out of it. And judging from the fussing baby noises drifting down from upstairs, Mary was present and alert. He could see the blue uniform of a paramedic on the stairwell. The paramedic glanced back at him and gave him a thumbs-up. Okay. So he didn't need to worry about the baby for the few minutes. A second paramedic was kneeling on the ground next to his officer. On the other side of Zee was Sergeant Thompson. When Thompson spotted his chief, he murmured something to the paramedic and headed their way. Paul opened the sliding door to let him in.

"Paul," Irene whispered. "I want to go upstairs and check on the baby. Make sure she's okay."

"No need for you to do that, Mrs. Martello," Thompson assured her in his comforting voice. "The other paramedic is checking on her right now."

Irene compressed her lips together. If Paul were to guess he would say that she was biting her tongue to keep from arguing. Poor Irene. He knew her desperate concern for the little Amish girl was tearing her up.

Still, he couldn't let her place herself in danger until he knew the scene was safe. He turned his attention on Thompson.

"Report, Sergeant."

Sergeant Thompson straightened. "It's like this, Chief," the officer began. "The intruder was neither the man that Jace had pointed out nor the bearded man you described."

Realizing that Thompson wasn't up-to-date on the information, he quickly filled him in on Carter's death. When he mentioned the other man that had been in the picture with Carter, Thompson pursed his lips and nodded. "Yeah, that seems about right. The intruder was young, and from what I could tell had dark hair. Medium build, but strong. He ran out the back door and jumped over the fence when I arrived. Sergeant Zee managed to Tase him, but he had already snuck up behind her and struck her pretty hard on the head. The paramedic thinks she probably has a concussion. He didn't have time to get to the child."

Well, that was something to be grateful for. As much as he wished the intruder had been caught, it was good to know that he could focus on one person without putting the other in danger. He turned and caught sight of Irene.

Her arms were crossed and her foot was tapping the floor. She was the very picture of impatience, possibly irritation. Being told that she couldn't go check up on a crying child had to go against the grain. But the baby was in good hands and didn't seem to be hysterical, even though he could still hear her fussing.

"I'm going to go talk with Sergeant Zee," he informed her, ignoring the storm clouds gathering on her brow. "Do me a favor, will you? Stay here until I get back. You can be my go-between if the paramedic needs anything."

He waited for her agreement. It was slow in coming, but he couldn't leave without knowing she'd remain where she was. She nodded, reluctance stamped all over her pretty features. That didn't matter. As long as she was safe, he could deal with whatever annoyance she was feeling.

Irene stood, indecision cluttering her mind. On the one hand, Paul had told her specifically to stay here. And it wasn't like she was needed upstairs at the minute. The paramedic was with Mary. And the little girl was making normal babbling noises. Plus, the attacker had scampered over the fence. So there was no need to be anxious.

But she was. Despite telling herself not to be silly, she couldn't stop the tremors that reverberated deep in her soul and made her stomach queasy. It was like being behind the wheel of a race car zooming out of control and off the track and then discovering that the brakes have failed. She knew she wanted the horror to stop and was powerless to make it happen. And that powerlessness tore at her whenever she heard anything that sounded like it could be a whimper coming from Mary upstairs while she was stuck down here, unable to do anything to help.

Irene didn't like feeling she wasn't in control. She'd been that way for months after Tony had died. And when she had gotten her life to where she felt it was manageable again, she had promised herself that never again would she allow herself to be in a situation where she felt so inadequate. So weak.

Like she was now.

Shaking her head fiercely, she tried to ward off the dismal thoughts. Feeling sorry for herself wouldn't help. She tapped the glass door. It was a heavy glass. It must have been soundproof, too. She was only a few feet away from the group outside on the deck, but she couldn't hear a word they were saying. Paul was talking now. She could see his lips moving. If she inched open the door, she'd be sure to hear his deep voice. She liked the way he talked, in that slow, comforting drawl. What was the word she was searching for? *Smooth.* That was it.

Smooth as hot fudge over vanilla ice cream, a friend had once described it. Irene rolled her eyes at the memory.

Thump.

Irene startled, her eyes shooting to the ceiling. Something had fallen. Something heavy. Mary was up there. No, Mary wouldn't make a crash like that. And she was in her crib.

Remembering how Matthew had managed to climb out of his crib at fifteen months, Irene wasn't reassured.

She didn't need to worry. There was a paramedic up there with her.

A second later, Mary started crying.

That wasn't a cry. That was a more a scream…of terror.

Forgetting her promise to Paul, Irene shot up the stairs without any thought to the possible danger. The sound of her steps was drowned out by Mary's howls. There was a baby upstairs who was hurt, terrified or both.

Irene reached the top of the stairs and pivoted to the right, toward the shrieks. And nearly stumbled over the body of the paramedic.

She very nearly lost her lunch right then and there. She didn't need a medical degree to know the man was dead. There was a hole in the middle of his forehead, and his eyes were staring straight ahead. She hadn't heard a gun, but she knew about silencers. She'd just never seen one—or the effects of one—up close before.

Paul. She needed Paul.

Mary shrieked again. Hysterical.

"Shut your mouth, brat," an angry voice growled. "Or I will do it for you. I ain't got time for this."

No time for Irene to get Paul. Mary could be dead, injured or gone before he arrived. Irene crept to the door of the room, eyes searching for a weapon the whole time. She passed another room with an open door. It was a bedroom, with a vase full of roses on the night-stand. She grabbed the vase. It was long and slender, shaped like a tube. She picked it up. It was heavy. Probably lead crystal. That would work. She didn't have the luxury of searching for the bathroom to empty it, so she dumped the roses and water in a soggy gush onto the carpet. She grimaced and mentally apologized to Zee, but she had no choice.

Whirling out into the hall, she saw a man heading the opposite direction carrying a straining Mary, her little mouth taped shut. Tears were pouring from her devastated eyes.

It was a man she'd probably have nightmares about for the rest of her life. Black Beard.

"Hey!"

Black Beard jerked back as if scalded. His shock

didn't last long. He swung in Irene's direction. Recognition flared in his dark eyes. His beard parted in the most hideous grin. It was filled with triumph. Irene realized she'd just given him the other thing he wanted aside from Mary—her.

Dropping the struggling toddler onto the floor beside him, the man surged toward Irene with a roar, huge arms open to grab her. Mary sat up, her little hands moving to the tape on her face. Irene pulled back from the man, but he still managed to grab a handful of her jacket. With a fierce yank, she pulled the slippery material from his meaty hands. He growled. Lunged again.

Acting on instinct, Irene tightened her fist around the vase. With a heave, she swung her arm around, slamming the side of the lead-crystal vase into the side of Black Beard's head with a satisfying clunk. The vase hit the floor. He staggered. Shook his head.

Irene hoped he'd stay distracted long enough for her to grab Mary and escape. She darted around him, putting herself between the toddler and her kidnapper. The child's small arms reached out for Irene. Unfortunately, Black Beard didn't remain stunned for long. Whirling, he fixed his eyes back on Irene.

Rage distorted his features.

Now what? She was literally stuck in the middle with nowhere to run.

"Irene!"

It was Paul! He must be looking for her.

The man whipped his gaze toward the stairs. He reached back and pulled a gun with a silencer on it from his waistband.

"He has a gun!" she shouted in warning. Grabbing Mary, Irene rushed back into the bedroom and slammed the door, locking it. Then she dove to the other side of the room, the weeping child still in her grip, seeking shelter.

And not a moment too soon. The lock of the door splintered, great chunks of the wood blowing inward. Black Beard had shot out the lock.

"Police! Surrender your weapon!"

Paul. *Oh, Lord. Please keep him safe.*

The prayer came out naturally. Because she knew only God could help.

Several more explosions in the hall. Gunfire. Then more crashes.

It wasn't until Mary patted her face that Irene realized she was weeping. For whom she didn't know. Mary? Paul? The paramedic? Maybe even herself. Or all of them. All she did know was that she was desperate to see if Paul was safe. But she knew she couldn't leave Mary alone. Mary. The sweet baby still had a piece of tape over her mouth, although she had worked it off enough so that she could breathe. Irene pulled it off the rest of the way, trying to be gentle.

Hugging the child close, Irene waited, her mouth dry. She tried to swallow past the lump in her throat. It was torture not knowing what was coming. The sound of running feet pounded past the door. But not toward the stairs, like she would have expected.

Her breathing sounded like a freight train to her own ears in the silence. She'd never really thought of silence as loud before. Now she longed to hear something to tell her that Paul had survived.

"Chief!"

"Up here, Thompson."

The sound of Paul's voice sent a flood of relief

through her. Her spine went soft, and she wilted against the wall, bringing Mary with her. The baby laid her unbonneted head against Irene's chest, sticking her thumb into her mouth and gently sucking.

"Irene? Irene!" Paul called, his voice frantic.

"We're fine," she yelled back. "I'll be there in a moment."

She half expected him to charge through the door, but then she heard another pair of feet stomping up the stairs.

"Is that...?"

"Yeah. He's dead. The intruder shot him point-blank, looks like."

They must be talking about the murdered paramedic. Irene felt sorrow for the man, wondering if he left a wife behind, or children. She knew all too well the suffering that they would go through.

"What about Jace's sister? And the kid?"

"She's fine. Said she'd be right out." His voice was calm, but she detected a slight edge to it. He was concerned. She needed to move.

Bracing herself with the wall, she stood. When she tried to set Mary down briefly, the child wound her chubby arms around her neck, burying her wet face into Irene's shoulder.

"Okay, then. I guess I won't put you down. Come on, Mary. Let's go."

Irene took one step. Paul pushed the busted door open. His skin had an ashen cast to it. At first, she thought he'd been hurt, after all. When he strode forward and pulled her and the child into his arms, she realized he'd been as concerned about her as she had been for him.

Strangely, Mary made no fuss in his embrace. Maybe because Irene was still holding her.

"Are you two really okay?" Paul pulled away, his gaze roaming over them.

"Fine. More scared than anything."

"I had no idea you were in trouble until I came inside and you were gone. Then I heard a crash."

She nodded. "He had shot the paramedic. But he must have used a silencer. And he taped Mary's mouth shut. Did you shoot him?"

She shuddered. She didn't think she could stand seeing one more dead body in the hallway. She was pretty sure she'd collapse into hysterics before the day was through.

Paul shook his head. "No. He ran into the room at the end of the hall and slammed the door. When I got in there, he'd already climbed out the window and down the ladder leaning against the side of the house. I imagine that's how he got in. I think the other guy was supposed to be the lookout while he got Mary."

It made sense.

"I'm taking her home with me."

She waited for the argument. It never came.

"Probably a good idea. And we'll keep a strong detail on your house. Which means that until further notice, you will have someone with you at all times. In the next day or so, we'll take Mary into Spartansburg and start searching for her family."

Relieved that he hadn't tried to dissuade her, she merely nodded.

"Irene…" She looked up, her relief fading at his drawn features. His voice held no trace of its usual drawl. "I don't have to tell you that this isn't over. We know for a fact that there are now two people, at least, after Mary. And they also want you out of the picture. Probably because you are the only real witness. We haven't been able to get a good description of the man who went after Zee. And the second man, the one with the beard? We still haven't identified him. As far as we can tell, he isn't in our database. We have nothing on him. I suspect he's going to want to keep it that way. And he's willing to kill to make it happen."

Chapter Seven

The next morning, Irene checked on Mary in the crib that she'd asked Paul to bring down from the attic. It was a school day, so her boys were both up. In fact, the two rascals peeped over the edge of the crib, fascinated. It amused her. It wasn't as if they'd never seen a baby girl before. They hung out with their cousin Ellie all the time. And Lieutenant Willis's wife, Maggie, often brought her twins over to play when the women got together.

Maybe it was because the poor thing was away from her mother. Or maybe it was because Irene was acting like her mother until the little girl's family was found. Either way, they were drawn to her.

"Mommy," AJ whispered, "are her mommy and daddy with my daddy?"

She froze. She hadn't allowed her mind to go there. All at once, emotion swamped her. "I don't know sweetie. I don't think so. But Chief Paul and I are going to find out."

He nodded, not taking his eyes off the sleeping girl.

Irene hustled her boys out of the room, but didn't close the door. She wanted to know if Mary woke up, and she didn't have a baby monitor anymore. The boys got dressed and ate their breakfast. She waved at them as they hurried to get on the bus. Deeper in the house, she could hear Paul's voice. She'd let him in right before checking on Mary. Was he on the phone? In the kitchen, she found Paul talking quietly to Seth Travis—Maggie's half brother. He was a good friend to most of the police department. He was also a paramedic. She heard the words "funeral" and "widow" and cringed. They were talking about the paramedic who'd been killed. Her heart broke for his family.

Before her thoughts grew too maudlin, she caught sight of two shopping bags Seth was holding. He broke off his conversation with Paul when he noticed her and moved her way.

"Hey, Irene. You okay after your ordeal yesterday?"

She smiled. She'd always liked Seth. "Yes, I'm fine, thanks. I'm sorry about your friend."

He compressed his lips, nodding. "Yeah. Me, too."

He hefted the bags in her direction, clearly not wanting to linger on the depressing subject. "Jess and I got these from Rebecca, Miles's fiancée. Her brother collected them for her." Something Amish, then. Rebecca's brother was still firmly entrenched in the Amish community, though he remained close to his sister, who had chosen a different life. And since Rebecca was best friends with Jess, Seth's wife, it made sense that he'd been the one to bring over the package.

"Did she say if anyone had mentioned a missing child?" It would be wonderful if they could find Mary's family right away.

Her hope was dashed as he slowly shook his head. "No. Sorry. But that doesn't mean that a family living on the outskirts of town couldn't have had a child kidnapped. This wasn't a church week, so there are plenty of families her brother said he hasn't had contact with in the past week or so."

Irene recalled hearing that the Amish went to worship services every other Sunday. They didn't have them in a church, but in community members' barns.

Taking the bag that Seth offered her, Irene held it open. Inside were several simple dresses like the ones that the Amish children she'd worked with wore. And a few bonnets.

"Tell her thank you. I think it would mean a great deal to Mary's family."

Seth nodded in acknowledgment and took his leave. "Jess and I have plans with my family this afternoon."

In the wake of his departure, she noticed Paul frowning as his dark eyes scanned over her. "What?"

"Are you sure you're up to this?"

She was slightly insulted. She wasn't a weakling. She'd dealt with hardship before, although never what Mary's family was contending with. It was her duty to help.

"Yes, of course I'm up to it." She couldn't help it that her voice came out a little sharp. It stung that he'd doubt her.

Paul stepped closer. She watched his hand raise, mesmerized as he slid the backs of his fingers down her cheek. "Irene, I didn't mean it to insult you. It's just that you have been attacked three times now in such a short time."

For a moment, she allowed herself to remain still, close enough that she could feel his warm breath on her face, smell the cinnamon gum he'd been chewing. But just a moment. Then she forced herself to step back.

"Right," he said. Was that disappointment? "Let's head out. We have a long day ahead of us."

Irene hurried to rouse Mary, who grumbled but allowed herself to be cleaned up and dressed. One of the dresses fit her perfectly. With care, she braided Mary's hair and put on her bonnet. She was adorable. And hungry. Mary's stomach was growling so Irene fed the tiny girl a simple breakfast and got together both a small ice chest with water and snacks to sustain them throughout the day and a backpack to act as a makeshift diaper bag. Was she forgetting anything? It had been several years since she'd needed to do this, and she was out of practice.

As she moved to the kitchen, the phone rang. She paused, apprehension heavy in her gut. Who would call at seven thirty on a Monday morning? Either something bad had happened, or...

Shaking her head as if she could dislodge the notion, she walked over to the phone and looked at the number display. Not a number she knew. She felt a moment of relief that it wasn't the school or her mother calling to report bad news, but anxiety quickly took its place as the answering machine clicked on and she waited to hear what the caller would say.

Paul stood in the doorway, his face confused. She'd never told him about the calls she'd received the other night. He opened his mouth—most likely to ask why she wasn't answering her phone. She shook her head.

Her voice ended, and it was followed by a beep. There was a pause, then a man's voice. "You won't get away with what you've done. I will make sure of that."

Click.

"Who was that?" Paul growled.

Irene looked at him. If anyone could help her, it was him. He'd already proved that keeping her safe was his priority. The desire to run into his arms rushed over her and was hard to resist.

Something dropped behind her, and both she and Paul whirled toward the crash. Mary had upended a box of CDs Irene kept on the floor near the player and was picking them up one by one, enthralled. No wonder—they wouldn't have been something she would've had access to in the Amish world.

Irene glanced around her house. It was no longer baby-proofed now that both her boys were in school. A frown settled on her face. That was something she'd need to take care of if Mary would be staying with her for long…but she still hoped that wouldn't be the case, for Mary's family's sake.

She sent up a cautious prayer. *Lord, help us find her family quickly.* Being in danger had sure given her a wake-up call to how much she needed God in her life.

Paul was still waiting for her reply. She told him about the phone calls and wasn't surprised when he hit the roof over the fact that she hadn't mentioned them before.

"How am I supposed to protect you when you keep secrets like that?"

She grimaced. He had a point. "I didn't intend to keep any secrets. I truly did forget about the calls when someone started creeping around my house."

Grumbling, Paul walked into the other room. She could hear him talking on his cell phone. When he returned, his usual calm demeanor was back in place. Funny, how she seemed to be the one who kept making him lose his cool.

"Okay, here's what we'll do. I am having your phone

calls monitored. If we can trace the caller, that would be great. I would also appreciate if you kept me apprised of any other suspicious attempts to contact you—including through social media or email. Deal?"

"Absolutely." She wasn't a fool.

"Okay. There's nothing more we can do right now, so let's get on the road."

Paul had made coffee and placed it in travel mugs. Irene added cream and sugar to hers, then donned her coat and stuck her gloves into her pockets. Carrying Mary in her arms, with the diaper bag slung over her shoulder, she followed Paul out to his cruiser. She saw him grab the cooler of food she'd packed. When they got to the cruiser, she noticed for the first time that he had a car seat in the back seat. She raised her eyebrow. He shrugged.

"When Seth texted that he'd be coming over with the clothes, I asked him to stop at the hospital and pick it up. They keep them for emergencies. I installed it while you were busy." He opened her door, and she slipped into the passenger seat. A jolt of electricity shot up her arm when her bare hand came into contact with his. Averting her eyes, she scolded herself silently for letting him get to her.

Did he feel it, too? No, she didn't want to know. Still, the temptation to sneak a peek at his handsome profile when he joined her in the confines of the vehicle got the better of her. His face was bland. Which meant he was probably unaffected by her presence.

She was *not* disappointed by that. Definitely not. The last person she wanted to be interested in her was Paul Kennedy.

* * *

The route through Spartansburg, Pennsylvania, was one winding curve after another. The main road was paved, but the majority of the smaller roads shooting off from them were dirt and gravel. Many of the signs with the street names were faded beyond readability. Some of the signs were missing completely.

On the way into town, they stopped at several of the farms, getting out and carrying Mary up to the houses to see if anyone recognized her.

"I don't know of any *kinder* that have gone missing," one woman said kindly, her hand resting on the shoulder of her own child, a boy of only five or six. He leaned against his mother's side, wide blue eyes staring up at the strangers.

"Thanks for your time," Paul said, trying to keep the frustration from showing in his voice.

At the next house, Mary put up a fuss when they got her out of her seat, wailing and twisting until Irene set her on the ground to let her walk. Even then, she folded her little arms across her chest and refused to move, a definite pout forming, pushing out her lower lip.

Paul was amazed at how calm and gentle Irene remained, no matter how stubborn the little girl got.

This time, when the small group managed to make it up to the house, the husband and wife were both there. Paul was disappointed but unsurprised when they denied knowing the child.

"You might find someone who knows more at the diner in town, ain't so?" The young husband glanced to his wife for confirmation.

"Ja." She nodded her head emphatically. "That is a *gut* idea. Many people go through there every day,

and some of them are traveling. They might have heard something from another town."

Finally, an idea he could run with. For the first time that morning he felt a bit of anticipation. He thanked the couple, then he and Irene returned a fractious Mary to her car seat. He aimed the cruiser back toward town. Mary continued fussing.

"It's okay, baby," Irene crooned. "I have something for you." Opening the cooler she'd laid at her feet, she dug around inside until she retrieved a green sippy cup with a triumphant "Aha!"

Mary tugged the offered cup out of the Irene's hand and started drinking, making loud slurping sounds.

He snickered, then shot a glance at Irene and was rewarded by a smile that shot his pulse into orbit. When was the last time he'd shared such a simple moment with her?

Reality crashed down on him. He knew he had feelings for her, but he couldn't allow them to grow. There was too much baggage in his past for a classy woman like her. Plus, once she knew of his secret battles, she might be repulsed. And he wouldn't blame her. Not one bit. He returned his eyes to the road ahead.

Ten minutes later, he parked in front of the diner. Irene got out and released Mary from her seat. She put the wiggly child down to let her walk, but kept a tight grip on her little hand. Paul held the door for Irene, then followed her inside.

Letting his eyes adjust for a moment, Paul turned his attention to their quest and began talking with the nearest stranger. Soon, his hope and patience were rewarded. Although no one recognized Mary, a new bit of information came to light.

"I don't know of anyone around here who is missing a daughter with Down syndrome," one woman said, wiping her hands on her simple apron as she left the kitchen area.

"Well, now, hold on, Ruth." A tall, lanky man unfolded himself from the chair where he'd been sitting, enjoying a large breakfast of biscuits and sausage gravy. "I didn't think anything of it before, but remember what Carl said?" He glanced around the restaurant at the mix of Englisch and Amish folk gathered. A couple of the Amish people nodded their heads, troubled frowns gathering on their brows.

A tingle went up his spine. Something had happened. Something that might just have a bearing on his case and, hopefully, lead them to getting that sweet baby back to her family. Irene was leaning forward, her eyes intent. She was holding Mary again. The child had her head against Irene's shoulder with a thumb in her mouth, sucking loudly. Her other little hand played with a ribbon hanging down from her starched white bonnet.

"What did you hear? Please, anything could help us." He swallowed back his frustration. The hesitation to share information in front of him was obvious. He understood that the Amish felt uncomfortable discussing community problems with the secular authorities, but come on. Surely, everyone would want to work together to get a child home?

"I do not know all the details," one of the Amish men began, drawing his words out slowly, as if weighing each one. "There was an accident at an Amish farm. A fire, I seem to recall. One of the *kinder* couldn't be located after it was out. The whole community searched.

It was thought the young one had died in the fire. I recall hearing she had Down syndrome."

Irene gasped, her hands moving to cradle Mary closer. Paul could almost hear her thoughts. She was putting herself in the mother's place. Feeling the grief in her heart. That was one of the things he'd always found so amazing about Irene. She was the most empathetic person he'd ever known. That's why he'd run so fast from her all those years ago. He couldn't risk dragging her down with him.

Now was not the time to reminisce, he scolded himself. Now was the time for action. He needed to get this child home and find the kidnappers before they could hurt either Irene or Mary again.

"Okay, so where can we find this family?" Paul asked, thinking the sooner the better.

The woman named Ruth spoke up. "I don't think they live around here. Samuel?" She looked back at the man who'd talked about the fire.

"*Nee.* Carl Zook had heard about them from his brother. He said they were from Ohio, but he didn't know the family himself."

Ohio. They needed to get back in the car. Even as he thought that, Paul noticed the way Irene's shoulders sank. She would be away from her boys longer. It couldn't be helped. They would do what they needed to.

"Maybe we could talk with this Carl fellow before driving to Ohio?" Irene asked, her voice soft. Mary had fallen asleep.

"*Ja*, that would be a *gut* idea." Ruth nodded. "He keeps to himself. I don't know if he will talk with you. His place is a little out-of-the-way. But Samuel can give you directions."

Samuel grunted, then accepted the paper and pen she handed him. He proceeded to draw a map on the paper. The directions were rather convoluted. Paul would have much preferred to use the GPS, but no one in the restaurant knew Carl's exact address.

This would have to do.

Thus equipped, they thanked the crowd gathered and turned to depart.

"Young man."

Paul pivoted to face Ruth again. He was a bit tickled to be referred to as "young man." He'd started to feel every one of his thirty-two years lately.

Ruth moved to him, her hand gently touching the sleeping child. "Have faith. Gott is *gut*. He will help you. You must trust Him."

Paul was moved. "I do, ma'am. Every day, I do."

She gave a satisfied nod, then shifted her head to assess Irene. "And you?"

Irene bit her lip. Paul really felt for her. He knew from Jace that her faith had taken a beating since Tony had died. He couldn't blame her. His own heart had felt bruised when he'd lost his friend. But he had never lost faith. She had. Would she ever get it back?

"I haven't trusted God for a while," she admitted. Paul was shocked. Irene had always been a private person, especially when it came to her faith. "I thought He had abandoned me. But I am reevaluating that now."

What? Paul felt his jaw drop at this admission. A tiny spark of joy ignited in his heart. He'd been praying for her to find her lost faith for the past three years, but never had he imagined a conversation such as this one.

"*Gut*, child. Gott will not abandon you. You must

always remember that. He is always there. Even when we cannot feel Him."

"Thank you." Irene's whisper was rich with feeling.

Paul guided them back out to the cruiser. He almost bumped into a fellow scurrying along the sidewalk, hands deep in the pockets of a camouflage coat. The man mumbled an apology, but never slowed down.

Some people. Paul shook his head, disgusted at the fellow's rudeness, then dismissed it from his mind. Too many other things to focus on.

Irene immediately set about tucking Mary back into the car seat.

He had the oddest sensation that they were being watched. The hairs on the back of his neck prickled. He glanced around in a full circle. Nothing.

He didn't relax.

"Get in the car," he commanded.

Irene was startled, but complied without question. He got in and started the engine. He drove away, constantly looking in the mirrors and searching the horizon.

"Paul, what is it? You're scaring me." Irene followed his gaze, her own face growing pale.

"I don't know if anything's wrong. All I know is that I have the feeling I am missing something. No clue what, though. Keep your eyes and ears open, will you?"

"Always." Irene sighed and settled back in her seat. "So where are we going?"

Paul handed her the map. "Here, you look at it. I can't while I'm driving. Samuel said that Carl lived up past Buells Corners. Hopefully, he'll be able to tell us where Mary's family is. And that will put us one step closer to finding the people responsible for the kidnapping, and for murdering the paramedic yesterday." *The people who are also after you.* He didn't say the last part. "Read the directions off to me."

She did so.

They weren't as bad as he'd thought at first. Within twenty minutes, they were pulling onto the road that should take them to Carl's house.

They swung into his dirt driveway and Paul cut the engine. Everything was still. He would have expected more activity on a Monday morning. The folks back at the diner said Carl worked from home. Some kind of furniture business out in his barn.

His intuition was going haywire.

"Stay in the car."

Without looking to see if she would do as he ordered, Paul left the cruiser, locking the doors behind him. Then he approached the house, one hand over his service weapon so he could draw it quickly if necessary. His feet made tracks in the day-old snow as he climbed the stairs.

The door was open. Not much, only an inch, but more than a person would leave open on a freezing cold December day. He moved to the door, already dreading what he would find inside the old farmhouse. With all his heart, he hoped he was wrong.

"Mr. Zook? Are you home? Hello?" he didn't expect an answer and he didn't get one.

He put his hand on the door and gave it a gentle push. It swung open, creaking eerily on its hinges. Peering inside, he saw an immaculate house sparsely decorated.

He also saw a body on the floor, a pool of blood spreading out around it.

Chapter Eight

The back door was wide-open.

Whoever had been here had left in a hurry. Probably when they'd pulled up.

Irene! He abandoned his calm and drew his service weapon. Then he raced back outside and off the porch. He ran straight to the car and hopped in. Irene was staring at him, blue eyes wide and alarmed. He didn't have time to calm her. If Carl's shooter had hung around, then she was a sitting duck in the cruiser. Someone standing outside with a gun could pick her off at any moment. It made him want to rush her indoors.

But he had no idea if the shooter was still inside the house, waiting for her.

"You need to stay down. Carl Zook has been shot. I have no idea if he's alive, but I don't want to leave you here as a target. I'm going to call for backup. Corry is only ten miles away. The Corry police can be here in a relatively short time."

Irene's face had lost all color. But she met his gaze squarely. She shocked him by reaching out and placing one slim hand on his cheek. He swallowed and covered her hand with his. If he lived to be a hundred, he would always treasure that small gesture.

"Paul, be careful."

He smiled. It felt wobbly. "I will. But y'all need to get out of sight so I don't worry."

Without another word, she scrambled into the back seat with Mary, unhooked the little girl and brought her down on the floor with her to play a rousing game of patty-cake. The sight mesmerized him. He'd seen her with her boys. She was a wonderful mother. The thought of her sitting and playing with his child, too, sneaked into his mind.

He shoved the thought away. *Enough.* He wasn't accomplishing anything. There were too many blind spots inside the car. Paul let himself out of the cruiser and crouched beside it. Keeping low, he brought out his phone and called the police. He would have to wait for them to arrive before he went over the scene. While he was anxious to check it out, if he got himself shot he'd leave Irene and Mary in more danger than they were in now.

So he waited. And prayed.

By the time he heard sirens indicating the police had arrived, his leg was cramped. He stumbled against the cruiser briefly when he stood, but managed to steady himself. He saw Irene watching him from her position on the floor. She was so beautiful. Frightened, pale, angry. It didn't matter. Seeing her and knowing she was well was a balm to his soul.

He would do whatever was necessary to keep her safe. It was more than duty. She was a woman in a million, and he would do right by her—as a friend, since he knew he'd blown his chance of them ever being anything more.

"Chief Kennedy?"

He faced the female officer approaching him. "Yes, Officer."

"Lieutenant Nickols," she introduced herself, pointing to the rectangular pin bearing her name. "Have you checked the scene yet?"

As if he were a rookie? He held in a smile. "No, Lieutenant. I have a woman and child in my vehicle. I couldn't risk their lives."

She was surprised, understandably so. Not many civilians were taken to crime scenes. To her credit, she just nodded and began the search with her partner. Between the two of them, they determined that the house was safe.

They also checked on Carl Zook.

"Hey, Chief!" Lieutenant Nickols yelled out. "This guy's alive! I got a pulse here. Not a strong one, but it's there."

Thank you, Jesus.

While they were searching, the ambulance arrived.

The crew immediately started to work on the injured man.

Before they could load him on a stretcher and transfer him to the ambulance, a buggy rolled into the driveway.

It was getting really crowded now.

Irene and Mary had moved into the kitchen. That way, Paul had a clear view of them as he assisted the local department. He switched his attention from Irene to the woman hopping down from the buggy and running into the house.

"Whoa!" The male officer, Dudak, stepped in front of her, halting her entrance. "This is a crime scene."

"This is my house!" She shoved past him, then stumbled to a stop as she saw the man on the floor. "Dat! What are you doing to him?"

Paul moved forward. "I'm sorry, miss. I came here to talk to your father and found him. He'd been shot." He held up his hands in a placating gesture when her face paled and she looked like she might faint. "He's alive! Do we have your permission to transport him to the hospital? He will die if we don't."

Boy, he hated to be so harsh.

As he was talking, she went down on her knees next to her father and began to sob. A hand landed on Paul's arm. Irene. She squeezed his biceps. He could feel the warmth of her hand through his shirt. "I'll help," she whispered plopping Mary on the floor with a couple of toys she pulled out of the bag on her shoulder.

As he watched, she went down beside the young woman, putting her arm around her shoulders. She whispered to her. The woman struggled to control herself and listened. Finally, she wiped her tears and nodded.

Irene cast a look back and winked. Paul smiled. Was there another woman who could even compare to her? He doubted it. She amazed him with her strength and her compassion.

"It's okay," she called, obviously unaware of the completely inappropriate thoughts flying around in his head. "She'll let you take him to the hospital."

The ambulance crew didn't waste any time. Within minutes, Carl was loaded into the ambulance and headed to the nearest hospital.

His daughter prepared to follow. As she stood in the doorway, she paused. "I'm sorry. What did you want to talk to my *dat* about?"

Paul hated to add to her concern. Especially since Carl may have been shot because he had knowledge about Mary. Somehow, someone had clued in to the fact that he and Irene were coming to talk with the man. He was sure of it. Paul didn't have a shred of evidence, but his instincts told him he was dead on target.

"This child." Irene beat him to it. "She was kidnapped and we're trying to find her family. We think her name is Mary. The people in town thought that she may belong to a family in Ohio. A family that thought she'd died in a fire last week."

"*Ja.* I know that story. They lost their youngest daughter, Mary Ann Lapp."

Mary stopped playing on the floor and stood. She walked over to the woman and smiled. Paul caught his breath. He exchanged excited glances with Irene. They were finally getting somewhere.

Paul squatted down beside the toddler. She backed up a little, still a little shy around him and men in general, no doubt. "Mary Ann?"

Her sweet face split into a wide grin, blossoming like a flower in the sunshine. His heart melted. Then she brought her shoulders up and giggled, and he was enchanted.

"It's nice to meet you, Mary Ann."

She giggled again.

He heard a sigh. Irene. When he looked up, there were tears in her eyes. Alarmed, he stood and took her hand. "Irene? You okay?"

"Right as rain." She laughed and wiped her eyes

with her free hand. It was amazing how ebullient he felt just because she hadn't pulled away from him. "Silly of me, I know. But it seems like we might actually find her parents."

Without thinking about it, he leaned forward and touched his lips to her forehead. That was really stupid. But it had felt right.

She blinked up at him.

He didn't give her time to decide if he'd gone too far.

"I believe we will find them, Irene. God has a plan for Mary Ann. Just like He has one for you and me." Huh. He probably should have phrased that differently. That sounded like God had a plan for them as a couple. He liked the sound of that more than he should.

Miss Zook was already nodding vigorously.

"*Ja.* Gott has a plan. You have to trust Him."

Irene shook her head, her expression bemused. "I'm trying. In the meantime, do you know where we might find Mary Ann's family?"

"Well, now, I don't know the family myself. Somewhere in Holmes County, I know that much."

Paul could see the discouragement starting to take root inside Irene as Miss Zook hurried out the door, anxious to go with her father. Officer Dudak escorted her to the ambulance.

Mary Ann was occupied for the moment, fascinated by the dust motes dancing in the stream of light coming through the window. Every so often, she'd try to catch the particles, then laughed when she couldn't. What a wonder the world was to a child. He almost envied that simplicity.

He looked up, and was startled to see Irene fighting tears.

"Irene?" She'd been so happy just a second before.

She wiped her eyes. "Sorry. I'm glad that we're getting somewhere, but my heart aches at what her parents are going through."

He took advantage of the child's distraction to comfort the woman.

Gently, he pulled Irene into his arms, ignoring the startled glance he got from Officer Dudak, returning from outside. What did he care for that man's disapproval when someone—a very special someone—was hurting inside?

Irene held herself stiff for a moment, arms crossed in front of her like a shield. He wasn't giving up. He held her close with one arm across her back. The other hand rubbed slow circles up near her neck. He was rewarded when she relaxed, leaning her head against his shoulder.

For a moment, he forgot his intentions as the sweet, airy aroma of her shampoo assaulted his senses. He had started to lower his head, to breathe in her scent, when realization rushed upon him with a chill. What was he doing? He had no right to feel this way about a woman of her caliber.

But he did.

What was she doing?

Irene felt a change in the way Paul held her. Tension emanated from him. Embarrassed heat flooded her face at the idea that he might think she had read too much into his actions.

She wasn't the vulnerable girl he'd known so many years ago. She was made of stronger stuff and could handle whatever was thrown at her, thank you very much. Hadn't she already proved that?

She pulled out of his arms abruptly. He let her go, his arms dropping to his side. Did he look hurt?

"I'm good," she announced.

His dark gaze roamed her face, questioning. She shivered.

"Irene." Paul's voice was low, keeping his words private between the two of them. "I promise I won't give up. We will keep searching for her family. It might take some time, but we will find them."

She swallowed, transfixed by the intensity of his voice. She believed him. In that moment, it was so clear. No matter what had happened so many years ago, she trusted him now. It would be so easy to fall for him, deeper than when they were teenagers. He had become a man who kept his word and who served those around him tirelessly.

He was also a cop.

That was the thing, the one thing, she couldn't overlook. No matter how her stomach fluttered in his presence or how safe he made her feel, she couldn't— wouldn't—put herself or her children through that torment again.

Ignoring the sorrow bubbling up inside, she took a step back. She needed to put space between them.

"Irene…" Paul shook his head and sighed. She had the feeling he knew exactly what she was doing. "I need to touch base with these guys." He jerked his thumb in the direction of the Corry officers.

She raised her eyebrows.

"They can keep us in the loop on what they find. And I need to be in on the interview with Carl if and when he wakes up. He might be able to give us some details, both on Mary Ann's family and on the man who shot him."

Irene frowned. "Do you think it was the man who was staring at us at church?"

Paul considered. "Yeah, I do. He was in the picture with Carter, and, like I said before, I think he phoned Carter to tell him we were coming. I also believe he was the man who attacked Sergeant Zee."

Irene clenched her jaw in frustration. When would this awful ordeal end? And how many more good people would be hurt before then. She nodded toward the others. "Go ahead."

He touched her hand, then sauntered over to talk with the other officers.

She wanted to scream, she was so frustrated. *Why, God? Haven't I been through enough?* Unbidden, verses came to her mind.

Blessed be the God and Father of our Lord Jesus Christ, the Father of mercies and God of all comfort, who comforts us in all our affliction so that we will be able to comfort those who are in any affliction with the comfort with which we ourselves are comforted by God. For just as the sufferings of Christ are ours in abundance, so also our comfort is abundant through Christ. 2 Corinthians 1:3-5.

Wow. She couldn't believe she remembered that—she had learned it so long ago. But the question was did she believe it? Where was God when she had been trying to put her life back together? Where was He when her babies asked for their daddy? Or when she lay alone in her bed at night weeping for her husband? God hadn't comforted her then.

Because you would not let Him.

The stark truth of that thought hit her hard. She had hardened her heart to God. Whether deliberately or not, she had turned away, refusing to accept His comfort. His strength. Oh, she still would have suffered even if she'd kept her heart open. There was no escaping that. But she recalled vividly the comfort her family had taken in the knowledge that they would see Ellie again after her sister's death. How they had stood together.

She had rejected it all when Tony died. Suddenly, she was ashamed of herself. What kind of example was that for her little ones?

God, I am so sorry for shutting You out. I know danger is stalking me now. Help me to rely on You, no matter what happens.

Peace flowed into her, like a balm on her raw spirit.

A hand tugged at her pant leg…followed by a whimper. Mary Ann.

She squatted down to put her eyes on a level with the little girl. Mary Ann whined again, then patted her mouth. She was so cute in her little white bonnet.

"You're probably getting hungry, aren't you, sweetie?"

The cooler was in the car. Maybe she should go get Paul before running outside for it? He was deep in serious discussion with the officers, though.

Mary Ann whimpered again. What should she do? She'd overheard the other two officers talking a bit ago. They had said they didn't think the perp had hung around. Did that mean the danger had passed? After all, they had checked all the buildings, and had seen no sign of the shooter. Not to mention how long she and Paul had sat in the car without being attacked. Why would the shooter stick around with so many cops roaming through the house and property? She looked down again into Mary Ann's pleading eyes.

She needed to get her food.

"Okay, Mary Ann? I need you to stay here, okay? I'm going to get you some food."

Mary Ann babbled something. Whether it was just baby babble or Pennsylvania Dutch, Irene had no clue. But she needed to know that the Amish child understood her.

"Can you sit down? Right here?"

Mary Ann plopped down on her bottom, wobbling a bit as she did so.

Relief coursed through Irene. The child understood. "Okay, honey. You stay here. I will be back quickly with something to eat."

She stood and walked to the front door. Paul and the officers had moved to the kitchen. She could hear them talking. The words "forced entrance" and "probably didn't know the perp" floated to where she stood. Poor Carl. To be taken unaware in the supposed security of his own home.

She slipped through the door. If she was quick, Paul would never know she'd gone to the car. She raced across the lawn to his cruiser. Opening the passenger door, she reached in and grabbed the lightweight cooler.

She had just straightened when the first shot came. It slammed into the door she'd been holding on to.

Irene screamed. Dropping the cooler, she darted behind the vehicle, chased by the sound of shot number two. She ducked down low and did a funny squatting walk along the rear of the cruiser, keeping her head below the trunk line. Her hands skimmed the cold bumper to help her keep her balance. Shot number three. The right rear tire took the slug, hissing as the air whooshed out.

"Irene!"

Paul.

He and Dudak raced out. Nickols was probably keeping Mary Ann inside, safe.

"Irene! Where are you?"

Paul called again. She could hear the fear rumbling in his deep voice. He couldn't see her, she realized.

"I'm behind your car!" she yelled back, still keeping low. "I'm fine."

Besides being scared out of her wits, that was.

The Lord is with you, she reminded herself. *Lord, please protect us all. Keep Paul safe.*

For even now, he was racing toward the back of the car, his eyes searching the horizon, service weapon ready. He dashed around the car to the back end. He slipped the arm not holding the gun around her and squeezed.

"You okay?" he queried urgently, gaze skimming over her. His face, she noted, was pale.

Ouch. She hated that she was the one to cause him such fear.

"I'm fine. Terrified, but unhurt."

She waited for the lecture. She even wanted it, because she knew it would be well deserved. What she got, however, was another squeeze and a kiss on the forehead.

They waited for another shot.

None came. She could hear Mary Ann screaming inside the house. Instinctively, she tried to stand, to go and comfort the child, but Paul wouldn't let her move. Reluctantly, she agreed. Mary Ann was hungry and scared, but she was safe. They were not. Not yet.

After ten minutes with no more shots, Paul called the other officer over. They kept Irene sandwiched between them and, gripping her elbows, fast-walked her back to the house. Their service weapons were out, and they were focused on the trees.

The moment Irene was inside, Mary Ann rushed at her. Irene realized with a pang of regret that the cooler was still outside, on the snowy ground where she'd dropped it. She wasn't about to go after it.

Paul and Dudak turned to the door.

"Wait, Paul! Where are you going?"

He was so busy scanning the trees he didn't even look her way. "We need to search the tree line."

Before she could protest, he was gone. Chasing after a killer.

Chapter Nine

Paul motioned Dudak to split off to the left. If this criminal had any brains he'd be long gone by now. Really, he should have left as soon as Paul's cruiser pulled up to the house. Instead, he'd stuck around long enough to go after Irene again. It wasn't smart or logical. In fact, it spoke of someone more concerned with a personal vendetta than keeping under the radar.

Paul zigzagged through the trees, his eyes constantly scanning the brush and the treetops for any sign of movement. Any noise that might lead them to the killer's hiding spot.

Paul already had a pretty good guess what the man looked like. He thought back to the picture in Niko Carter's wallet. That dark-haired guy and the bearded man were after Irene. He had a feeling this was no longer just about Mary Ann.

The search was fruitless.

No sightings. No clues. Nothing that led them nearer to closing the case and stopping the people who had Irene in their sights.

After about an hour, they had to admit defeat. The

shooter had managed to elude them. Again. Paul was starting to get pretty irritated at showing up too late. As he walked back to where Irene was waiting, he kept going over the day's events in his mind.

How had the shooter known that they were going out to talk with Carl Zook? It seemed like too much of a coincidence that he was shot the same day that they would come asking questions—just minutes before their arrival. Somehow, the sniper had made the connection that they would come after him.

Again, the question reverberated in his mind. How?

He had found a way to spy on them and knew that they would be coming out to talk with people about the case today. Had the cruiser been bugged? He'd better search his vehicle, just in case.

Ten minutes later, he frowned in frustration at his car. Nothing. Suddenly, the image of the young man slamming into him outside the diner crossed his mind. It no longer seemed like a coincidence. If he'd gone back inside, it was possible that the locals were still talking of Zook. Yeah. That would fit. He'd left after them, but if the man knew the area well, he might have been able to take a quicker route.

From the yard, he could hear Mary Ann hollering. He spotted the cooler lying upside down on the ground and mentally connected the dots. The kid must be hungry. That was probably why Irene had come outside in the first place. He paused and listened. Yep. She didn't sound hurt or scared. Just mad. Nothing gets a kid mad like an empty belly. He'd watched his sister's kid enough to have learned that the first rule of peace in the house was to keep children well fed. He detoured slightly and picked up the forgotten cooler before resuming his trek to the house.

Immediately, his thoughts returned to analyzing what he knew about the case. It was what he did best…fitting the pieces together. He was so consumed with the clues rattling around in his mind as he walked into Carl's house that he was unprepared when Irene bounded out of the kitchen and threw herself into his arms.

He was unprepared, but not displeased. Dropping the cooler, for a moment he allowed himself the pleasure of holding her. Just a moment. Then he resolutely stepped back. But he couldn't completely distance himself. One look into those blue eyes swimming with tears, and he was lost again.

"Hey, now." He cupped her face in his hands and used the pads of his thumbs to wipe away the moisture. Then he playfully tugged a lock of her dark red hair. "What's this? I'm fine, Red, just dandy."

"Red." She sniffed and let him catch the slightest glimpse of a smile. "You haven't called me that since high school."

It had slipped out without his permission. A slip like that might make one think his feelings, so long buried, were still as strong as they'd once been. But he knew that couldn't be the case. Irene Martello was way out of his league.

"I was so scared when you ran out there, Paul. What if you'd been shot?"

It was a valid concern. He regretted that she'd had to deal with it, but there was no other choice.

"I'm sorry, but you understand we had to see if we could catch this joker?"

She nodded and some of his tension faded. She

seemed to be taking everything in stride. Not something he would have expected from her, which meant he'd probably catch it later.

That was fine. As long as she and Mary Ann were safe.

His phone rang. He grabbed it off the clip on his belt without removing his gaze from the beautiful woman before him, now feeding the little girl. He allowed a grin to escape at the way the kid ate, dropping crumbs everywhere. She must have really been hungry.

"Kennedy here."

"Chief Kennedy." The voice was unfamiliar. She identified herself as a nurse from the hospital. "Mr. Zook woke up as they prepped him for surgery and spoke with his daughter. She is now insisting that she has information for you, and refuses to tell it to the staff here. She will only talk to you. Says it's police business."

"Be there soon."

He disconnected and turned to find the three adults in the room watching him. He didn't want to step on any toes here—this shooting was not in his precinct. But the fact that Irene had been shot at... Well, he dared anyone to try to stop him from finding the creep that had thought that was a good idea. This went far beyond whose precinct it was. And if Miss Zook had information that could help him, he wanted to know it right away.

"Okay, folks." He kept his voice at an easy drawl. No need to antagonize anyone. "The hospital called. Miss Zook is asking me to come there. She has some information. I do believe we should move this party to the hospital. See what she has to say."

Officer Dudak scowled. Before he opened his mouth, Paul knew he'd gotten his hackles raised.

"Now, look here, Chief. This is our area. We thank you for your help, but we can handle it."

Paul raised his hands. He was willing to try to placate the man, but this was one time he wasn't budging. "I'm not trying to home in on your investigation. However—" he indicated the child playing on the floor "—this intersects with one of my cases. I have a cop in the hospital and a murdered paramedic." He drilled Dudak with a stare. "And one of my friends has been shot at multiple times. I think this is a good time to work together."

Dudak raised his brows, then shifted his glare between Paul and Irene. His glance mellowed and his face cleared. "Ah, I see. All right. Can't say I like it, but I get it now."

Apparently, it didn't matter how much he tried to deny it. The other man had picked up on Paul's feelings for the beautiful redhead standing so close to him. Had Irene picked up on the insinuation? She looked startled, then a flush swept into her face. She dipped her head, and her hair swung forward. He could no longer see her face. Was she embarrassed because she knew how he felt? Was there any chance she was feeling the same? Or was she upset at any speculation because she wasn't feeling anything for him?

It didn't matter now. Feelings could be sorted out later. Her safety was the priority right now. And that meant he needed to get to the hospital.

"As soon as I change this tire, I'll follow you guys," Paul stated, promptly ending the discussion. They nodded. Officer Dudak stepped forward to assist. In the span of fifteen minutes, both cars were on the road again.

At the hospital, they found a couple of spots in the side lot. Miss Zook was waiting for them in the bustling hospital waiting room. All around her, people played on iPods or sat texting on smart phones.

As they entered, the energy in the room shifted. People sat straighter and averted their eyes. *Nothing charged the tension in a room like the arrival of three police officers in full gear.* Paul bit back a smile. He wondered if any of the people in the room had a reason to fear the arrival of the police, but let his suspicions slide. People just didn't know how to react to them.

Miss Zook immediately made a beeline to them. Or rather, to Paul. "I need to talk with you."

He nodded. "That's why we're here. Let's step out to the lobby, shall we? It might be more private there."

The small group moved into the area between the two sets of sliding doors. Irene and a babbling Mary Ann trailed behind the cops and Miss Zook. The stream of people passing the doors continued and they received quite a few curious stares, but at least it was quiet. They could converse in relative privacy.

Miss Zook watched Irene for a minute.

"It's okay," Paul assured her. "You can talk in front of Irene."

"Ja," she said, her voice soft. "I was thinking about the *kind*."

"She was stolen from her home." Paul kept his words gentle. But all of the sudden he thought about his own niece, who was just a toddler. Or Dan and Maggie's twins. The idea of living with the death or the disappearance of a child pierced through him. What if Irene had to do that? He knew her sons were her whole world. He had to banish those thoughts if he wanted to keep his mind clear. "We're trying to reunite her with her parents. I think your father knew something about what was happening."

"I think you are right." The girl wrapped her arms around herself and shivered.

Paul's heart twisted. The poor thing. Did she have anyone other than her father? She couldn't have been more than eighteen. Old enough to be married, but since she still lived with her father, he doubted she was. Although, since Amish didn't wear wedding rings, he couldn't be sure.

"Miss Zook, what did your father say before he went into surgery?"

Dudak shifted his feet restlessly and opened his mouth as if to speak. Paul shot him a warning glance. The young officer snapped his mouth shut, though he didn't look happy. That was just fine. He could be unhappy, as long as he kept his mouth shut.

Finally, Miss Zook seemed to come to the decision to trust him. "He didn't know the man who shot him. Said he was a strange Englischer. Young. With brown hair and a jacket like hunters wear."

Paul felt another piece click into place. The description matched the young man who'd bumped into him outside the diner. He was right about that connection.

Miss Zook kept talking. "The man said Dat was talking too much. And that he was too late. They'd already got another little girl."

They'd kidnapped another child?

Irene reeled from the horrible news. In her distraction, she squeezed the child she was holding. Mary Ann squirmed and cried in protest.

"Sorry, honey. I didn't mean to do that." Irene kissed the top of the bonnet and set the wriggling child on the ground. Mary Ann immediately moved away and pulled herself up on the bench stationed against the wall.

"Wait." Paul sounded as shocked as she was. "Do you have any idea where this child was stolen from?"

She was already shaking her head. "*Nee.* I asked, but Dat didn't know. The man said that, then shot him. I think he meant to kill him."

"Yeah, good thing our shooter is a lousy shot." The male officer smirked as he elbowed his partner. She, Irene was happy to note, directed a disapproving frown his way.

Paul gave him the fiercest scowl she'd ever seen on his face. Whoa. She was seeing a side to Paul that she'd forgotten about. He always seemed so in control of himself that she'd forgotten he'd had a temper and no tolerance for cruelty or stupidity.

The officer's comment certainly seemed to fall into one of those categories.

"What?" The officer looked affronted. "All I'm saying is that we're dealing with someone who's not used to using a gun. His target was only a few feet away, but he couldn't kill him. And how many times did he shoot at the redhead there? Yet she wasn't even nicked."

Offended at the tactless comments, Irene was tempted to put him in his place. Paul's expression, however, caught her attention. The scowl had melted into thoughtfulness. Tactless or not, something the man said had resonated with Paul.

"You may be right about that, Dudak."

Even knowing he had a point didn't make her like him any more than she currently did.

"Miss Zook, I am going to talk with the Corry police chief. See if we can't get someone to watch your father while he's here."

Her brow furrowed. "While he's here. When he gets released, I don't think Dat will want Englischers guarding him on his own property."

"That's understandable, but here he's still under our guard."

A minute later, the young Amish woman left to go wait on news of her father's condition. The three cops converged to discuss the next step in the investigation.

It suddenly struck Irene as she listened to the conversation just how exhausted she was. She didn't remember being this drained when Matthew was going through colic. And that was almost three months of limited sleep at night while dealing with an energetic toddler all day long.

Letting the police officers and Paul handle the nitty-gritty details, she moved like a sleepwalker to the bench and sat down beside Mary Ann. The little girl abandoned the umbrella stand she'd been examining and climbed up to sit on Irene's lap. She lifted her little hands and patted Irene's cheeks. Her hands were so soft and cool. Affection welled up inside Irene. And longing. Right at that moment, all she wanted was to go home and hug her boys. Hearing that another child was gone broke her heart.

Mary Ann pushed her hands against Irene's cheeks and drew her head down.

Irene looked into her round brown eyes. "Yes, pumpkin? Do you want something?"

The girl tilted her head and pursed her lips. Her little brow wrinkled. Oh, she was the sweetest little thing.

"Mam?"

Irene hadn't thought her heart could break any more, but hearing that first word she'd ever heard from the child broke through the dam. Tears pooled in her eyes. She blinked them back, not wanting to scare the precious child.

"I know you miss your *mam*, sweetie." She sniffed. Her voice sounded thick and fuzzy. She cleared her throat. *God, please help us find her parents.* "We're going to find her. Paul will get you back to your family."

"Yes, I will."

She hadn't heard him approach. The other officers were leaving. The door swooshed behind them. She raised an eyebrow at Paul. His eyes were soft and deep. And the affection and emotion she saw in them reached out and touched a chord deep in her soul. Shoving such ridiculous emotions away, she lifted Mary Ann off her lap and stood.

"Do you need to stay here and wait for Carl to wake up or something like that?" She hoped not.

He shook his head, his gaze never leaving her face. Warmth crept into her cheeks. She needed to stop reacting like a silly schoolgirl every time he looked at her. It was getting seriously annoying.

"The Corry police will take care of that. They promised to keep us in the loop."

She wanted to wilt. Just melt right into a relieved puddle on the floor. But then she reminded herself that the day wasn't over yet. They might be finished at the hospital, but there was still plenty to do.

"What now?" She pulled herself together and straightened her spine. This was not about her. It was about the little girl holding on to her leg. The child trusted her to get her home. And Irene would do that. *Paul and I will do that*, she amended. Because she would get nowhere without him. *Or without God.*

Even a week ago that thought would have been scoffed at. But now she realized she needed to hold tight to God to keep her sanity.

Paul smiled, a slight half grin that lifted one corner of his mouth. But it still made her feel better. He lifted a hand as if to touch her, then let it drop.

She was not disappointed, she told herself.

"Now we head back to LaMar Pond. I know we need to travel to Ohio. But I refuse to just drive out there without any idea of where we're going. We're going to see if we can find out more about any families named Lapp that recently lost a child. Or had a severe fire on their property. At the same time, I need to put out some feelers for another missing little girl. Come on, let's go home. You can call your mom on the way."

Finally.

They moved out to the car. Paul hit the button to unlock the doors. Irene didn't wait for him to open her door, instead reaching out and pulling the door wide-open.

She stopped.

"Do you hear something?" She leaned her head toward the car, trying to catch the elusive sound.

It sounded familiar. Like a clock ticking.

Her world stopped as fear held her tight in its grip.

"Irene, move!"

Paul grabbed her hand and yanked her and Mary Ann away from the car. "Run!"

She didn't need to be told twice. They were half-way across the lot when the door blew off the car. Paul grabbed Mary Ann from her and shoved Irene forward. She fell, catching herself on her hands. They were scraped raw on the icy parking lot. She barely felt the pain. Mary Ann was screaming. Paul had wrapped himself around the panicked child as he'd gone to the ground.

Mary Ann was terrified and angry. But she was alive.

Irene looked back and promptly gagged.

The car was still there, smoking. The passenger seat, the seat she'd been about to sit in, was gone.

Chapter Ten

There'd been a bomb planted in her seat. Paul was still shaking, fifteen minutes later. He berated himself for not seeing the trap. The car had been out of his line of sight for more than long enough to be tampered with. Knowing that, he should have approached more cautiously. *That's what being consumed with concern for a woman will get you*, he scolded himself.

They were alive, though. He was amazed they were all uninjured. Shaken, but not hurt. He gave praise where it was due.

"Thank You, Jesus, for protecting us."

Irene nodded. "I'm thinking He is watching over us."

Well, at least there was one positive thing about this.

Mary Ann's shrieking had subsided into pitiful crying interspersed with hiccups. She was sitting in Irene's lap, thumb in her mouth. Her bonnet was slightly askew. He reached down and plucked gently at the top, straightening it. Irene smiled and hugged the girl closer.

Security from the hospital poured out of the building. Great. Now they would be stuck here even longer, letting the perp put more and more distance between them. Who knew how completely he'd be able to disappear if they didn't go after him now?

Still, Paul tamped down his impatience as they were prodded and poked by the hospital staff to be sure they weren't suffering any hidden injuries.

By the time they were declared injury-free, the Erie Bomb Squad had arrived. Paul was glad to see Trevor Stone leading the crew. Trevor was a shy young man, but Paul had learned to trust his judgment.

"What do we have, Trevor?" he said as he approached the young man. Trevor raised a hand in greeting and pushed his glasses back on his nose.

"Chief. This is a very sophisticated device. See those wires?" He pointed to the wires hanging out of the car where the door had been. Paul couldn't help it. His glance slid farther to where the passenger seat ought to be. He shuddered. Ten seconds more and Irene would have been there.

Don't go there, man. She's fine. You're all fine. Focus on Trevor. "Okay, yeah. I see them."

Trevor continued. "Whoever this dude is, he knows his explosives—and how to use them with precision. This was designed to take out just the passenger seat. Not the entire car. And it was remotely controlled."

Paul straightened, a new horror blossoming in his chest. "You mean he was here, watching?"

"Yeah, afraid so. He had to have been. The countdown didn't start until he pushed the button."

Paul swiveled his head to check on Irene. She was still there. He nodded at the security guard closest to him, and the man jogged over. "That woman is in danger. You stay right with her."

There may have been something in his voice, but

the man didn't argue, just ambled away to stand guard over Irene.

And over his heart.

He did not just think that.

"He waited until Irene was getting ready to sit, and then he pushed the button." It was hard to say the words, but he didn't back down from the challenge. Right now, he was Irene's best chance to survive, and she was counting on him to keep his head in the game.

"That's my guess."

Dudak and his partner stepped closer. At some level he'd been aware of them searching the parking lot. "What can we do, Chief?"

"Search the perimeter. Trevor here will give you the range of the remote. Extend your search past that. Any clues will be helpful."

They jogged out. He turned to the hospital personnel. "Are there security cameras in this section of the parking lot?"

When they admitted that there were, he said he wanted a look at the files as soon as possible.

"Chief."

He turned back to Trevor. The troubled expression on the man's face did nothing to quell the dread brewing inside him.

"Spit it out, Trevor. I need to know what I'm dealing with."

Trevor pulled a section of the explosive device from the car. It looked so harmless just sitting in his hand. Not like something that had the ability to rip a body to pieces.

"This device here? I saw it frequently when I was an EOD specialist for the army."

Explosives ordnance disposal specialist. Paul whistled. That type of job took guts and a rock-steady spirit. Those soldiers saw far too much carnage. Paul's respect for Trevor skyrocketed.

Then he frowned. "You're saying that we are looking for someone with a background in explosives, possibly ex-military?"

"I'd almost guarantee it, sir."

Great.

He called Parker and had him come to pick up Irene and Mary Ann. Irene started to argue. He placed a finger against her lips, stopping her midword.

"Red, you're tired, and who knows how exhausted that baby is. You both need a good meal and some sleep. And at your house, she can be free to walk around a bit more. I will be there tonight to keep watch. Parker will stay with you the entire time until I arrive, so you'll not be alone."

She nodded, although judging by the expression on her face, she wasn't happy about it. Still, some of the tension had eased from her shoulders when he'd said he'd be at her house later.

Warning signs went off in his brain. The last thing he wanted was for her to grow too attached to him. Too dependent. He didn't deserve that kind of trust. As soon as this case was done, life needed to go back to the way it had been.

Maybe it was about time he let her into the darker side of his past. He cringed, imagining the look of disgust that was sure to grow on her lovely face once she knew the real Paul Kennedy. It wasn't a story he enjoyed telling. The only person alive who knew all of it was Jace. He didn't even think his own mom and sister had figured out the whole truth.

Yet, as unappealing as it was, he needed to tell her. But not now.

He was relieved when Parker arrived thirty-five minutes later to take Irene home. Thompson arrived, too. Presumably to give Paul a ride back to LaMar Pond when he finished at the hospital. As he walked back to the hospital to view the file from the camera, he saw the tow truck arrive to take his vehicle away.

He stopped and watched it. It was just a car. But right now, it was a reminder to him of just how very precious life was.

This was getting him nowhere. He needed to see if the security cameras had caught anything useful. Only then would he be able to get back to Irene. He could really go for a cup of hot, strong black coffee. The stuff in the thermos he'd made that morning was cold by now. Not to mention he had no idea if the perp had tampered with it. He grimaced. He could really use some coffee. If for no other reason than the caffeine might give him a boost to help him through the next few hours.

When they entered the hospital, Thompson excused himself. Paul frowned, but didn't say anything. His frown turned into a grin several minutes later when Thompson rejoined him and handed his chief a hot cup of coffee from the cafeteria.

"You read my mind," Paul exclaimed. Thompson grinned.

Going through the footage was tedious work. They had to view numerous frames before they found the section that corresponded with their arrival at the hospital.

"There. We're pulling in now." He pointed at the

screen, seeing the two police cruisers pulling in and parking side by side. He watched as he got out and then walked around to let Irene out. She retrieved Mary Ann. They appeared to be talking. He couldn't even remember what they had been talking about.

They moved out of the camera view. A few minutes passed. Suddenly, Paul noticed movement in the trees.

"Look! On the right!" Was that him?

Yep. It sure was. A young man on a motorcycle flew across the road and swerved into the parking lot. In fluid movements, he was off the bike and removed his helmet before he set to work on Paul's car. There was no other movement on that side of the lot. They'd parked there to be away from others, little knowing that their perp would be bold enough to approach out in the open.

Within moments, Paul's lock had been jimmied open and the bomb was in place. This was no amateur. As Trevor had surmised, the man was a pro. This was very obviously not the first bomb he'd ever handled.

When he was finished, their bomber cleaned up all traces of his presence and hopped back on the bike. As he hefted his helmet in one hand, he looked straight at the camera and jerked his right arm up in an arrogant salute, the movement sharp and precise. He knew exactly where the camera was and that they would look for him afterward. He wanted Paul to know who had killed Irene. Paul couldn't hold back the shudder that rolled through him.

He wanted to close his eyes and forget about the scene replaying on the screen, though of course he couldn't. Irene was counting on him. He forced himself to focus.

"Go back to where he was looking at the camera,"

Paul ground out, fury boiling up inside him. He choked back the bile that was thick in his throat.

The screen froze on the man's face.

"Bingo." Paul narrowed his gaze at the image before him. In his mind, he was seeing a younger version of the same face, standing in the photograph beside Niko Carter. "I am going to find you and put you away for a long time, my friend. It's time you learned the meaning of justice."

Irene walked into her house and wanted to weep. Her mother walked out of the kitchen, wiping her hands on a dish towel, Izzy at her heels. Mary Ann squealed at the sight of the dog. Irene set her down, knowing that the dog would watch over her. The scent of her mother's meat loaf permeated the air.

Her mother made the best meat loaf.

"Mom, when did you get here?"

"Well, is that any way to greet your mother?" Vera smiled, taking the sting out of her words. "The boys were getting restless, so I brought them over."

Irene hugged her mom, holding on until she got her emotions under control.

"*Please* don't take this the wrong way, Mom. I am really happy to see you. And I can't wait to see the boys. But it's not safe for you to be here right now. Someone's after me. They planted a bomb in Paul's car."

Vera gasped, her wrinkled hand flying to cover her pearly lipsticked mouth. "Oh, no! Are you okay? You don't seem hurt. What about Paul? Was he injured?"

Irene placed a hand on her mother's shoulder. Troubled tears clouded the older woman's eyes. Irene understood. There was more than just fear in that look.

Vera Tucker still mourned the daughter who had been killed twelve years before. She probably always would. Irene wasn't sure you could ever completely heal from something like that.

"Easy, Mom. Everyone's okay. Paul's not hurt and he will be here after he finishes collecting evidence."

"Mommy!"

The somber mood was dispelled as two whirlwinds swept into the room. Irene bent to embrace both of her sons, inhaling their little-boy scent. It brought with it its own form of comfort.

"Hey, guys. Were you good for Granny?"

"I was." Matthew poked a thumb into his chest. Then he turned it toward his brother. "Not him, though. He didn't wash his hands before he licked the bowl."

Irene listened to their chatter as they set the table and sat down to eat. She asked Parker to bring in the high chair stored in the garage. When asked if he wanted to join them for supper, he refused politely.

"Smells good, ma'am, but I'm on duty. It would be more than my life was worth if the chief thought I wasn't protecting you properly." He went back out to scan the perimeter again.

Irene blushed. Her mother flashed a satisfied grin her way.

"You can get those thoughts out of your mind, Mom. There's nothing going on between Paul and me."

Liar, her mind whispered. She ignored it.

"I didn't say anything. Although if anything were to develop between you two, there'd be nothing wrong with that. You've been alone for three years now. That's more than enough time to mourn. Now it's time for you to move on."

Move on. How did one do that?

After dinner, she helped her mother clean up the dinner dishes. There were leftovers. Although Irene protested, her mom insisted she keep them.

"It's only me at home," Vera reasoned. "I made enough for you and the boys to have another meal. And if I remember correctly, Paul enjoys my meat loaf, too."

Irene rolled her eyes, ignoring her mom's blatant matchmaking. If only her mom knew how impossible such a match would be. Irene didn't want to tell her mom how broken she was, though. It would only cause her more heartache. Her mom had enough tragedies in her past. She didn't need to add Irene's problems to her burdens.

Parker walked Vera out to her car and then returned to his watch. Irene was thankful for his presence, but worry still chewed at her mind, nibbling away her confidence bit by bit. The criminals after her had attacked her so many times, despite the protection around her. What was to keep them from coming through one policeman to get her?

Soft weeping caught her attention, distracting her from her concern for Parker. She quickly tracked the sound back to the crib in the bedroom, Izzy on her heels. Mary Ann was holding tight to one of Matthew's stuffed animals, his favorite crocodile. Hours earlier, Irene had watched as he'd handed it to her solemnly. Irene had swallowed tears at that one. Matthew loved that animal.

"She needs it more, Mommy. 'Cause she don't have her mommy here."

Her sweet boy. He made her so proud and broke her heart at the same time.

AJ had swung his arm around his little brother's shoulders when he noticed his brother's lip had started to quiver. "Come on, Matthew," AJ had said, very mature. "You can sleep with Bubba."

Matthew had perked up. Bubba was AJ's prized stuffed cow. No one got to touch Bubba.

"Really?"

A sniffle brought her back to the present. Lowering the side, Irene reached in and lifted the small girl from the bed. Her bonnet had been removed, and her braids swung free over her shoulders, wisps of brown hair escaping from them.

"It's all right, Mary Ann. I'm here." She kept her voice soft, placing a kiss on the child's forehead.

"Mam." Mary Ann sobbed, burying her face in Irene's shoulder. "Me *mam.*"

Tears spurted from Irene's own eyes. "I know, baby. I know you want your *mam.* We'll get you home just as soon as we can." Sitting in the rocking chair, she slowly rocked the baby back to sleep.

As she was replacing her in the crib, her phone dinged.

Paul had sent a message. On my way soon.

Ok. Mom left meat loaf. She hit Send on the message.

A minute later there was another ping. This time she grinned at the message. I'm telling Thompson to use his siren. Your mom's meat loaf is the best.

Irene watched out the window, waiting for him to arrive. She'd taken some Tylenol for the headache she felt coming on. The dull throb was just beginning to ebb when headlights turned into her driveway. Parker got up and joined the men at the car. She saw them chat for a few minutes before Parker waved and strode down to his own vehicle and left.

Thompson stayed in the car. Paul moved up to the door and knocked.

Irene became aware of Izzy pressing up against her side, fluffy tail slapping the ground with a thump-thump as she wagged it.

"I know, girl. I like him, too," Irene whispered, petting the dog's sleek head.

She opened the door and he stepped inside. More than anything she wanted him to pull her into his arms, the way he'd done earlier. But he didn't, and she wasn't about to make a move toward him. It wasn't like she really wanted him to hug her. She reminded herself that she had no room in her life for another cop. And he was apparently trying to keep his distance, as well.

But his face… It seemed to have aged since that morning. Weariness emanated from him. When had she ever seen Paul so tired, so drawn? The answer was never. He'd always seemed to have the energy and drive of ten men. Now he looked like he was ready to fall over.

"Hey, you look beat. Come into the kitchen and get some meat loaf."

He nodded, but had yet to say anything.

In the kitchen, she motioned for him to sit at the table. He complied, his movements weary. Now she was really concerned.

She set a plate of warm meat loaf and a baked potato before him and pulled a large frosted mug from the freezer. She filled it with milk and handed it to him. He tipped his head and drained most of the glass, setting it back on the table with an exaggerated "ah." Just like her kids did.

A laugh escaped her. "More?"

"Please. I needed that."

Finally, he spoke. She realized a grin was tugging at her lips and turned to hide it.

Soon, all inclination to grin faded. As he ate, Paul related what he'd found.

"It doesn't make sense. Isn't going after me in such a public way counterintuitive? Wouldn't the kidnappers want to be staying under the radar?"

Paul nodded. "This is more than a random reaction, Irene. I think that we have some sort of kidnapping organization here. I need to contact the surrounding precincts. Both to see if they can lend us some manpower, and to let them know of the possibility of a kidnapping ring. I think the man who planted that bomb has gone rogue. And I think he's ex-military."

The room tilted. She had been leaning against the counter. Now she stood upright abruptly.

"Which means he's someone with training."

"Yeah." Paul finished his meal and took his plate to the sink. "Tomorrow, I want to head into the station and see if I can find out who he is. Also, I need to find out as much info as I can about the new missing child and Mary Ann's family. Do you think you'd be ready to make a trip Wednesday morning to Ohio?"

She thought of something. "My boss has been really lenient about me taking time off. But I do need to go to the meeting tomorrow."

He tilted his head. "What meeting? I don't remember anything about a meeting."

"I had forgotten about it. But it's for the family I was

visiting when I first saw the bearded man. Tomorrow at four." She waited anxiously.

His face grew fierce. "You're kidding, right? How on earth can you go to a meeting when all this is going on?"

Her own temper rose. "I don't want to lose my job! Others can handle the rest of the visits. I was brought on board after they were started. This case is all mine. No one else knows the family yet."

He scowled. "You're not going alone."

She opened her mouth. He shook his head. "No way, Irene. It's completely nuts, but I will let you go if I can go with you."

She huffed, but secretly was relieved. "I wasn't going to argue."

"One more thing. My cruiser is not in shape to be driven. We'll have to use your car."

She started to wash the dishes. The air crackled between them. Tension, attraction, or both? As much as she tried to deny it, she could feel something brewing between them. *Lord, help me to guard my heart.*

After drying her hands on the towel hanging on the stove, she turned to find him watching her. Her breath caught in her throat. There was so much tenderness, so much longing in that look, it robbed her of all thought. Then he straightened and the expression was gone. Had she imagined it?

"How about some coffee?" she asked, trying to ease the electric current between them.

He smiled. A slow, easy smile that made her pulse hike. "There's never a bad time for coffee."

She smiled back as she reached for the button on the Keurig.

"Irene, stop!" Paul's shout reached her a moment too

late, just as she touched the machine. Sparks flew out in every direction. A jolt shot through her fingertips at the same moment that Paul grabbed the broom from the corner and swept the machine from the countertop and into the empty sink.

Paul grabbed the fire extinguisher off the wall and used it to douse the smoking coffee maker.

For the second time that day, she'd escaped death because of Paul's quick thinking. She knew in her bones this was no accident. Just as she knew the person responsible wouldn't give up. What she didn't know was if she'd survive the next time.

Chapter Eleven

Irene sat, dazed, as the smell of smoke filled the air. The smoke detector let out four shrill beeps before Paul yanked it off the wall, silencing it. Then Paul rushed to her side and called to her. She felt his warm hand on her shoulder as he gently shook her.

"Irene? Irene! Come on, Red. Can you hear me? Are you okay?"

She turned her head, stunned, and stared into his concerned gaze. "I'm fine. My hand feels funny, but the numbness is already fading." She looked down at her shocked hand, amazed to find it looked completely normal. It felt like the tips of her fingers had been singed off.

She took in the countertop. The foam from the fire extinguisher had started to dissipate, but she could tell it would leave a mess behind it. The Keurig was damaged beyond repair. It had never had problems before. The machine was only three months old. Jace and Melanie had given it to her on her last birthday.

"That was no accident." Her words were not a question. They left a bitter taste on her tongue. Fury and anguish battled for control. Not from the incident itself. No, her feeling of helpless anger was more due to the fact that someone had violated her home, had come into her personal space and tried to do her and her family harm. That was the final straw for her.

"I know." Paul surveyed the machine grimly. "Which means that our guy knows you survived his earlier attempt. The fact that he was bold enough to come and sabotage this machine terrifies me, Irene. I don't have enough manpower to watch your house when you're not here. And I'm afraid he'll go after your family to get to you."

She froze. Her boys. Paul was right. The wacko coming after her was vicious enough to use her children against her.

"What do I do?" Was that wobbly voice hers? She sounded like she was all of ten years old. Honestly, she couldn't take any more. *Lord, why? I'm trying to trust You again, but this doesn't make it easy.* Even as she cried out to her God, she knew she had enough faith to continue to trust and believe.

Paul paced, rubbing his hand across his chin as he considered his options. Finally, he nodded. "Your mom…her house is protected with a security system, right?"

She sat up. "Yes. She had it put in several years ago, when someone was after Melanie."

He stopped pacing and faced her, shoving his hands in his back pockets. "Yeah, I remember that. Irene, I think you should call your mom. Let her know you, the boys and Mary Ann are coming and why. I don't want her to be taken off guard. There will be continued police protection, but the security system will alert us to any intruders or issues during the day when no one is home. And if I remember right, the retired fire chief is across the street. He knows the drill. Shouldn't mind keeping an eye on the place."

Irene didn't even hesitate. She called her mom, who immediately agreed. Irene hated bringing her problems home to her mother's door, but knew it was necessary to protect them all. Paul had gone outside to let Thompson in on what had happened. By the time Irene had woken the boys, the two cops had reviewed the kitchen scene and confirmed that the coffee maker had been tampered with.

She heard Thompson mutter, "This dude is either brave or stupid, Chief, messing with your coffee."

"You got that right," Paul replied, his familiar drawl back in place.

Shaking her head, Irene went to hurry the boys along.

"We can take Izzy, right, Mom?" Matthew asked, his lower lip pushed out in a slight pout.

"Of course, buddy. Izzy's family." She tousled his hair.

"What about the girls?" AJ queried, pushing his glasses up on his little nose.

Oh, boy. That one wasn't going to go over well with her mom. The "girls" were Jelly Bean and Oreo, a couple of rats the boys had gotten from Jace last year. Irene hadn't been pleased. Their grandmother had pitched a fit when she'd seen them. But if they stayed here, who knew when they'd get back? And she wasn't about to return twice a day to feed them. She made an executive decision.

"Get their food together, and we'll take them. Make sure you have everything they'll need for several days."

She monitored the boys packing for a few minutes before hurrying to pack for herself and Mary Ann. Within an hour, they were ready to go.

Irene opened the hatchback and whistled. Izzy hopped up inside. Irene couldn't help remembering that only a few days ago they'd opened the door to find Mary Ann hidden inside. Shivering, she shut the door and climbed into the driver's seat. Should she have let Paul drive?

He was looking comfortable in the passenger seat. She had never thought of asking. She glanced back at the seat behind them. Her sons were situated on either side of Mary Ann, taking turns making her laugh. The rats were safely in their cage on the floor at AJ's feet.

The moment she backed out of the driveway and started down the road, Thompson pulled away from the curb and followed her. The plan was that he would give Paul a ride home once she and the children were situated.

It was a testament to how serious the situation was that her mother saw the rat cage coming into her house and didn't say anything. Her complexion turned a little green, and one slender, blue-veined hand pressed her mouth as if she were feeling ill. Still, she didn't protest.

"Sorry, Mom." Irene muttered, guilt swamping her.

"Never you mind, Irene. We'll do whatever we need to. All that matters is that you and the kids stay safe."

That was the end of the conversation. The rats were soon safely tucked away in the boys' usual room. The room that had once belonged to her sister, she reflected.

Paul didn't stay inside long after they arrived. He and Thompson did a thorough check of the house and grounds to make sure everything was safe and that the security system was working well. Irene knew a cruiser would be parked outside all night.

Paul himself would be going home. She was embarrassed to realize how much she didn't want him to leave. But she knew it was best. He didn't have a vehicle here, and he really needed some sleep. He looked like he wanted to say something.

"What?" she asked.

He sighed, a sound of pure frustration. "Oh, nothing that won't keep."

She knew him better than that. Whatever he wanted to tell her, it was important. At least to him. Although she doubted it had anything to do with her safety. If it did, he would have said it, whether her mom was within listening distance or not.

Well, whatever it was, it didn't matter now. He had gone home, and she was safe inside here. It was better this way.

But even as she shut the door behind him, she had to ignore the sense of loneliness that swept in.

All he wanted was a cup of coffee. Paul made his way out to the office coffee station and poured some in his favorite travel mug. It was hot. That was good. Already his morning was looking brighter. He took a tentative sip. Ugh. He made a gagging face at Lieutenant Dan Willis, who smirked back at him.

"Sorry, Chief. Parker made the coffee."

He just knew that Dan was laughing at him, which was cruel. He lifted his mug in Dan's direction. "This is not coffee. I think it might be watered-down diesel fuel."

Parker sauntered in. "Anything to get your engine running."

"Oh, man," Paul groaned. "Bad coffee and terrible jokes. What did I do to deserve this?"

Both officers chuckled.

A few minutes later, Dan was all business. "Sir? I think you need to see this."

Paul's stomach tightened. It was either really good news or really bad. Dan moved over so he could get a look at the information on his monitor. Paul whistled quietly. Gazing back at them from the computer screen was the image of a young man in a US Army uniform. Private William Sharps, EOD specialist. Dishonorable discharge.

There was a string of minor complaints. He had done a year in prison around two years ago. And he had been ordered by a judge to undergo counseling after assaulting a girlfriend, something he never completed.

Paul scanned the information. One comment stuck out. His commanding officer had said he was "a brilliant young man with a short fuse and a profound lack of empathy. He seems to enjoy other people's pain."

Not a good thing to find in a soldier. And definitely not a person you'd want chasing you. Yet that was the man who had it in for Irene. Why? Paul was still working on that one, although he believed that Carter's death was the event that tipped Sharps over the edge.

"Lieutenant Willis," he addressed Dan, "please see that this information is sent to all surrounding precincts. This man is dangerous, and is responsible for at least two attempted murders. Oh, and he is highly skilled at setting off explosives, so caution is advised."

Dan nodded and stood. Paul knew his officers. Dan was the model of efficiency. Paul could trust that his orders would be carried out to the letter and that Dan would advise him of any responses or changes in quick order.

His next plan of action was to track down Mary Ann's family. After a half hour, he was more than frustrated. Lapp was an extremely popular name in that particular part of the country.

He began to check with the local police in the area to find out if there were any fires involving Amish families where a young child with Down syndrome was supposedly killed. That turned out to be quite a project. There were three departments in cities within the county and five police departments from counties near enough to have been involved.

He spent the better part of the morning and his entire lunch hour on the phone chasing down leads. He came away with nothing. His frustration grew. Irene needed him to solve this fast. Her very life depended upon it. What a time for Jace and Miles to be out of the area at a trial. He could have really used them about now.

Finally, his diligence paid off. There had been four suspicious fires in the past two weeks throughout the region. Three of them involved Amish in some way. As to casualties, that was a little confusion. Two or more of them seemed to have resulted in at least one death. But that was all gossip. There were no coroner reports, only local talk. At least two of them seemed to be connected to the name Lapp, but even that was unclear. Still, it was more than he'd had an hour ago.

Paul caught sight of the clock on the wall and exclaimed in dismay. It was two thirty. He'd promised Irene he'd arrive no later than three fifteen so she'd be at the meeting on time.

He worked feverishly for the next half hour before

calling it a day. Parker would give him a ride out to Vera's house so Parker could spell Jackson on watch duty.

No sooner had he arrived than Irene ran out the door, red laptop bag over her shoulder and two travel mugs in her hand. Two? He grinned as he stepped from Parker's cruiser and was handed a travel mug.

"Dan called and said your coffee at the station was below par this morning," she announced by way of greeting.

"Hey!" Parker mock-glowered at her. "I do my best."

"Sorry." She didn't look apologetic. Smug, yes. Sorry, no. "At least you're a good cop. That's the important thing."

Parker grinned.

"You ready to move out?" *Silly question, Kennedy. She's here with her bag, isn't she?*

"Yeah. The sooner this meeting is over, the better I'll feel about it. I get the willies just thinking of going near that place."

Who wouldn't? Paul kept that thought to himself, not wanting to dampen her high spirits. She'd had enough put on her shoulders in the past few days to make anyone depressed. This upbeat Irene was the Irene he used to know.

He was pretty sure some of the cheer was forced. That was fine, too. She was brave and trying to keep a positive outlook. In a way, so was he.

He got into her SUV with her and buckled himself in. Glancing up, he caught the tender look in her eyes before she shifted her gaze. Did she have feelings for him, too? The brief surge of hope was drowned out by the knowledge that he couldn't allow her to become attached to him.

Soon, very soon, he'd have to talk with her about his past. So she would know why this relationship developing between them could never go anywhere. He'd feel pretty ridiculous if she said that she was sorry, but the feelings were all on his side. Though maybe that would be preferable. The last thing he wanted was to break her heart.

His was another story. He had the feeling it was too late for him.

Pull yourself together, Kennedy. These maudlin thoughts will get you nowhere.

Pulling himself straighter in his seat, he spent the rest of the ride to the Zilchers' house filling her in on what he'd learned that day. He'd been tempted to wait, but felt that would be unfair. She deserved to know. To his relief, she seemed to take it all in stride.

"So you were right. About Sharps being military, I mean," she mused. "I didn't think he'd pick up knowledge about explosives and that sort of thing off the street."

She flipped on the blinker and turned onto the street where the Zilchers lived. All conversation died. Her posture grew taut. He could see her slim fingers clench on the wheel. She pulled into the driveway behind the other cars and put the car in Park, yet made no move to get out. Her gaze shifted toward the other house. The crime-scene tape was still up. The blinds were shut.

Paul leaned over and covered her hand with his. She jumped, then snorted.

"I can't believe I'm being this stupid."

"Hey." He caught her chin in his hand and turned her face to his. The glimmer of tears in her eyes was almost his undoing. Man, he wished he had the right to take her in his arms and kiss those tears away. Or the ability to tell her with absolute certainty that everything would be fine. He did what he could. "Irene, you're not being stupid. You have been so brave, so strong, these past few days, I am filled with admiration for you. And you are not alone here. I will be with you the entire time."

She nodded, throwing her shoulders back and lifting her chin. "Right. Let's do this." She turned to open the door, then cut a shy glance back at him. "Thanks. It means a lot that you're here."

"Who else will be inside?"

She stopped and tilted her head to consider, then ticked off the participants on her fingers. Altogether, there would be four other people besides them and the family at the table. He relaxed. That many people made it highly unlikely that Sharps would attack here. He told her so.

"Still, you have your gun, right?"

He grinned at the question and patted the service weapon in its holster. "Right here."

"Then we're good. Let's go."

They exited the vehicle together.

The meeting went smoothly. The parents and other educators were initially intimidated by the presence of an armed police officer. But after a few minutes the meeting grew so intense that they forgot about him.

About forty minutes into the meeting, Paul excused himself to the kitchen when Dan called. He listened as his lieutenant explained that they had managed to find the link between Sharps and Carter. Turned out the two were second cousins and had grown up together. The best they could figure out was that one of them had recruited the other to the kidnapping ring.

Five minutes later, Paul could hear that the meeting was breaking up. He peered through the doorway and his blood ran cold. The seat where Irene had sat just a few minutes ago was empty.

"Gotta go." He hung up as he dashed through the door. The startled team members stared at him, mouths wide-open. He didn't care. "Where's Irene?"

His voice came out hard. Almost angry.

"Our meeting is done. She needed to make a call to her office. I think she went out to the back porch."

Paul tore through the house to the porch. No Irene. Her phone was lying on the wooden deck. He picked the phone up and then turned to scan in all directions. Something caught his attention. Was that movement in the abandoned house? It was too shadowy to know for sure—the blinds were still down—but his instinct was screaming at him that Irene was there. And not by herself.

He called Dan back. "Irene's gone. I think the perp has taken her to the crime-scene house. I'm going in. No time to wait for backup, so get here quick."

He disconnected before Dan could answer, already moving toward the house. He had no idea what he would find. But he knew that if he needed to put himself in front of a bullet to save Irene, he wouldn't even hesitate.

Chapter Twelve

Irene struggled to break free as she was dragged through the line of trees to the house that would haunt her forever. One of Black Beard's meaty hands was across her mouth and nose. If she started to lag, he tightened his grip and she suddenly found herself unable to breathe. She had no choice but to keep up with the brutal man. Branches scraped her face, abusing her tender skin. A trickle dripped down her cheek. She was bleeding.

At the back door to his former house, he thrust her inside. She noted that the crime-scene tape had been cut. She saw only darkness for a minute or two until her eyes began to adjust to the dim light.

Black Beard kicked the door behind him shut. The sound was so final that Irene cringed. The imagery of a casket lid being shut flashed into her mind. She waggled her head as much as the man's hold would allow to dislodge the image. Such thoughts would only serve to keep her locked in fear, unable to act. She refused to be a victim.

A human-sized shadow moved toward them until

Irene was finally able to see the woman who stood before her. It took her a moment, but then her eyes flared wide as recognition sent shock waves through her.

The woman she'd been so concerned about less than a week ago stood before her. Except now there was no sign of an Amish bonnet. Of Amish anything. This woman was completely Englisch, from her skinny jeans and oversize sweater to her edgy haircut, heavy eye makeup and double pierced ears. The young woman shook her head when she saw Irene. Her shoulders slumped. She was the picture of dejection.

"Oh, Eddie," she whispered. "Why would you go and do something this stupid?"

Eddie? This monster holding her had an ordinary, pleasant name like "Eddie"?

"I don't want to hear it, Brenda." Irene shivered at the angry growl so close to her ears.

"Well, you're gonna hear about it. We coulda got the money Billy stashed and ran. He said to meet him, not go grabbing anyone else."

"Billy! I'm sick of listening to Billy. He's gonna get us all caught the way he's been chasing after this one. And for what? Because his cousin went and got himself killed. I say, we get rid of her, then there's no one left who can identify us. And then he'll have to start playing by the rules again. We can start over again in another state."

Brenda crossed her arms and glared.

Irene held her breath. She was getting an awful lot of information here. Which meant that neither of them expected her to live to share it with the authorities. But, surely, Paul had to be looking for her.

Brenda started talking. "I'm done, Eddie Dillinger.

You can take your money and leave. I ain't never gonna put on another of those dresses and bonnets again."

"You're as much of a pain as your loser boyfriend was. I don't need you."

Without warning, Eddie reached into his coat pocket and brought out a gun. Brenda had time to open her mouth, gaping like a fish, before he pulled the trigger. She screamed and grabbed her stomach before falling to the floor, crying in pain.

"And now, it's time I took care of you," he said to Irene, his acrid breath fanning across her face as he pushed his face against the side of hers. She struggled not to gag.

Before he could lift the gun again, it was shot out of his hand. Irene found herself suddenly free as the big man howled and cradled his injured hand.

Paul stepped into the room, his expression tight and grim. He advanced slowly, his service weapon never wavering off the man.

"I called for backup. They should be here within five minutes."

It was actually only four minutes until backup arrived, and they were followed closely by an ambulance. Irene hadn't been harmed, no doubt thanks to Paul's quick intervention. And God's protection. She may have doubted in the past, but now she was sure He was looking after her. How else would she have survived all this?

Physically, she was fine. Emotionally, though, she was starting to feel wrung out. As for the two kidnappers, they both needed treatment. It would be touch and go with the woman named Brenda. She'd taken a hit to her abdomen. Even as Irene watched from the sidelines, Brenda kept fading in and out of consciousness. Eddie, however, would definitely live to stand trial. He was handcuffed, both hands in front, his injured hand bandaged. He was also yelling angrily at everyone he looked at. Irene cringed at the foul language coming out of his mouth.

Eddie caught her watching him. A sneer curled his lip under the thick beard. She could see his teeth. The sudden thought struck her that he could be considered an attractive man, but one hardly noticed because of the anger and cruelty emanating from him.

"You ain't safe yet, pretty girl." Eddie spit in her direction. "Billy'll hunt you down and gut you like a deer. It's only a matter of time."

Paul stepped into the room, "That's enough."

His voice was harder than Irene had ever heard it. She started at the sound of it. She wasn't the only one. The man who'd been throwing threats and insults her way seconds ago subsided, although he continued to glower as one of the police officers lead him away.

Irene couldn't remember ever seeing Paul this angry, either. Paul didn't get angry. He was so calm nothing ever ruffled his feathers or got the better of him. *Except when I'm in trouble.*

Not ready to deal with that thought yet, Irene continued to watch as Brenda was loaded onto a stretcher and wheeled out the door. She really hoped the girl would survive. It would mean she would go to jail, yes, but even in jail, one could find redemption. The Lord could work anywhere, she was beginning to understand.

Quietly, she murmured a prayer for the woman's healing and conversion.

"Amen."

Irene nearly jumped out of her skin at Paul's deep voice so close to her ear. She had been so preoccupied with Brenda's situation she hadn't paid any attention to where Paul was in the room. Not that she'd forgotten about him. She knew he was there. And felt safer because of it.

"Can I ask you why you didn't let me know where you were going before heading to the back porch alone?"

Was he mad at her? He didn't sound mad. Just calm. Which meant nothing.

She gazed into his eyes and breathed a sigh of relief. What she saw there was warmth and concern. He had been worried, she knew that.

"I wasn't planning on leaving the house." She felt inclined to defend herself. "I just needed a little privacy to make a call. The house next door was still abandoned, or so I had thought. There were no vehicles in the driveway, no hint that anyone was there. I was done with my call and had turned to return inside when he grabbed me from behind and yanked me down the steps."

Paul brushed a hand down the side of her head. "Your brother would have my head if I let anything happen to you."

She stiffened at the thought that his concern for her was all due to his friendship with Jace.

Then he touched her chin, turning her head to look at him again. "And I would have been pretty upset myself."

Softening, she leaned into the hand on her face. What was she doing? She didn't want to encourage his affections…did she? She was growing more confused by the moment. To regain her equilibrium, she took a step away and laughed shakily.

"I'll try not to get into trouble again."

Paul frowned, but let her go. "Do that. In the meantime, are you finished with the meeting? Can we go? I want to be at the hospital when that woman comes out of surgery."

Good grief. She had completely forgotten about her clients.

"Almost done. I am so happy that I'm the service coordinator and not a therapist. Sweet kid, I just don't think I could go back there every week. I do need to collect my things. Then we can go."

It was funny how life went on around you even when your world was being torn upside down.

Before heading to the hospital, Paul drove Irene back to her mother's house so she could change. Every house on her mother's block was in full Christmas mode. Which was not surprising, as they were just over three weeks out. Mrs. Tucker's house was ablaze with lights and a lavishly decorated tree sat in the front window. She even had the two evergreens in the front yard decked out.

Man, he hadn't decorated for Christmas for years. It hadn't made sense, him being a bachelor and all. He celebrated his Savior every day in his heart. The decorations wouldn't change that. No, that seemed like something a family would do. A family he'd always assumed he'd never have.

But now he was starting to want a family.

Correction. He wanted Irene's family. He wanted to see *her* smiling at him every day, not some random woman his matchmaking mother or sister claimed would make a good wife. Because as much as he denied it, he knew that the feelings he'd once had for the teenage Irene were growing again. Only stronger and deeper.

He had to find William Sharps. Once the threat to Irene was gone, he could move on. Either with or without her. He'd seen her withdrawal earlier. She obviously had misgivings about getting closer to him.

Well, who wouldn't? Especially given their past together. And she didn't know the worst about him. Not yet. But he was determined that she would. Tonight. He'd tell her tonight.

But not now. Right now, they needed to go to the hospital. He knew he could leave her here at her mother's house. Zee had been approved to return to work, so he had her watching the school AJ and Matthew attended. They were home now. Parker was coming to take over the watch. And some of the other officers had dropped off a new cruiser for him to use while his was being fixed up. He wouldn't leave her, though. He didn't care what anyone thought. He was taking no more chances with Irene. Or her family.

Irene walked out the front door and took his breath away. Her gorgeous red hair was hidden under a warm wool hat, but it didn't matter. She still looked just as beautiful as she was, inside and out. She was strong and confident, and he sensed her newly rediscovered relationship with God had brought her some peace. She glowed with it. And his heart ached.

In each hand, she held a new travel mug. Exactly what his tired brain needed. Caffeine.

Paul jumped out of his side to walk around to her door and open it. It was the gentlemanly thing to do. And it got him his coffee faster. She handed him his mug as she folded herself neatly into her seat. It smelled wonderful.

"Thanks for the coffee." He slid into his seat and fastened his belt. "It's not anything fancy, right? Not like the tutti-frutti stuff you like."

"Please—" she added an extra flair to her eye-roll "—I know you better than that, Paul Kennedy. Yours is black, and way too strong for my liking. And mine's not fancy. It's just coffee with English toffee creamer. You should try it. It's yummy."

"Yeah, no thanks."

Still, he chuckled at the face she made.

Then it was down to business. He couldn't let himself get distracted before the case was fully closed. There was too much of a risk that she'd be attacked again.

At the hospital, they were directed to wait. And wait.

Finally, they were given the word that Brenda had survived the surgery. They waited a couple more hours before they were allowed to go in. It was almost nine. Visiting hours had ended. Paul had bought them both something to eat from the cafeteria although neither felt much like eating.

They entered the ultrasterile room together. Paul had instructed that Brenda be put in a private room with a guard at all times. The less contact she had with any of the other patients, the better. Irene situated herself in a chair near the wall. Paul moved to stand at the side of her bed.

Brenda's eyelids fluttered open about three-quarters of the way. She still looked drowsy from the anesthesia. When she saw Paul in his uniform, a gentle sigh left her.

"Knew you'd come see me," she mumbled, her voice thick. "Eddie dead?"

"No, ma'am. Eddie's been arrested for kidnapping and at least one murder and another attempted murder."

"He killed the paramedic," she said tonelessly. "And I think he would have killed the redhead if you hadn't interrupted him."

"And he tried to kill you, too. As for the kidnapping, you will be under arrest when you leave here." He recited her rights. She nodded her understanding. "I need you to tell me about the kidnapping operation. Is there another child you've kidnapped recently?"

He expected resistance, but Brenda had apparently given up.

"We had to take another kid to replace the one you cops are protecting. Folks already paid half for her. Got her from an Amish family in Indiana. We were supposed to go to the new safe house and meet up with Billy before delivering her to her new family. When we didn't show up, Billy probably took her and collected the rest of the money himself."

She gave up the address for the new parents without demur when asked.

"Why were you back at the house?"

Her lids fluttered shut again. He was afraid she'd fallen asleep. She answered though, much to his relief. "Had to leave quickly last week. Turns out Billy left money there that we didn't know about. He was out that day. Didn't know we'd left it behind till later."

"Who put the little girl in the SUV?"

Irene tensed. He heard her chair creak as she leaned forward.

"I did." Her eyes opened again, and she looked past him to Irene. "I saw your face when you came to the house. You looked so nice. Eddie was angry at me. I had kidnapped the kid, but didn't know she had Down syndrome. Eddie saw her face and he flew off the handle. Said no one would want her. Hit me. I fell and cut my head." Now that she said it, he could see the scabbed cut on the side of her head. That explained the blood they'd found on Mary Ann. And on the floor. "I knew he would kill her if the family said they wouldn't take her."

Irene paled.

"Then why did he go after her and try to kidnap her again?" He could see her energy was fading, but he needed the answers while she was willing to give them.

"He thought it would be easier to get her than to try and find a new child in another Amish community. When he couldn't grab her, Billy said there was no choice but to find someone else. But that the redhead still had seen too much."

Irene.

"What was your role in the operation?"

"I'm so tired," she mumbled.

"You can sleep when you answer."

A tear slipped down her wan cheek. "The guys would cause some kind of accident—usually a fire. Always in some out-of-the-way community. That way it was unlikely fire inspectors and coroners would be involved. While everyone was running around trying to put the fire out, I would go in and find the youngest child. I dressed in Amish clothing, so no one would pay attention to me. I could walk in and walk out with the kid. But after Niko died, I was done. I shouldn't have ever agreed to it, and will feel guilty until I die."

"Why'd you agree to it?" Irene asked from her chair. She got up and walked over to stare down at the woman on the bed. There was pity in her gaze. But also anger and accusation. Paul knew he should be mad at her for interfering with his interrogation. But, in his mind, she had earned a right to ask the question.

"I didn't want to." Brenda kept her eyes closed. "But my guy, Niko, said if we didn't get the money, we'd never be able to marry and have a life together. Now he's gone, and nothing matters anymore."

"How many children have you taken?" Paul barked.

"Not that many. Eight. Maybe ten. Hard to remember. The one I put in your car was from Ohio. I don't remember exactly where. Somewhere in Holmes County."

It confirmed their information.

"What about the new child? Where is she from?"

"Oh, I remember that one very clearly. Mostly because I had already decided to get out of it and turn Eddie in." She rattled off an address in Indiana.

A minute later, the nurse came in and shooed them out.

It was a somber duo who returned to the Tucker house that evening. They didn't talk as they went inside. Vera had left the coffeepot on. Irene poured Paul a cup, then started to make herself a pot of tea.

"Why do people do it, Paul?"

Huh?

"What, Red? Why do people do what?" He took a long swallow of coffee. At this rate, he'd be up until three in the morning.

"Why do people make such dumb choices? That day when Eddie came chasing after me with the gun…if Brenda and Niko had just walked away, he'd be alive and she wouldn't be on her way to prison. They'd be poor, sure, but at least they'd have a chance."

This was the opening he needed to tell her. Nervousness settled over him. He couldn't shake it off.

"Well, Irene. Many people make really dumb choices. I've made some myself." She turned to face him. He wished she wouldn't. Looking at her face as he confessed his failings would be hard. But he was a man of honor now, and he wouldn't back down. "You remember that night when I left you behind at the dance?"

Yeah, she remembered. He saw the way her mouth tightened. But she didn't back away.

"You were the best thing in my life, Irene. You and Jace. But there were things about me you didn't know. That I couldn't tell you. I know you wondered why I never invited you to my house, to meet my parents." She nodded. "Well, I was ashamed. See, my mom, she's great. But my dad, well…"

He stood and paced to the door leading outside. *Give me strength, Lord.* "My dad had issues. Bad ones. Back then, he'd lost his job and become discouraged. Turned to alcohol. And later to drugs. He ended up in prison for vehicular homicide while driving drunk. And he died there."

Facing her, he saw the compassion in her eyes. That would change when she heard the rest. "You'd think I would have learned, right? I was so ashamed of what he'd done, but when I was fourteen, I started to get into his alcohol stash." Yeah, she saw where this was headed. He saw her grow pale. "I hid it for years, but I was an alcoholic by the time I was sixteen."

He couldn't face her and turned away. "I knew you were special. From the first time I saw you, I knew it. And I knew I wasn't worthy of you. Then your sister died, and you needed me to be someone you could lean on. I couldn't stand to see you in pain. That night, though, well, some of the other kids had snuck alcohol into the dance. And I didn't turn away from the temptation. I was pretty drunk, but still lucid enough, when one of the guys asked how my girlfriend would react seeing me drunk after her sister died because of drugs."

A soft sob sounded behind him. He flinched. "I had never been as ashamed of my father as I was of myself in that moment. I wasn't worthy of you. And never would be. I knew you'd be safe, that your friends would make sure you got home, so I walked out and didn't look back. I wasn't going to make you see me like that—I wasn't going to put you anywhere near me while I was so out of control." He'd hated leaving her behind, even then. But he'd known it was the right thing to do. Then and now, she deserved so much better than him.

"I never touched a drop of alcohol after that. Not once in all these years. And Jace helped me reconcile with God. Then we moved, and I started over."

Footsteps. She walked over and joined him at the door. Put a hand on his arm. He didn't turn to look at her, just bowed his head and finished his story. "I moved back years later, and you had moved on. I was happy for you, Irene. I really was. Tony was a great man, an honest cop and a good friend. He made you as happy as you deserve to be—something that I could never do. I can't ever let down my guard. I was weak once. I refuse to let that happen again."

There was nothing more to be said. He set his cup in the dishwasher and left, knowing that between the security system and the cop on duty, she would be fine until morning. Which gave him time to get his head back in the game.

Chapter Thirteen

Paul picked up Irene at the assigned time. Mary Ann was remaining at her mother's house this time. Sergeant Zee was there with her, and another officer was keeping watch on the outside. Today, they were searching for the other child.

Irene had tried to talk at first—regular chitchat, probably intended to get them back to normal—but he had given her short answers, so now they drove in silence. He tried to tell himself he was fine with the divide growing between them, but he wasn't. It was unbelievable how much you could miss someone when they were sitting right next to you.

Deliberately, he turned on the radio. More to drown out his own thoughts than anything else. He was amazed that she didn't seem to be disgusted with him after what he'd told her. How could she not be?

He came to a stop at a red light.

Jace never judged you. Why should she?

He blinked, momentarily dazzled by the epiphany. An epiphany cut short by a small beep from the car behind them. Oops. The light was green. It must have been green for a while for someone to honk their horn at a police car.

"I can't believe someone just honked at you!" Irene exclaimed, surprised out of her silence. Feeling a bit lighter, he chuckled and rolled down the window to wave at the annoyed driver.

"Nah. I was woolgathering when I should have been paying closer attention. Besides, it's not like they whaled on the horn. It was a polite beep."

He grinned at her snort, much happier than he'd been an hour ago.

Two hours later, they arrived at their destination—a large two-story brick house just outside of Pittsburgh, currently housing an Amish child who'd been stolen from her family. There were two cars in the drive, which had been meticulously shoveled. The house was completely decked out for Christmas, even more than Mrs. Tucker's. There was even a plastic sleigh on the roof.

"I hate that we're going to break their hearts." Although Irene wasn't facing him, the sadness in her voice was clear. He covered her hand with his, resealing the connection he'd almost destroyed.

"I don't want to sound cruel, Irene, but the truth is that we have to. Somewhere, there's a mother and father mourning for their daughter."

She nodded. When she finally faced him, her blue eyes were clear. "Thanks for letting me come."

"You kidding me? Like I'd leave you unguarded again. Uh-uh. You're stuck with me until this man gunning for you is put behind bars."

She flashed a smile his way. "Thanks, Paul. Okay. Let's go do this thing."

It was a hard visit. The parents were belligerent at

first. They called their lawyer, who told them to do nothing until she arrived. So they were stuck waiting until she did. The animosity seething from the new parents was almost tangible. The little girl, however, was delightful—from the little they saw of her.

"How old do you think she is," Paul whispered to Irene when the woman left the room to take the little girl upstairs for a nap. To Paul's thinking, the kid hadn't looked in the least sleepy. Most likely, her new parents wanted to get her away from them. Couldn't blame them. Unfortunately, it wouldn't help.

"She's not much more than a year," Irene whispered back. "Not much language yet, and she's still not quite walking steady."

The man sitting across from them glared, and they lapsed into silence.

Finally, the lawyer arrived. The first thing she did was question Irene's presence. Paul had already thought that one through.

"Irene is a special-education teacher trained to interact with emotionally fragile children—and we had reason to believe that might be the case here. The child that the kidnapping organization had originally planned to sell to your clients had been treated so harshly by men that only women were able to get near her." All true.

The mother's eyes grew wide with horror. "There was another child? What do you mean?"

Despite the pang of sympathy that struck him, he did his job.

"They kidnapped another girl, but didn't realize until afterward that she had Down syndrome. They didn't want to chance you backing out and demanding your money be returned. They stole the baby upstairs from Indiana, leaving her parents to think she'd been killed."

The look the woman gave her husband said it all. She wouldn't have accepted Mary Ann. Paul tightened his lips, holding his anger inside.

At that point, the lawyer demanded to see the couple's paperwork. Paul raised his eyebrows. He suspected that the couple had done the "adoption" without the lawyer. Her frown grew deeper as she read. The adoptive parents must have been able to gauge her expression because they were ashen by the time she looked up. "Christine. Jim. I am so sorry. None of these papers would hold up in court. They are a complete mockery. I wish you had consulted me before you started the adoption process."

He had been right. Not that there was any joy in it.

"But she is still ours, right?" Christine demanded. "We paid them ten thousand dollars. Doesn't that count for anything?"

Some of his sympathy vanished. "It doesn't matter how much you paid for her," Paul cut in. "The child was kidnapped from her real parents."

Her face grew red. "I don't mean to be unfeeling toward her birth parents. I really don't. But they already think she's dead. Please, we love her. She's our heart now."

"Christine." The lawyer's voice was unyielding. "You need to go get the child now. She is not yours, and if you don't give her up, the police are well within their rights to charge you with conspiracy to kidnap."

That finally got through to the weeping couple. Paul and Irene stood by grimly while they woke the child, crying over her. The wife held on tight at the last moment. Her husband eased the child out of her resisting arms and handed the baby to Irene. He caught his wife as she collapsed, sobbing.

"You need to go now," he ordered.

Paul held Irene's elbow as she carried the baby to the car. The little girl cried as she was buckled into the car seat. Irene sat in back with her to try to comfort the child as best as she could. What a rough few days the little one had been through.

Fortunately, they didn't have to go all the way back to Indiana to return her. Brenda had given them the family's name and address and Paul had sent two officers to Indiana to fetch the parents. They had left the night before. Sergeant Jackson had sent him a text saying they were on their way back earlier that morning. By the time they arrived at the station, they were already there.

Paul led Irene and the girl into the station. A sudden cry rent the room. "Edith!"

The baby in Irene's arms wiggled like a worm, desperate to get down. The moment Irene set her down, she was off, running on unsteady legs into her *mam*'s arms. The little family huddled close together, speaking in Pennsylvania Dutch together as if they were alone.

Paul noticed that the officers all had silly, sappy smiles on their faces. He had started to shake his head when he realized he was grinning, too. Irene wasn't just smiling. She was radiant at the sight of the parents being reunited with their child.

"Danke. Danke," the parents said to him and Irene as they made to go home with their child. "We thought our Edith was dead. Gott has blessed us. Our daughter is alive. *Danke* for finding her."

One family reunited. One to go.

And one killer still on the loose.

* * *

Joy was amazing. It energized you and wore you out at the same time.

Irene slipped into bed that night so exhausted she was sure she'd never get to sleep. But soon she was nodding off. That's when the nightmares came. Nightmares of men with black beards chasing her. Strangers wearing hooded sweatshirts shooting at her. Walking into the kitchen and her mother telling her someone had kidnapped the boys as she cooked pancakes for breakfast.

Irene woke up, fear pumping through her blood, the urge to run still fighting with reality.

The children are safe. There is a police officer right outside. She checked on her boys and Mary Ann anyway. They were all three snug in their beds, asleep.

What to do now? Going back to bed was out of the question. As much as she needed more sleep, she dreaded the prospect of another nightmare.

The unsettled feeling continued as she went to the kitchen to fix herself a cup of tea, hoping it might settle her down. She filled the kettle and put it on the stove. While she was waiting, she let her thoughts wonder. Over Mary Ann. Her boys. Paul. What was she feeling toward him? And how was he feeling toward her? She reviewed his story about his past. It didn't bother her as much as he'd expected it to, that was clear. The thing was, she knew that people had weaknesses. And she also knew Paul. His strength. His dedication. He was an honest man who had fallen once. Of course, she could forgive him for that. But forgiving him wasn't the same as trusting him with her heart. He was still a cop—was that an obstacle she'd ever be able to overcome?

As she pondered, her gaze fell on her mother's well-worn Bible.

When had she last read the Word of God? Contrition touched her heart. *Sorry, Lord.*

Pulling the book off the table, she held it reverently in her hands for a few minutes. When her tea was ready, she carried the Bible to the table with her and opened it randomly. It fell open to Matthew. The Sermon on the Mount. Her gaze landed on Matthew 5:4.

"Blessed are those who mourn—they will be comforted."

At that moment, she felt God's presence stronger than she had in the past three years. She had mourned. And if she let Him, her God would comfort her. She remained at the table for another hour, her tea forgotten as she deliberately set about spending time with the Lord and allowing Him to minister to her broken heart.

Irene was ready and waiting by the time Paul picked her up at eight. The boys had eaten breakfast and gone to school with Sergeant Zee. Irene couldn't quite bring herself to call the woman "Claire," even though she'd been invited to. For some reason, she felt safer sending her boys off with efficient Sergeant Zee than with the friendly, vivacious Claire. Strange, but that's the way a mother's heart worked sometimes.

Mary Ann was finishing up her breakfast, too. Rather, she was throwing her breakfast. Irene was busy cleaning the cereal up off the floor when the doorbell rang. Her pulse skittered.

"Okay, baby girl, we gotta get you all cleaned up and pretty. Hopefully, we'll find your parents today." She was careful not to say *mam* or *dat* so she wouldn't get the toddler worked up.

"Pow, Pow." Mary Ann shrieked happily.

Pow? Irene wrinkled her brow and searched through her vocabulary. Then it hit her. Mary Ann was trying to say "Paul," but the baby couldn't manage the *l* sound yet. Irene racked her brain for other words she'd heard Mary Ann say. There were only a handful, which wasn't odd. Maybe she had said words that were unclear and in Pennsylvania Dutch. Or maybe she had a language delay due to the Down syndrome. Either way, Irene didn't know how well her parents would take that one of her first words was the name of an Englisch cop. Well, they probably wouldn't care, she decided. They'd be so overjoyed at getting their baby back it wouldn't matter what she said.

Irene and Mary Ann went out to meet Paul. His eyes were covered with dark sunglasses today. She missed seeing his eyes, but had to admit he was gorgeous. Flushing, she put the baby in the car seat, wishing she hadn't braided her hair so it could provide some shielding to her red cheeks. She felt like a schoolgirl.

"Morning, Red." There was that smooth-as-velvet drawl.

It was going to be a long day.

"Good morning, Paul."

In the end, it wasn't as long a day as they'd expected. Mary Ann traveled very well, and kept up a long string of giggles and babbling from the back seat. Several times, Paul and Irene exchanged grins at the noises.

The trip was around five hours long, due to stops to eat or to get out and let Mary Ann stretch her legs or have her diaper changed. At one stop, Irene offered Paul a tin of homemade cookies, courtesy of her mom. As he took one, their fingers touched. Electricity shot up her arm. This time, she didn't pull away. This time, she stayed where she was and watched him as he watched her, unable to look away.

He's going to kiss me, she thought. *Maybe? Yes*. His head moved closer.

"Irene?"

Was he asking for permission? She didn't know what to do. It didn't matter. He seemed to take her lack of response as consent. His head came closer. She felt his breath on her lips.

"Pow! Pow!" Mary Ann toddled over and pushed herself in between them, jabbering away.

They'd almost kissed! She was in mortal danger, they were on a mission, and they'd almost kissed! What were they thinking?

She couldn't regret it, though. Her blood was still hammering in her veins.

"Well," she said, to relieve the tension, "at least we know she's not afraid of you anymore."

"Pow?" Paul frowned quizzically.

"That's how she says 'Paul,'" Irene relied gently.

His eyes widened. Then he did something that melted her heart. He leaned over and kissed the bonneted head. When he looked back at her, his eyes were shining.

That's how he'd look when his child said "Daddy" for the first time.

She shouldn't go there. Maybe when the case was behind them. But, for now, she needed to remember that there was a man out there whose mission it was to end her life. It was only a matter of time before he attacked again.

Chapter Fourteen

They arrived in Holmes County, Ohio, after one o'clock in the afternoon. Irene was amazed. She had thought there was a large Amish population where she lived. Here, though, the Amish community was bristling with activity. Buggies were everywhere.

It didn't take long to find the first address on Paul's list. It was quite a distance from most of the houses, but Irene wasn't surprised by that. According to Brenda, one of the criteria for the children they kidnapped was that the family lived out of the way. This place definitely qualified.

The woman who came to the door watched them warily. She wasn't exactly unhelpful, but neither was she able to give them any new information. Yes, their family had suffered an accident lately. Some of the local kids had been smoking in the barn. No one had died. They'd lost some farm equipment. She didn't recognize Mary Ann, nor was she aware of any missing children with Down syndrome.

Irene sighed, discouraged, as they started driving again.

"Hey, now, don't do that." Paul reached out and put his hand on her shoulder, squeezing gently. "We now have one less place on our list. Which means the probability of one the next houses being the right one has gone up proportionally."

Irene laughed, shaking her head. "You've been spending too much time with Miles. That's the sort of geeky thing he would say."

Paul laughed with her. There was no rancor in the words or the laughter. The sergeant was dear to them all.

The next house was much the same as the first, although this time there were several children about and a couple of youths working in the barn. They were very kind. Irene liked them immensely.

But they were not Mary Ann's family.

"I will pray that Gott will lead you to the right family," the woman said.

"Thank you. We appreciate it," Irene returned. Paul raised an eyebrow. She smiled back. She had meant every word.

They returned to the car and resumed driving. By now, Mary Ann had grown tired of traveling. She cried and tried to wiggle out of her seat. When she couldn't get free, she shrieked. Irene was afraid she'd have a headache before they arrived at the next place.

But arrive they did.

"Are we interrupting some kind of event, do you think?"

There were buggies and people everywhere. Kids and adults. Despite the cold weather, there was a crowd of people outside. On one side of the house was a large hill. She could see children sledding on it.

"I don't know. I guess we'll find out." Paul said.

Sighing, she nodded and got out of the car. Their arrival had a domino effect. People stopped what they were doing to watch the unknown Englischers get out of the police cruiser. Irene immediately went to the back to retrieve Mary Ann. The child's shrieks filled the air as Irene opened the door.

If they didn't have someone's attention before, they had it now.

Thankfully, the crying stopped abruptly when Irene unstrapped her from the car seat. As soon as Irene reappeared with a suddenly smiling Mary Ann in her arms a murmur spread through the crowd. Irene saw one of the children run into the house.

"Mam!" the child yelled.

Within seconds, the door flew open, and adults spilled from the house. In the front was a pretty Amish woman with a black dress and red hair peeping out from under her bonnet. Her pale cheeks were wet, tears flooding down them. Right behind her came a man, crying, as well.

Mary Ann saw them and reacted as if she'd been electrified. She shrieked and shook and struggled in Irene's arms. Irene set her down. "Mam. Da. Mam. Da." The words tumbled out of her little mouth, over and over.

Her parents rushed to their baby and knelt to embrace her, paying no attention to the snow. Their reaction, the love and joy on the faces, was so similar to that of Edith's parents.

"We knew our baby was not dead," Mary Ann's father stated, rising to greet the newcomers. "How did you find her?"

Irene let Paul take the lead on this one. She was overcome watching the touching reunion.

"She was kidnapped by people who wanted to sell her in an adoption scam."

Both parents gaped at Paul, apparently dumbfounded.

"How did you rescue her?" Mrs. Lapp whispered, her face distraught.

Irene finally spoke up. "One of the kidnappers had a change of heart. She hid Mary Ann in my car when I left it unlocked."

She decided not to go into the rest—such as Eddie's plans for disposing of Mary Ann.

Paul rubbed her shoulder. Reassurance?

All too soon it was time to go. She suddenly realized how much she was going to miss Mary Ann.

"Can I give her a hug? To say goodbye?"

Mary Ann's mother nodded and stepped back slightly so Irene could move in closer. Irene squatted near the little girl. "Hey, Mary Ann, I need a hug. Paul and I are going bye-bye."

Mary Ann put up her tiny arms, and Irene wrapped her in one last hug. As much as she'd miss her, she was at total peace. This was exactly where the precious child belonged.

Irene set her down and looked into her sweet face. "You be good, darling girl."

When Irene stood, Mary Ann seemed to search for something. Then her arms raised again. "Pow. Pow."

As long as she lived, she knew she'd never forget the sudden sweetness on his face. Or the way his deep eyes glistened. He copied the posture Irene had used to embrace the child and pulled her into his arms. "Bye, Mary Ann." Then he moved so they were nose to nose. He whispered, but his words were still audible. "I promised we'd find your *mam* and *dat*. Be happy, sweetheart."

"Pow." She patted his face.

They returned to the car and started driving back home. The drive was silent. Irene was too wrung out to speak. And worried. Now that they had found Mary Ann's parents, they only had one more task. And that was to find Billy—before he found her.

Pensive, she sighed. Paul reached out and covered her hand with his. He didn't say anything, but she was grateful for the comfort. If only she could make her nerves settle down.

Billy Sharps was out there somewhere. And she knew he wasn't going to give up.

They still had to find the man targeting Irene. Paul felt as if the stakes had just been raised. Billy had no remaining coconspirators, the money he'd left at the house had been taken as evidence and the children he'd stolen had been returned. His officers had interviewed Eddie. He'd agreed to cooperate in return for a lighter sentence and give the authorities all the information on the families who'd bought the children.

That left Billy to focus his vengeance on Irene. Paul could see her out of his periphery. Tension held her body stiff, her face grim. He had a pretty good idea that Billy was on her mind, too.

They were pulling into a town. He could see a restaurant on the left side. His stomach had grumbled for the past half hour, and he'd seen her rub hers. Making a split-second decision, he pulled into a spot on the street, as close to the streetlight as he could get.

"Come on. We need to stretch our legs. Might as well eat."

It was an Amish-run restaurant. He grinned in anticipation. No one cooked like Amish women. This would be a treat, even if they still needed to be careful.

Paul requested one of the tables near the window. He made sure that he sat where he could see the car the entire meal. He didn't want another bomb planted. Or any kind of tracking device. Now that he knew the perp was ex-military, that opened the door to all kinds of modes of attack. He needed to be on his guard.

The food was all homemade, delicious and there was lots of it. They declined dessert, and got up. As they walked to the door, Paul reached out and took hold of Irene's hand. He had no idea how she'd respond. Pull away? Let her hand stay in his?

She sent him a saucy smile and a tilted eyebrow. That was fine. It was progress.

Outside the restaurant, though, he dropped her hand as they approached the car. He kept her close to the building so he could shield her.

It seemed like forever before they reached the cruiser. Soon he'd be able to relax. Not yet.

A shadow moved.

"Down!"

Paul shoved Irene to the ground and threw himself on top of her. Not a second too soon. The closest vehicle next to theirs—a buggy—exploded, sending waves of heat over them. The wheels flew through the air.

People started screaming. The restaurant patrons streamed out the door in an angry mass. When no further blasts seemed to be coming, Paul sat up carefully.

Irene remained where she lay on the ground, coughing weakly. At a quick once-over, she appeared uninjured.

"Irene! Are you okay?" He seemed to be asking that question a lot lately.

"Yeah." She sat up, dazed, and stared stunned at the burning buggy. "Was anyone in that thing? Where is the horse?"

"I put my horse in the barn out back," a shaky voice replied.

They looked up to see a middle-aged man, watching his mode of transportation burn before his eyes. Paul stood and faced the crowd, making sure to keep himself between them and Irene. Her back was to the building, so there was little chance that anyone would be able to sneak in behind her.

Irene wilted, leaning back against the bricks. He felt the same way. The destruction was senseless and cruel, but at least everyone had survived—it would have been horrible if any person or horse had been killed in the blast.

"Did anyone see anything? Anyone acting suspicious near the buggy in the past hour, or anyone running after it blew?"

"Ja," a soft voice replied. "I saw someone." A young woman wearing a pale dress stepped forward, shivering. Cold? Or fear? She was wearing a coat and gloves, making it likely that she had already been outside before the blast. No one seemed to have grabbed a coat when they left the restaurant.

Paul motioned the girl forward. He wasn't moving from Irene. If there was a sniper out there, they'd have to go through him first. No one touched his woman. He was tired of trying to pretend he didn't love her. Well, he did, whether or not she felt the same way. He would stand by her and protect her while she remained in danger. Or longer, if she allowed him to remain in her life.

The girl had come to stand before him. She tried to remain still, although he could discern telltale signs of nervousness—twisting her hands, chewing her lip, her eyes darting around.

"It's okay, miss. You're not in any trouble. But the man responsible for this is a dangerous criminal and we need to catch him as soon as possible. He has been kidnapping Amish children and selling them. My companion and I have just come from returning one of those children to her family."

An angry murmur spread through the crowd. Children were to be protected. The idea of stealing a child was repugnant.

"I didn't see him put anything in the buggy. But right before it happened, I saw a man standing over there—" She pointed to an area off to the left. He would have been blocked from Paul's view by the buggy. "As you came out, he pointed something at the buggy. I thought it was a cell phone. He touched it with his other hand, and then the buggy exploded."

"How is it that you weren't hurt by it?" Paul was struck with how close the teenager had come to being seriously injured.

"I was standing on the other side of that truck. I could see everything through its window."

"Did you see him leave?" Paul really hoped she had.

"*Nee.* I mean no. I looked up and he was gone." She looked worried.

"It's okay," he reassured her. "Can you tell me anything about what he looked like?"

Even before she described him, Paul knew what she'd say. She'd seen a dark-haired man in a camouflage coat. William Sharps.

Paul and Irene were both exhausted by the time they reached Mrs. Tucker's house that evening. Paul walked her inside.

"Chief Paul! Mommy!" Matthew skidded to a halt before them and threw his arms around first his mother and then the chief. Paul started to do his customary rubbing of the boy's head, but stopped, affection stealing over him. Instead, he bent down and returned Matthew's hug. Matthew grinned.

Paul started to straighten, then noticed AJ standing at his side, his face serious. AJ was harder to read. Did he want a hug? Paul didn't know what to do. He decided to leave it up to the seven-year-old and opened his arms. Immediately, AJ's thin face lit up and he bounded in to accept a hug, gripping Paul tightly in return.

Paul had made up his mind earlier to go straight home and leave Irene to have some personal time with her sons. So when Vera invited him to stay and have a piece of pecan pie and a cup of fresh coffee, he opened his mouth to decline.

Irene's soft hand on his arm stopped him.

"Paul, we'd love to have you join us." She added a soft smile meant only for him. He forgot how to breathe. "Stay."

Wordlessly, he nodded.

Pecan pie was his absolute favorite. And yet this time, he never tasted a bite. His focus was all on the beautiful redhead seated next to him. He would gladly remain by her side for the rest of his days. As far as he was concerned, there'd never be another woman for him.

It was some time later when he looked around to see Vera herding the boys off to their baths. They both came over to give Paul and their mother another hug before following their grandmother.

Paul stood up. He needed to take his leave.

As they moved together to the front door, his phone rang. It was Jackson.

"Jackson. What's going on?" He kept his eyes on Irene as he talked.

"Hey, Chief. We just got a report that Sharps might have been spotted near the Indiana border."

That grabbed his attention. His brow wrinkled as he processed this new information. "Indiana? Not Pennsylvania?"

"That's what the report said. It wasn't a definite sighting, but the timing's right."

He hung up and related the news to Irene. "I'm still going to have you watched and the house kept under surveillance. Even if it's him leaving the area for now, I don't think he'll stay gone. The Indiana police are keeping a watch for him, also."

"You'll get him." Irene flashed that soft smile up at him. The one that made him feel invincible and weak at the knees simultaneously. "I know you will, Paul. I have faith in you."

He couldn't take any more. He reached out and pulled her gently into his arms, the way he'd wanted to so many times. He held his breath, waiting for her to resist or pull back. She did neither, melting into his arms. Softly, he allowed his lips to touch hers. A sigh left her.

Gaining confidence, he kissed her again, letting the sweet kiss linger.

When they parted, her cheeks were pink and her eyes were shining.

Touching the side of her face, he turned and walked out the door, knowing he'd dream of this moment all night.

Chapter Fifteen

Irene waved at the officer sitting across the street in his cruiser the next afternoon as she left her office and headed toward her car to drive to a meeting. Paul had reluctantly agreed to let her go to work, as long as an officer trailed her. The Erie precinct had sent several officers to help provide coverage. One of them was Lieutenant Crane. He didn't wave back. She shrugged. He wasn't there to be social. She squinted, trying to see him better.

Nope. The glare from the sun was too sharp. She could see his position but not his face. She slowed her walk. A sudden chill fell over her. She continued rapidly on stiff legs to where her SUV was parked. She could almost feel icy fingers touching her neck and couldn't keep her shoulders from twitching.

Her thoughts flew back to the officer who was on duty to protect her. Even if he wasn't feeling friendly, he should have acknowledged her presence. Maybe he hadn't seen her wave? She cut her eyes to the cruiser. He was sitting in the same position as before.

Something was not right.

She reached her vehicle and began to get in, then hesitated. Miles's fiancée, Rebecca, had been attacked by someone hiding in her car back in October, she remembered. Her legs shook as she peered in her windows. Some of the tension fled as she ascertained that no one was in her car.

But that didn't mean there was no danger.

She dove into the vehicle, hitting the lock button as soon as the door slammed behind her. Then she leaned her head back against the headrest and let out a shuddering breath. But she couldn't rest easy yet. Turning her car on, she jabbed the phone button on the dashboard. Her phone was in her back pocket, but it was close enough for the Bluetooth signal to pick up.

"Number?" the computerized voice queried.

Breathlessly, she gave Paul's number, rooting around in her purse for her sunglasses. Her instinct told her to get out of there, but with the way the sun was reflecting off the snow, she knew she'd never be able to drive without shades. Blue eyes were just that sensitive.

A moment later she sighed in resignation. Voice mail. Well, she'd leave the message as she drove away. Setting her sunglasses on the bridge of her nose, she clutched the gearshift to put the car in Reverse.

And shrieked as something hit her window. Her shriek melded with the beep from the voice mail.

Turning her head, she saw a gun pointing right at her.

Private William Sharps had found her. She could still take her chances and put the car in Reverse, hoping to get away before he shot her. Then she saw what he had in his other hand, and her heart stopped beating.

Matthew's stuffed crocodile. He'd never lose sight of it.

Terrified that this man had her kids, she rolled the window down.

"Smart lady," he sneered. "Get out of the car and come with me if you want your brats to live."

"What do want from me?" She hated the quaver in her voice, but she was still composed enough to realize that whatever was said was being recorded in Paul's voice mail. It was her only hope of getting out of this alive. She knew without a doubt that the man in front of her planned to kill her. And probably her children, too.

Lord, help us. Please guide me.

The sneer hardened into a look of pure hatred. "It's all your fault. If not for you, Niko would still be alive, and we'd be on our way to being rich men."

"You know the police are after you." His eyes blazed at her words, and she hoped the anger provoked him into saying something—revealing an important clue. She had to give Paul as much as information as she could. "Your friend Eddie is in jail. You don't want to add another murder to your list of offenses."

He let out a crack of harsh laughter. It grated along her sensitive nerves. "Yeah, Eddie's probably told them everything. What a weak fool! He wanted to go into hiding again. Said we'd start again in another state. Plenty of desperate people all over the country willing to pay for children. You were too close with the police, he said. It was too risky to continue to work the operation in Pennsylvania. But what about what I wanted?"

She didn't answer. The malevolent stare he leveled at her said he didn't care what she thought. He'd made up his mind.

He kicked the door. She jumped, her pulse leaping. "Get out. You're going to do exactly what I say if you want your kids to survive. They'll be orphans, but they may live. *If* you follow my directions."

At that, she knew it was doubtful that she would be rescued in time. But she wasn't giving up. Not while there was a chance that her babies would survive.

She must have hesitated too long. He kicked the door again and pointed the gun straight at her head.

"I have no problem with shooting you right here in the middle of the street. But if I do, your kids won't survive the day."

Numbly, she opened the door and stepped down. She didn't even take the time to turn off the engine. Who knew what would set him off? She suspected he wouldn't really shoot her out in the open. Judging by the angle at which he was standing, he was trying to hide the gun from any passersby. Plus, there was no silencer on it, so chances were he'd be seen if he shot her and ran. No, he was bluffing, though she couldn't exactly call his bluff. Not if her goal was to get both herself and AJ and Matthew out of this horrific nightmare alive.

No sooner had she stepped away from her vehicle than her right elbow was yanked into his side. Her skin crawled at being in such close proximity to a killer. His long legs kept up a brisk pace and she was forced to jog along at his side, the click of her boot heels loud in the silence. Once, she tripped.

His grip tightened, and he pulled her arm behind her at a painful angle.

Near the side of the parking lot, he stopped next to an old pickup truck. It was so rusted she could barely tell what the original color had been. He forced her up into the cab, shoving her over so he could climb up beside her. He gave her one final shove. Hard. Just for spite, she was sure of it. Her knee knocked over a can of Diet Coke. It spilled across the passenger seat. Her head cracked against the window. She bit her lip to keep from crying out and tasted blood.

Sharps slammed his door shut, then reached behind his seat and pulled out a roll of duct tape. Instinctively, she drew back. He slapped her, then grabbed both wrists in one large hand. The tape made a loud, tearing noise as he wound it around and around her wrists tight enough that she worried about losing circulation. When he was satisfied that she couldn't escape, he started the engine and began to drive.

Sharps drove one-handed, the other hand holding the gun. It was positioned low enough that bystanders couldn't see it. But Irene never forgot that it was there. Add to that, he had no heat in the truck, and her seat was wet. Soon, she was shivering from a combination of terror and the cold seeping into her body. Her mind was unable to formulate clear thoughts. She should pray, but nothing was coming. Instead, her mind kept up a litany of *Help, Lord. Help.*

It was all she could do. She trusted that God understood, and that He would take care of the rest.

Finally, Sharps pulled off the main road and up a side street. She knew this road. It dead-ended at an old lumber mill that had been closed for over ten years.

Apparently, Sharps had found another use for it.

Shudders were racking her slender frame continuously by this point. Her jaw was aching from her chattering teeth grinding against each other.

Sharps stopped the truck next to the boarded-up building and got out. He dragged her across the seat without any thought to her bound hands. When she fell out of the truck and landed in a heap at his feet, he kicked her, then yanked her upright.

"Okay, woman," he growled. "It's time you got what was coming to you."

He pushed her forward. She cried out as her heel caught in a crack and her ankle twisted. He didn't care, just kept herding her toward the building. Inside, the only positive thing she could determine was that the building was slightly warmer than outside. She was so frozen, though, she wasn't sure she'd ever truly be warm again.

Not that she had all that long to feel cold.

Her frantic gaze searched the shadows for any sign of her babies. But neither AJ nor Matthew was anywhere to be seen.

Was she too late?

"Where are my sons?" she demanded, fear forgotten in her concern for her children.

He laughed, a horrible sound. "I ain't got your kids. Never did. Followed them this morning and the little one dropped the animal. Knew I could use it as bait. You weren't so smart, were ya? Now I have you here, and no one knows any better."

He didn't have her boys. That meant she could fight back without them being in danger.

Lord, help me. And please let Paul find me. I love him, Lord. And I think he loves me.

Her hands were still bound. As Sharps advanced on her, she backed away, looking around for anything she might use to defend herself. As she passed a rickety shelf unit, she noticed a pile of old straw and insulation that was being used for a mouse's nest. Her wrists were bound, but she could still use her hands. Before she could talk herself out of it, she grabbed it up in her fists and threw it directly at his eyes. A mouse fell out of the debris and landed on him, biting his cheek in its fright.

Sharps shrieked, waving his arms to rid himself of both the rodent and the debris in his eyes.

Irene didn't stick around to watch. Whirling, she took off as fast as her boots would let her run.

Not fast enough. Within seconds, she heard him charging after her.

There was a room ahead of her. She ran in and shoved the door shut, locking it with the slide latch.

He banged on the door. Each bang brought a shower of dust. The door frame shook. It wouldn't last long under the onslaught.

And then he would catch her.

Paul glanced at the clock on the wall. Three fifteen. Irene would be at work for another hour. He knew she had a meeting this afternoon. Officer Crane was watching her. Paul frowned as he realized that Crane should have reported in already.

A knock on the door startled him. His head shot up. His two new hires were waiting for him. He waved them in. Officer Lily Shepherd entered, followed by Officer Gabe McLachlan. Both had neutral expressions, but he could read the apprehension in their eyes. He smothered a grin. Facing the new chief was always a harrowing experience. Part of him was tempted to growl at them just to see their reactions. Of course, he wouldn't. He'd been the new guy before. And he'd also been the one shown mercy, so he would do likewise.

"Relax, you two. I just wanted to review a few details before you go on duty for the first time here."

Shepherd's shoulders dipped just a little, some of the tightness flowing out. McLachlan grinned and shook his head. Paul smiled back. He couldn't help it. His gut feeling was that they would both be assets to his team.

"Sit down. I want to see how you're settling in."

They had both attended an orientation. He knew neither officer was from the area. Shepherd had started out in Chicago. Her record working the streets there was impressive. Mac was from the other side of Pittsburgh.

They each grabbed a chair in front of the desk and sat, waiting for him to begin.

Paul lowered himself into his chair and reached for the files on the desk. His eyes went to the clock again. Almost three twenty. His gut screamed that something was wrong—it wasn't like Crane to be late checking in. He'd known the Erie officer for years. He hadn't become chief by ignoring his instincts. He considered them a gift from God to help him perform his duties.

"Hold on a minute, guys." He grabbed his phone. "I need to check in with Crane for a moment."

He didn't wait for them to agree.

The light on his phone was blinking. He pushed the button and tapped in his access code to unlock it. He smiled, relief leaking through his system. A voice mail. Well, Crane must have called in and he hadn't heard the phone ring. That was fine.

He tapped the voice-mail icon and held the phone up to his ear to listen in.

The smile slid off his face. He heard Irene gasp. Why didn't she say something? Then fear plowed into his brain. Someone was talking. The voice was unfamiliar, but the menace was clear.

"Smart lady. Get out of the car and come with me if you want your brats to live."

Sharps had Irene! And possibly her kids!

It took all his will to force himself to stand and listen to the rest of the message, hoping against hope the killer would reveal a location or some other pertinent detail. Nothing.

He had no time to waste. The moment the call was done, he was around his desk and heading to the door.

"You two, with me," he barked to the startled officers. Both Shepherd and Mac rose immediately and followed without question. "Jackson!"

Gavin Jackson looked up from his desk.

"Let all precincts know. Billy Sharps has Irene. Parker." He pointed a finger at the brown-haired sergeant. His finger shook, but he ignored it, as well as the agony pulsing through his system. If Irene died, he wasn't sure how he'd cope with that. "You need to check in with Zee at Mrs. Tucker's house. If they are there and safe, let me know. Tell Zee no one leaves. They may be in danger."

Parker nodded and reached for his phone.

"Thompson!" he barked. "Go back to the hospital and see if the woman in custody, Brenda, knows of another possible place Sharps might take someone. Anything she can think of may help. Move, people! Lives are in danger!"

The officers scattered, their faces grim. Irene Martello was well liked by all of them. And even if she had been a stranger, Paul knew he could count on every single one of them to put their lives on the line to protect her. It was their calling. And they were all dedicated to it.

"You two—" He waved a finger between McLachlan and Shepherd. "I want you with me."

They didn't question him. They may have been newly hired, but both had strong service records.

He didn't bother weighing the pros and cons of siren or no siren. He was going in hot. Irene needed him. He would die before he let her down. Cars parted, moving to the side of the road to allow his cruiser with its blazing red-and-blue lights to pass.

Paul's phone rang. Parker's name flashed up on the display. Paul jabbed the phone button, putting him on speaker.

"Yeah, Parker. What do you have?"

"Chief, I talked with Zee. Mrs. Tucker and the kids are safe. The doors are bolted."

"Good. Keep me informed of any developments."

"You got it." A pause. "Chief? We'll be praying for Irene. And for you."

Paul had to swallow around the lump that had gathered in his throat. "Thanks, Ryan. It means a lot."

He caught McLachlan's puzzled glance in the mirror. Well, now was not the time or place to spill his heart. Lord willing, he'd be able to find Irene. Alive. And if he did, he'd never let his past cause him to keep his heart from her again. Right now, however, he needed to focus. Praying silently, he drove to where Irene worked. Her car was still there in the parking lot. His mouth went dry. The driver's door was wide-open, and the motor was still running. Irene was nowhere to be seen.

He pulled behind Crane's cruiser. "McLachlan. Shepherd. Go search that SUV. Make note of any signs of struggle. Anything we can use."

Meanwhile, he opened his own door and stood, letting his training and experience kick in. Scanning the area, he judged that the danger here was gone, then went to check on Crane. He had a bad feeling about it. Crane was an older officer with decades of experience. He wouldn't have let Irene go with a stranger. Even if he'd been distracted or away from his car, the sight of her door being open would have clued him in that something was wrong.

So it was no surprise to find that the cheerful grandfather of two had been shot. Twice. There was a gash along the side of his head. And the other bullet was in his chest. His Kevlar vest had stopped it from killing him. Even as he watched, Paul could see his friend's chest rising and falling. The passenger window was shattered, glass strewn all over the seat. Paul opened the passenger door. He could hear Crane breathe. And groan. It sounded beautiful.

"Hold on, buddy. I'm calling for help." Paul immediately thumbed the radio on his shoulder and called in for an ambulance.

He heard feet running behind him.

"Sir!" Shepherd halted, her eyes excited. "Mac found something, sir!"

And indeed, Mac had found something.

"See these tracks, sir?" Mac pointed at a fresh set of tire tracks, not yet covered by snow. "They're recent, because it snowed up until almost three. And there are footprints."

Paul squatted. "Yep. See these? Heels. Like those fancy boots Irene wears."

"Exactly. And they both stop near the same side of the tracks. It looks like he must have had her get into his vehicle, then he got in the same side. But she was walking, so she was alive. And, I found this."

He handed Paul a small piece of paper. Paul almost crowed with delight. It was a gas receipt from a nearby gas station. From less than two hours ago.

"Outstanding work, you two," he praised them, feeling the first ray of hope. "If we can get a description of the vehicle, we'll be able to put out an alert."

Trying not to let his excitement get away with him, Paul ordered Mac to remain on the scene until the paramedics came. "I'm going to have Parker meet you at the hospital. I want you to search with him as soon as we have more information. Shepherd," he said as he turned to the woman beside him. "You're with me. I hope we won't need to call on your experience, but I want someone with sniper training, just in case."

Her eyes were shadowed, but she nodded in agreement.

They were off. Fortunately, the clerk at the gas station did remember the truck. Although there had been a lot of traffic at the time in question, most of the customers had been women in smaller vehicles or SUV drivers out Christmas shopping. The only man to fit Sharps's description had made himself even more memorable by acting suspiciously while at the pumps. So much so that she had secretly written down the make and model of the full-size pickup truck he was driving and the license plate. When he came in, he'd been rude, but hadn't done anything else, so she had set the number aside.

Paul thanked her and immediately put out an alert for the vehicle and driver. If all went well, they'd be able to track him down fast.

Paul just prayed it was in time.

Chapter Sixteen

Paul's phone rang. He snatched it out of his pocket. It was McLachlan.

"Mac, what do ya got?"

"Chief, Parker and I are just leaving the hospital. The girlfriend remembered our guy talking to his cousin about an old lumberyard they could use as a secret base if things ever went south. She was pretty sure it was within an hour of here."

Paul thought for a moment. "I know of a couple. One near Cochranton. Another close to Meadville."

He called the others, having them divide up, searching all possibilities.

He headed for Meadville, hating the fact that it might be a wild-goose chase. But until he had more facts, it was all he could do.

His phone buzzed again. It was Jackson. He jabbed the phone button with more force than necessary. Shepherd shot him a wide-eyed glance, then her expression went flat again.

"Chief!" Jackson's voice was sharper than usual, highlighting the strain they were all feeling. "The Cochranton police said that truck was spotted in Cochranton earlier this morning. It was crossing the bridge. Heading away from where the old lumber mill is."

"On my way."

Paul flipped on his siren, then did a U-turn at the next intersection. Shepherd used the radio to advise the others of the new information. Paul swerved onto the route that would take them to Cochranton. It was a relief that the road crews had recently been through there. The roads were relatively clear, letting him go at a normal speed. Unfortunately, he couldn't go any faster than that. There were so many twists and turns in these Pennsylvania roads. One turn taken too fast and they'd be stuck in a ditch. Which would mean he wouldn't be able to get to Irene.

It took less than thirty minutes, but it was the longest drive he'd ever experienced. The woman he loved, and if he was honest with himself, had loved since high school, was in danger. *Please, Lord. Keep her safe.*

As they approached the old mill, he turned off his sirens. No use letting the madman holding Irene know that he'd been located. Pulling off before the mill, he and Shepherd exited the cruiser and walked into the yard.

The truck was there.

Paul could have cried, his relief was so great.

But it was too early to celebrate. Irene was still inside with Sharps. Mac and Parker jogged quietly into sight. He heard Shepherd quietly talking into her radio, letting the other teams know their status. Jackson's voice replied he was en route. Approximate arrival in five minutes. Good. His team was coming in. There would be no escape for this villain.

Scooting close to the building, he motioned for the others to spread out, covering all the exits. When they complied, he moved. Gently he opened the door a mere inch, listening for any clues as to the location of Sharps and Irene.

Deep inside the structure, a man was yelling. Although he couldn't make out all the words, he could understand enough. Vile, angry threats of torture and death.

He'd never been so happy to hear such awful language in his life. It meant Irene was still alive. And fighting. Because she was evidently hiding.

Banging. Loud banging. A fist on wood.

A shot.

The acid in his stomach churned. What had been shot?

More yelling. Enraged.

It was time to get in there. Indicating to Shepherd that he needed her to come with him, he entered the lumber mill. The smell of dust, mold and rotting wood was overpowering. There was also the tangy smell that told him rodents had taken up residence.

"See if you can sneak up behind him. If need be, I will distract him, giving you a chance to shoot," he whispered. Shepherd's face was troubled. He reinforced his priority. "Irene is the most important thing here. Her safety, and the safety of my officers, has to be my focus."

Understanding dawned. Yes, he would sacrifice himself for Irene to live. There was never any doubt that he'd do that. Willingly. She nodded.

He followed the sounds and his heart froze as a woman cried out.

Irene.

Paul broke into a run. Sharps had Irene by the hair and was dragging her out from behind an old filing cabinet. His gun was in his other hand. He yanked Irene to him and started to lift the gun.

Paul had to act, now.

"Sharps!" he shouted, breaking the man's focus. "Police! Let her go!"

Former Private William Sharps whirled, still holding Irene. "Back off! I'll kill her!" he screamed. Paul knew he was serious. There was no sign of Shepherd yet. She may not have been able to find a way around. It was a chilling possibility. He needed to give her more time. There was no way he could shoot Sharps right now without hitting Irene.

"Killing her won't bring your cousin back. It was never our intention that he die. No one else needs to die here."

Sharps sneered. "Like you're just gonna let me go? Don't come any closer!"

Paul stopped. He had been inching forward.

"I ain't afraid to use this gun! I already killed one cop today, so I know there's no way out for me."

Irene paled. Paul could see the shudder that went through her. She had probably wondered about Crane.

"He's not dead!" Paul said, using his most reasonable voice, which was a challenge, because he was shouting inside. "You didn't kill a cop, you just injured him. He's on his way to the hospital now."

He hoped.

The young man scowled, but then his grip on the gun tightened. And his grip on Irene. "No. I don't believe you. You'd say anything to get me to let her go."

He placed the gun against Irene's temple. Her eyes closed, lips moving. She was praying. Sweat beaded on his forehead.

A door's squeaky hinges creaked behind them. Sharps whirled, pointing the gun in that direction even as he hauled Irene closer, his arm around her throat. Paul shot the gun out of his hand at the same moment that Irene slammed the heel of her boot against his shin. He howled, releasing her.

"Irene! Run!" Paul ordered, his voice hoarse.

She took off toward the door. Parker was there, waiting for her. He grabbed her and pulled her outside.

"Don't worry about me!" she yelled. "Go help Paul!"

There was nothing he could do about the tiny burst of pleasure that shot through him at the evidence that she was concerned for him. He focused on the man in front of him. Sharps was clutching his hand to his stomach, blood dripping on the sawdust-covered floor.

Paul eased closer, gun still pointed at him. "It's over, Billy. Put your hands up."

Sharps let out a whimper and began to raise his hands. Paul stepped closer. He was less than two feet away. The killer started gagging, his throat working as he made retching sounds and started to bend over. In the next moment, he hurtled himself at Paul, a blade glinting in his hands.

Paul felt the sudden stabbing pain, then heard a shot from behind. Sharps slipped off Paul and onto the ground, screaming.

Shepherd had hit her target.

Too bad she was too late.

Paul felt himself topple over and was out before he hit the ground.

* * *

What was going on in there?

Irene paced, worrying her lower lip between her teeth. Paul had told her to run, so she had. She knew that the worst thing she could have done at a time like this would have been to stay and distract him and the other cops. Staying would have inhibited their ability to respond to the threat Sharps represented.

She knew that in her head, but in her heart, she felt she had abandoned Paul. The man who had stepped up to be her protector. The man who—and now she could admit it—she'd fallen in love with.

Something was wrong. She'd heard a shot, and there'd been screaming. Then another shot. Now the police officers around her were all converging on the building.

One phrase penetrated her mind. *The chief's been injured.*

A dark chasm opened inside her. Paul had been hurt. She had no idea how bad. Was he even still alive? She tried to get to the building, but the officer at the door wouldn't let her through.

"Sorry, Mrs. Martello," the young woman said quietly. "This is a crime scene. And I can't let you contaminate it."

Irene stared at her. Even in her grief, she recognized a kindred soul. This woman had seen love and loss before. She understood. "Is he... I mean is Paul—"

She couldn't say the words. They were too raw, would make it too real.

"No. He's not dead. He's been stabbed, and is losing a lot of blood. That's all I can tell you."

She hated it, but Irene had to be satisfied with that

until the ambulance arrived. When it pulled up, Seth got out with Sydney. He squeezed her shoulder as they walked past. They seemed to be inside forever. When they exited, carrying Paul on a stretcher, she gasped. A dark stain had spread out across his shirt. His shoulder was covered with several layers of thick bandages. It must have been bleeding heavily. She knew her first aid. You apply bandages and pressure until the bleeding stopped. The ragged sound of his breathing was loud. Everyone was silent as he passed. His ashen complexion terrified her.

Tears ran down her face, but she ignored them. Her heart was breaking.

Not again. She thought she'd die from the pain of losing Tony. She couldn't bear to lose Paul, too. Oh, why had she opened herself up to this kind of grief again?

She wished Jace were back. She could really use her big brother right about now.

She began to step toward the stretcher and was stopped by a hand touching her arm. Jackson stood beside her. She was aware of Dan Willis taking position on her other side. Other officers moved in every direction. Everyone was pale, their eyes as somber as she had ever seen them. Paul was a man who commanded great respect and affection in those who worked with him.

"Irene."

She looked over at Dan.

"He needs to get to the hospital quickly," Dan said.

"I'm going with him." It wasn't a question. She wouldn't give way on this one. Not a chance. To her surprise, no one argued. Or maybe that was not surprising. They were very observant. No doubt, everyone knew that she was falling for the chief.

"I figured" was all Dan said. He helped her into the ambulance. She was aware dimly of the vehicle moving, its siren blaring, but her attention was focused on the dear man in front of her.

The ride to the hospital seemed to take forever. Irene held Paul's hand in hers, eyes glued to his pale face. He stirred once, opening those deep, dark eyes to see her.

"Irene," he murmured as his lids drifted shut again. "My Irene."

Her throat constricted. In her mind, she replayed her memories of Paul. Paul laughing in high school. Paul charming as he flirted with her. Paul cold and distant as he avoided her after he left her at the dance. Paul standing up next to Jace on his wedding day. Paul holding her face as he kissed her. Was that really only last night?

So many memories in her life were centered around this man. The thought of him suddenly disappearing from her life was devastating. But, if he lived, she would always have the worry hanging over her that this could happen again. What if he got hurt? What if he didn't come home? Maybe she'd been naive once, thinking such things didn't happen in LaMar Pond. But she had seen too much in the past few years to believe that anymore.

They arrived at the hospital, and she walked beside the stretcher as it was brought in through the emergency room entrance. Then she was left behind as the man she loved was wheeled into surgery. She called her mom, holding back tears as she talked to her babies. Her mom wanted to come, but Irene convinced her to stay home. This wasn't a place for kids.

For the next two hours, she paced aimlessly across the waiting room. The room began to fill with people.

Paul's officers. Their wives. Dan came in and gave her a crushing hug. She held on for a moment, needing the connection. When she pulled back, her face was wet and his eyes were too bright. Parker and Jackson stood together, not talking though she had the impression they were giving each other support. The two new cops—she couldn't remember their names—also stood together. The woman wore a shuttered expression. Brooding. Her companion's face was openly concerned for Paul and—she guessed—for his fellow officer.

Melanie and Maggie sat with her, offering whatever comfort they could.

She felt apart from it all. Oh, none of them had done anything to leave her out. In her numbness, she had a disconnected feeling. Would she ever be able to feel anything again?

"Irene."

And just like that, she shattered.

Jace was back. She hadn't heard him come up to her, but there he and Miles were. Weeping, she flung herself into his arms and buried her head in her brother's shoulder. Her tears turned into great heaving sobs. Jace wrapped his strong arms around her, rocking her as if she were a baby instead of a twenty-nine-year-old woman.

She had no clue how long she cried. When she finally lifted her head, she was almost dizzy from it.

"When did you get back?"

Jace brushed a hair back from her face, almost like a parent. She'd made the same motion with her children.

"Not long ago. We came straight here from the airport." Jace kissed her forehead.

Irene opened her mouth and forgot what she wanted

to say. She had just noticed that all the officers had come and gathered around her and Jace. Not to gawk. There was something almost protective in their stance, and their expressions were full of compassion.

She felt stupid, letting herself lose control in front of Paul's colleagues.

Then she realized something. "Wait, Jace. Paul's mom and sister. Did anyone call them?"

Jackson responded. "I did. Mrs. Kennedy is on her way. Cammie is catching the first plane. They should both be here by this evening."

Good. She couldn't imagine not being able to be there if one of her children needed her.

Talking ceased when the doctor entered the waiting room. His face appeared solemn, but it was softened by the tiniest smile curling at the edges.

"I'm assuming that you folks are all here for Chief Kennedy?"

As one they nodded.

"How is he, Doctor?" Irene stepped forward. If any of the cops felt it odd that she was the one asking, none of them said anything. They seemed to accept it as her right. So how obvious had her feelings been, anyway?

"The surgery went well. Chief Kennedy was very fortunate. The knife missed the carotid artery. The muscle damage was minimal. He will need lots of rest, but should make a complete recovery."

The cheer that went up was so enthusiastic that Irene expected someone to run in and yell at them to quiet down. No one did, though. Weakness invaded her knees. She stumbled over to a chair and sat, leaning her head back against the wall and closing her eyes. The seat next to her creaked. She opened one eye, then closed it again when she saw Jace. He seemed to understand that she didn't want to talk.

Through the next hour, the officers went in to see Paul, two at a time. His mother arrived and was rushed in.

She came out and walked over to Irene. "My dear," she said, and patted Irene's cheek. "Paul is asking for you."

Irene wished with all her heart she could say no. She realized what she needed to do, and it would be like tearing out her own heart. She knew it would hurt him, too.

Instead, she nodded and walked on numb legs to his room. She opened the door. His eyes were closed. She was able to convince herself that he was asleep. His lids drifted up and he met her gaze. Her heart sank.

Here goes. She entered the room. He smiled, a great open smile. When she didn't return it, his smile faded. Confusion twisted his face.

"Irene. I wanted to see you. Make sure you weren't hurt."

Her heart was beating so fast. "I'm fine. You saved my life."

"Irene, come here. I want to talk with you."

Her feet were leaden. She moved to the side of his bed.

"Today, when I knew you were in danger, I knew I had to tell you that I loved you. That I wanted a chance with you…"

She shook her head. No, no, no. This was all wrong. She had to stop it.

Paul's face paled. "You can't tell me you don't love me. I know you do."

He was right, she couldn't tell him that she didn't. "I won't lie to you. I have feelings for you. Strong ones. But I can't go through this again. I can't be a cop's wife again, living with the uncertainty. It would destroy me."

"Irene." Paul reached out his hand to her. His eyes swam with tears.

She couldn't stand it. Shaking her head, she backed up, then walked out of the room, tears on her cheeks. Her shoulders shook when she heard him call her name. She ignored it and kept walking, knowing Jace was at her side. His glance kept going between her and down the hall where his best friend lay.

Poor Jace. She hadn't meant to put him in this position, and yet she couldn't do anything about it. "Take me home, Jace."

His mouth tightened, but he nodded. He took her home and dropped her off. Their mother and her children greeted her.

She answered their questions without emotion, feeling empty inside.

She had left her heart at the hospital.

Chapter Seventeen

Irene pulled into Gina Martello's driveway and shut off the engine. She sat for a moment, staring blindly out the front windshield. Her last client for the day had canceled, allowing her to leave work early. Her sons and her mother-in-law weren't expecting her for another thirty minutes. She could go in and grab the boys, and maybe they could pick up a pizza on the way home. It would be a special treat for them. Yes. That's exactly what she would do.

She didn't move.

Paul. Two weeks had passed since she'd left him in the hospital. Christmas was four days away.

What was he doing tonight? Was he still at work, neck-deep in a new case? She could picture him, strolling around the police station as if he had no cares, whistling the theme song for the Andy Griffith Show.

How she missed him.

He had said he loved her. His eyes had been filled with that love the last time she'd seen him. And pain. Pain from his wound, true. But even more pain because she had rejected him.

But it was the right move, wasn't it? After all, did she really need to risk her heart again?

Her mind flashed back to a conversation she'd had with Jace two nights ago. He'd told her she was being dumb, letting the past ruin her chances for love again.

"I just want to be happy," she'd shot back.

"Because you're so happy now?" he'd countered. "Really? Are you?"

She couldn't answer. It didn't matter. He kept talking. "When are you going to realize that we are always in danger of losing those we love? We have lost Dad, Ellie and Tony. We didn't have any choice about that. But you have a choice. Paul is still very much alive. Do you really want to lose him, too?"

Did she?

Too late.

The truth sank in deep. It was too late. She was already soul-deep in love with the man. How had it happened? She had tried to protect her heart, and it hadn't mattered in the end. She had fallen.

Now both of their hearts were broken.

Not to mention the suffering of her boys. Oh, they didn't say anything. A mother knew when her children were sad, though. She could tell they missed Paul. He would have made a wonderful father for them.

Stop it! What's done is done.

Impatient with her maudlin thoughts, Irene got out of the car, slamming the door shut. And closing her mind to thoughts of Paul. Of his strength and courage. Of his gentleness. That deep voice…

Enough!

She stamped through the snow on the walkway up to the door and let herself in. She could hear muted voices in the playroom. An Italian aria was playing in the kitchen. She followed the music.

Gina was baking cookies.

A wave of love for her late husband's mother flooded her. The woman had become more than an in-law. She was a true friend. Just then, the older woman seemed to become aware of Irene and turned, a welcoming smile on her face.

"Irene! Did I lose track of the time?" Gina turned to glance at the clock on the wall.

"No, I got off early."

Gina started to speak, then she narrowed her eyes at Irene and pursed her lips.

Irene knew that look. The woman was dying to say something and was trying to hold her tongue. "What?"

"What? What do you mean 'what'?"

Irene rolled her eyes. "Come on, Gina. You know you want to say something."

The woman held her tongue for another ten seconds before she gave in. "Ah, me. You know I love you like a dear daughter, Irene? I don't like to see you unhappy. Or the boys."

Irene walked over and kissed her cheek. "We're fine, Gina. Or we will be."

"You are in love with Tony's boss, Paul. I can see it."

Irene opened her mouth to deny it, but couldn't. Distress filled her. The last thing she wanted to do was cause her mother-in-law pain. How would the woman feel knowing she had let another man into her heart? Fearfully, she gazed at the woman.

Gina gave her a gentle smile in return. It was a bittersweet smile.

"Irene, my son loved you with all his heart. Until the

day he died, you and the boys were his everything. I know you loved him, too." Irene's heart thumped hard in her chest. Where was this headed? Gina continued. "I will always miss my Tony. I wish he were here to see his sons grow. It breaks my heart to know he won't. But you are young. If God has given you a second chance at love, who are you to deny it? Or to deny my grandsons the blessing a good stepfather would bring?"

"But Gina," Irene choked out. "Paul is the chief of police. How can I love a cop again? How could I survive the worry, the pain again?"

Gina clucked her tongue. "Shame on you! Where is your faith? God will always see you through. You can't live without pain. Or love. That's life. Embrace it, Irene. It is a gift."

It's a gift.

Irene pondered and struggled with those words until Christmas Eve. Each day, each moment, the conviction grew inside her. She had made a mistake to reject Paul. He had a dangerous job, but being with him would be worth the risk. There was a hole in her heart without him at her side.

Was she too late?

She'd soon find out, she thought, as she pulled into the church parking lot for the late-night service. She arrived early. The choir performed Christmas music for an hour before the service began. Her boys had taken a late-afternoon nap so they would be able to last through the service. Paul was already there. She recognized his car the minute she pulled in. Her insides began to quake. Would she be able to ask him for another chance? And how would she handle it if he rejected her?

Jace and Mel pulled into the lot at the same time. Her mom had driven in with them. Together, the small group moved inside the church, alight with decorations and candles. People smiled and greeted them as they passed. Irene acknowledged each greeting, though she didn't stop. She had a goal in mind.

Paul was sitting near the front. Alone. Not for long.

Setting her jaw, Irene started to lead the group toward him. At first Jace looked startled, and then a satisfied smile settled over his face as he saw where she was headed. She ignored him. Nothing mattered other than getting to Paul. Her heart ached at the slump of his shoulders. She had put that there. He had taken many blows in life, but she had never seen him dejected. It was a posture she never wanted to see again.

She reached his row. He still hadn't looked up. Sucking in a deep breath, she started to enter.

Jace stopped at the row behind them and ushered their mother into it ahead of them. Melanie followed, holding a sleeping Ellie in her arms. Jace moved in after them. As he moved behind Paul, he tapped his boss and best friend's left shoulder. Paul turned his head to see Jace.

Irene slipped into the seat beside him. Matthew looked around her and saw who was sitting there.

"Chief Paul!"

The exclamation brought Paul's head swinging around in shock.

His startled gaze connected with Irene's. He opened his mouth. Closed it again. Then he blinked his eyes, fast. And swallowed.

Overcome, Irene bit her lip. One tear slipped past

her eyelids even though she tried to hold it back. Paul lifted a trembling hand and wiped it away.

She smiled. It was all she was capable of at the moment.

AJ and Matthew scooted passed her to hug Paul. He embraced them both. Then the boys repositioned themselves so one was on either side of him. Irene was forced to make room for Matthew. She didn't mind, though. The look of startled joy in Paul's eyes was all she needed.

They had yet to speak a word. Halfway through the service, Jace leaned forward and scooped Matthew up in his arms, settling the boy back with him. To her surprise, the child didn't fuss. Immediately, Paul moved closer to Irene. Her breath caught as he took her hand in his.

He held her hand through the remainder of the service. Joy swirled through her at the touch. Every now and then, she squeezed his hand and he returned the gesture. Just to let her overwhelmed heart know that he was really there, accepting her and loving her back, despite the way she'd hurt him. God was so good. So faithful. Despite her weakness and her failings, He was giving her a second chance.

She was really here. Beside him.

He'd been a bear to be around the past few days. He was man enough to admit it and feel bad about it. He hadn't been tempted to whistle even once since he'd been stabbed. All because she was gone. He had been furious with her at first. He knew she loved him. He'd seen it in her expression in the ambulance. For a short while, he'd allowed himself to believe they had a chance.

Then she'd crushed him and walked away like what they had didn't matter.

And now she was here. And he was holding her hand. He squeezed again. She reciprocated, and his world righted itself. He hadn't thought much about it when Jace had sat behind him. He hadn't realized that Irene had slipped in beside him until he had heard Matthew. He'd never forget the way his whole being had seized up in joy and hope.

For the first time in almost a week, Paul felt whole again.

When the service ended, Paul looked back at Jace and raised his brows.

Jace grinned.

"Hey, munchkins. Why don't I take you home? If your mom gives me her keys, then Chief Paul can drive her home. Okay?"

Good old Jace. He understood him well.

"Why wouldn't Mommy drive us home?" Matthew scrunched up his nose and peered at his uncle.

"Don't be such a baby," AJ scolded. "Mommy and Chief Paul have adult things to talk about."

Matthew pushed out his lower lip. An eruption was imminent.

"Come on boys. We'll talk in the car."

With a few grumbles from Matthew, the others left. Paul hadn't missed the blush on Irene's face as she'd handed over her keys. They sat quietly for a few minutes as the others in the church began to drift out to their cars. The pastor came in to lock the doors.

When he saw Paul and Irene, he smiled. "Would you like me to come back in a few minutes to lock up?"

"That would be wonderful."

The pastor left them quietly.

Finally, it was just the two of them. It should have felt weird to have this conversation in a church. It didn't, though. Because he knew that God was with them in this moment, on this holy night. He wanted His blessing on them.

"Paul," Irene began in a hushed voice. "Oh, Paul, I was so stupid."

"Irene." He moved slightly away so that he could turn to her, raising his leg so his hip and thigh were against the back of the pew bench, his knee bent. She did the same. They sat facing each other, knee to knee. But he never released her hand. "I have missed you so much. Every day. I have to know. Did you change your mind? Because I don't think I could handle that kind of rejection from you again."

Tears misted her eyes. She nodded.

"I was so afraid," she admitted. "You were right. I did—do—love you. With all my heart. And it terrified me."

"Because of Tony." If his voice was a little flat, he couldn't help it. Tony had been a good man and a friend. He had also been a cop, and it had gotten him killed. Paul didn't think he could walk away from being a cop. Not because his love for Irene was shallow. It wasn't. His love for this sweet woman was overwhelming, part of his marrow. Being a cop, though, was what he believed his God called him to be. One didn't just abandon God's calling.

Irene flinched slightly at his tone. "Yes. Don't shut

me out," she begged when he shifted slightly away. "I was wrong."

He stilled. Hope again took root.

"I thought that if I walked away from you, then I would be spared going through that kind of pain again. But I wasn't. I was hurting every day that we were apart. Even though you were still alive I was in pain because I was too stubborn to give you a chance. And I finally realized that I was wasting the time we do have. My brother reminded me that the next breath is never guaranteed."

Paul scooted in again, the emotion in his chest choking him. He reached out and ran his free hand through her glorious red hair. The soft strands sifted through his fingers. He'd thought he'd never be able to touch her hair again, to smell her light, floral perfume.

"Irene," he murmured when he could finally speak. "I have loved you since I was a senior in high school. I know I made mistakes with you. But I have never loved you more than I do right now."

The tears she'd been fighting finally broke through and rolled down her cheeks. He released her hands and gently wiped the wetness from her face. She was smiling by the time he was done.

"Paul Kennedy, I don't know why God has blessed me a second time, but I do love you." She leaned forward until their foreheads touched. They sat like that for several minutes.

A throat clearing made them break apart.

"Sorry, folks," the pastor said, "but I really do need to lock up."

Quietly, they stood, and Paul helped Irene into her coat. When she looked up at him, he couldn't resist stopping long enough to drop a chaste kiss onto her soft lips. She sighed.

The drive home was filled with murmured conversation. Paul didn't stay long after he dropped her off. Mostly because he had some planning to do for Christmas day. Jace being present was also a factor. He ignored his best friend's smirk as he kissed Irene quickly at the door and drove home.

He all but ran up the walkway and into his house when he arrived. Irene loved him!

Thank You, Jesus!

There's was no way he was going to be able to sleep now. He glanced at the clock. It was after ten. Well, as long as he had the energy...

He wrapped up the presents he had bought the boys last week.

Then he made a phone call to a friend. Yes, it was late at night, but the moment his old buddy heard what he needed, he was more than happy to assist. Paul hung up the phone and felt a moment of doubt. Did he dare take this step? Would it backfire? He'd find out in a few hours.

He hardly slept all night. Too keyed up. But by nine in the morning, he was done waiting. He knew that Irene and the boys would be off to her mom's at one o'clock, so he had time.

Irene let him in with a smile and a blush when he arrived. He understood. Even though the feelings between them had been growing for some time, their mutual acknowledgment was still shiny and new.

"Chief Paul!"

Laughing, Paul set the presents on the table in the hall and bent to scoop up the boys. What a joy they were! He chuckled again as their eyes widened when he handed them each their presents. He didn't usually give them gifts. Gifts were from family members. Irene shot him a speculative glance.

The boys were thrilled with their new remote-control cars. They hurled themselves at Paul, thanking him. Then they ran off to the kitchen to play with them. Snatching up Irene's hand, he pulled her into the living room. They could still hear the squeals and shouts coming from the other room, accompanied by barks from the dog.

Stopping in front of the tree, Paul faced Irene. She looked at him, her brow arched. How he loved her! Getting down on one knee, he drew out a ring. She gasped.

"My buddy Dex owns a jewelry store. I called him last night, and he opened the doors for me." He sucked in a deep breath. "Irene, I know it hasn't been a long time. But like I said, I have loved you for half of my life. These past two weeks without you have been some of the hardest I have ever known. I don't want to go another day without knowing that I have the right to finally call you mine."

"Oh!" Irene covered her mouth with her hand, but not before he glimpsed the smile that was coming out like the sun after a long, hard rain. It grew into a grin.

"Yes!" Irene held her shaking hand out to him. He put the ring right where it belonged. And then she was in his arms. Right where she belonged.

Epilogue

Irene stood in the bride room with her mother, Gina, Melanie, Maggie and Paul's sister, Cammie. Paul's mother was with Cammie's husband, Allen, keeping watch over the children while the women got ready for the ceremony. She couldn't believe this day was finally here. Of course, she and Paul hadn't had a long engagement. A little shy of three months. But it had felt like a lifetime, waiting for the day they could start their lives together.

"Do you have something borrowed?" Melanie asked.

Irene held her hand to her necklace. "Gina's lent me her pearls."

Gina Martello gave her a misty smile. "They look gorgeous on you."

Mel nodded. "And I gave you the earrings." The something blue.

Irene held her hand to her veil. "And Mom's veil." There was something old.

"Oh! Don't you dare make me cry!" her mother wailed softly. Her eyes were already watering even though there was a smile on her face.

"And your dress is something new." Mel grinned in satisfaction before hugging her sister-in-law gently. "Let's go get you married."

The ladies filed down into their positions. LaMar Pond policemen were present to escort the mothers to their seats before returning to stand near the groom. Claire Zerosky was lovely as she sat near the front, strumming on a harp. Seated near her was Miles, resplendent in his dress uniform, complete with its shiny sergeant insignia. He had agreed to interpret for Rebecca and Jess, who were both deaf. Rebecca and Jess were already seated with Seth. Irene grinned as she saw Rebecca blow Miles a kiss. He winked back at her.

It was time.

When Claire began the wedding march, Irene quivered. Excitement and joy burst through her as she watched the bridesmaids move towards the front. A very pregnant Maggie went first. Dan met her in the middle and escorted her the rest of the way. Cammie followed, to be met by Jackson. Next went Melanie, her maid of honor, to be met by Jace.

The guests let out a combined "aww" as the flower girls made their way up the aisle. Cammie's four-year-old daughter waved at her grandmother as she walked, completely forgetting that she was supposed to be scattering the rose petals nestled in her basket. It was Maggie's daughter, Siobhan, however, who stole the show. Always willing to perform, she was in her element. She threw rose petals helter-skelter and waved with abandon. More than one guest ended up with petals in their hair. No one minded, though.

The smiles grew as Rory followed his twin sister, his face very serious under a mop of dark curls as he carried the wedding rings on a small satin pillow. The three youngsters were precious. Absolutely adorable.

But not, in Irene's eyes, as adorable as the two young men standing at either side of her. Jace had offered to walk her down the aisle. But when AJ and Matthew heard about it, they shut down the idea.

"She's our mommy," AJ had stated. "And Chief Paul will be our new daddy. It should be us. 'Cause we're gonna be a family."

She'd nearly come undone at those sweet words. Paul had cleared his throat and embraced the boys, one at a time. "I think you two would be the perfect choice. How 'bout it, Jace? Best man?"

Jace had wiped his own eye. "Yeah, man. I am anyway."

Now she nodded at her boys. While she held her bouquet in her hand, each little boy held on to an elbow. The guests that had smiled at Cammie and the twins grew teary eyed as Irene's sons walked her down the aisle to Paul.

Finally, she stood before her groom, breathless and expectant. She smiled through her own tears as she saw him blink. She wasn't the only one affected by the beauty of this moment. From now on, they would be together. More than that, her heart overflowed with gratitude that her sons, soon to be his children, too, would once again have an earthly father to guide them. She whispered a quiet prayer of gratitude to God. She knew Paul felt the same. Just the night before, he'd admitted that he was overwhelmed. Never had he believed he would be the recipient of such a gift. She made herself a promise that she would never take what they'd been blessed with for granted, and instead would cherish it every day for the rest of their lives.

The ceremony was exquisite. Irene listened with joy as Paul said his vows in his strong, deep voice. When it was her turn, she didn't hesitate. She repeated the words that would bind her to this brave man with vibrant intensity, meaning them from the depths of her soul. When the rings were in place and blessed, her heart grew so full she could barely breathe.

At last the time came when they were announced husband and wife.

"You may now kiss the bride."

The bride. His bride.

Paul cupped Irene's face in his hands as if it were the most precious thing in the world. She quivered with the anticipation of his kiss. When his lips touched hers, she sighed, melting into the kiss.

After all the heartache and despair they had both endured, God had brought them healing and love.

After several heartbeats, they drew apart and shared a smile meant only for each other.

The pastor indicated they should turn and face the congregation.

"I now present to you Mr. and Mrs. Paul Kennedy."

As their friends and family smiled and clapped, Paul and Irene faced the congregation with AJ and Matthew in front of them. Together, the four stood, a family at last.

* * * * *

WE HOPE YOU
ENJOYED THIS BOOK!

Love Inspired®

New beginnings. Happy endings.
Discover uplifting inspirational
romance.

Look for six new Love Inspired
books available every month,
wherever books are sold!

LIHALO2019

Love Inspired®

Save $1.00

on the purchase of ANY
Love Inspired or
Love Inspired Suspense book.

Available wherever books are sold,
including most bookstores, supermarkets,
drugstores and discount stores.

Save $1.00

on the purchase of ANY Love Inspired or Love Inspired Suspense book.

Coupon valid until February 28, 2020.
Redeemable at participating retail outlets in the U.S. and Canada only.
Limit one coupon per customer.

52616512

Canadian Retailers: Harlequin Enterprises Limited will pay the face value of this coupon plus 10.25¢ if submitted by customer for this product only. Any other use constitutes fraud. Coupon is nonassignable. Void if taxed, prohibited or restricted by law. Consumer must pay any government taxes. Void if copied. Inmar Promotional Services ("IPS") customers submit coupons and proof of sales to Harlequin Enterprises Limited, P.O. Box 31000, Scarborough, ON M1R 0E7, Canada. Non-IPS retailer—for reimbursement submit coupons and proof of sales directly to Harlequin Enterprises Limited, Retail Marketing Department, 22 Adelaide St. West, 40th Floor, Toronto, Ontario M5H 4E3, Canada.

U.S. Retailers: Harlequin Enterprises Limited will pay the face value of this coupon plus 8¢ if submitted by customer for this product only. Any other use constitutes fraud. Coupon is nonassignable. Void if taxed, prohibited or restricted by law. Consumer must pay any government taxes. Void if copied. For reimbursement submit coupons and proof of sales directly to Harlequin Enterprises, Ltd 482, NCH Marketing Services, P.O. Box 880001, El Paso, TX 88588-0001, U.S.A. Cash value 1/100 cents.

5 65373 00076 2   (8100)0 12434

® and ™ are trademarks owned and used by the trademark owner and/or its licensee.

© 2019 Harlequin Enterprises Limited

LICOUP47016R

SPECIAL EXCERPT FROM

Love Inspired®

Christmastime brings a single mom and her baby back home, but reconnecting with her high school sweetheart, now a wounded veteran, puts her darkest secret at risk.

Read on for a sneak preview of
The Secret Christmas Child *by Lee Tobin McClain, the first book in her new Rescue Haven miniseries.*

He reached out a hand, meaning to shake hers, but she grasped his and held it. Looked into his eyes. "Reese, I'm sorry about what happened before."

He narrowed his eyes and frowned at her. "You mean...after I went into the service?"

She nodded and swallowed hard. "Something happened, and I couldn't...I couldn't keep the promise I made."

That something being another guy, Izzy's father. He drew in a breath. Was he going to hold on to his grudge, or his hurt feelings, about what had happened?

Looking into her eyes, he breathed out the last of his anger. Like Corbin had said, everyone was a sinner. "It's understood."

"Thank you," she said simply. She held his gaze for another moment and then looked down and away.

She was still holding on to his hand, and slowly, he twisted and opened his hand until their palms were flat together. Pressed between them as close as he'd like to be pressed to Gabby.

The only light in the room came from the kitchen and

LIEXP1019

the dying fire. Outside the windows, snow had started to fall, blanketing the little house in solitude.

This night with her family had been one of the best he'd had in a long time. Made him realize how much he missed having a family.

Gabby's hand against his felt small and delicate, but he knew better. He slipped his own hand to the side and captured hers, tracing his thumb along the calluses.

He heard her breath hitch and looked quickly at her face.

Her eyes were wide, her lips parted and moist.

Without looking away, acting on impulse, he slowly lifted her hand to his lips and kissed each fingertip.

Her breath hitched and came faster, and his sense of himself as a man, a man who could have an effect on a woman, swelled, almost making him giddy.

This was Gabby, and the truth burst inside him: he'd never gotten over her, never stopped wishing they could be together, that they could make that family they'd dreamed of as kids. That was why he'd gotten so angry when she'd strayed: because the dream she'd shattered had been so big, so bright and shining.

In the back of his mind, a voice of caution scolded and warned. She'd gone out with his cousin. She'd had a child with another man. What had been so major in his emotional life hadn't been so big in hers.

He shouldn't trust her. And he definitely shouldn't kiss her. But when had he ever done what he should?

Don't miss
The Secret Christmas Child *by Lee Tobin McClain,*
available December 2019 wherever
Love Inspired® books and ebooks are sold.

www.LoveInspired.com

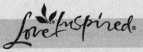
"Are the *kinder* okay?"

"Yes, they'll be fine." Uncomfortable with his small intrusion into her family, she said, "Kevin had a bad dream and woke us up."

"Because of the rain?"

She wanted to say that was silly but, glad she could be honest with Michael, she said, "It's possible."

"Rebuilding a structure is easy. Rebuilding one's sense of security isn't."

"That sounds like the voice of experience."

"My parents died when I was young, and both my twin brother and I had to learn not to expect something horrible was going to happen without warning."

"I'm sorry. I should have asked more about you and the other volunteers. I've been wrapped up in my own tragedy."

"At times like this, nobody expects you to be thinking of anything but getting a roof over your *kinder*'s heads."

He didn't reach out to touch her, but she was aware of every inch of him so close to her. His quiet strength had awed her from the beginning. As she'd come to know him better, his fundamental decency had impressed her more. He was a man she believed she could trust.

She shoved that thought aside. Trusting any man would be the worst thing she could do after seeing what Mamm had endured during her marriage and then struggling to help her sister escape her abusive husband.

"I'm glad you understand why I must focus on rebuilding a life for the children." The simple statement left no room for misinterpretation. "The flood will always be a part of us, but I want to help them learn how to live with their memories."

"I can't imagine what it was like."

"I can't forget what it was like."

Normally she would have been bothered by someone having sympathy for her, but if pitying her kept Michael from looking at her with his brown puppy-dog eyes that urged her to trust him, she'd accept it. She couldn't trust any man, because she wouldn't let the children spend their lives witnessing what she had.

Don't miss
An Amish Christmas Promise *by Jo Ann Brown,*
available December 2019 wherever
Love Inspired® books and ebooks are sold.

LoveInspired.com

Love Inspired®

Discover wholesome and uplifting stories of faith, forgiveness and hope.

Join our social communities to connect with other readers who share your love!

Sign up for the Love Inspired newsletter at **LoveInspired.com** to be the first to find out about upcoming titles, special promotions and exclusive content.

CONNECT WITH US AT:

Facebook.com/groups/HarlequinConnection

 Facebook.com/LoveInspiredBooks

Twitter.com/LoveInspiredBks

LISOCIAL2019